THE 120 DAYS OF SODOM

THE 120 DAYS OF SODOM

OR THE SCHOOL OF LIBERTINAGE

BY MARQUIS DE SADE

ISBN: 978-1-968194-21-5

Contents

Note

The 120 Days of Sodom, or the School of Licentiousness (Les 120 journées de Sodome ou l'école du libertinage) is a novel by the French writer and nobleman Donatien Alphonse François, Marquis de Sade, written in 1785. It tells the story of four wealthy male libertines who resolve to experience the ultimate sexual gratification in orgies. To do this, they seal themselves away for four months in an inaccessible castle with a harem of 46 victims, mostly young male and females, and engage four women brothel keepers to tell the stories of their lives and adventures. The women's narratives form an inspiration for the sexual abuse and torture of the victims, which gradually mounts in intensity and ends in their slaughter. The work remained unpublished until the twentieth century. In recent times it has been translated into many languages, including English, Japanese and German. Due to its themes of sexual violence and extreme cruelty, it has frequently been banned.

Introduction

The extensive wars wherewith Louis XIV was burdened during his reign, while draining the State's treasury and exhausting the substance of the people, none the less contained the secret that led to the prosperity of a swarm of those bloodsuckers who are always on the watch for public calamities, which, instead of appeasing, they promote or invent so as, precisely, to be able to profit from them the more advantageously. The end of this so very sublime reign was perhaps one of the periods in the history of the French Empire when one saw the emergence of the greatest number of these mysterious fortunes whose origins are as obscure as the lust and debauchery that accompany them. It was toward the close of this period, and not long before the Regent sought, by means of the famous tribunal which goes under the name of the Chambre de Justice, to flush this multitude of traffickers, that four of them conceived the idea for the singular revels whereof we are going to give an account. One must not suppose that it was exclusively the low-born and vulgar sort which did this swindling; gentlemen of the highest note led the pack. The Duc de Blangis and his brother the Bishop of X***, each of whom had thuswise amassed immense fortunes, are in themselves solid proof that, like the others, the nobility neglected no opportunities to take this road to wealth. These two illustrious figures, through their pleasures and business closely associated with the celebrated Durcet and the Président de Curval, were the first to hit upon the debauch we propose to chronicle, and having communicated the scheme to their two friends, all four agreed to assume the major roles in these unusual orgies.

For above six years these four libertines, kindred through their wealth and tastes, had thought to strengthen their ties by means of alliances in which debauchery had by far a heavier part than any of the other motives that ordinarily serve as a basis for such bonds.

What they arranged was as follows: the Duc de Blangis, thrice a widower and sire of two daughters one wife had given him, having noticed that the Président de Curval appeared interested in marrying the elder of these girls, despite the familiarities he knew perfectly well her father had indulged in with her, the Duc, I say, suddenly conceived the idea of a triple alliance.

"You want Julie for your wife," said he to Curval, "I give her to you unhesitatingly and put but one condition to the match: that you'll not be jealous when, although your wife, she continues to show me the same complaisance she always has in the past; what is more, I'd have you lend your voice to mine in persuading our good Durcet to give me his daughter Constance, for whom, I must confess, I have developed roughly the same feelings you have formed for Julie."

"But," said Curval, "you are surely aware that Durcet, just as libertine as you..."

"I know all that's to be known," the Duc rejoined. "In this age, and with our manner of thinking, is one halted by such things? do you think I seek a wife in order to have a mistress? I want a wife that my whims may be served, I want her to veil, to cover an infinite number of little secret debauches the cloak of marriage wonderfully conceals. In a word, I want her for the reasons you want my daughter -- do you fancy I am ignorant of your object and desires? We libertines wed women to hold slaves: as wives they are rendered more submissive than mistresses, and you know the value we set upon despotism in the joys we pursue."

It was at this point Durcet entered. His two friends related their conversation and, delighted by an overture which promptly induced him to avow the sentiments he too had conceived for Adelaide, the Président's, Durcet accepted the Duc as his son-in-law, provided he might become Curval's. The three marriages were speedily concluded, the dowries were immense, the wedding contracts identical.

No less culpable than his two colleagues, the Président had admitted to Durcet, who betrayed no displeasure upon learning it, that he maintained a little clandestine commerce with his own daughter; the three fathers, each wishing not only to preserve his rights, but noticing here the possibility of extending them, commonly agreed that the three young ladies, bound to their husbands by goods and homes only, would not in body belong more to one than to any of them, and the severest punishments were prescribed for her who should take it into her head not to comply with any of the conditions whereunto she was subject.

They were on the eve of realizing their plan when the Bishop of X***, already closebound through pleasure shared with his brother's two friends, proposed contributing a fourth element to the alliance should the other three gentlemen consent to his participation in the affair. This element, the Duc's second daughter and hence the Bishop's niece, was already more thoroughly his property than was generally imagined. He had effected connections with his sister-in-law and the two brothers knew beyond all shadow of doubt that the existence of this maiden, who was called Aline, was far more accurately to be ascribed to the Bishop than to the Duc; the former who, from the time she left the cradle, had taken the girl into his keeping, had not, as one may well suppose, stood idle as the years brought her charms to flower. And so, upon this head, he was his colleagues' equal, and the article he offered to put on the market was in an equal degree damaged or degraded; but as Aline's attractions and tender youth outshone even those of her three companions, she was unhesitatingly made a part of the bargain. As had the other three, the Bishop yielded her up, but retained the rights to her use; and so each of our four characters thus found himself husband to four wives. Thus there resulted an arrangement which, for the reader's convenience, we shall recapitulate:

The Duc, Julie's father, became the husband of Constance, Durcet's daughter;

Durcet, Constance's father, became the husband of Adelaide, the Président's daughter;

The Président, Adelaide's father, became the husband of Julie, the Duc's elder daughter;

And the Bishop, Aline's uncle and father, became the husband of the other three females by ceding this same Aline to his friends, the while retaining the same rights over her.

It was at a superb estate of the Duc, situated in the Bourbonnais, that these happy matches were made, and I leave to the reader to fancy how they were consummated and in what orgies; obliged as we are to describe others, we shall forego the pleasure of picturing these.

Upon their return to Paris, our four friends' association became only the firmer; and as our next task is to make the reader familiar with them, before proceeding to individual and more searching developments, a few details of their lubricious arrangements will serve, it seems to me, to shed a preliminary light upon the character of these debauchees.

The society had created a common fund, which each of its members took his turn administering for six months; the sums, allocated for nothing but expenses in the interests of pleasure, were vast. Their excessive wealth put the most unusual things within their reach, and the reader ought not be surprised to hear that two million were annually disbursed to obtain good cheer and lust's satisfaction.

Four accomplished procuresses to recruit women, and a similar number of pimps to scout out men, had the sole duty to range both the capital and the provinces and bring back everything, in the one gender and in the other, that could best satisfy their sensuality's demands. Four supper parties were held regularly every week in four different country houses located at four extremities of Paris. At the first of these gatherings, the one exclusively given over to the pleasures of sodomy, only men were present; there would always be at hand sixteen young men, ranging in age from twenty to thirty, whose immense faculties permitted our four heroes, in feminine guise, to taste the most agreeable delights. The youths were selected solely upon the basis of the size of their member, and it almost became necessary that this superb limb be of such magnificence that it could never have penetrated any woman; this was an essential clause, and as naught was spared by way of expense, only very rarely would it fail to be fulfilled. But simultaneously to sample every pleasure, to these sixteen husbands was joined the same quantity of boys, much younger, whose purpose was to assume the office of women. These lads were from twelve to eighteen years old, and to be chosen for service each had to possess a freshness, a face, graces, charms, an air, an innocence, a candor which are far beyond what our brush could possibly paint. No woman was admitted to these masculine orgies, in the course of which everything of the lewdest invented in Sodom and Gomorrah was executed.

At the second supper were girls of superior class who, upon these occasions forced to give up their proud ostentation and the customary insolence of their bearing, were constrained, in return for their hire, to abandon themselves to the most irregular caprices, and often even to the outrages our libertines were pleased to inflict upon them. Twelve of these girls would appear, and as Paris could not have furnished a fresh supply of them as often as would have been necessary, these evenings were interspersed with others at which were admitted, only in the same number as the well-bred ladies, women ranging from procuresses up through the class of officers' wives. There are above four or five thousand in Paris who belong to one or the other of the two latter classes and whom need or lust obliges to attend soirees of this kind; one has but to have good agents to find them, and our libertines, who were splendidly represented, would frequently come across miraculous specimens. But it was in vain one was honest or a decent woman, one had to submit everything: our Lordships' libertinage, of a variety that never brooks limits, would overwhelm with horrors and infamies whatever, whether by Nature or social convention, ought to have been exempt from such ordeals. Once one was there, one had to be ready for anything, and as our four villains had every taste that accompanies the lowest, most crapulous debauch, this fundamental acqui-escence to their desires was not by any means a matter of inconsequence.

The guests at the third supper were the vilest, foulest creatures that can possibly be met with. To him who has some acquaintance with debauchery's extravagances, this refinement will appear wholly understandable; 'tis most voluptuous to wallow, so to speak, in filth with persons of this category; these exercises offer the completest abandon, the most monstrous intemperance, the most total abasement, and these pleasures, compared with those tasted the evening before, or with the distinguished individuals in whose company we have tasted them, have a way of lending a sharp spice to earlier activities. At these third suppers, debauch being more thorough, nothing was omitted that might render it complex and piquant. A hundred whores would appear in the course of six hours, and only too often something less than the full hundred would leave the games. But there is nothing to be gained by hurrying our story or by broaching subjects which can only receive adequate treatment in the sequel.

As for the fourth supper, it was reserved for young maids; only those between the ages of seven and fifteen were permitted. Their condition in life was of no importance, what counted was their looks: they had to be charming; as for their virginity, authentic evidence was required. Oh, incredible refinement of libertinage! It was not, assuredly, that they wished to pluck all those roses, and how indeed could they have done so? for those untouched flowers were always a score in number, and of our four libertines only two were capable of proceeding to the act, one of the remaining two, the financier, being absolutely incapable of an erec-tion, and the Bishop being absolutely unable to take his pleasure save in a fashion which, yes, I agree, may dishonor a virgin but which, however, always leaves her perfectly intact. No matter; the twenty maiden-heads had to be there, and those which were not impaired by our quartet of masters became, before their eyes, the prey of certain of their valets just as depraved as they, whom they kept constantly at beck and call for more than one reason.

Apart from these four supper parties there was another, a secret and private one held every Friday, involving many fewer persons but surely costing a great deal more. The participants were restricted to four young and high-born damsels who, by means of strategy and money, had been abducted from their parents' homes. Our libertines' wives nearly always had a share in this debauch, and their extreme submissiveness, their docile attentions, their services made it more of a success each time. As for the genial atmosphere at these suppers, it goes without saying that even greater profusion than delicacy reigned there; not one of these meals cost less than ten thousand francs, and neighboring countries as well as all France were ransacked so that what was of the rarest and most exquisite might be assembled together. Fine and abundant wines and liqueurs were there, and even during the winter they had fruits of every season; in a word, one may be certain that the table of the world's greatest monarch was not dressed with as much luxury nor served with equal magnificence.

But now let us retrace our steps and do our best to portray one by one each of our four heroes -- to describe each not in terms of the beautiful, not in a manner that would seduce or captivate the reader, but simply with the brush strokes of Nature which, despite all her disorder, is often sublime, indeed even when she is at her most depraved. For -- and why not say so in passing -- if crime lacks the kind of delicacy one finds in virtue, is not the former always more sublime, does it not unfailingly have a character of grandeur and sublimity which surpasses, and will always make it preferable to, the monotonous and lackluster charms of virtue? Will you protest the greater usefulness of this or of that, is it for us to scan Nature's laws, ours to determine whether, vice being just as necessary to Nature as is virtue, she perhaps does not implant in us, in equal quantity, the penchant for one or the other, depending upon her respective needs? But let us proceed.

The Duc de Blangis, at eighteen the master of an already colossal fortune which his later speculations much increased, experienced all the difficulties which descend like a cloud of locusts upon a rich and influential young man who need not deny himself anything; it almost always happens in such cases that the extent of one's vices, and one stints oneself that much less the more one has the means to procure oneself everything. Had the Duc received a few elementary qualities from Nature, they might possibly have counter-balanced the dangers which beset him in his position, but this curious mother, who sometimes seems to collaborate with chance in order that the latter may favor every vice she gives to those certain beings of whom she expects attentions very different from those virtue supposes, and this because she has just as much need of the one as of the other, Nature, I say, in destining Blangis for immense wealth, had meticulously endowed him with every impulse, every inspiration required for its abuse. Together with a tenebrous and very evil mind, she had accorded him a heart of flint and an utterly criminal soul, and these were accompanied by the disorders in tastes and irregularity of whim whence were born the dreadful libertinage to which the Duc was in no common measure addicted. Born treacherous, harsh, imperious, barbaric, selfish as lavish in the pursuit of pleasure as miserly when it were a question of useful spending, a liar, a gourmand, a drunk, a dastard, a sodomite, fond of incest, given to murdering, to arson, to theft, no, not a single virtue compensated that host of vices. Why, what am I saying! not only did he never so much as dream of a single virtue, he beheld them all with horror, and he was frequently heard to say that to be truly happy in this world a man ought not merely fling himself into every vice, but should never permit himself one virtue, and that it was not simply a matter of always doing evil, but also and above all of never doing good.

"Oh, there are plenty of people," the Duc used to observe, "who never misbehave save when passion spurs them to ill; later, the fire gone out of them, their now calm spirit peacefully returns to the path of virtue and, thus passing their life going from strife to error and from error to remorse, they end their days in such a way there is no telling just what roles they have enacted on earth. Such persons," he would continue, "must surely be miserable: forever drifting, continually undecided, their entire life is spent detesting in the morning what they did the evening before. Certain to repent of the pleasures they taste, they take their delight in quaking, in such sort they become at once virtuous in crime and criminal in virtue. "However," our hero would add, "my more solid character is a stranger to these contradictions; I do my choosing without hesitation, and as I am always sure to find pleasure in the choice I make, never does regret arise to dull its charm. Firm in my principles because those I formed are sound and were formed very early, I always act in accordance with them; they have made me understand the emptiness and nullity of virtue; I hate virtue, and never will I be seen resorting to it. They have persuaded me that through vice alone is man capable of experiencing this moral and physical vibration which is the source of the most delicious voluptuousness; so I give myself over to vice. I was still very young when I learned to hold religion's fantasies in contempt, being perfectly convinced that the existence of a creator is a revolting absurdity in which not even children continue to believe. I have no need to thwart my inclinations in order to flatter some god; these instincts were given me by Nature, and it would be to irritate her were I to resist them; if she gave me bad ones, that is because they were necessary to her designs. I am in her hands but a machine which she runs as she likes, and not one of my crimes does not serve her: the more she urges me to commit them, the more of them she needs; I should be a fool to disobey her. Thus, nothing but the law stands in my way, but I defy the law, my gold and my prestige keep me well beyond reach of those vulgar instruments of repression which should be employed only upon the common sort."

If one were to raise the objection that, nevertheless, all men possess ideas of the just and the unjust which can only be the product of Nature, since these notions are found in every people and even amongst the uncivilized, the Duc would reply affirmatively, saying that yes, those ideas have never been anything if not relative, that the stronger has always considered exceedingly just what the weaker regarded as flagrantly unjust, and that it takes no more than the mere reversal of their positions for each to be able to change his way of thinking too; whence the Duc would conclude that nothing is really just but what makes for pleasure, and what is unjust is the cause of pain; that in taking a hundred louis from a man's pocket, he was doing something very just for himself, although the victim of the robbery might have to regard the action with another eye; that all these notions therefore being very arbitrary, a fool he who would allow himself to become their thrall. It was by means of arguments in this kind the Duc used to justify his transgressions, and as he was a man of greatest possible wit, his arguments had a decisive ring. And so, modeling his conduct upon his philosophy, the Duc had, from his most tender youth, abandoned himself unrestrainedly to the most shameful extravagances, and to the most extraordinary ones. His father, having died young and, as I indicated, left him in control of a huge fortune, had however stipulated in his will that the young man's mother should, while she lived, be allowed to enjoy a large share of this legacy. Such a condition was not in displeasing Blangis: poison appearing to be the only way to avoid having to subscribe to this article, the knave straightway decided to make use of it. But this was the period when he was only making his first steps in a vicious career; not daring to act himself, he brought one of his sisters, with whom he was carrying on a criminal intrigue, to take charge of the execution, assuring her that if she were to succeed, he would see to it that she would be the beneficiary of that part of the fortune whereof death would deprive their mother. However, the young lady was horrified by this proposal, and the Duc, observing that this ill-confided secret was perhaps going to betray him, decided on the spot to extend his plans to include the sister he had hoped to have for an accomplice; he conducted both women to one of his properties whence the two unfortunate ones never returned. Nothing quite encourages as does one's first unpunished crime. This hurdle once cleared, an open field seemed to beckon to the Duc. Immediately any person whomsoever showed opposition to his desires, poison was employed forthwith. From necessary murders he soon passed to those of pure pleasure; he was captivated by that regrettable folly which causes us to find delight in the sufferings of others; he noticed that a violent commotion inflicted upon any kind of an adversary is answered by a vibrant thrill in our own nervous system; the effect of this vibration, arousing the animal spirits which flow within these nerves' con-cavities, obliges them to exert pressure on the erector nerves and to produce in accordance with this perturbation what is termed a lubricious sensation. Consequently, he set about committing 10 thefts and murders in the name of debauchery and libertinage, just as someone else would be content, in order to inflame these same passions, to chase a whore or two. At the age of twenty-three, he and three of his companions in vice, whom he had indoctrinated with his philosophy, made up a party whose aim was to go out and stop a public coach on the highway, to rape the men among the travelers along with the women, to assassinate them afterward, to make off with their victims' money (the conspirators certainly had no need of this), and to be back that same night, all three of them, at the Opera

Ball in order to have a sound alibi. This crime took place, ah, yes: two charming maids were violated and massacred in their mother's arms; to this was joined an endless list of other horrors, and no one dared suspect the Duc. Weary of the delightful wife his father had bestowed upon him before dying, the young Blangis wasted no time uniting her shade to his mother's, to his sister's, and to those of all his other victims. Why all this? to be able to marry a girl, wealthy, to be sure, but publicly dishonored and whom he knew full well was her brother's mistress. The person in question was the mother of Aline, one of the figures in our novel we mentioned above. This second wife, soon sacrificed like the first, gave way to a third, who followed hard on the heels of the second. It was rumored abroad that the Duc's huge construction was responsible for the undoing of all his wives, and as this gigantic tale corresponded in every point to its gigantic inspiration, the Duc let the opinion take root and veil the truth. That dreadful colossus did indeed make one think of Hercules or a centaur: Blangis stood five foot eleven inches tall, had limbs of great strength and energy, powerful sinews, elastic nerves, in addition to that a proud and masculine visage, great dark eyes, handsome black eyelashes, an aquiline nose, fine teeth, a quality of health and exuberance, broad shoulders, a heavy chest but a well-proportioned figure withal, splendid hips, superb buttocks, the handsomest leg in the world, an iron temperament, the strength of a horse, the member of a veritable mule, wondrously hirsute, blessed with the ability to eject its sperm any number of times within a given day and at will, even at the age of fifty, which was his age at the time, a virtually constant erection in this member whose dimensions were an exact eight inches for circumference and twelve for length over-all, and there you have the portrait of the Duc de Blangis, drawn as accurately as if you'd wielded the pencil yourself. But if this masterpiece of Nature was violent in its desires, what was it like, Great God! when crowned by drunken 11 voluptuousness? 'Twas a man no longer, 'twas a raging tiger. Woe unto him who happened then to be serving its passions; frightful cries, atrocious blasphemies sprang from the Duc's swollen breast, flames seemed to dart from his eyes, he foamed at the mouth, he whinnied like a stallion, you'd have taken him for the very god of lust. Whatever then was his manner of having his pleasure, his hands necessarily strayed, roamed continually, and he had been more than once seen to strangle woman to death at the instant of his perfidious discharge. His presence of mind once restored, his frenzy was immediately replaced by the most complete indifference to the infamies wherewith he had just indulged himself, and of this indifference, of this kind of apathy, further sparks of lechery would be born almost at once.

In his youth, the Duc had been known to discharge as often as eighteen times a day, and that without appearing one jot more fatigued after the final than after the initial ejaculation. Seven or eight crises within the

same interval still held no terrors for him, his half a century of years notwithstanding. For roughly twenty-five years he had accustomed himself
to passive sodomy, and he withstood its assaults with the identical vigor
characterized his manner of delivering them actively when, the very
next moment, it pleased him to exchange roles. He had once wagered he
could sustain fifty-five attacks in a day, and so he had. Furnished, as we
have pointed out, with prodigious strength, he needed only one hand to
violate a girl, and he had proved it upon several occasions. One day he
boasted he could squeeze the life out of a horse with his legs; he mounted
the beast, it collapsed at the instant he had predicted. His prowess at the
table outshone, if that is possible, what he demonstrated upon the bed.
There's no imagining what had come to be the quantity of the food he
consumed. He regularly ate three meals a day, and they were all three
exceedingly prolonged and exceedingly copious, and it was as nothing
to him to toss down his usual ten bottles of Burgundy; he had drunk up
to thirty, and needed but to be challenged and he would set out for the
mark of fifty; but his intoxication taking on the tinge of his passions, and
liqueurs or wines having heated his brain, he would wax furious, and
they would be obliged to tie him down. And despite all that, would you
believe it? a steadfast child might have hurled this giant into a panic; true
indeed it is that the spirit often poorly corresponds with the fleshy sheath
enveloping it: as soon as Blangis discovered he could no longer use his
treachery or his deceit to make away with his enemy, he would become
timid and cowardly, and the mere thought of even the mildest combat,
but fought on equal terms, would have sent him fleeing to the ends of
the earth. He had nevertheless, in keeping with custom, been in one or
two campaigns, but had acquitted himself so disgracefully he had retired
from the service at once. Justifying his turpitude with equal amounts
of cleverness and effrontery, he loudly proclaimed that his poltroonery
being nothing other than the desire to preserve himself, it were perfectly
impossible for anyone in his right senses to condemn it for a fault.

Keep in mind the identical moral traits; next, adapt them to an entity
from the physical point of view infinitely inferior to the one we just
described; there you have the portrait of the Bishop of X***, the Duc de
Blangis' brother. The same black soul, the same penchant for crime, the
same contempt for religion, the same atheism, the same deception and
cunning, a yet more supple and adroit mind, however, and more art in
guiding his victims to their doom, but a slender figure, not heavy, no, a
little thin body, wavering health, very delicate nerves, a greater fastidi-
ousness in the pursuit of pleasure, mediocre prowess, a most ordinary
member, even small, but deft, profoundly skilled in management, each
time yielding so little that his incessantly inflamed imagination would
render him capable of tasting delight quite as frequently as his brother;
his sensations were of a remarkable acuteness, he would experience an

irritation so prodigious he would often fall into a deep swoon upon discharging, and he almost always temporarily lost consciousness when doing so.

He was forty-five, had delicate features, rather attractive eyes but a foul mouth and ugly teeth, a hairless pallid body, a small but well-shaped ass, and a prick five inches around and six in length. An idolater of active and passive sodomy, but eminently of the latter, he spent his life having himself buggered, and this pleasure, which never requires much expense of energy, was best suited to the modesty of his means. We will speak of his other tastes in good time. With what regards those of the table, he carried them nearly as far as the Duc, but went about the matter with somewhat more sensuality. Monseigneur, no less a criminal than his elder brother, possessed characteristics which had doubtless permitted him to match the celebrated feats of the hero we painted a moment ago; we will content ourselves with citing one of them, 'twill be enough to make the reader see of what such a man may be capable, and what he was prepared and disposed to do, having done the following:

One of his friends, a man powerful and rich, had formerly had an intrigue with a young noblewoman who had borne him two children, a girl and a boy. He had, however, never been able to wed her, and the maiden had become another's wife. The unlucky girl's lover died while still young, but the owner howbeit of a tremendous fortune; having no kin to provide for, it occurred to him to bequeath all he had to the two ill-fated children his affair had produced.

On his deathbed, he made the Bishop privy to his intentions and entrusted him with these two immense endowments: he divided the sum, put them in two purses, and gave them to the Bishop, confiding the two orphans' education to this man of God and enlisting him to pass on to each what was to be his when they attained their majority. At the same time he enjoyed the prelate to invest his wards' funds, so that in the meantime they would double in size. He also affirmed that it was his design to leave his offsprings' mother in eternal ignorance of what he was doing for them, and he absolutely insisted that none of this should ever be mentioned to her. These arrangements concluded, the dying man closed his eyes, and Monseigneur found himself master of about a million in banknotes, and of two children. The scoundrel was not long deliberating his next step: the dying man had spoken to no one but him, the mother was to know nothing, the children were only four or five years old. He circulated the intelligence that his friend, upon expiring, had left his fortune to the poor; the rascal acquired it the same day. But to ruin those wretched children did not suffice; furnished with authority by their father, the Bishop -- who never committed one crime without instantly conceiving another -- had the children removed from the remote pension in which they were being brought up, and placed them under the roof of certain people in his hire, from the outset having resolved soon to make them serve his perfidious lust. He waited until they were thirteen; the little boy was the first to arrive at that age: the Bishop put him to use, bent him to all his debauches, and as he was extremely pretty, sported with him for a week. But the little girl fared less well: she reached the prescribed age, but was very ugly, a fact which had no mitigating effect upon the good Bishop's lubricious fury. His desires appeased, he feared lest these children, left alive, would someday discover something of the secret of their interests. Therefore, he conducted them to an estate belonging to his brother and, sure of recapturing, by means of a new crime, the sparks of lechery enjoyment had just caused him to lose, he immolated both of them to his ferocious passions, and accompanied their death with episodes so piquant and so cruel that his voluptuousness was reborn in the midst of the torments wherewith he beset them. The thing is, unhappily, only too well known: there is no libertine at least a little steeped in vice who is not aware of the great sway murder exerts over the senses, and how voluptuously it determines a discharge. And that is a general truth whereof it were well the reader be early advised before undertaking the perusal of a work which will surely attempt an ample development of this system.

Henceforth at ease in the face of whatever might transpire, Monseigneur returned to Paris to enjoy the fruit of his misdeeds, and without the least qualms about having counteracted the intentions of a man who, in his present situation, was in no state to derive either pain or pleasure therefrom.

The Président de Curval was a pillar of society; almost sixty years of age, and worn by debauchery to a singular degree, he offered the eye not much more than a skeleton. He was tall, he was dry, thin, had two blue lusterless eyes, a livid and unwholesome mouth, a prominent chin, a long nose. Hairy as a satyr, flat-backed, with slack, drooping buttocks that rather resembled a pair of dirty rags flapping upon his upper thighs; the skin of those buttocks was, thanks to whipstrokes, so deadened and toughened that you could seize up a handful and knead it without his feeling a thing. In the center of it all there was displayed -- no need to spread those cheeks -- an immense orifice whose enormous diameter, odor, and color bore a closer resemblance to the depths of a well-freighted privy than to an asshole; and, crowning touch to these allurements, there was numbered among this sodomizing pig's little idiosyncrasies that of always leaving this particular part of himself in such a state of uncleanliness that one was at all times able to observe there a rim or pad a good two inches thick. Below a belly as wrinkled as it was livid and gummy, one perceived, within a forest of hairs, a tool which, in its erectile condition, might have been about eight inches long and seven around; but this condition had come to be the most rare and to procure it a furious sequence of things was the necessary preliminary. Nevertheless, the event occurred at least two or three times each week, and upon these occasions the Président would glide into every hole to be found, indiscriminately, although that of a young lad's behind was infinitely the most precious to him. The head of the Président's device was now at all times exposed, for he had had himself circumcised, a ceremony which largely facilitates enjoyment and to which all pleasure-loving persons ought to submit. But one of the purposes of the same operation is to keep this privity cleaner; nothing of the sort in Curval's case: this part of him was just as filthy as the other: this uncapped head, naturally quite thick to begin with, was thus made at least an inch ampler in circumference. Similarly untidy about all the rest of his person, the Président, who furthermore had tastes at the very least as nasty as his appearance, had become a figure whose rather malodorous vicinity might not have succeeded in pleasing everyone. However, his colleagues were not at all of the sort to be scandalized by such trifles, and they simply avoided discussing the matter with him. Few mortals had been as free in their behavior or as debauches as the Président; but, entirely jaded, absolutely besotted, all that remained to him was the depravation and lewd profligacy of libertinage. Above three hours of excess, and of the most outrageous excess, were needed before one could hope to inspire a voluptuous reaction in him. As for his emission, although in Curval the phenomenon was far more frequent than erection, and could be observed once every day, it was, all the same, so difficult to obtain, or it never occurred save as an aftermath to things so strange and often so cruel or so unclean, that the agents of his pleasure not uncommonly renounced the struggle, fainting by the wayside, the which would give birth in him to a kind of lubricious anger and this, through its effects, would now and again triumph where his efforts had failed. Curval was to such a point mired down in the morass of vice and libertinage that it had become virtually impossible for him to think or speak of anything else. He unendingly had the most appalling expressions in his mouth, just as he had the vilest designs in his heart, and these with surpassing energy he mingled with blasphemies and imprecations supplied him by his true horror, a sentiment he shared with his companions, for everything that smacked of religion. This disorder of mind, yet further augmented by the almost continual intoxication in which he was fond of keeping himself, had during the 16 past few years given him an air of imbecility and prostration which, he would declare, made for his most cherished delight.

Born as great a gourmand as a drunk, he alone was fit to keep abreast of the Duc, and in the course of this tale we will behold him to perform wonders which will no doubt astonish the most veteran eaters.

It had been ten years since Curval had ceased to discharge his judicial duties; it was not simply that he was no longer fit to carry them out, but I even believe that while he had been, he may have been asked to leave these matters alone for the rest of his life.

Curval had led a very libertine life, every sort of perversion was familiar to him, and those who knew him personally had the strong suspicion he owed his vast fortune to nothing other than two or three murders. However that may be, it is, in the light of the following story, highly probable that this variety of extravagance had the power to stir him deeply, and it is this adventure, which attracted some unfortunate publicity, that was responsible for his exclusion from the Court. We are going to relate the episode in order to give the reader an idea of his character.

There dwelled in the neighborhood of Curval's town house a miserable street porter who, the father of a charming little girl, was ridiculous enough to be a person of sensibility. Twenty messages of every kind had already arrived containing proposals relating to the poor fellow's daughter; he and his wife had remained unshaken despite this barrage aimed at their corruption, and Curval, the source of these embassies, only irritated by the growing number of refusals they had evoked, knew not what tack to take in order to get his hands upon the girl and to subject her to his libidinous caprices, until it struck to him that by simply having the father broken he would lead the daughter to his bed. The thing was as nicely conceived as executed. Two or three bullies in the Président's pay intervened in the suit, and before the month was out, the wretched porter was enmeshed in an imaginary crime which seemed to have been committed at his door and which got him speedily lodged in one of the Conciergerie's dungeons. The Président, as one would expect, soon took charge of the case, and, having no desire to permit it to drag on, arranged in the space of three days, thanks to his knavery and his gold, to have the unlucky porter condemned to be broken on the wheel, without the culprit ever having committed any crime but that of wishing to preserve his honor and safeguard his daughter's.

Meanwhile, the solicitations were renewed. The mother was brought in, it was explained to her that she alone had it in her power to save her husband, that if she were to satisfy the Président, what could be clearer than that he would thereupon snatch her husband from the dreadful fate awaiting him. Further hesitation was impossible; the woman made inquiries; Curval knew perfectly well to whom she addressed herself, the counsels were his creatures, and they gave her unambiguous replies: she ought not waste a moment. The poor woman herself brought her daughter weeping to her judge's feet; the latter could not have been more liberal with his promises, nor have been less eager to keep his word. Not only did he fear lest, were he to deal honorably and spare the husband, the man might go and raise an uproar upon discovering the price that had been paid to save his life, but the scoundrel even found a further delight, a yet keener one, in arranging to have himself given what he wished without being obliged to make any return.

This thought led to others; numerous criminal possibilities entered his head, and their effect was to increase his perfidious lubricity. And this is how he set about the matter so as to put the maximum of infamy and piquancy into the scene:

His mansion stood facing a spot where criminals are sometimes executed in Paris, and as this particular offense had been committed in that quarter of the city, he won assurance the punishment would be meted out on this particular square. The wretch's wife and daughter arrived at the Président's home at the appointed hour; all windows overlooking the square were well shuttered, so that, from the apartments where he amused himself with his victims, nothing at all could be seen of what was going on outside. Apprised of the exact minute of the execution, the rascal selected it for the deflowering of the little girl who was held in her mother's arms, and everything was so happily arranged that Curval discharged into the child's ass the moment her father expired. Instantly he'd completed his business, "Come have a look," quoth he, opening a window looking upon the square, "come see how well I've kept my bargain," and one of his two princesses saw her father, the other her husband, delivering up his soul to the headsman's steel.

Both collapsed in a faint, but Curval had provided for everything: this swoon was their agony, they'd both been poisoned, and nevermore opened their eyes. Notwithstanding the precautions he had taken to swathe the whole of this exploit in the most profound mystery, something did indeed transpire: nothing was known of the women's death, but there existed a lively suspicion he had been untruthful in connection with the husband's case. His motive was half-known, and his eventual retirement from the bench was the outcome. As of this moment, no longer having to maintain appearances, Curval flung himself into a new ocean of errors and crimes. He sent everywhere for victims to sacrifice to the perversity of his tastes. Through an atrocious refinement of cruelty, but one, however, very easily understood, the downtrodden classes were those upon which he most enjoyed hurling the effects of his raging perfidy. He had several minions who were abroad night and day, scouring attics and hovels, tracking down whatever of the most destitute misery might be able to provide, and under the pretext of dispensing aid, either he envenomed his catch -- to give poison was one of his most delectable pastimes -- or he lured it to his house and slew it upon the altar of his perverse preferences. Men, women, children: anything was fuel to his rage, and at its bidding he performed excesses which would have got his head between block and blade a thousand times over were it not for the silver he distributed and the esteem he enjoyed, factors whereby he was a thousand times protected. One may well imagine such a being had no more religion than his two confreres; he without doubt detested it as sovereignly as they, but in years past had done more to wither it in others, for, in the days when his mind had been sound, it had also been clever, and he had put it to good use writing against religion; he was the author of a several works whose influence had been prodigious, and these successes, always present in his memory, still constituted one of his dearest delights.

The more we multiply the objects of our enjoyments...

...the years of a sickly childhood.

Durcet is fifty-three; he is small, short, broad, thickset; an agreeable, hearty face; a very white skin; his entire body, and principally his hips and buttocks, absolutely like a woman's; his ass is cool and fresh, chubby, firm, and dimpled, but excessively agape, owing to the habit of sodomy; his prick is extraordinarily small, 'tis scarcely two inches around, no more than four inches long; it has entirely ceased to stiffen; his discharges are rare and uneasy, far from abundant and always preceded by spasms which hurl him into a kind of furor which, in turn, conducts him to crime; he has a chest like a woman's, a sweet, pleasant voice and, when in society, the best-bred manners, although his mind is without question as depraved as his colleagues'; a schoolmate of the Duc, they still sport together every day, and one of Durcet's loftiest pleasures is to have his anus tickled by the Duc's enormous member.

And such, dear reader, are the four villains in whose company I am going to have you pass a few months. I have done my best to describe them; if, as I have wished, I have made you familiar with even their most secret depths, nothing in the tale of their various follies will astonish you. I have not been able to enter into minute detail with what regards their tastes -- to have done so now would have been to impair the value and to harm the main scheme of this work. But as we move progressively along, you will have but to keep an attentive eye upon our heroes, and you'll have no trouble discerning their characteristic peccadilloes and the particular type of voluptuous mania which best suits each of them. Roughly all we can say at the present time is that they were generally susceptible of an enthusiasm for sodomy, that the four of them had themselves buggered regularly, and that they all four worshiped behinds.

The Duc, however, relative to the immensity of his weapon and, doubtless, more through cruelty than from taste, still fucked cunts with the greatest pleasure.

So also did the Président, but less frequently.

As for the Bishop, such was his supreme loathing for them the mere sight of one might have kept him limp for six months. He had never in all his life fucked but one, that belonging to his sister-in-law, and expressly to beget a child wherewith some day to procure himself the pleasures of incest; we have seen how well he succeeded.

As regards Durcet, he certainly idolized the ass with as much fervor as the Bishop, but his enjoyment of it was more accessory; his favorite attacks were directed toward a third sanctuary -- this mystery will be unveiled in the sequel. But on with the portraits essential to the intelligence of this work, and let us now give our reader an idea of these worthy husbands' four wives.

What a contrast! Constance, the Duc's wife and the daughter of Durcet, was a tall woman, slender, lovely as a picture, and modeled as if the Graces had taken pleasure in embellishing her, but the elegance of her figure in no way detracted from her freshness, she was not for that the less plumply fleshed, and the most delicious forms graced by a skin fairer than the lily, often induced one to suppose that, no, it had been Love itself who had undertaken her formation. Her face was a trifle long, her features wonderfully noble, more majesty than gentleness was in her look, more grandeur than subtlety. Her eyes were large, black, and full of fire; her mouth extremely small and ornamented by the finest teeth imaginable, she had a narrow, supple tongue, of the loveliest pink, and her breath was sweeter still than the scent of a rose. She was full-breasted, her bosom was buxom, fair as alabaster and as firm. Her back was turned in an extraordinary way, its lines sweeping deliciously down to the most artistically and the most precisely cleft ass Nature has produced in a long time. Nothing could have been more perfectly round, not very large, but firm, white, dimpled; and when it was opened, what used to peep out but the cleanest, most winsome, most delicate hole. A nuance of tenderest pink had shaded this ass, charming asylum of lubricity's sweetest pleasures, but, great God! it was not for long to preserve so many charms! Four or five attacks, and the Duc had spoiled all those graces, how quickly had they gone, and soon after her marriage Constance was become no more than the image of a beautiful lily wherefrom the tempest has of late stripped the petals away. Two round and perfectly molded thighs supported another temple, in all likelihood less delicious, but, to inclined to worship there, offering so many allurements it would be in vain were my pen to strive to describe them. Constance was almost a virgin when the Duc married her, and her father, the only man who had known her, had, as they say, left that side of her perfectly intact. The most beautiful black hair -- falling in natural curls to below her shoulders and, when one wished it thus, reaching down to the pretty fur, of the same color, which shaded that voluptuous little cunt -- made for a further adornment I might have been guilty of omitting, and lent this angelic creature, aged about twenty-two, all the charms Nature is able to lavish upon a woman. To all these amenities Constance joined a fair and agreeable wit, a spirit somewhat more elevated than it ought to have been, considering the melancholy situation fate had awarded her, for thereby she was enabled to sense all its horrors and, doubtless, she would have been happier if furnished with less delicate perceptions.

Durcet, who had raised her more as if she were a courtesan than his daughter, and who had been much more concerned to give her talents than manners, had all the same never been able totally to destroy the principles of rectitude and of virtue it seemed Nature had been pleased to engrave in her heart. She had no formal religion, no one had ever mentioned such a thing to her, the exercise of a belief was not to be tolerated in her father's household, but all that had not blotted out this modesty, this natural humility which has nothing to do with theological chimeras, and which, when it dwells in an upright, decent, and sensitive soul, is very difficult to obliterate. Never had she stepped out of her father's house, and the scoundrel had forced her, beginning at the age of twelve, to serve his crapulous pleasures. She found a world of difference in those the Duc imbibed with her, her body was noticeably altered by those formidable dimensions, and the day after the Duc had despoiled her of her maidenhead, sodomistically speaking, she had fallen dangerously ill. They believed her rectum had been irreparably damaged; but her youth, her health, and some salutary local remedies soon restored the use of that forbidden avenue to the Duc, and the luckless Constance, forced to accustom herself to this daily torture, and it was but one amongst others, entirely recovered and became adjusted to everything.

Adelaide, Durcet's wife and the daughter of the Président, had a beauty which was perhaps superior to Constance's, but of an entirely different sort. She was twenty, small and slender, of an extremely slight and delicate build, of classic loveliness, had the finest blond hair to be seen. An interesting air, a look of sensibility distributed everywhere about her, and above all in her features, gave her the quality of a heroine in a romance. Her exceptionally large eyes were blue, they expressed at once tenderness and decency; two long but narrow and remarkably drawn eyebrows adorned a forehead not very high but of such noble charm one might have thought this were modesty's very temple. Her nose, thin, a little pinched at the top, descended to assume a semi-aquiline contour; her lips inclined toward the thin, were of a bright, ripe red; a little large, her mouth was the unique flaw in this celestial physiognomy, but when it opened, there shone thirty-two pearls Nature seemed to have sown amidst roses. Her neck was a shade long, attached in a singular way, through what one judged a natural habit, her head was ever so faintly bent toward her right shoulder, especially when she was listening; but with what grace did not this interesting attitude endow her! Her breasts were small, very round, very firm, well-elevated, but there was barely enough there to fill the hand. They were like two little apples a frolicking Cupid had fetched hither from his mother's garden. Her chest was a bit narrow, it was also a very delicate chest, her belly was satin smooth, a little blond mound not much garnished with hair served as peristyle to the temple in which Venus seemed to call out for an homage. This temple was narrow to such a point you could not insert a finger therein without eliciting a cry from Adelaide; nevertheless, two lustrums had revolved since the time when, thanks to the Président, the poor child had ceased to be a virgin, either in that place or in the delicious part it remains for us to sketch. Oh, what were the attractions this second sanctuary possessed, what a flow in the line of her back, how magnificently were those buttocks cut, what whiteness there, and what dazzling rose blush! But all on all, it was on the small side. Delicate in all her lines, she was rather the sketch than the model of beauty, it seemed as though Nature had only wished to indicate in Adelaide what she had so majestically articulated in Constance. Peer into that appetizing behind, and lo! a rosebud would offer itself to your gaze, and it was in all its bloom and in the most tender pink Nature wished you to behold it; but narrow? tiny? it had only been at the price of infinite labors the Président had navigated through those straits, and he had only renewed these assaults successfully two or three times.

Durcet, less exacting, gave her little affliction in this point, but, since becoming his wife, in exchange for how many other cruel complaisances, with what a quantity of other perilous submissions had she not been obliged to purchase this little kindness? And, furthermore, turned over to the four libertines, as by their mutual consent she was, how many other cruel ordeals had she not to undergo, both of the species Durcet spared her, and of every other.

Adelaide had the mind her face suggested, that is to say, an extremely romantic mind, solitary places were the ones she preferred, and once there, she would shed involuntary tears -- tears to which we do not pay sufficient heed -- tears apparently torn from Nature by foreboding. She was recently bereft of a friend, a girl she idolized, and this frightful loss constantly haunted her imagination. As she was thoroughly acquainted with her father, as she knew to what extents he carried his wild behavior, she was persuaded her young friend had fallen prey to the Président's villainies, for he had never managed to induce the missing person to accord him certain privileges. The thing was not unlikely. Adelaide imagined the same would someday befall her; nor was that improbable. The Président, in her regard, had not paid the same attention to the problem of religion Durcet had in the interests of Constance, no, he had allowed all that nonsense to be born, to be fomented, supposing that his writings and his discourses would easily destroy it. He was mistaken: religion is the nourishment upon which a soul such as Adelaide's feeds. In vain the Président had preached, in vain he had made her read books, the young lady had remained a believer, and all these extravagances, which she did not share, which she hated, of which she was the victim, fell far short of disabusing her about illusions which continued to make for her life's happiness. She would go and hide herself to pray to God, she'd perform Christian duties on the sly, and was unfailingly and very severely punished, either by her father or her husband, when surprised in the act by the one or the other.

Adelaide patiently endured it all, fully convinced Heaven would someday reward her. Her character was as gentle as her spirit, and her benevolence, one of the virtues for which her father most detested her, went to the point of extreme. Curval, whom that vile class of the poverty-stricken irritated, sought only to humiliate it, to further depress it, or to wring victims from it; his generous daughter, on the other hand, would have foregone her own necessities to procure them for the poor, and she had often been espied stealing off to take to the needy sums which were intended for her pleasures. Durcet and the Président finally succeeded in scolding and pounding good manners into her, and in ridding her of this corrupt practice by withholding absolutely all means whereby she could resume it. Adelaide, having nothing left but her tears to bestow upon the poor, went none the less to sprinkle them upon their woes, and her powerless howbeit staunchly sensitive spirit was incapable of ceasing to be virtuous. One day she learned that some poor woman was to come to prostitute her daughter to the Président because extreme need bade her do so; the enchanted old rake was already preparing himself for the kind of pleasure-taking he liked best. Adelaide had one of her dresses sold and immediately got the money put it in the mother's hands; by means of this small assistance and some sort of a sermon, she diverted the woman from the she was about to commit. Hearing of what she had done, the Président proceeded to such violences with her -- his daughter was not yet married at the time -- that she was a fortnight abed; but all that was to no avail: nothing could put a stop to this gentle soul's tender impulses.

Julie, the Président's wife, the Duc's elder daughter, would have eclipsed the two preceding women were it not for something which many behold as a capital defect, but which had perhaps in itself aroused Curval's passion for her, so true it is that the effects of passion are unpredictable, nay, inconceivable, and that their disorder, the outcome of disgust and satiety, can only be matched by their irregular flights. Julie was tall, well made although quite fat and fleshy, had the most lovely brown eyes in the world, a charming nose, striking and gracious features, the most beautiful chestnut brown hair, a fair body of the most appetizing fullness, an ass which might easily have served as model to the one Praxiteles sculpted, her cunt was hot, strait, and yielded as agreeable a sensation as such a locale ever may; her legs were handsome, her feet charming, but she had the worst-decked mouth, the foulest teeth, and was by habit so dirty in every other part of her body, and principally at the two temples of lubricity, that no other being, let me repeat it, no other being but the Président, himself subject to the same shortcomings and unquestionably fond of them, nay, no one else, despite her allurements, could have put up with Julie. Curval, however, was mad about her; his most divine pleasures were gathered upon that stinking mouth, to kiss it plunged him into delirium, and as for her natural uncleanliness, far from rebuking her for it, to the contrary he encouraged her in it, and had finally got her

accustomed to a perfect divorce from water. To these faults Julie added
a few others, but they were surely less disagreeable: she was a vast eater,
she had a leaning toward drunkenness, little virtue, and I believe that had
she dared try it, whoredom would have held little by way of terror for
her. Brought up by the Duc in a total abandon of principles and manners,
she adopted a whore's philosophy, and she was probably an apt student of
all its tenets; but, through yet another very curious effect of libertinage,
it often happens that a woman who shares our faults pleases us a great
deal less in our pleasures than one who is full of naught but virtues: the
first resembles us, we scandalize her not; the other is terrified, and there
is one very certain charm more.

Despite his proportions, the Duc had sported with his daughter, but
he had had to wait until she was fifteen, and even so had not been able to
prevent Julie from being considerably damaged by the adventure, indeed,
so much so that, eager to marry her off, he had been forced to put a term
to pleasure-taking of this variety and to be content with delights less
dangerous for her, but at least as fatiguing. Julie gained little by gaining
the Président, whose prick, as we know, was exceedingly thick and, furthermore, however much she was dirty from neglect of herself, she could
not in any wise keep up with a filthiness in debauch such as the one that
distinguished the Président, her beloved spouse.

Aline, Julie's younger sister and really the daughter of the Bishop,
possessed habits and defects and a character very unlike her sister's.

She was the most youthful of the four, she had just become eighteen; she had a fetching, exuberantly healthy, and almost pert little
countenance; a little turned-up nose; brown eyes full of expression and
vivacity; a delicious mouth; a most shapely though somewhat tall figure,
well-fleshed; the skin a bit dark but soft and fine; ass rather on the ample
side but well-molded, a pair of the most voluptuous buttocks that ever a
libertine eye may behold, the love mound brown-haired and pretty, the
cunt a trifle low or, as they say, à l'anglaise, but as tight as one might wish,
and when she was presented to the assembly she was thoroughly a maid.
And she still was at the time the party we are to chronicle got under way,
and we shall see in what manner her maidenhead was annihilated. As for
the first fruits of her ass, the Bishop had been peacefully plucking them
every day for the past eight years, but without, however, arousing in his
dear daughter much of a taste for these exercises: she, despite her mischievous and randy air, only cooperated out of obedience and had never
hinted that she shared the slightest pleasure in the infamies whose daily
victim she was. The Bishop had left her in the most profound ignorance,
scarcely did she know how to read or write, and she had absolutely no
idea of religion's existence; her mind was natural, it was that of a child,
she would give droll replies, she liked to play, she loved her sister a great
deal, detested the Bishop out of all measure, and feared the Duc as she

dreaded fire. On the wedding day, when she discovered herself naked and surrounded by the four men, she wept, and moreover did all that was asked of her, acting without pleasure as without ill-temper. She was sober, very clean, and having no other fault but that of laziness, nonchalance reigned in all her movements and doings and everywhere about her person, despite the liveliness announced by her bright eyes. She abhorred the Président almost as much as she hated her uncle, and Durcet, who treated her with no excess of consideration, nevertheless seemed to be the only one for whom she appeared to have no repugnance.

These were the eight principal characters in whose company we are going to enable you to live, good reader. It is now time to divulge the object of singular pleasures that were proposed.

It is commonly accepted amongst authentic libertines that the sensations communicated by the organs of hearing are the most flattering and those impressions are the liveliest; as a consequence, our four villains, who were of a mind to have voluptuousness implant itself in the very core of their beings as deeply and as overwhelmingly as ever it could penetrate, had, to this end, devised something quite clever indeed.

It was this: after having immured themselves within everything that was best able to satisfy the senses through lust, after having established this situation, the plan was to have described to them, in the greatest detail and in due order, every one of debauchery's extravagances, all its divagations, all its ramifications, all its contingencies, all of what is termed in libertine language its passions. There is simply no conceiving the degree to which man varies them when his imagination grows inflamed; excessive may be the differences between men that is created by all their other manias, by all their other tastes, but in this case it is even more so, and he who should succeed in isolating and categorizing and detailing these follies would perhaps perform one of the most splendid labors which might be undertaken in the study of manners, and perhaps one of the most interesting. It would thus be a question of finding some individuals capable of providing an account of all these excesses, then of analyzing them, of extending them, of itemizing them, of graduating them, and of running a story through it all, to provide coherence and amusement. Such was the decision adopted. After innumerable inquiries and investigations, they located four women who had attained their prime -- that was necessary, experience was the fundamental thing here -- four women, I say, who, having spent their lives in the most furious debauchery, had reached the state where they could provide an exact account of all these matters; and, as care had been taken to select four endowed with a certain eloquence and a fitting turn of mind, after much discussion, recording, and arranging, all four were ready to insert, each into the adventures of her life, all the most extraordinary vagaries of debauch, and to do so in such an order and at such a pace that the first, for example, would work into the tale of her life's activities the one hundred and fifty simple passions and the least esoteric or most ordinary deviations; the second, within the same framework, an equal number of more unusual passions involving one or more men with one or several women; the third was also to introduce into her narration one hundred and fifty of the most criminal whimsies and those which most outrage the laws of both Nature and religion; and as all these excesses lead to murder and as these murders committed through libertinage are infinitely various and are just as numerous as the occasions upon which the libertine's inflamed imagination adopts different tortures, the fourth was to adorn the events of her life with a meticulous report upon one hundred and fifty assorted examples of them. In the meantime, our libertines, surrounded, as at the outset I indicated, by their wives and also by other objects in every kind, were to pay close heed, were to be mentally heated, and were to end by extinguishing, by means of either their wives or those various objects, the conflagration the storytellers were to have lit. There is surely nothing more voluptuous in this project than the luxurious manner whereby it was carried out, and they are both this manner and these several recitations which are to compose this work; wherewith, having said this much, I advise the overmodest to lay my book aside at once if he would not be scandalized, for 'tis already clear there's not much of the chaste in our plan, and we dare hold ourselves answerable in advance that there'll be still less in its execution. Insomuch as the four actresses we have been speaking of play a most essential role in these memoirs, we believe, even were we to have to beg the reader's forgiveness therefor, we should still feel obliged to describe them; they will narrate, they will act: such being the case, is it possible that they remain unknown? Banish all expectation of beauties portrayed, although there were doubtless in the plans provisions for employing these four creatures physically as well as morally; be that as it may, neither their charms nor their years were the deciding factors, but rather their minds and their experience only that counted, and with what regards the latter, our friends could not possibly have made better choices.

Madame Duclos was she to whom they entrusted the relating of the one hundred and fifty simple passions; the woman who went by this name was forty-eight years of age, still in fairly good condition and preserving the vestiges of beauty; she had very handsome eyes, an exceedingly fair skin, and one of the most splendid and plumpest asses that could ever favor your gaze; a mouth both clean and fresh, superb breasts, and pretty brown hair, a heavy figure but a noble one, and all the looks and tone of a brilliant whore. She had spent her life, as shall be observed, in places and under circumstances where indeed she had been obliged to study what she is going to relate, and to see her was to realize she must have gone to the task with wit and verve, with ease and interest.

Madame Champville was a tall woman about fifty, slender, well made, having the most voluptuous quality in her look and bearing; a faithful devotee of Sappho, she had that kind of expression even in her slightest movements, in her simplest gestures, in her least words. She had ruined herself for the sake of keeping girls and, had it not been for this predilection to which she generally sacrificed everything she was able to earn abroad, she might have been comfortably well to do. For a long time she had been in public service, and during recent years had been making her way as an outfitter in her turn, but had confined herself to a limited practice, her clients being reliable rakehells of a certain age; never did she receive young men, and this prudent conduct was lucrative and did something to improve her affairs. She had been blond, but a more venerable tint, and that of wisdom, was beginning to color her hair; her eyes were still exceedingly attractive, blue, and they contained a most agreeable expressiveness. Her mouth was lovely, still fresh, missing no teeth as yet, she was flat-chested but had a belly which was good, but had never aroused envy, her mound was rather prominent, and her clitoris protruded three inches when well warmed; tickle this part of her and one was certain to see her fly into an ecstasy in no time, and especially if the service was rendered by a female. Her ass was very flabby and worn from use, entirely soft, wrinkled, withered, and so toughened by the libidinous customs she in recounting her history will explain to us, that one could do everything one wished without her feeling anything there. One strange and assuredly very rare thing, above all in Paris: she was as much a maid on this side as a girl emerging from a convent, and perhaps, had it not been for the accursed part she put to use with people who cared for nothing but the extraordinary and whom, consequently, that side pleased, perhaps, I say, had it not been for that part, this singular virginity might have perished with her.

Madame Martaine, a portly matron of fifty-two, very well preserved and very healthy and blessed with the biggest and most beautiful rump one could wish for, boasted the precise opposite by way of adventure. She had devoted her life to sodomitical debauch, and was so well familiarized therewith she tasted absolutely no joy save therefrom. A natural deformity (she had also been blessed with an obstruction) having prevented her from knowing any other, she had given herself over to this kind of pleasure, led to it both by her inability to do anything else and by early habit, in consideration of which she clung fast to this lubricity wherein 'twas declared she was yet delicious, ready to brave come what might, dreading nothing. The most monstrous engines were as naught to her, in fact such were the ones she preferred, and the sequel to these papers will perhaps reveal her still giving valorous fight beneath the standards of Sodom, as the most intrepid of buggresses. Her features were gracious enough, but signs of languor and of decline were beginning to mar her attractions, and but for the plumpness sustaining her yet, she might have been thought timeworn and frayed.

As for Madame Desgranges, she was vice and lust personified; tall, thin, fifty-six, ghostly pale and emaciated, dead dull eyes, dead lips, she offered an image of crime about to perish for lack of strength. She had once upon a time been brunette, there were some who even maintained she'd had a beautiful body; not long thereafter it had become a mere skeleton capable of inspiring nothing but disgust. Her ass, withered, worn, marked, torn, more resembled marbled paper than human skin, and its hole was so gaping, sprung, and rugose that the bulkiest machines could, without her knowing a thing, penetrate it dry. By way of crowning graces, this generous Cytherean athlete, wounded in several combats, was missing one nipple and three fingers. She limped, and was without six teeth and an eye. We may perhaps learn by what order of attacks she had been so mistreated; but one thing is certain: nothing she had suffered had induced her to mend her ways, and if her body was the picture of ugliness, her was the depository of all the most unheard of vices and crimes: an arsonist, a parricide, a sodomite, a tribade, a murderess, a poisoner, guilty of incest, of rape, of theft, of abortions, and of sacrileges, one might truthfully affirm that there is not a single crime in the world this villain had not committed herself, or had others commit for her. Her present calling was procuring; she was one of society's most heavily titled furnishers, and as to much experience she joined a more or less agreeable prattle, she had been chosen to fill the role of fourth storyteller, that is to say, the one in whose story the greatest number of infamies and horrors were to be combined. Who better than a creature who had performed them all could have played this part?

These women once found, and found in every article to be such as was desired, the friends turned their attentions to accessories. They had from the outset planned to surround themselves with a large number of lust-inspiring objects of either sex, but when it was brought to their attention that the only setting in which this lubricious roister could conveniently be held was that same château in Switzerland belonging to Durcet, the one in which he had dispatched little Elvire, when, I say, it was remarked that this château of only moderate size would not be able to lodge so great a throng of inhabitants, and that, what was more, it might well prove unwise or dangerous to bring along such a host, the list of subjects was trimmed to thirty-two in all, the storytellers included: to wit: four of that class, eight young girls, eight young boys, eight men endowed with monstrous members, for the delights of passive sodomy, and four female servants. But thoroughness went into the recruiting of all that; a year was devoted to these details, an enormous amount of money too, and these are the measures they employed to obtain the most delicious specimens of all France could offer in the way of eight little girls: sixteen intelligent procuresses, each accompanied by two lieutenants, were sent into the sixteen major provinces of France, while a seventeenth was occupied with the same work in Paris only. Each of these outfitters was given a rendezvous at one of the Duc's estates on the outskirts of Paris, and all of them were to appear there, during the same week, exactly ten months after the date of their departure -- this was the period they were given for searching. Each was to bring back nine subjects, which came to a total of one hundred and fifty-three girls, from which one hundred and fifty-three a choice of only eight was to be made.

The procuresses were instructed to emphasize high birth, virtuous-ness, and the most delicious visage possible; they were to conduct their researches so as to draw material chiefly from eminent families, and were not to hand over any girl without being able to prove that she had been forcibly abducted from either a convent housing pensionnaires of quality, or from the home of a family, and that a family of distinction. Whatever was not superior to the class of bourgeoisie, and what from these upper classes was not both very virtuous and wholly virgin and impeccably beautiful, would be refused without mercy; spies were posted to survey these women's proceedings and to supply the society with exhaustive and prompt reports of what they were doing.

For each suitable subject found, they were paid thirty thousand francs, the agents assuming all expenses. The costs were incredible. With respect to age, it was fixed at from twelve to fifteen; anything above or between was pitilessly rejected. At the same time, under identical circumstances, with the same means, at the same expense, seventeen ages of sodomy likewise scoured the capital and the provinces in search of little boys, and their rendezvous was set for a month after the selection of the girls. As for the young men whom we propose henceforth to designate as fuckers, the size of the member was the sole criterion: nothing under ten or eleven inches long by seven or eight around was acceptable. Eight men labored throughout the kingdom to supply this demand, and their rendezvous was scheduled to fall a month after the little boys'. While the story of how these selections were made and received is not our foremost concern, it might not be inappropriate at this point to insert a word on the subject in order to bring out yet a little more of our four heroes' genius; it seems to me that nothing which serves to enlarge the reader's understanding of these figures and to shed light upon a party as extraordinary as the one we are going to describe, can be judged irrelevant.

The time for the assembling of the little girls having arrived, every-one converged upon the Duc's estate. Some few procuresses having been unable to fill their quota of nine, some others having lost their charges en route, either by illness or flight, only one hundred and thirty of them were present at the rendezvous, but what charms, great God! never, I believe, have so many charms been seen gathered together in one place. Thirteen days were given over to this examination, and each day ten of them were inspected. The four friends gathered in a circle, and in its middle was placed the little girl, dressed as she had been seized; the procuress responsible for her capture recited her history. If something of the conditions of high birth or virtue were wanting, the inquiry went no deeper, the child was forthwith rejected, without appeal, and sent on her way, and the purveyor lost all that she had spent in connection with her. Next, having provided all the vital particulars, the procuress was asked to retire, and the child was interrogated in order to determine whether what had just been alleged were true. If all seemed well, the procuress was called in again, and she lifted the girl's skirts from behind, so as to expose her buttocks to the group; this was the first thing it wished to examine. The slightest defect in this part was grounds for immediate rejection; if on the contrary naught were amiss here, she was ordered to strip, or was stripped, and, naked, she passed and passed again, five or six times over, from one of our libertines to the other, she was turned about, she was turned the other way, she was fingered, she was handled, they sniffed, they spread, they peeped, they examined the state of the goods, was it new, was it used, but did all this coolly and without permitting the senses' illusion to upset any aspect of the examination. This done, the child was led away, and beside her name inscribed upon a ballot, the examiners wrote passed or failed and signed their names; these ballots were then dropped into a box, the voters refraining from communicating their opinions to one another; all the girls examined, the box was opened: in order to be accepted, a girl had to have our four friend's names in her favor. The absence of one name was enough to exclude her instantly and, in every instance, inexorably, as I have said: the unsuitable ones were kicked directly out, set at large, alone and without a guide, save when, as happened with perhaps a dozen, our libertines frolicked with them after the choices had been made and before turning them over to their procuresses.

This round resulted in the exclusion of fifty candidates, the other eighty were gone over afresh, but with much greater exactitude and severity; the least defect warranted instantaneous dismissal. One, lovely as the day, was weeded out because one of her teeth grew a shade higher from the gum than the rest; more than twenty others were refused because they were daughters of nothing better than bourgeois. Thirty were eliminated during this second round, hence only fifty were left. The friends resolved not to continue to the third round until having first being relieved of some fuck through these fifty aspirants' own ministry, this in order that the senses' perfect calm could insure saner and sounder choice. Each of the quartet encompassed himself by a team of twelve or thirteen children; members of each team adopted varying attitudes, teams were shifted, everything was brought off with such dexterity, there was, in a word, so much lubricity in the doing that sperm flow, temperatures subsided, and another thirty disappeared from the race. Twenty remained; that was still a dozen too many. Further expedients to procure calm were resorted to, every means wherefrom one would suppose disgust could be born was employed, but the twenty still remained, and how might one have subtracted from a number of creatures so wonderfully celestial you would have declared they were the very work of a divinity? Equal in beauty, something else had to discovered which could at least award eight of them some kind of superiority over the twelve others, and what the Président then proposed was worthy indeed of all the disorder of his mind. That made no difference; the suggestion was accepted: it had to do with finding out which of them would best do something the chosen eight would be often called upon to do. Four days sufficed amply to decide this question, and at last twelve were given their leave, but not blankly as in the case of the others; they provided a week's complete and exhaustive amusement, then were put into the keeping of the procuresses who soon made a pretty penny from the prostitution of creatures as distinguished as these. As for the successful eight, they were installed in a convent to keep until the day of departure, and in order to reserve until the designated period the pleasure of enjoying them, the four colleagues did not touch them before then.

I'll not be so foolhardy as to attempt to describe these beauties: they were all of them superior in an equal degree: my brush strokes would necessarily be monotonous; I shall be content to give their names and to affirm that upon my word it is perfectly impossible to obtain an idea of such an assemblage of graces, of attractions, of perfections, and that had Nature wished to give Man an idea of what her greatest and wisest art can create, she would not have presented him with other models.

The first was named Augustine: she was fifteen, the daughter of a Languedoc baron, and had been kidnapped from a convent in Montpellier.

The second was named Fanny: she was the daughter of a counselor to the parliament of Brittany and had been abducted from her father's own château.

The third was named Zelmire: she was fifteen years old, she was the Comte de Terville's daughter, and he idolized her. He had taken her hunting with him on one of his estates in Beauce and, having left her alone in the forest for a moment, she had been pounced upon at once. She was only a child and, with a dowry of four hundred thousand francs, was the following year to have married a very great lord. It was she who most wept and grieved at the horror of her fate.

The fourth was named Sophie: she was fourteen and was the daughter of a rather well-to-do gentleman who lived on his estate in Berry. She had been seized while on a walk with her mother, who, seeking to defend her, was flung into a river, where she expired before her daughter's eyes.

The fifth was named Colombe: she was from Paris, the child of a counselor to Parliament; she was thirteen and had been kidnapped while returning in the evening to her convent with a governess, after leaving a children's ball. The governess had been stabbed to death.

The sixth was named Hébé: she was just twelve, the daughter of a cavalry captain, a nobleman who lived in Orléans. The youngster had been enticed and carried away from the convent where she was being brought up; two nuns had been bought. You could not hope to find anything more seductive or sweeter.

The seventh was named Rosette: she was thirteen and was the child of the Lieutenant-General of Chalon-sur-Saône. Her father had just died, she was with her mother in the countryside near the city, and was captured within sight of her relatives by agents disguised as thieves.

The last was named Mimi or Michette: she was twelve, she was the daughter of the Marquis de Sénanges and had been kidnapped on her father's estate in the Bourbonnais while on a carriage drive which she had been allowed to take with two or three women from the château. The women were murdered. It will be remarked that the preparations for these revels cost much money and many crimes; to such people, treasure means exceedingly little, and as for crime, one was then living in an age when it was not by any means probed and punished the way it is nowadays. Hence everything succeeded, and so prettily that, the inquests amounting to virtually nothing at all, our libertines were never troubled by consequences.

The time drew nigh for the examination of the little boys. Easier to obtain, their number was greater. The pimps produced one hundred and fifty of them, and it will surely be no exaggeration if I affirm that they at least equaled the little girls, as much in their innocence, and their elevated rank. Thirty thousand francs were paid for each of them, the same sum given for the girls, but the entrepreneurs risked nothing, because this game being more delicate and far more to the taste of our epicures, it had been decided that no one would be put in danger of losing his expenses, that while the lads with whom it was impossible to come to terms would be rejected, as they would be put to some use they would also be paid for.

Their examination was conducted like that of the girls, ten were verified each day, but with the very wise precaution which had been a little too much neglected with the girls, with the precaution, I say, of always preceding the examination by a discharge arranged with the aid of the ten who were under present scrutiny. The others were half of a mind to bar the Président from the ceremony, they were wary of the depravation of his tastes; they had feared, in the selection of the girls, being made the dupes of his accursed predilection for infamy and degradation: he promised to keep himself in check, and if he kept his word, it is unlikely he did so without difficulty, for when once a damaged or diseased imagination becomes accustomed to these species of outrages against good taste and Nature, outrages which so deliciously flatter it, it is no easy matter to restore such a person to the path of righteousness: it seems as if the desire to satisfy his longing displaces reason in his judgments. Scorning what is truly beautiful, no longer cherishing but what is frightful, desire's pronouncements correspond to its criteria, and the return to truer sentiments would appear to him to be a wrong done those principles whence he should be most sorry to stray. One hundred hopefuls were found unanimously approved when the initial séances were over, and these decisions had to be five times reconsidered in order to arrive at the small group alone to be accepted. Thrice in succession fifty survived the balloting, and then, to reduce that number to the stipulated eight, the jurors were compelled to resort to unusual measures in order somehow to lessen the appeal of idols still glamorous despite everything they had been able to do to them. The idea occurred to them to dress the boys as girls: twenty-five were eliminated by this trick which, lending to a sex they worshiped the garb of one to which they had become indifferent, depreciated their value and ruined almost all the illusion. But nothing could alter the voting on the twenty-five that were left. 'Twas all in vain, in vain they spattered their fuck about, in vain they wrote their names upon the ballots at the same moment they discharged, in vain they put to use the expedient adopted with the little girls, the twenty-five proved irreducible every time, and at last they agreed to have them draw lots. Here are the names they gave the lucky ones who remained, their age, their birth, and a word or two about their adventures; their portraits? I cry off: Cupid's own features were surely no more delicate, and the models Albani sought from which to choose traits for his divine angels must certainly have been inferior by far.

Zélamir was thirteen years old: he was the only son of a gentleman out of Poitou who had been bringing him up with the greatest care. Escorted by a single domestic, he had been sent to Poitiers to visit a kinsman; our rogues ambushed them, slew the domestic, and made off with the child.

Cupidon was the same age: he had been a pupil in a school at La Flèche, and was the son of a gentleman dwelling in the vicinity of that town. A trap was laid for the boy, he was kidnapped while on an outing the students used to take on Sundays. He was the prettiest pupil in the entire collège.

Narcisse was twelve; he was a Knight of Malta. He had been abducted in Rouen, where his father filled an honorable post compatible with his nobility; the boy was en route to the Collège de Louis-le-Grand at Paris, he was waylaid and seized while on the road.

Zéphyr, the most delicious of the eight, it being supposed that their excessive beauty might allow the possibility of a choice, was from Paris; he was pursuing his studies there, in a famous pension. His father, a ranking officer, did all in his power to get his son back, and failed; money had seduced the headmaster of the school, who delivered seven specimens, of whom six were refused. Zéphyr had set the Duc's head to spinning, and the latter protested that were it to have cost a million to bugger the boy he would have paid it in cash on the spot. He reserved to himself the lad's initiation, and it was generally granted him. O tender and delicate child, what disproportion and what a dreadful fate were in store for you!

Céladon was the son of a magistrate of Nancy; he was captured at Lunéville, whither he had gone to visit his aunt. He had just attained his fourteenth year. In this case a girl was used to bait the trap.

Céladon and she were introduced, the little wench drew him into the snare by feigning love for him; he was negligently chaperoned, the stroke was successful.

Adonis was fifteen; he was ravished at Plessis, where he was enrolled in school. He was the son of a judge of the assize courts who raised a great hue and cry, but all to no avail, the capture had been so nicely planned no one knew a thing about it. Curval, who had been mad about the child for two years, had made his acquaintance at his father's house, and it was he who had supplied the means and information necessary to debauch him. The others were greatly surprised to find such sensible good taste in a head so depraved as Curval's, and he, most proud, profited from the event to show his colleagues that, as was plainly to be seen, he still could boast a sometimes fine palate. The child recognized him and fell to weeping, but the Président consoled him with the assurance it would be to him would befall the deflowering, and while uttering these comforting words, he wobbled his enormous engine against those frail little buttocks. Curval asked the assembly for the boy; his request was unopposed.

Hyacinthe was fourteen years old; he was the son of a retired officer living in a small city in Champagne. He adored hunting and was taken while afield, his father having been so imprudent as to allow him to set out alone.

Giton was twelve; he was kidnapped at Versailles from amidst of the page boys at the King's stables. He was the son of a man of consequence from the Nivernais, who not six months prior had brought him to Versailles. He was very simply abducted while walking alone on the avenue de Saint-Cloud. He became the Bishop's passion, and to the Bishop was the prize decreed.

Those, thus, were the masculine deities our libertines prepared for their lubricity; we will see in due time and place the use to which they were put. One hundred and forty-two subjects remained, but whereas there had been much trifling over the eight, there was none with this game: not one of the defeated candidates was dismissed until he had served some purpose.

Our libertines spent a month with them at the Duc's château. As they were on the eve of setting forth, as all the practical arrangements were completed, the company had little else to do but amuse itself until the day of departure. When at last they were thoroughly fed up with their sport, they fell upon a pleasant means for disposing of what had provided it: that was to sell the boys to a Turkish pirate, a scheme whereby no trace of them would be left and a part of the costs would be recovered. They were sent in small groups to a place near Monaco, the Turk came to get them and lead them off into slavery, doubtless a dreadful fate, but one whereby, none the less, our four villains were hugely entertained.

And now came the moment of choosing the fuckers. Those of this class who failed to meet the standards were the cause of no embarrassment; being mature and reasonable men, it was enough to pay them for their trouble, their traveling expenses, and send them home. The eight experts who had contracted to furnish the fuckers had, furthermore, many fewer obstacles to surmount, since the specifications were by and large concrete and the conditions made no difference at all. Thus it was fifty came to the rendezvous; from amongst the twenty biggest, the eight youngest and most attractive were singled out, and since in the sequel mention will almost never be made save of the four biggest of the eight, I shall restrict myself to naming these.

Hercule, with a body hewn in the image of the god whose name he had been given, was twenty-six years of age and was endowed with a member eight and one-quarter inches around by thirteen long. Nothing more beautiful nor more majestic has ever been seen; this tool was almost always upright, and with only eight discharges, so tests revealed, it could fill a pint measure to the brim. Hercule was also very gentle, very sweet, and had an interesting countenance.

Antinoüs, so named because, like Hadrian's favorite, he had, together with the world's prettiest prick, its most voluptuous ass, and that exceedingly rare. Antinoüs wielded a device measuring eight inches in circumference and twelve in length. He was thirty and had a face worthy of his other features.

Bum-Cleaver lugged a club so amusingly shaped it was nearly impossible for him to perform an embuggery without splitting the ass, whence came the name he bore. The head of his prick resembled the heart of an ox, it was eight and three-eights inches around; behind it, the shaft measured only eight, but was crooked and had such a curve it neatly tore the anus when penetrating it, and this quality, very precious to libertines as jaded as ours, had made him singularly sought after.

Invictus, so named because, no matter what he did, his erection was perpetual, was furnished with an engine eleven inches long and seven and fifteen-sixteenths inches around. Greater ones, who had difficulty stiffening, had been turned away to make room for him who, regardless of the quantity of discharges he produced in a day, rose heavenward at the slightest touch.

The other four were of about the same dimensions and the same shape. The forty-two rejected candidates provided a fortnight's entertainment and, after the friends had put them through their paces and worn them to the bone, they were well rewarded and bidden adieu.

Nothing now remained but the choice of the four ladies-in-waiting, and this final stage was without doubt the most picturesque. The Président was not the only one whose tastes were depraved; his three friends, and especially Durcet, were indeed a little tainted by his accursed, crapulous, and debauched mania which causes one to find a greater, more piquant attraction in an old, disgusting, and filthy object than in what Nature has fashioned most divinely. Explaining this fancy would probably be difficult, but it exists in many people;

Nature's disorder carries with it a kind of sting which operates upon the high-keyed sort with perhaps as much and even more force than do her most regular beauties; it has been proven, moreover, that when one's prick is aloft, it is horror, villainy, the appalling, that pleases; well, where are they more emphatically present than in a vitiated object? If 'tis the filthy thing which pleases in the lubricious act, then certainly the more filthy the thing, the more it should please, and it is surely much filthier in the corrupted than in the intact and perfect object.

No, as to that there's no doubt. Furthermore, beauty belongs to the sphere of the simple, the ordinary, whilst ugliness is something extraordinary, and there is no question but that every ardent imagination prefers in lubricity the extraordinary to the commonplace. Beauty, health never strike one save in a simple way; ugliness, degradation deal a far stouter blow, the commotion they create is much stronger, the resultant agitation must hence be more lively; in the light of all this, there should be no cause for astonishment in the fact that an immense crowd of people prefer to take their pleasure with an aged, ugly, and even stinking crone and will refuse a fresh and pretty girl, no more reason to be astonished by that, I say, than at a man who for his promenades prefers the mountains' arid and rugged terrain to the monotonous pathways of the plains. All these matters depend upon our tastes in this connection than it is in our power to alter the form of our bodies.

Be that as it may, such, as I have said, was the dominating taste of the Président and, to tell the truth, the taste which came near to predominating in his three confreres, for when it came to choosing female servants, their views were identical, and we are about to see from this choice that its making bespoke the constitutional disorder and depravation to which we have just alluded.

The most painstaking search was initiated in Paris; the four creatures needed were finally located; however loathsome may be their portraits, the reader will none the less permit me to draw them: that I do so is essential to that aspect of manners the elucidation of which is one of the principal aims of this work.

Marie was the name of the first one; she had been servant of a notorious brigand quite recently put to death on the wheel, whipping and
branding had been her penalty. She was fifty-eight years old, had almost
no hair left, her nose stood askew, her eyes were dull and rheumy, her
mouth large and filled with her thirty-two teeth, yes, they were all there,
but all were yellow as sulphur; she was tall, raw-boned, having whelped
fourteen children, all fourteen of whom, said she, she'd strangled from
fear they'd turn out ne'er-do-wells. Her belly rippled like the waves of the
sea, and one of her buttocks was devoured by an abscess.

The second was known as Louison; she was sixty, stunted, hunchbacked, blind in one eye, and lame, but she had a fine ass for her age and
her skin was still in fairly good repair. She was as wicked as the devil and
forever ready to commit any horror and every extravagance one could
possibly demand of her.

Thérèse was sixty-two; she was tall, thin, looked like a skeleton, not a
hair was left on her head, not a tooth in her mouth, and from this opening
in her body she exhaled an odor capable of flooring any bystander. Her
ass was peppered with wounds, and her buttocks were so prodigiously
slack one could have furled the skin around a walking stick; the hole in
this splendid ass resembled the crater of a volcano what for width, and
for aroma the pit of a privy; in all her life, Thérèse declared, she had
never once wiped her ass, whence we have proof positive that the shit
of her infancy yet clung there. As for her vagina, it was the receptacle of
everything ungodly, of every horror, a veritable sepulcher whose fetidity
was enough to make you faint away. She had one twisted arm and limped
in one leg.

The fourth was called Fanchon; six times she had been hanged in
effigy, and not a crime exists in this world she had not committed. She
was sixty-nine, she was flat-nosed, short, and heavy; she squinted, had
almost no forehead, had nothing but two old teeth in her stinking maw,
and they were ready to fall out, an erysipelas blazed all over her ass and
hemorrhoids the size of your fist hung from her anus, a frightful chancre
consumed her vagina, and one of her thighs had been entirely burned.
She was dead drunk three-quarters of the year, and in that condition,
her stomach being very weak, she vomited over everything. Despite the
batch of hemorrhoids adorning it, her asshole was naturally so large that
all unawares she blew driblets and farts and often more besides. Apart
from acting as servants in the luxurious recreation palace the four friends
had in mind, these women were also to lend a hand at all the convoca-
tions and render all the lubricious services and ministrations that might
be required of them.

As soon as all these matters had been decided and the summer having
already begun, they turned their thoughts to the transporting of the
various objects which were, during the four months' sojourn on Durcet's

estate, to render its inhabitation comfortable and agreeable. A vast store of furniture and mirrors, of viands and wines and liqueurs of all kinds were ordered borne thither, workmen were sent there, and little by little the numerous subjects were conducted to the château where Durcet, who had gone ahead, received, lodged, and established them as they arrived.

But the moment has come to give the reader a description of the renowned temple appointed for so many luxurious sacrifices throughout the projected four-month season. He will observe with what great care they had chosen a remote and isolated retreat, as if silence, distance, and stillness were libertinage's potent vehicles, and as if everything which through these qualities instills a religious terror in the senses had necessarily and evidently to bestow additional charm upon lust. We are going to picture this retreat not as once it was, but in the state of embellishment and yet more perfect solitude that resulted from our four friends' efforts.

To reach the place one had first to get to Basel; at that city you crossed the Rhine, beyond which the road became steadily narrower until you had to abandon your carriage. Soon afterward you entered the Black Forest, you plunged about fifteen leagues into it, ascended a difficult, tortuous road that, without a guide, would be absolutely impracticable. By and by you caught sight of a sinister and mean hamlet of charcoal burners and gamekeepers; there began the territory Durcet owned, and the hamlet was his; as this little village's population was composed almost entirely of thieves or smugglers, Durcet easily befriended it, and his first order to the inhabitants was expressly to enjoin them under no circumstances to allow anyone whomsoever to pass on toward the château after the 1st of November, the date by which the entire society was to be assembled in it. He distributed weapons to his faithful vassals, granted them certain privileges they had been long soliciting, and the barrier was lowered. That done, and the gates tightly sealed, one will see by the following description how difficult of access was Silling, the name Durcet's château bore.

Having passed the village, you begin to scale a mountain almost as high as the Saint-Bernard and infinitely more difficult to ascend, for the only way to reach the summit is by foot; not that the route is forbidden to pack mules, but such are the precipices which everywhere border the one so very narrow path that must be followed, that you run the greatest danger if you ride; six of the mules used to transport supplies and food perished, taking with them two laborers who had though to mount astride them. Five full hours are required to reach the top of the mountain, and there you come upon another extraordinary feature which, owing to the precautions that had been taken, became a new barrier so insurmountable that none but birds might have overcome it: the topographical accident we refer to is a crevice above sixty yards wide which splits the crest into northern and southern parts, with the result that, after having climbed up the mountain, it is impossible, without great skill, to go back down it.

Durcet had united these two parts, between which a precipice fell to the depth of a thousand feet and more, by a fine wooden bridge which was destroyed immediately the last of the crew had arrived, and from this moment on, all possibility of communicating with the Château of Silling ceased. For, cross the bridge and you come down into a little plain about four acres in area; the plain is surrounded on all sides by sheer crags rising to the clouds, crags which envelop the plain within a faultless screen. The passage known as the bridge path is hence the only one by which you may descend into or communicate with the little plain; the bridge removed or destroyed, there is not on this earth a single being, of no matter what species you may imagine, capable of gaining this small plot of level land.

And it is in the center of this flat space so well surrounded, so solidly protected, that one finds Durcet's château. Yet another wall, thirty feet high, girds it; beyond the wall a moat filled with water and exceedingly deep defends a last tall and winding enclosure; a low and strait postern finally leads into the great inner court around which all the living quarters are built, and they are very capacious, very well furnished thanks to the arrangements latterly concluded; one discovers a long gallery on the first floor. I would have it remarked that the description I am about to give of the apartments corresponds not to what in former times they may have been, but to the manner in which they had just been rearranged and distributed in accordance with our libertines' common conception. From the gallery you moved into a very attractive dining hall provided with buffets shaped like towers which, communicating with the kitchen, made it possible to serve the company its food hot, promptly, and without the help of any waiters. From this dining hall, hung in tapestries, warmed by heating devices, furnished with ottomans, with excellent armchairs, and with everything which could make it both comfortable and pleasing to the eye, you passed into a large living room or salon, simple, plain, but exceedingly warm and equipped with the very best furniture; adjacent to this room was an assembly chamber intended for the storytellers' narrations. This was, so to speak, the lists for the projected jousts, the seat of the lubricious conclaves, and as it had been decorated accordingly, it merits something by way of a special description.

Its shape was semicircular; set into the curving wall were four niches whose surfaces were faced with large mirrors, and each was provided with an excellent ottoman; these four recesses were so constructed that each faced the center of the circle; the diameter was formed by a throne, raised four feet above the floor and with its back to the flat wall, and it was intended for the storyteller; in this position she was not only well before the four niches intended for her auditors, but, the circle being small, was close enough to them to insure their hearing every word she said, for she was placed like an actor in a theater, and the audience in their niches found themselves situated as if observing a spectacle in an amphitheater. Steps led down from the throne, upon them were to sit the objects of debauchery brought in to soothe any sensory irritation provoked by the recitals; these several tiers, like the throne, were upholstered in black velvet edged with gold fringe, and the niches were furnished with similar and likewise enriched material, but in color dark blue. At the back of each niche was a little door leading into an adjoining closet which was to be used at times when, having summoned the desired subject from the steps, one preferred not to execute before everyone the delight for whose execution one had summoned that subject. These closets were provided with couches and with all the other furnishing required for every kind of impurity. On either side of the central throne an isolated column rose to the ceiling; these two columns were designed to support the subject in whom some misconduct might merit correction. All the instruments necessary to meting it out hung from hooks attached to the columns, and this imposing sight served to maintain the subordination so indispensable to parties of this nature, a subordination whence is born almost all the charm of the voluptuousness in persecutors' souls.

One could walk from this semicircular room directly to a chamber which formed the end of this part of the living quarters. This chamber was a kind of boudoir, it was soundproof and secluded, but very warm within, very dark during the day, and its purpose was for private interviews and secluded contests, or for certain other secret delights which will be unveiled in the sequel. To reach the other wing, one had to retrace one's footsteps, and once in the gallery, at the end of which an exceedingly handsome chapel was visible, one entered the opposite wing which completed the circuit of the inner courtyard. You discovered a splendid antechamber adjoined by four superb apartments, each having a boudoir and wash cabinets; splendid Turkish beds canopied in three-colored damask with matching furniture adorned these suites whose boudoirs offered everything and more of the most sensual that lubricity might fancy. These four units, exceptionally well-heated and comfortable, were intended for the four colleagues, who were perfectly lodged therein. In that the protocols stipulated that their wives were to occupy the same quarters, no separate space was set aside for them.

Upstairs, the second story contained about the same number of apartments, but they were otherwise divided; you first came upon, to one side, a vast room bordered by eight niches, each having a little bed -- these were the girls' quarters, and beside them were two small chambers for the old women who were to have charge of them. Further along, a pair of pretty rooms had been set aside for two of the storytellers. Now turning about and going in the other direction, you found a similar eight-niched room for the little boys; by it were two rooms for the duennas appointed to supervise them; and beyond these were two more rooms, also alike, for the two storytellers. Eight cheerful rooms, as fine as anything you have yet seen, formed the eight fuckers' quarter, although these individuals were destined to do very little sleeping in their own beds. Below, on the ground floor, were the kitchens and, near them, six small chambers for the six persons to whom the preparation of food had been confided; amongst them were three cooks renowned for their art; they were all females, women having been preferred for a pleasure outing like this one, and I believe the decision was just. The cooks were assisted by three robust young scullery maids, but none of the kitchen staff was to appear at the revels, that was not its purpose, and if the rules imposed in this connection were violated, 'tis merely because libertinage stops at nothing, and the true way of extending and multiplying one's desires is to attempt to impose checks upon them. One of these three underlings was to look after the numerous livestock which had been fetched to the château --with the exception of the four aged ladies who were meant for household duties, there were no domestics save for these three cooks and their seconds. But depravity, cruelty, disgust, infamy, all those passions anticipated or experienced, had erected another locality whereof it is a matter of urgency that we give the sketch, for the laws essential to the proper unfolding of our tale demand that we depict it with thoroughness now.

A fatal stone there was which, cunningly made, could be raised from below the step of the altar in the little Christian temple we discerned from the gallery; beneath that stone one beheld a spiral stairway, very narrow and very steep, whose three hundred steps could convey you down into the bowels of the earth, to a kind of vaulted dungeon, closed by triple doors of iron, and in which was displayed everything the cruelest art and the most refined barbarity could invent of the most atrocious, as much for gripping one with terror as for proceeding to horrors. And there below, what tranquility! to what degree might not the villain be reassured who brought his victim there! What had he to fear? He was out of France, in a safe province, in the depths of an uninhabitable forest, within this forest in a redoubt which, owing to the measures he had taken, only the birds of the air could approach, and he was in the depth of the earth's entrails. Woe, a hundred times woe to the unlucky creature who in the midst of such abandonment were to find himself at the mercy of a villain lawless and without religion, whom crime amused, and whose only interest lay in his passions, who heeded naught, had nothing to obey but the imperious decrees of his perfidious lusts. I know not what will transpire in that nether place, but this I may say without doing our tale a disservice, that when a description of the dungeon was given the Duc, he reacted by discharging three times in succession.

Everything being ready at last, everything perfectly disposed, the subjects installed, the Duc, the Bishop, Curval, and their wives, with the four second-ranking fuckers in their train, set off (Durcet and his wife, together with all the rest, having arrived beforehand, as we have previously noted), and not without infinite difficulty, finally reached the château on the evening of the 29th of October. Immediately they crossed it, Durcet had the bridge cut. But that was not all: having inspected the place, the Duc decided that, since all the provisions were within the fortress, and since therefore they had no need to leave it, it were necessary, in order to forestall external attack, which was little dreaded, and escapes from within, the possibilities of which were less unlikely, it were necessary, I say, to have walled shut all the gates, all the passages whereby the château-might be penetrated, and absolutely to enclose themselves inside their retreat as within a besieged citadel, without leaving the least entrance to an enemy, the least egress to a deserter. The recommendation was put into effect, they barricaded themselves to such an extent there was no longer any trace left of where the exits had been; and then they settled down comfortably inside.

After the provisions we have just cited had been taken, the two days still remaining before the 1st of November were devoted to resting the subjects, that they might make a fresh appearance at the scenes of debauchery soon to begin, and during this interval the four friends labored over a code of laws which, as soon as it was brought to perfection and signed, was promulgated to those concerned. Before advancing to the matter, it is essential that these articles of government be made known to the reader who, after the exact description we have given him of everything, will now have no more to do than follow the story, lightly and voluptuously, his mind impeded by nothing, his memory embarrassed by no unexpected intrusions.

Statutes

The company shall rise every day at ten o'clock in the morning, at which time the four fuckers who have not been in duty during the night shall come to pay the friends a visit and shall each bring a little boy; they shall pass from one bedchamber to another, successively. They shall perform as bidden by the friends' likings and desires, but during the preliminaries the little boys shall serve only as a tempting prospect, for it has been decided and planned that the eight maidenheads of the little girls' cunts shall remain intact until the month of December, and their asses shall likewise remain in bond, as shall the asses of the eight little boys, until the month of January, at which times the respective seals shall be broken, and this in order to allow voluptuousness to become irritated by the augmentation of a desire incessantly inflamed and never satisfied, a state which must necessarily lead to that certain lascivious fury the friends shall strive to provoke, considering it one of lubricity's most highly delectable situations.

At eleven o'clock, the friends shall repair to the quarters appointed for the little girls. In that place will be served breakfast consisting of chocolate, or of roasts cooked in Spanish wine, or of other appropriate restoratives. This breakfast shall be served by the eight little girls, naked, aided by the two elders, Marie and Louison, assigned to the seraglio of girls, the other two elders being assigned to that of the boys. If, during this breakfast, the friends are moved to commit impudicities with the little girls, before or after, the latter shall lend themselves thereunto with the resignation prescribed to them, and wherein they shall not be found wanting without severe punishment being the consequence. But it is agreed that at this hour there shall be undertaken no secret or private exercises, and that if a moment's wantonizing be desired, it shall be conducted openly and before the public present at the morning meal.

These little girls shall adopt the general custom of kneeling at all times whenever they see or meet a friend, and they shall remain thus until told to stand; they, the wives, and the elders shall alone be subject to these regulations, wherefrom the others are dispensed, but everyone shall be bound never to address the friends save as my Lord.

Before leaving the girls' apartments, that one of the friends who is invested with the month's stewardship (it being intended that for the space of a month one friend shall be in general supervision of everything, each friend acceding to the office in his turn and in the following order: Durcet during November, the Bishop during December, the Président during January, the Duc during February), he, then, who is the month's presiding officer, before leaving the girls' quarters, shall inspect them all, to determine whether they are in the state wherein they have been instructed to maintain themselves, whereof the elders shall be each morning apprised and which will be determined by the need that exists for them to keep in such and such a state.

As it is strictly forbidden to relieve oneself anywhere save in the chapel, which has been outfitted and intended for this purpose, and forbidden to go there without individual and special permission, the which shall be often refused, and for good reason, the month's presiding officer shall scrupulously examine, immediately after breakfast, all the girls' water closets, and in the case of a contravention discovered in the one above-designated place or in the other, the delinquent shall be condemned to suffer the penalty of death.

The friends shall move from there into the little boys' apartments in order to perform the same inspections and similarly to pronounce capital punishment against offenders. The four little boys who have not been that morning with the friends, shall now receive them when they enter their chamber and shall untrouser themselves before them, the other four shall remain standing in attention, awaiting the orders which are given them.

Messieurs may or may not indulge in lewd byplay with the four they have not until now seen during the day, but whatever they do shall be done publicly; no intimate commerce shall be held at this hour.

At one o'clock, those of the girls or the boys, of mature and of young years, who have obtained permission to satisfy urgent needs, that is to say, the heavier sort, and this permission shall never be put most sparingly accorded, and at the most to a third of the subjects, those, we repeat, shall betake themselves to the chapel where everything has been artistically arranged for the voluptuous delights falling under this head. In this place they will find the four friends who shall wait for them until two o'clock and never any longer, and who shall distribute and adjust them as they judge proper to the delights of this order which they may be moved to taste.

From two to three the first two tables shall be served: they shall dine simultaneously, one in the girls' large apartment, the other in that of the young boys: the three kitchen servants shall serve these two tables. At the first shall sit the eight little girls and the four elders; at the second the four wives, the eight little boys, and the four storytellers. During their meal, Messieurs will be pleased to gather in the living room where they will chat together until three o'clock. Just before this hour, the eight fuckers shall make their appearance here, as well clothed and as well adorned as it is in their power to be.

At three shall be served the masters' dinner, and the honor to be present there shall be enjoyed by none but the eight fuckers; this meal shall be served by the four wives, entirely naked, aided by the four elders, clad as sorceresses; to the latter shall fall the task of bringing the plates from the towers into which the servants, on the other side, shall have put them, and the plates shall be handed to wives, who shall deposit them on the table. The eight fuckers, in the course of the dinner, will be at liberty to handle and touch the unclothed bodies of the wives in whatever manner and to whatever extent they please, without the said wives being permitted to refuse or defend themselves; the fuckers will even be able to go to the point of employing insults and of thickening their sticks by apostrophizing them with all the invectives they may see fit to pronounce.

The friends shall rise from the table at five, at which time these Messieurs only (the fuckers shall retire until the hour of general assembly), these Messieurs only, I say, shall pass into the salon, where two little boys and two little girls, who shall be changed daily, shall, in a state of nudity, serve them coffee and liqueur; nor shall it be at this point in the day's activities Messieurs shall permit themselves diversions which might enervate them; conversation shall be limited to simple jesting.

Shortly before six o'clock, the four children who have been serving, shall withdraw and go promptly to dress themselves. At exactly six, Messieurs shall pass into the assembly chamber heretofore described. They shall each of them repair to their respective alcoves, and the following distribution shall be observed by the others: upon the throne shall be the storyteller, the tiers below the throne shall be occupied by the sixteen children, so arranged that four of them, that is to say, two girls and two boys, shall be situated directly opposite each niche; each niche shall have before it a like quatrain; this quatrain shall be specially allocated to the niche before which it is placed, the niches alongside being excluded from making any claims upon it, and these quatrains shall be diversified each day, never shall the same niche have the same quatrain. Each child in each quatrain shall have one end of a chain of artificial flowers secured to his arm, the other end of the chain leading to the niche, so that when the niche's proprietor wishes any given child in his quatrain, he has but to tug the garland, and the child shall come running and fling himself at the master's feet.

Above the quatrain shall be situate an elder, attached to the quatrain, and responsive to the orders of the chief of that quatrain's niche.

The three storytellers who are not on active service as raconteurs during the month shall be seated upon a bench at the foot of the throne, assigned to no one but yet ready to do anyone's bidding. The four fuckers appointed to spend the night with the friends may be absent from the assembly; they shall be in their rooms, busy grooming themselves for the coming night, at which time great feats shall be regularly expected of them. With respect to the four others, they shall be each one at the feet of one of the friends, who shall be in his niche and upon his couch beside that one of the wives whose turn it is to be with any given husband. This wife shall be at all times naked, the fucker shall wear a closefitting singlet and shorts of taffeta, pink in color, the month's storyteller shall be attired as an elegant courtesan, as shall be her three companions, the little boys and the little girls of the quatrains shall always be differently and splendidly costumed, one quatrain in Asiatic style, one in Spanish, another in Turkish garb, a fourth in Greek, and on the following day otherwise; but all these costumes shall be of taffeta or of lawn; at no time shall the lower half of the body be discomfited by any raiment, and the removal of a pin shall suffice to bare it completely.

As for the elders, they shall alternately interpret the Graeae, nuns, fairies, sorceresses, and upon occasion, widows. The doors to the closets contiguous to the niches shall be kept at a warm temperature by stoves, and shall be garnished with all the appurtenances required for various debauches. Four candles shall burn in each of the closets, and fifty in the auditorium.

Punctually at six o'clock, the storyteller shall begin her story, which the friends may interrupt at any point and as frequently as they please; this narration shall last until ten o'clock in the evening, and during this time, as its object is to inflame the imagination, every lubricity will be permitted, save however for those which might be prejudicial to the approved schedule of deflowerings, which shall be at all times rigorously observed; apart from this, Messieurs may do what they like with their fucker, wife, quatrain, quatrain elder, and even with the storytellers if this whim move them, and that either in their niche or in the adjacent closet. The narration shall be suspended for as long as the pleasures of him whose needs interrupt it continue, and when he shall have done and be sated, the tale shall be resumed.

The evening meal shall be served at ten. The wives, the storytellers, and the eight little girls shall without delay proceed to dine by themselves, women never being admitted to the men's supper, and the friends shall sup with the four fuckers not scheduled for night duty, and with four little boys. Aided by the elders, the four other boys shall serve.

The evening meal concluded, Messieurs shall pass into the salon for the celebration of what are to be called the orgies. Everyone shall convene there, both those who have supped apart and those who have supped with the friends, the four fuckers chosen for the night's service being excepted.

The salon shall be heated to an unusual temperature, and illuminated by chandeliers. All present shall be naked: storytellers, wives, little girls, little boys, elders, fuckers, friends, everything shall be pell-mell, everyone shall be sprawled on the floor and, after the example of animals, shall change, shall commingle, entwine, couple incestuously, adulterously, sodomistically, deflowerings being at all times banned, the company shall give itself over to every excess and to every debauch which may best warm the mind. When 'tis time for these deflowerings, it shall be at this moment and in these circumstances that those operations shall be performed, and once a child shall be initiate, it shall be available for every enjoyment, in all manners and at all times.

The orgies shall cease at precisely two in the morning, the four fuckers designated for nocturnal exercise shall come, in elegant undress, to lead away each of them the friend wherewith he is to bed, each friend shall be provided also with one of the wives or with a deflowered subject, when deflowered subjects there be, or with a storyteller, or with an elder to pass the night 'twixt her and his fucker, and all this according to his disposition, whereunto but one clause is put, that he submit himself to prudent arrangements whence it may result that each friend varies his companions every night, or is able so to do.

Such shall be the daily order of procedure. In addition, each week of the seventeen prescribed as the period of the sojourn at the château shall be marked by a festival. There shall be, first of all, marriages, full particulars relating to which shall be made available in due time and place. But as the first of these matches shall be made between the youngest of the children, who are not able to consummate them, they will in no wise disturb the schedule established for the deflorations. Marriages between adults being all post-defloratory, their consummation will damage nothing since, in acting, the friends shall be enjoying only what has been enjoyed already.

The four elders, to be held answerable for the behavior of their four children, shall, when it is faulty, report it to the month's presiding officer, and each Saturday there shall take place a common meting out of punishments, at the time of the orgies. An exact list of accumulating delinquencies shall be kept until then.

With what regards misbehavior on the part of the storytellers, their punishments shall be one-half that of the children, because their talents are to some purpose, and talent must always be respected. As for errors in the conduct of the wives, they shall always be rewarded by punishment double that given the children.

Should any subject in some way refuse anything demanded of him, even when incapacitated or when that thing is impossible, he shall be punished with utmost severity; 'tis for him to provide, for him to discover ways and means.

The least display of mirth, or the least evidence given of disrespect or lack of submission during the debauch activities, shall be esteemed one of the gravest of faults and shall be one of the most cruelly punished.

Any man taken flagrante delicto with a woman shall punished by the loss of a limb when authorization to enjoy this woman has not hitherto been granted him.

The slightest religious act on the part of any subject, whomsoever he be, whatsoever be that act, shall be punished by death.

Messieurs are expressly enjoined at all gatherings to employ none but the most lascivious language, remarks indicative of the greatest debauchery, expressions of the filthiest, the most harsh, and the most blasphemous.

The name of God shall never be uttered save when accompanied by invectives or imprecations, and thus qualified it shall be repeated as often as possible.

With respect to their tone, it shall at all times be exceedingly brutal, exceedingly harsh, and exceedingly imperious when addressing the wives and the little girls, but wheedling, whorish, and depraved when addressing the men whom the friends, by adopting with them the role of women, should regard as their husbands.

Any friend who fails to comply with any one of these articles, or who may take it into his head to act in accordance with a single glimmer of common sense or moderation and above all to spend a single day without retiring dead drunk to bed, shall be fined ten thousand francs.

Whenever a friend experiences the need to relieve himself heavily, a woman from that class he considers fitting shall be obliged to accompany him, to attend to those duties he shall during this activity indicate to her.

No subject, whether male or female, shall be allowed to fulfill duties of cleanliness whatsoever they may be, and above all those consequent upon the heavy need relieved, without express permission from the month's presiding officer, and if it be refused him, and if despite that refusal he surrender to this need, his punishment shall be of the very rudest.

The four wives shall have no prerogatives of any kind over the other women; on the contrary, they shall at all times be treated with a maximum of rigor and inhumanity, and they shall be frequently employed upon the vilest and most painful enterprises, such as for example the cleaning of the private and common privies established in the chapel. These privies shall be emptied only once every week, but always by them, and they shall be severely punished if they resist the work or accomplish it poorly.

Should a subject attempt evasion while the assembly is sitting, he shall be punished by death instantly, whomsoever he be.

The cooks and their assistants shall be respected, and those of the friends who violate this article shall pay a fine of one thousand gold louis. With regard to these fines, they shall all be specially employed, upon the return to France, for the initial expenses incidental to a new party, either in this same kind, or in another.

These affairs being settled and these regulations published on the 30th, the Duc spent the morning of the 31st inspecting everything, having the statutes repeated aloud, and scrupulously examining the premises to see whether they were susceptible to assault or favorable to escape.

Having concluded that one would have to have wings or the devil's powers to get out or in, he reported his findings to the society and devoted the evening to haranguing the women. By his order they were all convoked in the auditorium, and having mounted that kind of tribune or throne intended for the storyteller, here more or less is the speech he delivered to them.

"Feeble, enfettered creatures destined solely for our pleasures, I trust you have not deluded yourselves into supposing that the equally abso-lute and ridiculous ascendancy given you in the outside world would be accorded you in this place; a thousand times more subjugated than would be slaves, you must expect naught but humiliation, and obedience is that one virtue whose use I recommend to you: it and no other befits your present state. Above all, do not take it into your heads to rely in the least upon your charms; we are utterly indifferent to those snares and, you may depend on it, such bait will fail with us. Ceaselessly bear in mind that we will make use of you all, but that not a single one of you need beguile herself into imagining that she is able to inspire any feeling of pity in us. Roused in fury against the altars that have been able to snatch from us some few grains of incense, our pride and our libertinage shatter them as soon as the illusion has satisfied our senses, and contempt almost always followed by hatred instantly assumes the pre-eminence hitherto occupied by our imagination. What, furthermore, might you offer that we do not know by heart already? what will you tender us that we shall not grind beneath our heels, often at the very moment delirium transports us?

"Useless to conceal it from you: your service will be arduous, it will be painful and rigorous, and the slightest delinquencies will be requited immediately with corporal and afflicting punishments; hence, I must recommend to you prompt exactness, submissiveness, and a total self-abnegation that you be enabled to heed naught but our desires; let them be your only laws, fly to do their bidding, anticipate them, cause them to be born. Not that you have much to gain by this conduct, but simply because, by not observing it, you will have a great deal to lose.

"Give a thought to your circumstances, think what you are, what we are, and may these reflections cause you to quake -- you are beyond the borders of France in the depths of an uninhabitable forest, high amongst naked mountains; the paths that brought you here were destroyed behind you as you advanced along them. You are enclosed in an impregnable citadel; no one on earth knows you are here; you are beyond the reach of your friends, of your kin: insofar as the world is concerned, you are already dead, and if yet you breathe, 'tis by our pleasure, and for it only. And what are the persons to whom you are now subordinated? Beings of a profound and recognized criminality, who have no god but their lubricity, no laws but their depravity, no care but for their debauch, godless, unprincipled, unbelieving profligates, of whom the least criminal is soiled by more infamies than you could number, and in whose eyes the life of a woman --what do I say, the life of a woman? the lives of all women who dwell on the face of the earth, are as insignificant as the crushing of a fly. There will, doubtless, be few you, without the flutter of an eyelash lend yourselves to them all, and faced with whatever it may be, show patience, submission, and courage. If unhappily, some amongst you succumb to our passions' intemperance, let her adjust bravely to her fate: we are not going to exist forever in this world, and the most fortunate thing that can befall a woman is to die young. Our ordinances have been read to you: they are very wise and well-designed for your safety and for our pleasures; obey them blindly, and expect the worst from us should we be irritated by your misbehavior. Several amongst you have ties with us, I know, and perhaps they embolden you, and perhaps you hope for indulgence on this account; you would be most gravely mistaken were you to put much store by them: no blood attachment is sacred in the view of people like ourselves, and the more they seem so to you, the more their rupture will stimulate the perversity in our spirits. Daughters, wives, it is to you, then, I address myself at present: expect us to grant you no prerogative, you are herewith advised that you will be treated with an even greater severity than the others, and that specifically to point out to you with what scorn we view the bonds whereby you perhaps think us constrained.

"Moreover, do not simply wait for us to specify the orders we would have you execute: a gesture, a glance, often simply one of our internal feelings will announce our desire, and you will be as harshly punished for not having divined it as you would be were you, after having been notified, to ignore that desire or flout it. It is up to you to interpret our movements, our glances, our gestures, to interpret our expressions, and above all not to be mistaken as to our desires. Let us suppose, for example, this desire were to see a particular part of your body and that, through clumsiness, you were to exhibit some other -- you appreciate to what extent such contempt would be upsetting to our imaginations, and you are aware of all that one risks by chilling the mind of a libertine who, let us presume, is expecting an ass for his discharge, and to whom some fool presents a cunt.

"By and large, offer your fronts very little to our sight; remember that this loathsome part, which only the alienation of her wits could have permitted Nature to create, is always the one we find most repugnant. And relative to your ass itself, there are precautions to observe: not only would you be well-advised, upon presenting it, to hide the odious lair which accompanies it, but it behooves you to avoid the display, at certain moments, of an ass in that certain state wherein other folk desire always to find it; you probably understand me; and furthermore, the four duennas will furnish you later on with instructions which will complete the explanation of everything.

"In short: shudder, tremble, anticipate, obey -- and with all that, if you are not very fortunate, perhaps you will not be completely miserable. No intrigues amongst you, no alliances, none of that ridiculous friendship between the girls which, by softening the heart in one sense, in another renders it both more ill-tempered and less well-disposed to the one and simple humiliation to which you are fated by us; consider that it is not at all as human beings we behold you, but exclusively as animals one feeds in return for their services, and which one withers with blows when they refuse to be put to use.

"You have seen with what stringency you are forbidden anything resembling any act of religion whatsoever. I warn you: few crimes will be more severely punished than this one. It is only too well known that in your midst there are yet a few fools unable to bring themselves to abjure this infamous God and abhor his worship; I would have you know that these imbeciles will be scrupulously examined, and there is no extremity they will not suffer who are so unlucky as to be taken in the act. Let them be persuaded, these stupid creatures, let them henceforth be convinced that in all the world there are not twenty persons today who cling to this mad notion of God's existence, and that the religion he invokes is nothing but a fable ludicrously invented by cheats and impostors, whose interest in deceiving us is only too clear at the present time. In fine, decide for yourselves: were there a God and were this God to have any power, would he permit the virtue which honors him, and which you profess, to be sacrificed to vice and libertinage as it is going to be? Would this all-powerful God permit a feeble creature like myself, who would, face to face with him, be as a mite in the eyes of an elephant, would he, I say, permit this feeble creature to insult him, to flout him, to defy him, to challenge him, to offend him as I do, wantonly, at my own sweet will, at every instant of the day?.

This little sermon concluded, the Duc descended from the chair and, with the exception of the four elders and the four narrators, who knew very well they were there as sacrificers and priestesses rather than as victims, except for those eight individuals, I say, everyone burst into tears, and the Duc, not much touched by the scene, left those enacting it to conjecture, jabber, and complain to each other, in perfect certainty the eight spies would render a thorough report of everything: and off he went to spend the night with Hercule, the member of the troupe of fuckers who had become his most intimate favorite in the capacity of a lover, little Zéphyr still having, as a mistress, the first place in his heart. In that upon the following morning everything was to begin, the mechanism was to start functioning, everyone accordingly completed final arrangements, went soundly to sleep, and on the morrow at the stroke of ten, the curtain rose upon a scene of libertinage which was to continue unimpeded, in strict compliance with prescription, until and including the 28th day of February.

And now, friend-reader, you must prepare your heart and your mind for the most impure tale that has ever been told since our world began, a book the likes of which are met with neither amongst the ancients nor amongst us moderns. Fancy, now, that all pleasure-taking either sanctioned by good manners or enjoined by that fool you speak of incessantly, of whom you know nothing and whom you call Nature; fancy, I say, that all these modes of taking pleasure will be expressly excluded from this anthology, of that whenever peradventure you do indeed encounter them here, they will always be accompanied by some crime or colored by some infamy.

Many of the extravagances you are about to see illustrated will doubtless displease you, yes, I am well aware of it, but there are amongst them a few which will warm you to the point of costing you some fuck, and that, reader, is all we ask of you; if we have not said everything, analyzed everything, tax us not with partiality, for you cannot expect us to have guessed what suits you best.

Rather, it is up to you to take what you please and leave the rest alone, another reader will do the same, and little by little, everyone will find himself satisfied. It is the story of the magnificent banquet: six hundred different plates offer themselves to your appetite; are you going to eat them all? No, surely not, but this prodigious variety enlarges the bounds of your choice and, delighted by this increase of possibilities, it surely never occurs to you to scold the Amphitryon who regales you.

Do likewise here: choose and let lie the rest without declaiming against that rest simply because it does not have the power to please you. Consider that it will enchant someone else, and be a philosopher.

As for the diversity, it is authentic, you may be sure of it; study closely that passion which to your first consideration seems perfectly to resemble another, and you will see that a difference does exist and that, however slightly it may be, it possesses precisely that refinement, that touch which distinguishes and characterizes the kind of libertinage wherewith we are here involved.

We have, moreover, blended these six hundred passions into the storytellers' narratives. That is one more thing whereof the reader were well to have foreknowledge: it would have been too monotonous to catalogue them one by one outside the body of the story. But as some reader not much learned in these matters might perhaps confuse the designated passions with the adventure or simple event in the narrator's life, each of these passions has been carefully distinguished by a marginal notation: a line, above which is the title that may be given the passion. This mark indicates the exact place where the account of the passions begins, and the end of the paragraph always indicates where it finishes.

But as numerous personages participate in a drama of this kind, notwithstanding the care we have taken in this introduction to describe and designate each one... we shall provide an index which will contain the name and age of every actor, together with a brief sketch of them all; so that should the reader, as he moves along, encounter what seems to him an unfamiliar figure, he will have merely to turn back to this index, and if this little aid to his memory suffice not, to the more thorough portraits given earlier.

Dramatis Personae

The Duc de Blangis, fifty, built like a satyr, endowed with a monstrous member and prodigious strength; he may be regarded as the depository of every vice and every crime. He has killed his mother, his sister, and three of his wives.

The Bishop of X*** is his brother; forty-five years old, more slender and more delicate than the Duc; a nasty mouth. He is deceitful, adroit, a faithful sectary of sodomy, active and passive, he has an absolute contempt for all other kinds of pleasure, he has brought about the cruel deaths of the two children whose sizable fortune was left in trust with him; he is a nervous type, so sensitive he nearly swoons upon discharging.

The Président de Curval, sixty; a tall, thin, lank man, with sunken, dead eyes, an unhealthy mouth, the walking image of low license and libertinage, frightfully dirty about his body and attaching voluptuousness thereto. He has been circumcised, his erection is rare and difficult, it does take place however, and he ejaculates almost every day. His tastes induce him to prefer men; all the same, he has no scorn for a maid. For singularities in his tastes, he has a fondness for old age and whatever is kin to him in filthiness. He is endowed with a member practically as thick as the Duc's. In late years he has seemed as though unstrung by debauchery, and he drinks a great deal. He owes his fortune solely to murders and is nominally guilty of one, a dreadful one, whose details are contained in his biography previously given. When discharging, he experiences a sort of lubricious rage; it drives him to cruel deeds.

Durcet, banker, fifty-three, a great friend of the Duc, and his schoolmate; he is short, squat, and chubby, but his body looks healthy, pretty, and lair. He has the figure of a woman and all a woman's tastes: by his little firmness deprived from giving women pleasure, he has imitated that sex and has himself fucked at any time of day or night. He is also rather fond of a good mouthing, 'tis the only expedient which is able to afford him an agent's pleasures. His pleasures are his only gods, and he is constantly prepared to sacrifice everything to them. He is clever, adroit, and has committed a profusion of crimes; he poisoned his mother, his wife, and her niece in order to assure his inheritance. His spirit is stoical, stalwart his heart, and absolutely insensible to pity. He no longer stiffens, his ejaculations are most rare; his instants of crisis are preceded by a kind of spasm which hurls him into a lubricious fury dangerous for those who are serving his passions.

Constance, the Duc's wife, Durcet's daughter; twenty-two years of age, she is a Roman beauty, with more majesty than finesse, plump, but well-constructed, a superb body, a unique ass, a model ass, hair and eyes very dark. She is not without brains or wit, and but too well senses the horror of her fate. A great fund of native virtue nothing has been able to destroy.

Adelaide, Durcet's wife, the Président's daughter; a pretty little object, she is twenty, blond, very tender eyes of a lovely, animated blue, she has about her everything of the romantic heroine. A long, well-attached neck, her one defect is her mouth, which is a shade large. Small breasts and a little ass, but all that, though delicate, is fair and well-molded. A mind given to fantasy, a tender heart, excessively virtuous and believing; she secretly performs her Christian duties.

Julie, the Président's wife, elder daughter of the Duc; she is twenty-four, fat, fleshy, with fine brown eyes, a pretty nose, striking and agreeable features, but an appalling mouth. She has little virtue and even pronounced tendencies to uncleanliness, alcoholism, gluttony, and whoredom. Her husband loves her for her defective mouth; this singularity appeals to the Président's tastes. She has never been given either principles or religion.

Aline, her younger sister, supposed daughter of the Duc, really one of the Duc's wives and the Bishop's child; she is eighteen, has a very agreeable and fetching countenance, abounding health, brown eyes, an upturned nose, a mischievous air although she is profoundly indolent and lazy. She seems as yet to have no temperament and most sincerely detests all the infamies she is victim of. The Bishop baptized her behind at the age of ten. She has been left in crass ignorance, knows neither how to read nor write, she abhors the Bishop and greatly fears the Duc. She is much attached to her sister, is sober and tidy, speaks oddly and like a child; her ass is charming.

Duclos, the first storyteller; forty-eight, preserves her looks, is in good physical health, has the finest ass to be seen. Brunette, full figure, very well fleshed.

Champville is fifty; she is slender, well made, has lascivious eyes, she is a tribade, and everything about her proclaims it. Her present trade is pimping. She was once fair-haired, has pretty eyes, is long in the clitoris and ticklish in that part, has an ass much worn from service, but is none the less untupped in that place.

Martaine is fifty-two; she's a procuress too, a matronly dame, hale and hearty; inner obstructions have prevented her from ever knowing any but Sodom's delights, for which indeed she seems to have been specially created, for, her age notwithstanding, she has the world's noblest ass; it is both broad and big and so habituated to introductions that she can accommodate the weightiest engines without the flutter of an eyelash. She has pretty features still, but they are beginning to fade.

Desgranges is fifty-six; she is even now the greatest villain who has ever lived; she is tall, slender, pale, and was once dark-haired, she is crime's personification. Her withered ass resembles marbled paper, or parchment, and its orifice is immense. She is one-dugged, is missing three fingers and six teeth, fructus belli. There exists not a single crime she has not perpetrated or engineered, her prattle is pleasing to the ear, she has wit, and is currently one of the outfitters most highly respected by society.

Marie, the first of the duennas, is the youngest at fifty-eight; she has been whipped and branded, and was a servant to thieves. Her eyes are lackluster and running, her nose crooked, her teeth yellow, one buttock's gnawed by an abscess. She has borne and killed fourteen children.

Louison, the second duenna, is sixty; she is small, lame, one-eyed, and hunchbacked, but for all that she has yet a very pretty ass. She is always ready for crime and is extremely wicked. She and Marie are appointed as governesses to the girls, and the two following to the boys.

Thérèse, aged sixty-two, looks like a skeleton, has no hair, no teeth, a stinking mouth, an ass seamed with scars, its hole is of excessively generous diameter. Filthy and fetid to an atrocious degree; she has a twisted arm, and she limps.

Fanchon, sixty-nine years old, has been six times hanged in effigy and has perpetrated every crime under the sun; she squints, is flat-nosed, short, heavy, has no forehead, two teeth only. An erysipelas covers her ass, a bunch of hemorrhoids hangs from her hole, a chancre is eating her womb, she has a burnt thigh, and a cancer gnaws her breast. She is constantly drunk and vomits, farts, and shits here, there, and everywhere all the time, and all unawares she is doing it.

HAREM OF LITTLE GIRLS

Augustine, daughter of a Languedoc baron, fifteen years old, alert and pretty little face.

Fanny, daughter of a Breton counselor, fourteen, a sweet and tender air.

Zelmire, daughter of the Comte de Terville, seigneur of Beauce, fifteen, a noble look and a very sensitive soul.

Sophie, daughter of a gentleman from Berry, charming features, fourteen years.

Colombe, daughter of a counselor to the Parliament of Paris, thirteen years old, exuberant health.

Hébé, daughter of an Orléans officer, a very libertine air, charming eyes, she is twelve.

Rosette and Michette, both look like lovely virgins. The first is thirteen and is the daughter of a Chalon-sur-Saône officer, the other is twelve and is a daughter of the Marquis de Sénanges; she was abducted from her father's estate in Bourbonnais.

Their figures, the rest of their features and chiefly their asses are beyond all description. They were chosen from amongst one hundred and fifty.

HAREM OF LITTLE BOYS

Zélamir, thirteen, son of a Poitou squire.

Cupidon, same age, son of a gentleman from near La Flèche.

Narcisse, twelve, son of a nobleman situated in Rouen, Knight of Malta.

Zéphyr, fifteen, son of a general living in Paris. He is destined for the Duc.

Céladon, son of a Nancy magistrate. He is fourteen.

Adonis, son of a judge of a Paris assize court; fifteen, destined for Curval.

Hyacinthe, fourteen, son of a retired officer dwelling in Champagne.

Giton, page to the King, twelve, son of a gentleman from the Nivernais.

No pen is capable of representing the graces, the features, and the charms of these eight children superior also to all the tongue is empowered to say, and chosen, as you know, from amongst a very large number.

EIGHT FUCKERS

Hercule, twenty-six, very pretty, but also a very mean character, the Duc's favorite; his prick measures eight and one-quarter inches around and thirteen in length. Plentiful discharge.

Antinoüs is thirty. A fine specimen of a man, his prick is eight inches around and twelve inches long.

Bum-Cleaver, twenty-eight years old, has the look of a satyr; his majestic prick is bent saber fashion, its head, or glans, is enormous, it is eight and three-eighths inches in circumference and the shaft eight in length. A fine curve to this majestic prick.

Invictus is twenty-five, he is exceedingly ugly, but healthy and vigorous; the great favorite of Curval, he is continually aroused, and his prick is seven and fifteen-sixteenths inches around by eleven inches long.

The four others measure from nine to ten and fifteen-sixteenths inches long, by from seven and a half and five-eights inches around, and they are from twenty-five to thirty years of age.

End of the Introduction. Omissions I have made in it:

I must say that Hercule and Invictus are, the one a very mean character and the other very ugly, and that not one of the eight has ever been able to enjoy either a man or a woman.

That the chapel is used for a toilet, and give details of this usage.

That the outfitters, male and female, had cutthroats with them and under their orders during their forays.

Give some few more details about the elders' breasts and speak of Fanchon's cancer. Also a few more touches to the descriptions of the children's faces.

PART THE FIRST

The First Day

THE 150 SIMPLE PASSIONS, OR THOSE BELONGING TO THE FIRST CLASS, COMPOSING THETHIRTY DAYS OF NOVEMBER PASSED IN HEARING THE NARRATION OF MADAME DUCLOS; INTERSPERSED AMONGST WHICH ARE THE SCANDALOUS DOINGS AT THE CHÂTEAU DURING THAT MONTH; ALL BEING SET DOWN IN THE FORM OF A JOURNAL.

The company rose the 1st of November at ten o'clock in the morning, as was specified in the statutes which Messieurs had mutually sworn faithfully to observe in every particular. The four fuckers who had not shared the friends' couches, at their waking hour brought Zéphyr to the Duc, Adonis to Curval, Narcisse to Durcet, and Zélamir to the Bishop.

All four children were very timid, even more awkward, but, encouraged by their guides, they very nicely carried out their tasks, and the Duc discharged. His three colleagues, more reserved and less prodigal with their fuck, had as much of it deposited in them as did the Duc, but distributed none of their own.

At eleven o'clock they passed into the women's quarters where the eight young sultanas appeared naked, and in this state served chocolate, aided and directed by Marie and Louison, who presided over this seraglio. There was a great deal of handling and colling, and the eight poor girls, wretched little victims of the most blatant lubricity, blushed, hid behind their hands, sought to protect their charms, and immediately displayed everything as soon as they observed that their modesty irritated and annoyed their masters. The Duc rose up like a shot and measured his engine's circumference against Michette's slender little waist: their difference did not exceed three inches. Durcet, the month's presiding officer, conducted the prescribed examinations and made the necessary searches; Hébé and Colombe were found to have lapsed, their punishment was pronounced at once and fixed for the following Saturday at orgy hour. They wept. No one was moved.

They proceeded to the boys' apartments. The four who had not appeared that morning, namely Cupidon, Céladon, Hyacinthe and Giton, bared their behinds in accordance with orders, and the sight provided an instant's amusement. Curval kissed them all on the mouth, and the Bishop spent a moment frigging their pricks while the Duc and Durcet were doing something else. The inspections were completed, no misconduct was discovered.

At one o'clock Messieurs betook themselves to the chapel where, as you know, the sanitary conveniences were installed. The calculation of requirements for the coming soiree having led to the refusal of a good number of requests, only Constance, Duclos, Augustine, Sophie, Zélamir, Cupidon, and Louison appeared; all the others had asked permission and had been instructed to hold back until evening. Our four friends, ranged around the same specially constructed seat, had these seven subjects take their seat one after another, and then retired when they had enough of this spectacle. They descended to the salon where, while the women dined, they gossiped and tattled until the time came for them to be served their meal. Each of the four friends placed himself between two fuckers, pursuant to the imposed rule that barred all women from their table, and the four naked wives, aided by the elders costumed as the Graeae, served them the most magnificent and the most succulent dinner it were possible to concoct. No one more delicate, more skilled than the cooks they had brought with them, and they were so well paid and so lavishly provided that everything could not fail to be a brilliant success. As the midday fare was to be less heavy than the evening meal, they were restricted to four superb courses, each composed of twelve plates. Burgundy wine arrived with the hors d'oeuvres, Bordeaux was served with the entrees, champagne with the roasts, Hermitage accompanied the entrements, Tokay and madeira were served with dessert.

Spirits rose little by little; the fuckers, whom the friends had granted every liberty with their wives, treated them somewhat untenderly. Constance was even a bit knocked about, rather beaten for having dawdled over bringing a dish to Hercule who, seeing himself well advanced in the Duc's good graces, fancied he might carry insolence to the point of drubbing and molesting his wife; the Duc thought this very amusing. Curval, in an ugly humor by the time dessert arrived, flung a plate at his wife's face, and it might have clove her head in two had she not ducked. Spying one of his neighbors stiffen, Durcet, though they were still at table, promptly unbuttoned his breeches and presented his ass. The neighbor drove his weapon home; the operation once concluded, they fell to drinking again as if nothing had happened. The Duc soon imitated his old friend's little infamy and wagered that, enormous as Invictus' prick might be, he could calmly down three bottles of wine while lying embuggered upon it. What effortlessness, what ease, what detachment in libertinage! He won what he had staked, and as they were not drunk on an empty stomach, as those three bottles fell upon at least fifteen others, the Duc's head began gently to swim. The first object upon which his eye alighted was his wife, weeping over the abuse she had sustained from Hercule, and this sight so inspired the Duc he lost not an instant doing to her things too excessive for us to describe as yet. The reader will notice how hampered we are in these beginnings, and how stumbling are our efforts to give a coherent account of these matters; we trust he will forgive us for leaving the curtain drawn over a considerable number of little details. We promise it will be raised later on.

Our champions finally made their way into the salon, where new pleasures and further delights were awaiting them. Coffee and liqueurs were distributed by a charming quartet made up of Adonis and Hyacinthe, two appealing little boys, and two pretty maids, Zelmire and Fanny. Thérèse, one of the duennas, supervised them, for it was decreed that wherever two or more children were gathered, a duenna was to be on hand. Our four libertines, half-drunk but none the less resolved to abide their laws, contended themselves with kisses, fingerings, but their libertine intelligence knew how to season these mild activities with all the refinements of debauch and lubricity. It was thought for a moment that the Bishop was going to have to surrender his fuck in exchange for the extraordinary things he was wringing from Hyacinthe, while Zelmire frigged him. His nerves were already aquiver, an impending crisis was beginning to take possession of his entire being, but he checked himself, the tempting objects ready to triumph over his senses were sent spinning and, knowing there was yet a full day's work ahead of him, the Bishop saved his best for the evening. Six different kinds of liqueur were drunk, three kinds of coffee, and the hour sounding at last, the two couples withdrew to dress.

Our friends took a fifteen minute nap, then moved into the throne room, the place where the auditors were to listen to the narrations.

The friends took their places upon their couches, the Duc having his beloved Hercule at his feet, near him, naked, Adelaide, Durcet's wife and the Président's daughter, and for quatrain opposite him, and linked to his niche by a chain of flowers, as has been explained, Zéphyr, Giton, Augustine, and Sophie costumed as shepherds, supervised by Louison as an old peasant woman playing the role of their mother.

At Curval's feet was Invictus, upon his couch lay Constance, the Duc's wife and Durcet's daughter, and for quatrain four little Spaniards, each sex dressed in its costume and as elegantly as possible: they were Adonis, Céladon, Fanny, and Zelmire; Fanchon clad as a duenna, watched over them.

The Bishop had Antinoüs at his feet, his niece Julie on his couch, and four little almost naked savages for quatrain. The boys: Cupidon and Narcisse; the girls: Hébé and Rosette; an old Amazon, interpreted by Thérèse, was in charge of them.

Durcet had Bum-Cleaver for fucker, near him reclined Aline, daughter of the Bishop, and in front of him were four little sultanas, the boys being dressed as girls, and this refinement to the last degree emphasized the enchanting visages of Zélamir, Hyacinthe, Colombe, and Michette. An old Arab slave, portrayed by Marie, presided over this quatrain.

The three storytellers, magnificently dressed as upper-class Parisian courtesans, were seated below the throne upon a couch, and Madame Duclos, the month's narrator, in very scanty and very elegant attire, well rouged and heavily bejeweled, having taken her place on the stage, thus began the story of what had occurred in her life, into which account she was, with all pertinent details, to insert the first one hundred and fifty passions designated by the title of simple passions:

'Tis no slight undertaking, Messieurs, to attempt to express oneself before a circle such as yours. Accustomed to all of the most subtle and most delicate that letters produce, how, one may wonder, will you be able to bear the ill-shaped periods and uncouth images of a humble creature like myself who has received no other education than the one supplied her by libertinage. But your indulgence reassures me; you ask for naught but the natural and true, and I dare say what of these I shall provide you will merit your attention.

My mother was twenty-five when she brought me into the world, and I was her second child; the first was also a daughter, by six years my elder. My mother's birth was not distinguished. She had been early bereft of both her father and mother, and as her parents had dwelled near the Récollet monastery in Paris, when she found herself an orphan, abandoned and without any resources, she obtained permission from these good fathers to come and ask for alms in their church. But as she had some youth and health, she soon attracted their notice, and gradually mounted from the church below to the rooms above, whence she soon descended with child. It was as a consequence of one such adventure my sister saw the light, and it is more likely that my own birth might rightly be ascribed to no other cause.

However, content with my mother's docility and seeing how she did make the community to prosper and flourish, the good fathers rewarded her works by granting her what might be earned from the rental of seats in their church; my mother no sooner obtained this post than, with her superior's leave, she married one of the house's water carriers who straightway, without the least repugnance, adopted my sister and me.

Born into the Church, I dwelled so to speak more in the House of God than in our own; I helped my mother arrange the chairs, I seconded the sacristans in their various operations, I would have said Mass had that been necessary, although I had not yet attained my fifth year.

One day, returning from my holy occupations, my sister asked me whether I had yet encountered Father Laurent....

I said I had not.

"Well, look out," said she, "he's on the watch for you, I know he is, he wants to show you what he showed me. Don't run away, look him straight in the eye without being afraid, he won't touch you, but he'll show you something very funny, and if you let him do it he'll pay you a lot. There are more than fifteen of us around here whom he's shown it to. That's what he likes best, and he's given a present to us all."

You may well imagine, Messieurs, that nothing more was needed, not only to keep me from fleeing Father Laurent, but to induce me to seek him out; at that age the voice of modesty is a whisper at best, and its silence until the time one has left the tutelage of Nature is certain proof, is it not, that this factitious sentiment is far less the product of that original mother's training than it is the fruit of education? I flew instantly to the church, and as I was crossing a little court located between the entrance of the churchyard and the monastery, I bumped squarely into Father Laurent. He was a monk about forty, with a very handsome face. He stopped me.

"Whither are you going, Françon?" he asked. "To arrange the chairs, Father."

"Never fear, never fear, your mother will attend to them," said he. "Come, come along with me," and he drew me toward a sequestered chamber hard by the place. "I am going to show you something you have never seen."

I follow him, we enter, he shuts the door and, having posted me directly opposite him:

"Well, Françon," says he, pulling a monstrous prick from his drawers, an instrument which nearly toppled me with fright; "tell me," he continues, frigging himself, "have you ever seen anything to equal it?... that's what they call a prick, my little one, yes, a prick... it's used for fucking, and what you're going to see, what's going to flow out of it in a moment or two, is the seed wherefrom you were created. I've shown it to your sister, I've shown it to all the little girls of your age, lend a hand, help it along, help get it out, do as your sister does, she's got it out of me twenty times or more....

I show them my prick, and then what do you suppose I do? I squirt the fuck in their face.... That's my passion, my child, I have no other... and you're about to behold it."

And at the same time I felt myself completely drenched in a white spray, it soaked me from head to foot, some drops of it had leapt even into my eyes, for my little head just came to the height of his fly. However, Laurent was gesticulating. "Ah! the pretty fuck, the dear fuck I am losing," he cried, "why, look at you! You're covered with it." And gradually regaining control of himself, he calmly put his tool away and decamped, slipping twenty sous into my hand and suggesting that I bring him any little companions I might happen to have.

As you may readily fancy, I could not have been more eager to run and tell everything to my sister; she wiped me dry, taking the greatest care to overlook none of the spots, and she who had enabled me to earn my little fortune did not fail to demand half of my wages. Instructed by this example, I did not fail, in the hope of a similar division of the spoils, to round up as many little girls for Father Laurent as I could find. But having brought him one with whom he was already familiar, he turned her away, the while giving me three sous by way of encouragement.

"I never see the same one twice, my child," he told me, "bring me some I don't know, never any of those who say they've already had dealings with me."

I managed more successfully; in the space of three months, I introduced Father Laurent to more than twenty new girls, with whom, for the sake of his pleasure, he employed the identical proceedings he had with me. Together with the stipulation that they be strangers to him, there was another relative for age, and it appeared to be of infinite importance: he had no use for anything younger than four or older than seven. And my little fortune could not have been faring better when my sister, noticing that I was encroaching upon her domain, threatened to divulge everything to my mother if I did not put a stop to this splendid commerce; I had to give up Father Laurent.

However, my functions continued to keep me in the neighborhood of the monastery; the same day I reached the age of seven I encountered a new lover whose preferred caprice, although very childish, was nevertheless somewhat more serious. This one was named Father Louis, he was older than Laurent, and had some unidentifiable quality in his bearing that was a great deal more libertine. He sidled up to me at the door of the church as I was entering it, and made me promise to come up to his room. At first I advanced a few objections, but once he had assured me that three years ago my sister had come for a visit and that he received little girls of my age every day, I went with him. Scarcely were we in his cell when he closed and bolted the door and, having poured some elixir into a goblet, made me swallow it and then two more copious measures too. This preparatory step taken, the reverend, more affectionate than his confrere, fell to kissing me and, chattering all the while, he untied my apron and, raising my skirt to my bodice, he laid hands, despite my faint strugglings, upon all the anterior parts he had just brought to light; and after having thoroughly fingered and considered them, he inquired of me whether I did not desire to piss. Singularly driven to this need by the strong dose he had a few moments earlier had me drink, I assured him the urge to do so was as powerful as ever it could be, but that I did not want to satisfy it in front of him.

"Oh, my goodness, do! Why yes, my little rascal," quoth the bawdy fellow, "by God yes, you'll piss in my presence and, what's worse, you'll piss upon me. Here it is," he went on, plucking his prick from his breeches, "here's the tool you're going to moisten, just piss on it a little."

And thereupon he lifted me up and set me on two chairs, one foot on one chair, the other foot on the other, he moved the chairs apart as far as was possible, then bade me squat. Holding me in this posture, he placed a container beneath me, established himself on a little stool about as high as the pot; his engine was in his hand, directly under my cunt. One of his hands supporting my haunches, he frigged himself with the other, and my mouth being at a level with his, he kissed it.

"Off you go, my little one, piss," cried he, "flood my prick with that enchanting liquid whose hot outpouring exerts such a sway over my senses. Piss, my heart, care not but to piss and try to inundate my fuck."

Louis became animated, excited himself, it was easy to see that this unusual operation was the one which all his senses most cherished; the sweetest, gentlest ecstasy crowned that very moment when the liquids wherewith he had swollen my stomach, gushed most abundantly out of me, and we simultaneously filled the same pot, he with fuck, I with urine. The exercise concluded, Louis delivered roughly the same speech to me I had heard from Laurent, he wished to make a procuress of his little whore, and this time, caring precious little for my sister's threats, I boldly guided every child I knew to dear Louis. He had every one of them do the same thing, and as he experienced no compunction upon seeing any one of them a second or third time, and as he always gave me separate payment, which had nothing to do with the additional fee I extracted from my little comrades, before six months had passed I found myself with a tidy little sum which was entirely my own; I had only to conceal knowledge of it from my sister.

"Duclos," the Président interrupted at this point, "we have, I believe, advised you that your narrations must be decorated with the most numerous and searching details; the precise way and extent to which we may judge how the passion you describe relates to human manners and man's character is determined by your willingness to disguise no circumstance; and, what is more, the least circumstance is apt to have an immense influence upon the procuring of that kind of sensory irritation we expect from your stories."

"Yes, my Lord," Duclos replied, "I have been advised to omit no detail and to enter into the most minute particulars whenever they serve to shed light upon the human personality, or upon the species of passion; have I neglected something in connection with this one?"

"You have," said the Président; "I have not the faintest notion of your second monk's prick, nor any idea of its discharge. In addition, did he frig your cunt, pray tell, and did he have you dandle his device? You see what I mean by neglected details."

"Your pardon, my Lord," said Duclos, "I shall repair these present mistakes and avoid them in the future. Father Louis possessed a very ordinary member, greater in its length than it was around and in general of a most common shape and turn; indeed, I do recall that he stiffened rather poorly and that it was not until the crisis arrived he took on a little firmness. No, he did not frig my cunt, he was content to enlarge it with his fingers as much as possible, so as to give free issue to the urine. He brought his prick very close two or three times, and his discharge was rapid, intense, and brief; nothing came from his mouth but the words: 'Ah, fuck! piss, my child, piss the pretty fountain, piss, d'ye hear, piss away, don't you see me come?' And, while saying that, he intermittently sprinkled kisses on my mouth. They were not excessively libertine."

"That's it, Duclos," said Durcet, "the Président was right; I could not visualize a thing on the basis of your first telling, but now I have your man well in view."

"One moment, Duclos," said the Bishop, upon seeing that she was about to proceed. "I have on my own account a need rather more pressing than to piss, it's had me in its grip for an age and I have the feeling it's got to go."

So saying he drew Narcisse to his alcove. Fire leapt from the prelate's eyes, his prick stood up against his belly, foam flecked his lips, it was confined fuck that wished absolutely to escape and which could not be liberated save by violent means. He dragged his niece and the little boy into his closet. Everything came to a pause; a discharge was regarded as something far too portentous not to suspend everything the moment someone was about to produce one; all was to concur to make it delicious. But upon this occasion Nature's will did not correspond with the Bishop's wishes, and several minutes after having retired to the closet, he emerged from it, furious, in the same state of erection and, addressing himself to Durcet, presiding officer for November:

"Put that odd little fellow down for some punishment on Saturday," he said, flinging the child ten feet away from him, "and make it severe, if you please."

It was apparent that the boy had not been able to satisfy Monseigneur, and Julie whispered in her father's ear what had happened.

"Well, by God, then take another," cried the Duc, "choose something from one of our quatrains if nothing in yours suits you."

"Ah, my satisfaction now would be far beyond the damned little that would have been sufficient a moment ago," said the prelate. "You know to what we are led by a thwarted desire; I'd prefer to restrain myself, but no undue leniency with that poor little fool ," he continued, "that's what I recommend..."

"But be at ease, my dear Bishop," said Durcet, "I promise you he'll get a good scolding, 'tis a fine idea to provide the others with an example. I'm sorry to see you in such a state; try something else; have yourself fucked."

"Monseigneur," spoke up Martaine, "I feel myself greatly disposed to satisfy you, were Your Excellency to wish it..."

"No, no, Christ, no!" the Bishop cried, "don't you know that there are a thousand occasions when one does not want a woman's asshole? I'll wait...let Duclos continue, I'll get rid of it tonight, I'll have to find the one I want. Proceed, Duclos."

And the friends having laughed right heartily at the Bishop's libertine frankness- "there are a thousand occasions when one does not want a woman's asshole"- the storyteller resumed in these terms:

It was not long after I had attained the age of seven that one day, following my custom of bringing one of my little comrades to Louis, I found another monk with him in his cell. As that had never happened before, I was surprised and wanted to leave, but Louis having reassured us, my little friend and I went boldly in.

"Well there, Geoffrey," Louis said to his companion, pushing me toward him, "did I not tell you that she was nice?"

"Why yes indeed, she is," said Geoffrey, taking me upon his knees and giving me a kiss. "How old are you, my little one?"

"Seven, Father."

"Just fifty years younger than I," said the good father, kissing me anew.

And during this little dialogue, the sirup was being prepared and, as it was customary, each of us swallowed three big glasses of it, but, as it was not customary for me to drink when I brought Louis a toy, because he only expected a sprinkling from the girl I brought, because I did not usually stay for the ceremony but used to leave at once, for all these reasons I was astonished by their actions, and in a tone of the most naive innocence I inquired:

"And why do you have me drink, good Father? do you want me to piss?"

"To be sure, we do, my child," quoth Geoffrey, who still had me squeezed between his thighs and whose hands were already straying over my front, "yes, you're to piss, and the adventure is to take place with me; it will be, perhaps, a little different from the other one you experienced here. Come into my cell, let's leave Father Louis with your little friend, and let's get to business ourselves; we'll return when all our needs are satisfied."

We left; before going, Louis told me in a whisper to be very obliging with his friend, and said I'd not regret it if I were. Geoffrey's cell was not far from Louis', and we reached it without being seen. No sooner inside than Geoffrey, having barricaded the door, told me to get rid of my skirts. I obeyed, he himself pulled my shift above my navel and, having seated me on the edge of his bed, he spread my thighs as wide as it were possible, at the same time thrusting me back in such a way my belly came into full view and my weight rested entirely upon the base of my spine. He besought me to keep in that position and to begin to piss immediately he gave one of my thighs a little slap with his hand. Then, scrutinizing me for a moment in this attitude, with one hand he separated the lips of my cunt, with the other he unbuttoned his breeches and with quick and energetic movements began to shake a dark, stunted little member which seemed not much inclined to respond to what was required of it. To give it some encouragement, our man set about doing his duty and proceeded to his chosen custom, the one which procured him the greatest possible titillation -- down he went on his knees, I say, between my legs, spent another instant peering into the little orifice I presented to his eye, several times applied his mouth to it, between his teeth muttering certain luxurious phrases I cannot remember because at the time I did not understand them, and continued to agitate that sullen little member, which, though fearfully bullied, did not budge. Finally, he sealed his lips to those of my cunt, I received the signal, and instantly draining what my bladder contained into the gentleman's mouth, I flooded him with a stream of urine he swallowed as fast as I launched it into his gullet. Whereupon his member unfurled, and its proudly lifted head throbbed against one of my thighs: I felt it bravely spray his debilitated manhood's sterile issue. Everything had been so well managed he swallowed the final drops at the same moment his prick, confused by his victory, wept bloody tears over it. Trembling in every limbs, Geoffrey got to his feet, and I observed that he no longer had for his idol, once the incense had been extinguished, the same religious fervor he had while delirium, inflaming his homage, still sustained its glory: he rather abruptly gave me twelve sous, opened the door without asking me, as had the others, to bring him girls (he was evidently furnished by someone else) and, pointing the way to his friend's cell, told me to go there, said that he was in a hurry, that he had his offices to perform, that he could not conduct me himself, and then shut his door without affording me the chance to answer him.

"Oh yes indeed!" said the Duc, "unnumbered are they who absolutely cannot bear the instant when the illusion is shattered. It seems as if one's pride suffers when one lets a woman see one in such a state of feebleness, and disgust would appear to be the result of the discomfiture one experiences at such moments."

"No," said Curval, whom Adonis, kneeling, was frigging, and whose hands were wandering over Zelmire, "no, my friend, pride has nothing to do with it, but the object which is in the profoundest sense devoid of all value save the one our lust endows it with, that object, I say, shows itself for what in truth it is once our lubricity has subsided. The more violent has been the irritation the more this object is stripped of its attraction when this irritation ceases to sustain it, just as we are more or less fatigued after greater or lesser exertion, and this aversion we thereupon sense is nothing but the sentiment of a glutted soul whereunto happiness is displeasing because happiness has just wearied it."

"But from this aversion, all the same," spoke up Durcet, "is often born a plan for revenge, whose fatal consequences have often been observed."

"Yes, but that's another matter," Curval replied, "and as the aftermath of these recitals will perhaps afford us examples of what you're saying, let's not anticipate through dissertations what will be naturally produced of itself."

"Président, be frank," said Durcet: "on the verge of running amuck yourself, I believe that at the present moment you prefer to prepare yourself to feel how one enjoys than to discuss how one becomes disgusted."

"Why, not at all, not a bit of it," said Curval, "I am as cool as ice... To be sure, yes," he continued, kissing Adonis' lips, "this child is charming... but he's not to be fucked; I know of nothing worse than your damnable regulations... one must reduce oneself to things... to things... Go on, Duclos, go on, continue, for I have the feeling I might perpetrate something foolish, and I want my illusion to remain intact at least until I go to bed."

The Président, perceiving his engine beginning to rebel, sent the two children back to their posts and, lying down beside Constance, who, pretty as she was, doubtless failed to stimulate him as much, he a second time besought Duclos to resume her story; she did at once, as follows:

I rejoined my little comrade. Louis had been serviced; not very well pleased, we both left the monastery, I almost resolved not to return again. Geoffrey's tone had wounded my little pride, and without probing further to determine the origins of my displeasure, I liked neither its apparent cause nor its consequences. However, it had been written in my destiny that I was to have yet a few more adventures in that pious retreat, and the example of my sister, who had, so she told me, done business with fourteen of its inhabitants, was to convince me that I was still far from the end of my tour. Three months after this last episode, I became aware of overtures being made to me by another one of these reverend fathers, this one a man of about sixty. He invented every kind of ruse to lure me to his room; one of them succeeded, so well in fact that one fine Sunday morning I found myself there, without knowing why or how it had happened. The old rascal, known as Father Henri, shut and locked the door as soon as I had crossed the threshold, and embraced me with exceeding warmth.

"Ah, little imp!" cried he, transported with joy, "I've got you now, you'll not escape me this time, ha!"

The weather was extremely cold at the time, my little nose was running as children's usually do in the winter; I drew out a handkerchief.

"What's this? What's this? Be careful there," warned Henri, "I'm the one who'll attend to that operation, my sweet."

And having stretched me out upon his bed with my head a little to one side, he sat down next to me and raised my head upon his lap. He peered avidly at me, his eyes seemed ready to devour the secretion oozing from my nose. "Oh, the pretty little snotface," said he, beginning to pant, "how I'm going to suck her." Therewith bending down over me, and taking my nose in his mouth, not only did he devour all the mucus between my nose and mouth, but he even lewdly darted the tip of his tongue into each of my nostrils, one after the other, and with such cleverness he provoked two or three sneezes which redoubled the flow he desired and was consuming so hungrily. But ask me for no details bearing upon this fellow, Messieurs, nothing appeared, and whether because he did nothing, or because he did it all in his drawers, there was nothing to be seen, and amidst the multitude of his kisses and lecherous lickings there was nothing outstanding which might have denoted an ecstasy, and consequently it is my opinion that he did not discharge. All my clothes were in place, even his hands stayed still, and I give you my word that this old libertine's fantasy might be performed upon the world's most respectable and least initiated girl without her being able to suppose there was anything lewd in it at all.

But the same could not be said of the one that chance presented to my consideration the same day I turned nine years old. Father Etienne, that was the libertine's name, had several times asked my sister to bring me to him, and she had got me to promise to go alone, for she was unwilling to accompany me, fearing lest my mother, who already scented something in the wind, might find out; well, I was planning to pay him a visit when, one day, I ran directly into him in a corner of the church, near the sacristy. His manner was so gracious, he argued so persuasively that he had no need to drag me away by main force. Father Etienne was about forty, a healthy, robust, strapping fellow. We were no sooner closeted together than he asked whether I knew how to frig a prick.

"Alas!" said I, blushing to the ears, "I don't even know what you're talking about."

"Well then I'll explain, my chit," said he, bestowing heartfelt kisses upon my mouth and eyes, "my unique pleasure in this world is to educate little girls, and the lessons I give are so excellent they prove unforgettable. Begin by removing your skirts, for if I am to teach you how you must proceed in order to give me pleasure, 'tis only fair that at the same time I teach you what to do in order to receive it, and that lesson cannot be a success if anything hinders us. Here we go. We shall begin with you. What you behold down here," said he, placing his hand on my mound, "is called a cunt, and this is what you must do in order to awaken very felicitous sensations in it. With one finger -- one will do -- lightly rub this little protuberance you feel here. It, by the way, is called the clitoris."

I followed instructions.

"There, you see, that way, my little one, while one hand is busy there, let one finger of your other hand gradually work its way into this delicious crack "

He adjusted my hands.

"That's the way, yes... Well! Don't you feel anything?" he asked, keeping me to my task.

"No, Father, I truly don't," I answered most naively.

"Ah, that's because you are still too young, but two years from now you'll see the pleasures it gives."

"Wait," I interrupted, "I think something's happening."

And with all imaginable vigor I rubbed the places he had pointed out.... Yes, sure enough, a few faint titillations convinced me that what I'd begun was worth continuing, and the extensive use I have made ever since of this relief-providing exercise has more than once persuaded me of my master's competence.

"And now 'tis my turn," said Etienne, "for your pleasures arouse my desires, and I simply must share them, my angel. Here we are; take this," he said, inviting me to grip a tool so monstrous my two little hands were scarce able to close around it, "take this, my child, 'tis called a prick, and this movement here," he went on, guiding my wrists in rapid jerks, "this action is called frigging. Thus, by means of this action you frig my prick. Go to it, my child, put all your strength to it. The more rapid and persistent your movements, the more you will hasten a moment which, believe me, I cherish. But bear one essential thing in mind," he added, all the while directing my flying hands, "be careful at all times to keep the tip uncovered. Never allow this skin, we call it the prepuce, to cover it over; were this prepuce to happen to cover this part, which we call the glans, all my pleasure would vanish. That's it; we're shortly going to see something, my little one," my teacher continued, "watch me do on you what you did on me."

And pressing himself against my chest as he spoke and as I kept in motion, he placed his hands so adroitly, he wriggled his fingers with such high art that pleasure rose at last to grip me, and it is without a shadow of a doubt to him I owe my initiation. And then, my head reeling, I abandoned my task, and the reverend, not yet ready to complete it, consented to forget his pleasure for a moment in order to devote himself exclusively to cultivating mine; and when he had caused me to taste it all, he had me resume the work my ecstasy had obliged me to interrupt, and very expressly enjoined me to keep my mind strictly on what I was about and to care for naught but him. I did so with all my soul. It was only just: I surely owed him my thanks. I went so merrily to work, and I observed all his instructions so faithfully that the monster, vanquished by such rapid vibrations, finally spewed forth all its rage and covered me with its venom. Thereupon Etienne seemed to go out of his mind, borne aloft in the most voluptuous delirium; ardently he kissed my mouth, he fondled and frigged my cunt, and the wildness in his speech still more emphatically declared his disorder. Gross expressions, mingling with others of the most endearing sort, characterized this transport, which lasted quite a while, and whence at last the gallant Etienne, so unlike his piss-swallowing colleague, emerged to tell me that I was charming, that he greatly hoped I would come back to see him, and that he would treat me every time as he was going to now: pressing a silver coin into my hand, he conducted me back to the place he had brought me from and left me wonderstruck, thrilled and enchanted with this latest good fortune. Feeling much better about the monastery, I decided to return to it often in the future, persuaded that the more I advanced in age, the more agreeable adventures I would meet with there. But destiny called me elsewhere; more important events awaited me in a new world, and upon returning to my house I learned news which was soon to sober the elation produced in me by the happy outcome of my latest experience.

Here a bell was heard struck in the salon; it announced supper. Whereupon Duclos, generally applauded for the auspicious little beginnings she had made, descended from the stage, and, after having made a few adjustments to repair the disorder all four of them seemed to be in, the friends turned their thoughts to new pleasures and hastened to find out what Comus held in store for them.

This meal was to be served by the eight little girls, naked. Having been wise enough to leave the auditorium a few minutes early, they stood ready the moment the masters entered these fresh surroundings. The table companions were to be twenty in number: the libertine quartet, the eight fuckers, the eight little boys. But, still furious with Narcisse, the

Bishop wished to veto his presence at the banquet, and as it was perfectly natural that they make allowances for one another's whims and observe a mutual tolerance, no one raised his voice to contest the sentence, and the poor little simpleton was confined alone in a dark closet to await that stage in the orgies when perhaps Monseigneur might be inclined to make friends with him again. The wives and the storytellers, dining apart, had concluded their meal in great haste in order to be ready for the orgies, the elders directed the movements of the eight little girls, and dinner was begun.

This meal, much heavier than the one which had been eaten earlier in the day, was served with far greater opulence and splendor. I began with a shellfish soup and hors d'oeuvres composed of twenty dishes; twenty entrees came on next, and soon gave way to another twenty lighter entrees made up entirely of breasts of chicken, of assorted game prepared in every possible way. This was offset by a serving of roasts; everything of the rarest imaginable was brought on. Next arrived some cold pastry, soon afterward twenty-six entremets of every description and form. The table was cleared, and what had just been removed was replaced by a whole array of cold and hot sugared pastries. Dessert finally appeared: a prodigious number and variety of fruits, though the season was winter, then ices, chocolate, and the liqueurs which were taken at table. As for the wines, they varied with each service: Burgundy accompanied the first; two kinds of Italian wine came with the second and third; Rhine wine with the fourth; with the fifth, Rhône wines; sparkling champagne with the sixth; two kinds of Greek wine with the other two courses. Spirits were prodigiously roused, for, as distinct from lunch, one was not granted permission during dinner to take the waitresses to task, or with that same severity; these creatures, being the very quintessence of what the company had to offer, had to be treated rather more sparingly but, on the other hand, the friends indulged in a furious round of impurities with them.

Half-drunk, the Duc said he would not touch another drop, from now it was Zelmire's urine or nothing, and he drained two large glasses of it which he obtained by having the child climb upon the table and squat over his plate. "Why, there's nothing to drinking weak young piss," said Curval and, calling Fanchon to him: "Come hither, venerable bitch, I'd slake my thirst at the very source." And thrusting his head between the old crone's legs, he greedily sucked up the impure floods of poisonous urine she darted into his stomach. And now their words grew heated, they argued various philosophical problems and considered several questions relating to manners; I leave it to the reader to imagine the purity of those discourses and the loftiness of their moralizing. The Duc undertook an encomium of libertinage, and proved that it was natural, and that the more numerous were its extravagances, the better they served the creator of us all. His opinion was generally acclaimed, enthusiastically applauded, and they rose to go and put into practice the doctrines which had just been established. Everything was ready in the orgy salon: the women were there, already naked, lying upon piles of pillows on the floor, strewn promiscuously amongst the young catamites who had hastened away from table a little after dessert. Our friends reeled in; two elders undressed them, and they fell upon the flock like wolves assailing a sheepfold. The Bishop, whose passions had been cruelly irritated by the obstacles they had encountered of late, laid hands on Antinoûs' sublime ass while Hercule skewered him, and vanquished by this latest sensation and by the important and doubtless so much desired service Antinoüs was rendering him, he finally spat out streams of semen so hard driven and so pungent he swooned in ecstasy. Bacchus' wiles had spellbound senses glutted from excess, numbed from luxury; our hero passed from his faint to a sleep so profound he had to be carried to his bed.

The Duc was having a marvelous time. Curval, recollecting what Martaine had offered the Bishop, stuffed her while he got his own ass stoppered.

A thousand other horrors, a thousand other infamies accompanied and succeeded those, and our three indomitable champions -- for the Bishop no longer was of this world -- our valorous athletes, I say, escorted by the four night-toiling fuckers who had not been at the revels but who now came to fetch them, retired with the same wives who had shared their couches during the story time.

Luckless victims of their brutality, upon whom it is only too likely they showered more outrages than caresses and who, it is equally probable, inspired in them more disgust than pleasure...

Such were the events that transpired on the first day.

The Second Day

The company rose at the customary hour. The Bishop, entirely recovered from his excess, and who, waking at four in the morning, was deeply shocked to find they had let him go to bed unaccompanied, had summoned Julie and his fucker for the night to come and occupy their posts. They answered the call instantly, and in their arms the libertine plunged back into the thick of new impurities.

When, in keeping with regulations, breakfast had been taken in the girls' quarters, Durcet went on his rounds, and, notwithstanding all the arguments he heard, further delinquencies appeared to his eyes. Michette was guilty of one kind of fault and Augustine, whom Curval had ordered to keep herself throughout the day in a certain state, was found in the absolutely opposite state; she declared she had forgotten, made a hundred apologies, and promised it would not happen again, but the quadrumvirate was inexorable, and both names were inscribed on the list of punishments to be executed come the first Saturday.

Highly dissatisfied with all these little girls' ineptness in the art of masturbation, annoyed by the effects of this awkwardness with which he had been obliged to put up the previous evening, Durcet proposed that one hour in the morning be set aside for giving them lessons, and that the friends take turns rising an hour early, the exercise period being set from nine until ten -- one friend would rise at nine every morning, I say, to participate in the training. It was decided that the supervisor would be seated comfortably in a chair in the middle of the harem and that each little girl, led forth and guided by Duclos, the best frigger in the castle, would demonstrate upon the friend, would direct the little girl's hand, her motion, would explain the intricacies of tempo, how much and how little speed was required and how that depended on the patient's condition, would also explain what attitudes and postures were most conducive to the operation's success; furthermore, punishments were fixed for her who at the end of a fortnight, despite the lessons, should fail of perfect proficiency in this art. It was emphasized to the little girls that, pursuant to the good ecclesiastic's doctrines, the glans was to be kept uncovered at all times, and that the hand not in action was meanwhile continually to be employed exciting the adjacent areas, this in keeping with the particular fancy of the patient.

The financier's proposal pleased everyone; Duclos was informed, she accepted her appointment, and that same day she set up a frigging dummy upon which, in their spare time, the little girls could exercise their wrists and maintain the necessary degrees of agility and suppleness. Hercule was given the same instructorship in the boys' chamber; they being, as always, more skilled in this technique than the girls, because in the case of boys it is merely a question of doing for others what they do unto themselves, a week was ample time to turn them into the most delicious corps of friggers you could ever hope to meet with. On this particular morning, not one of them was found at fault, and Narcisse's behavior of the previous day having brought about the refusal of all permissions, the chapel was empty save for Duclos, a pair of fuckers, Julie, Thérèse, Cupidon, and Zelmire. Curval was stiff as a ramrod, Adonis had inspired an astonishingly high temperature in him when, that morning, he had visited the boys, and it was generally thought he would erupt while watching Thérèse and the two fuckers manage their affairs; but he kept a grip upon himself.

The midday meal was the usual affair, but the Président, having drunk a singular amount and frolicked about even more while eating, became inflamed all over again when coffee was served by Augustine and Michette, Zélamir and Cupidon, directed by old Fanchon, whom out of whimsy they had commanded to be as naked as the children. From this

contrast Curval's new lubricious furor was born, and he gave himself over
to some choice extravagances at the expense of Zélamir and the duenna;
this riotous conduct finally cost him his fuck.

The Duc, pike aloft, closed in upon Augustine; he brayed, he swore,
he waxed unreasonable, and the poor little thing, all atremble, retreated
like a dove before the bird of prey ready to pounce upon it. He limited
himself, however, to a few libertine kisses, and was content to give her an
introductory lesson in advance of the ones she was to begin the following morning. The two others, less animated, having already started their
naps, our two champions imitated them, and the quartet did not wake
until six o'clock, the hour when the storytelling began in the throne room.

All the previous day's quatrains had been altered with respect to both
subjects and dress, and our friends had these couch companions: the Duc
shared his niche with Aline, the Bishop's daughter and consequently his
own niece; beside the Bishop lay his sister-in-law, Constance, the Duc's
wife and Durcet's daughter; Durcet was with Julie, the Duc's daughter, the
Président's wife; that he might be roused from sleep and roused to more,
Curval had with him Adelaide, Durcet's wife, one of the creatures in this
world it gave him the greatest pleasure to tease because of her virtue and
her piety. He opened up with a few scurrile jests and low pranks, and
having ordered her throughout the séance to maintain a posture that
sorted well with his tastes, but which the poor woman found very tiresome
to maintain, he threatened her with all his anger might produce were she
to budge or give him a moment's inconvenience. Everything being ready,
Duclos ascended the platform and resumed her narration in this wise:

Three days having elapsed since my mother had appeared at the
house, her husband, far more uneasy about his belongings and his money
than about her, took it into his head to enter her room, where it was
their custom to hide their most precious possessions; and what was his
astonishment when, instead of what he was seeking, he found nothing
but a note, written by my mother, advising him to make the best of his
loss because, having decided to leave him forever, and having no money
of her own, she had been forced to take all she had been able to make off
with. As for the rest, he was to blame himself and his hard use of her for
her departure and for her having left him with two daughters who were,
however, certainly worth as much as and possibly more than what she
had removed. But the old gaffer was far from judging equal what now
he had and what he had just lost, and the dismissal he graciously gave
us, together with the request we not even sleep in the house that night,
was convincing evidence some discrepancy existed between his way of
reckoning and my mother's.

Not much afflicted by a compliment which gave us full liberty to
launch forth unimpeded into the little mode of life that was beginning
to please us so much, my sister and I thought only to collect our few

belongings and to bid as swift a farewell to our dear stepfather as he had
seen fit to bid us. Without the loss of a minute, we withdrew, and while
waiting to decide how best to come to grips with our new destinies, we
took lodgings in a small room in the neighborhood. Our first thoughts
turned to what might be our mother's fate and whereabouts; we had not
the least doubt but that she had gone to the monastery, having decided
to live secretly with some father, or that she was being kept somewhere
in the vicinity, and this was the opinion we held, without being unduly
concerned, when a friar from the monastery brought us a note that bore
out our conjectures. The substance of the note was that we would be very
well advised, immediately night had fallen, to come to the monastery
and speak to the Father Superior, who was the note's author; he would
wait for us in the church until ten o'clock and would lead us to the place
presently occupied by our mother, whose actual happiness and peace he
would gladly have us share. He very energetically urged us not to fail to
come, and above all to conceal our movements with all possible care; for
it was essential our stepfather know nothing of what was being done in
behalf of both our mother and ourselves. My sister, fifteen years old at
the time and hence more clever and more reasonable than I, who was
but nine, after having dismissed the bearer of the letter and given him
the reply that she would ponder its contents, admitted she found all these
maneuvers very peculiar indeed.

"Françon," says she, "let's not go. There's something wrong with it.
If this were an honest proposal, why wouldn't Mother have either added
a few words or made some kind of sign. Father Adrien, her best friend,
left there almost three years ago, and since then she's only dropped in
at the monastery while passing by, and hasn't had any other regular
intrigue there. What would have led her to choose this place for hiding?
The Father Superior isn't her lover and never has been. I know, it's true
she has amused him two or three times, but he's not the man to lose his
head over a woman for that slender reason: he's even more inconstant and
brutal to women once his caprice is satisfied. And so why would he have
taken such an interest in our mother? There's something queer about it,
I tell you. I never liked that old Superior; he's wicked and harsh, and he's
a brute. Once he got me into his room, there were three more of them
there, and after what happened to me then I swore I'd never set foot in
the place again. If you take my advice, you'll leave all those nasty monks
alone. There's no reason why I shouldn't tell you so now, Françon, I have
an acquaintance, a good friend, I dare say; her name is Madame Guérin,
I've been going to her place for the past two years, and in all that time
not one week has gone by without her arranging something nice for me.
But none of those six-penny fucks like the ones at the monastery; I get
at least three crowns from every one. Here, there's proof of it," my sister
continued, showing me a purse containing more than ten louis, "you

can see I'm able to make my own way in the world. Well, my advice to you is to do what I do. Guérin will take you on, I'm sure of it, she got a glimpse of you a week ago when she came to fetch me for a party, and she told me to make you a proposal, and she said that, young as you are, she'd always find some way of placing you. Do like me, I tell you, and we'll be well off in no time. Now, that's all I've got to say to you; I'll pay your expenses for tonight, but from then on don't count on me, little sister. Each for himself in this world. That's what I say. I've earned that money with my body and my fingers, do the same yourself. And if you have any qualms, go talk it over with the devil, but don't come looking for me; well, I've told what I think, and I'll tell you now that I'd sooner stick my tongue two feet out than give you even a glass of water for nothing. As for Mother, I don't care what's happened to her, as a matter of fact, even if it's the worst I'm perfectly delighted, and all I hope is that the whore is far enough away so I'll never see her again for the rest of my life. I know all the things she did to prevent me from getting anywhere in the trade, and all the while she was giving me that fine advice, the bitch was doing things three times worse. So, may the devil take her and above all not bring her back, that's all I care."

Not having, to tell you the truth, a heart more tender, nor a soul much more generous than my sister's, it was in all good faith I echoed the invectives wherewith she pilloried that excellent mother, and thanking my sister for the helpful words she promised to speak in my behalf, I in my turn promised to follow her to this woman's house and, once I had been adopted, to put an end to my reliance on her. As for refusing to go to the monastery, we were fully agreed.

"If indeed she is happy, so much the better for her," I commented, "and in that case we can look out for our own welfare without having to go and submit to the same fate. And if it is a trap they're setting for us, we've got to avoid it."

Whereupon my sister embraced me.

"Splendid," said she, "I see you're a good girl. Don't worry, we're going to make a fortune. I'm pretty, so are you; we'll earn as much as we want, my chit, but don't become attached to anyone, remember that. One today, another tomorrow, you've got to be a whore, a whore in body and soul. As for myself," she went on, "I'm one now, such as you see me, and there isn't any confessional, or priest, or counsel, or threat that could ruin things for me. By Jesus, I'd go show my ass on the sidewalk as calmly and coolly as I'd drink a glass of wine. Imitate me, Françon, be amenable and you can get anything out of men; the trade's a little hard in the beginning, but you'll get along and things get better. So many men, so many tastes. At first you've got to expect it, one of them wants one thing, another wants something else. But that doesn't matter, you're there to please and give them service; the customer is always right. It doesn't take long, and then the money's in your pocket."

I admit I was amazed to hear such wild remarks from a girl so young, who had always seemed to me so decent. But as my heart beat in harmony with the spirits of what she said, I let her know at once that I was not only disposed to duplicate all her actions, but even prepared to go a great deal further if necessary. Delighted with me, she fell to embracing me again, and as it was growing late, we sent out for a chicken and some good wine and supped and slept together, having decided to present ourselves the very next morning at the establishment of Madame Guérin and to ask her to include us amongst her pensionnaires.

It was during that supper my sister taught me all I still did not know about libertinage. She showed herself naked to me, and I can warrant that she was one of the prettiest creatures there was in Paris at the time: the fairest of skin, the most agreeable plumpness, yet the most supple and intriguing figure, the loveliest blue eyes, and all the rest correspondingly fine. I also learned for how long Guérin had been promoting her interests, and with what great pleasure she procured her clients who, never tired of her, asked for her constantly. No sooner were we in bed than it occurred to us we had managed very badly in failing to give the Father Superior a reply, for our negligence might annoy him, and while we remained in this quarter of town it was important to humor him at least. But what was to be done? Eleven o'clock had struck; we resolved to let things take their course.

The adventure probably meant a great deal to the Superior, we supposed, and hence it was not difficult to surmise that he was laboring more in his own behalf than in that of the alleged happiness he had mentioned in his communication; at any rate, midnight had just sounded when we heard a soft knocking at our door. It was the Superior himself; he had been waiting for us, said he, since two in the afternoon, we should at least have given him a response, and, seating himself at our bedside, he informed us that our mother had decided to spend the rest of her days in a little secret apartment they had at the monastery and in which she was having the world's most cheerful time, improved by the company of all the house's bigwigs who would drop in to spend half the day with her and with another young woman, our mother's companion; it was simply up to us to come and increase the number, but, in that we were a little too young to stay on permanently, he would only contract us to a three-year's stint, at the end of which he swore we would be granted our freedom and a thousand crowns apiece; he added that he had been charged by our mother to assure us that we would be doing her a great kindness were we to come to share her solitude.

"Father," my sister said most imprudently, "we thank you for your proposal. But at our age we have no inclination to have ourselves locked up in a cloister in order to be whores for priests, we've had enough of that already."

The Superior renewed his arguments, he spoke with a heat and energy which illustrated his powerful desire to have the thing succeed; finally observing that it was destined to fail, he hurled himself almost in a fury upon my sister.

"Very well, little whore," he cried, "at least satisfy me once again before I take my leave."

And unbuttoning his breeches, he got astride her; she offered no resistance, persuaded that by allowing him to have his way she'd be rid of him all the sooner. And the smutty fellow, pinning her between his knees, began to brandish and then to abuse a tough and rather stout engine, advancing it to within a quarter of an inch of my sister's face.

"Pretty face," he gasped, "pretty little whore's face, how I'll soak it in my fuck, by sweet Jesus!"

And therewith the sluices opened, the sperm flew out, and the entirety of my sister's face, especially her nose and mouth, were covered with evidence of our visitor's libertinage, whose passion might not have been so cheaply satisfied had his design in coming to us met with success. More complacent now, the man of God's only thoughts were of escape; after having flung a crown upon the table and relit his lantern:

"You little fools, you are little tramps," he told us. "You are ruining your chances in this world; may Heaven punish your folly by causing you to fall on evil days, and may I have the pleasure of seeing you in misery; that would be my revenge, that is what I wish you."

My sister, busy wiping her face, paid him back his stupidities in kind, and, our door shutting behind the Superior, we spent the remainder of the night in peace.

"You've just seen one of his favorite stunts," said my sister. "He's mad about discharging in girls' faces. If he only confined himself to that... but the scoundrel has a good many other eccentricities, and some of them are so dangerous that I do indeed fear..."

But my sister was sleepy, she dozed off without completing her sentence, and the morrow bringing fresh adventures with it, we gave no more thought to that one.

We were up early; having prettied ourselves as much as possible, we set out for Madame Guérin's. That heroine lived in the rue Soli, in a very neat ground-floor apartment she shared with six tall young ladies between the ages of sixteen and twenty-two, all in splendid health, all very pretty. But, Messieurs, you will be so kind as to allow me to postpone giving their descriptions until the proper moment in my story arrives. Delighted by the project which brought my sister to her for a long stay, Madame Guérin greeted us cordially and with the greatest pleasure showed us our rooms.

"Young as you may find this child to be," my sister said as she introduced me, "she will serve you well, I guarantee it. She is mild-tempered, thoughtful, has a very good character, and the soul of a thoroughgoing whore. You must have a number of old lechers amongst your acquaintances who are fond of children; well this is just what they're looking for... put her to work."

Turning in my direction, Guérin asked me if I was willing to undertake anything.

"Yes, Madame," I answered with something of an indignant air, and it pleased her, "anything provided it pays."

We were introduced to our new companions, who already knew my sister very well and our of friendship for her promised to look after me. We all sat down to dine together, and such, in a few words, Messieurs, was how I became installed in my first brothel.

I was not to remain long unemployed; that same evening, an old businessman arrived wrapped up in a cloak; Guérin selected him for my first customer and arranged the match.

"Ah, this time," said she to the old libertine, leading me forth, "if it's still hairless you like them, Monsieur Duclos, you'll be delighted with the article, or your money back. Not a hair on her body."

"Indeed," said the old original, peering down at me, "it looks like a child, yes indeed. How old are you, little one?"

"Nine, Monsieur."

"Nine years old! ... Well, well! that's how I like them, Madame Guérin, that's how I like them, you know. I'd take them even younger if you had any around. Why, bless my soul, they're ready as soon as they're weaned."

And laughing good-naturedly at his remarks, Guérin withdrew, leaving us alone together. Then the old libertine came up and kissed me upon the mouth two or three times. With one of his hands guiding mine, he had me pull from his fly a little device that could not have been more limp; continuing to act more or less in silence, he untied my skirts, lay me upon the couch with my blouse raised high upon my chest, mounted astride my thighs which he had separated as far as possible; with one hand he pried open my little cunt while the other put all his strength into manipulating his meager machine. "Ah, pretty little bird," he said as he agitated himself and emitted sighs of pleasure, "ah, how I'd tame you if I were still able to, but I can't anymore. There's no remedy for it, in four year's time this bugger of a prick will have ceased to get stiff. Open up, open up, my dearest, spread your legs." And finally after fifteen minutes of struggle, I observed my man to sigh and pant with greater energy. A few oaths lent strength to his expression, and I felt the area surrounding my cunt inundated with the hot, scummy seed which the rascal, unable to shoot it inside, was attempting to tamp down with his fingertips.

He had no sooner done so than he was gone like a flash of lightning, and I was still cleaning myself when my gallant passed out on the door and into the street. And so it was I came, Messieurs, to be named Duclos;

the tradition in this house was for each girl to adopt the name of her firstcomer. I obeyed the custom.

"One moment there," said the Duc. "I delayed interrupting you until you came to a pause; you are at one now. Would you provide further information upon two matters: first, have you ever had any news of your mother, have you ever discovered what became of her?

Secondly, was there any cause for the antipathy you and your sister had for her, or would you say these feelings were naturally inculcate in you both? This relates to the problem of the human heart, and 'tis upon that we are concentrating our major efforts."

"My Lord," Duclos replied, "neither my sister nor I have ever heard the slightest word from that woman."

"Excellent," said the Duc, "in that case it's all very clear, wouldn't you say so, Durcet?"

"Incontestably," answered the banker. "Not a shadow of a doubt, and you are very fortunate you did not put your foot in that one. Neither of you would ever have got out."

"'Tis incredible," Curval commented, "what headway that mania has made with public."

"Why, no; after all, there's nothing more delicious," the Bishop replied.

"And the second point?" asked the Duc, addressing the storyteller.

"As for the second point, my Lord, that is to say, as for the reason for our antipathy, I'm afraid I should be hard pressed to account for it, but it was so violent in our two hearts that we both made the avowal that we would in all probability and very easily have poisoned her had we not managed, as it turned out, to be rid of her by other means. Our aversion had reached the ultimate degree of intensity, and as nothing overt occurred to give rise to it, I should judge it most likely that this sentiment was inspired in us by Nature."

"What doubt of it can there be?" said the Duc. "It happens every day that she implants the most violent inclination to commit what mortals call crimes, and had you poisoned her twenty times over, this act would never have been anything but the result of the penchant for crime Nature put in you, a penchant she wishes to draw your attention by endowing you with such a powerful hostility. It is madness to suppose one owes something to one's mother. And upon what, then, would gratitude be based? is one to be thankful that she discharged when someone once fucked her? That would suffice, to be sure. As for myself, I see therein naught but grounds for hatred and scorn. Does that mother of ours give us happiness in giving us life? ...Hardly. She casts us into a world beset with dangers, and once in it, 'tis for us to manage as best we can. I distinctly recall that, long ago, I had a mother who aroused in me much the same sentiments Duclos felt for hers: I abhorred her. As soon as I was in a position to do so, I dispatched her into the next world; may she roast there; never in my life have I tasted a keener delight than the one I knew when she closed her eyes for the last time."

At this point dreadful sobs were heard to come from one of the quatrains. It proved to be the Duc's; upon closer examination it was discovered that young Sophie had burst into tears. Provided with a heart unlike those villains', their conversation had brought to mind the cherished memory of her who had given her life, and who had perished in an effort to protect her while she was being abducted; this cruel vision offered itself to her tender imagination, a flood of tears ensued.

"Ah, by God, now!" said the Duc, "that's splendid. It's for mama you're crying, is it, my little snotface? Come here, come along, let me comfort you."

And the libertine, warmed by what had been happening, by these words of his, and by the effects they produced, displayed a thunderous prick which was apparently speeding toward a discharge. Marie, the quatrain's duenna, led the child forward all the same. Her tears flowed abundantly down her cheeks, the novice's dress she was wearing that day seemed to lend yet more charm to the sorrow which embellished her looks: it was impossible for a creature to be lovelier.

"By the Holy Bugger," quoth the Duc, springing up like one gone out of his mind, "what a pretty mouthful we have here. I'm going to do what Duclos has just described... smear some fuck on her cunt... Undress her."

And everyone silently awaited the issue of this little skirmish.

"Oh! my Lord, my Lord!" cried Sophie, casting herself at the Duc's feet, "at least respect my sorrow, I groan for my mother's fate, she was dear to me, she died defending me, I shall never see her again. Have pity upon my tears, grant me this one evening of respite."

"Why, fuck my eyes!" the Duc exclaimed, fondling his heaven-threatening prick, "I'd never have believed this scene could be so voluptuous. Off with her clothes, I tell you to take them off," he roared at Marie, "she should already be naked."

And Aline, lying upon the Duc's couch, shed warm tears, so did Adelaide, who was heard to utter a moan in Curval's alcove; the latter, in no wise partaking of that lovely creature's grief, violently scolded his playmate for having shifted from the position he had commanded her to keep, and, that done, turned an appreciative gaze upon the delicious scene whose outcome interested him exceedingly.

Sophie's clothes are removed without the faintest regard for her feelings, she is placed in the posture Duclos has just described, the Duc announces that he is about to discharge. But how is the thing to be done? What Duclos has just related had been performed by a man virtually incapable of an erection, and he had been able to direct his flabby prick's discharge wherever he wished. Such was not the case here: the threatful head of the Duc's engine had not the least inclination to lower the awful stare whereby it seemed bent on cowing heaven; it appeared necessary, so to speak, to place the child on high. No one knew what to do, and the more obstacles were encountered, the more the enraged Duc fumed and blasphemed. Desgranges finally came to the rescue; nothing that pertained to libertinage was unknown to that sage old dame. She caught up the child and set her so skillfully upon her knees that, whatever the stance the Duc might adopt, the end of his prick was sure to nudge her vagina. Two servants came up to hold Sophie's legs, and had it been her deflowering hour, never might she have displayed the merchandise to better advantage. But there was yet more to attend to: a clever hand was needed to cause the torrent to leap its banks and to direct the flood fairly to its destination. Blangis had no desire to entrust so important a matter to an untutored child.

"Take Julie," Durcet suggested, "she'll suit you; she's beginning to frig like an angel."

"Bah," muttered the Duc, "I know the clumsy bitch. And she knows her father. No, she'd be panic-stricken, she'd fumble it."

"Upon my soul, I do recommend a boy for the job," said Curval; "why not Hercule? His wrist is like a whip."

"I won't have anyone but Duclos," the Duc answered, "she's the best of our friggers, allow her to quit her post for a moment or two."

Duclos steps forward, beaming with pride to have been accorded so distinguished a preference. She rolls her sleeve to the elbow and grasps the nobleman's enormous instrument, she sets to rattling that spear, keeps the foreskin snapped broadly back, she moves it with such art, she agitates it by means of strokes so swift and simultaneously so perfectly attuned to the state she observes her patient to be in, that the bomb finally explodes upon the very hole it is to cover, inundating it. The Duc shrieks, swears, storms. Duclos is disconcerted not in the least, she gauges her movements by the degree of pleasure they produce. Antinos, properly situated for this function, delicately works the sperm into the vagina as proportionally it flows from the spigot, and the Duc, vanquished by the most delicious sensations, dying from joy, sees grow gradually slack, between his frigger's fingers, that high-spirited, mettlesome member whose ardor has just been so powerfully communicated to the rest of himself. He flings himself back upon his sofa, Duclos strides back to her throne, the child wipes herself, is consoled, and regains her quatrain, and the recital continues, leaving the spectators convinced of a truth wherewith, I believe, they have already been penetrated for a long time: that the idea of crime is able always to ignite the senses and lead us to lubricity.

I was greatly surprised, said Duclos, taking up the thread of her narrative, to see all my companions laugh when I returned, and ask me if I had wiped myself, and say a thousand other things which proved they knew perfectly well what had just happened. I was not long left in my quandary; leading me into a room adjacent to the one in which the parties ordinarily took place and in which a short while before I had been at work, my sister showed me a hole to see everything that transpired there. She told me that the young ladies found it diverting to watch what men did to their colleagues; I could come and do some spying whenever I wished, provided there was not someone already at the hole. For it not infrequently occurred, said she, that this respectable hole had a part in mysteries which would be disclosed to me later on. The week was not out before I took advantage of my opportunities: one morning someone came and asked for a girl named Rosalie, one of the most lovely blondes it were possible to behold; I was curious to see what was to be done to her. I hid myself and witnessed the following scene.

The man with whom she had to cope was no older than twenty-six or thirty. Immediately she entered, he had her sit down on a very high stool used especially for this ceremony. As soon as she was settled, he removed all her combs and hairpins and down all the way to the floor floated in a cloud the superb golden hair that adorned Rosalie's head. He drew a comb from his pocket, combed her hair, took handfuls of it, tangled it, kissed it, everything he did was accompanied by remarks praising the beauty of that hair in which he took such a keen and exclusive interest. At last, from out of his trousers he pulled a smart little prick, already quite stiff, and he promptly enveloped it in his Dulcinea's hair; once well wrapped, he began to fondle his dart and discharged, at the same time passing his other arm around Rosalie's neck and applying his lips to her mouth. He extricated his defunct engine, I saw that my companion's hair was matted with glistening fuck; she cleaned it, put it up again, and our lovers separated.

A month later, someone came in quest of my sister; this personage, I was told by the others, merited observing, for he had a most baroque specialty. He was a man of about fifty. Straightway he entered, without any preamble, without a caress, he exhibited his behind to my sister, who knew her part to perfection; he has her take her place on the bed, he backs toward her, she seizes that flaccid and wrinkled old ass, drives her five fingers into the orifice, and begins to struggle and battle and worry it with such force the bed creaks. Be that as it may, without bringing anything else to light, our man wriggles, twitches, follows my sister's movements, lends himself luxuriously to this fearful abuse, cries he is coming, comes, and affirms this is the greatest of all pleasures. He had indeed taken a furious buffeting, my sister was in a sweat; but what mild stuff! what lack of imagination!

Although the gentleman with whom I had to do not long afterward was hardly more difficult to satisfy, he at least seemed more voluptuous and, in my view, his mania had more of the libertine tincture. He was a heavy-set man of about forty-five, short, sturdy, but energetic and hearty. Never having met a person with his predilection, my first act, as soon as we were alone together, was to hoist my skirts to the navel: a dog confronted by a hickory stick could not have looked more unhappy: "Good God, dearie, let's not have any of your cunt, please put it away." So saying, he snatched down my skirts even more hastily than I had raised them. "These poor little whores," he mumbled, screwing up his face in a pout, "never have anything but cunts to show you. I may not be able to discharge this evening, thanks to that exhibition... unless I can succeed in getting the accursed image of that cunt out of my head." Whereupon he turned me about and methodically raised my petticoats from behind. Guiding me himself, and keeping my skirts raised at all times, he moved me about in order to observe how my buttocks bounced when I walked, and then he had me approach the bed, upon which he had me lie belly down. Next, with the most scrupulous attention he examined my ass, with one hand screening his eyes to avoid any glimpse of my cunt whereof, it appeared, he was in mortal terror. At last, having warned me to do all in my power to conceal that unworthy (I employ his expression) part from his sight, he brought both hands to bear on my ass and manipulated it lewdly and at length: he opened it, he closed it again, spread and squeezed it, sometimes he applied his mouth to it, and once or twice I even felt him press his lips to the hole; but he still had not touched himself, nothing could be discerned. None the less, he must have felt hidden pressures mount and readied himself for the denouement of his little ritual. "Lie down," he told me, tossing a few pillows on the floor, "yes, down there, that's it, that will do... with your legs well spread, the ass a shade higher, and the hole stretched as wide open as it will go; come now, wider still," he continued, noticing my docility. And then, taking a stool and placing it between my legs, he sat down in such a way that his prick, which he now dragged from his breeches and began to vibrate, was as it were at a level with the hole upon which he was to offer a libation. His movements now grew more rapid, with one hand he frigged himself, with the other he separated my buttocks, and a few adulatory commendations seasoned with a quantity of hard language constituted his speech. "Ah, bugger the Almighty, here 'tis, the lovely ass," he cried, "the sweet little hole, and how I'm going to wet it." He kept his word. I felt myself soaked; his ecstasy seemed to annihilate the libertine. Ah, how true it is that the homage rendered at this temple is always more ardent than the incense which is burned at the other; and my worshipper left after promising to return to see me again, for he averred I satisfied his desires very well. He did indeed come back the next day, but was untrue to me, his inconstancy led him to my sister's asshole; I observed them, saw everything: every aspect of the rite was absolutely the same, and my sister lent herself to it with the same good will.

"Did your sister have a handsome ass?" Durcet inquired.

"You may judge by one fact, my Lord," Duclos replied. "A famous painter commissioned to do a Venus with a magnificent behind asked her the following year to be his model after having, he said, consulted every procuress in Paris without finding anything to equal her."

"Well now, since she was fifteen and since we have a few girls of the same age here, compare her ass," the financier continued, "with some of the asses you see in this room."

Duclos' eyes came to rest upon Zelmire, and she told Durcet that it would be impossible, not only with respect to the ass, but even with respect to the face, to find anyone who bore a closer resemblance to her sister.

"In that case," said Durcet, "come here, Zelmire, present your cheeks."

She did indeed belong to his quatrain; the charming girl approached all atremble. She was placed at the foot of the couch, made to lie upon her belly, her rump was raised by means of cushions, the little hole was in plain sight. The lecher's prick begins to rise, he falls to kissing and fondling what lies under his nose. He orders Julie to frig him, she sets to work, his hands stray hither and yon, snatching at divers objects, lust heats his brain, under Julie's voluptuous treatment his little prick looks as if it were about to stiffen, the lecher swears, the fuck flows, and the bell sounds for dinner.

As the same profusion reigned at every meal, to have described one is to have described them all; but as almost everyone had discharged, there was a general need to recuperate strength, and therefore the friends drank a great deal at this supper. Zelmire, to whom they gave the sobriquet of Duclos' sister, was to an uncommon degree regaled during the subsequent orgies, and everyone simply had to kiss her ass. The Bishop left a puddle of fuck thereon, the three others restiffened over it, and they went to bed as they had the night before, that is to say, each with the wife he had had upon his couch, and with one of the four fuckers who had not appeared since the midday meal.

The Third Day

The Duc was abroad at nine o'clock. 'Twas he who volunteered to be the first to lend a hand in the lessons Duclos was to administer to the little girls. He installed himself in an armchair and for one long hour submitted to various fondlings, masturbations, pollutions, and to a wide variety of tricks performed by each of those little ones who, throughout it all, were guided and supervised by their mistress; and as may be readily imagined, his spirited temperament was furiously aroused by the ceremony. He was obliged to make unbelievable efforts to preserve his fuck from loss, but, more or less in control of himself, he managed to contain himself and returned to his friends in triumph, boasting that he'd just weathered an assault he defied any one of them to beat off as phlegmatically. That brought on considerable wagering, the stakes were high, a fine of fifty louis was ultimately imposed upon whoever discharged during the lessons.

Instead of taking breakfast and conducting searches, this morning was employed in drawing up a program for the seventeen orgies planned for the end of each week, in this way definitively to fix the dates of the deflowerings now that, after having become better acquainted with the subjects than they had been previously, they were able to pass legislation. In that this timetable in the most decisive manner regulated all the operations to be executed during the campaign, we have deemed it necessary to provide the reader with a copy: it seems to us that, once he has perused it and familiarized himself with the subjects' several destinies, he will be able to take a keener interest in their individual persons.

SCHEDULE OF WORKS TO BE ACCOMPLISHED DURING THE REMAINDER OF THE PART.

On the 7th of November, at which time the first week will have drawn a close, Messieurs shall proceed in the morning to the marriage of

Michette and Giton, and those two wedded individuals, whose age forbids them from conjoining, as is true in the cases of three following couples, shall be separated on their marriage night, for to closet them together would be as futile as this ridiculous ceremony which will serve only to create diversion during the day. That same evening, punishments which have accumulated and been entered on the list kept by the month's presiding officer shall be meted out.

On the 14th, Messieurs shall in the same way effect the marriage of Narcisse and Hébé, with the same clauses as those cited above.

On the 21st, in the same way, Colombe and Zélamir shall be married. On the 28th, Cupidon and Rosette.

On the 4th of December, Champville's narrations having prepared the way for the following enterprises, the Duc shall deflower Fanny.

On the 5th, the said Fanny shall be wedded to Hyacinthe who, in the presence of the company assembled, shall take his pleasure with his young wife. In such will consist the fifth week's festival, and the corrections shall take place in the evening as usual, because the marriages shall be celebrated in the morning.

On the 8th, Curval shall deflower Michette. On the 11th, the Duc shall deflower Sophie.

On the 12th, to celebrate the sixth week's festival, Sophie shall be married to Céladon, and the clauses cited for the above-mentioned marriage shall be made to apply to this one; this shall not be repeated for those to follow.

On the 15th, Curval shall deflower Hébé.

On the 18th, the Duc shall deflower Zelmire, and on the 19th, in order to celebrate the seventh week's festival, Adonis shall marry Zelmire.

On the 20th, Curval shall deflower Colombe.

On the 25th, Christmas Day, the Duc shall deflower Augustine, and on the 26th, for the eighth week's festival, Zéphyr shall marry Augustine.

On the 29th, Curval shall deflower Rosette, and all the foregoing arrangements have been made to insure that Curval, less well membered than the Duc, be provided with more youthful girls.

On the 1st of January, the first day of the year and one upon which Martaine's newly begun narration will influence imaginations to consider new pleasures, the sodomistic deflorations shall be inaugurated, and shall proceed in the following order:

On the 1st of January, the Duc shall sound Hébé's ass.

On the 2nd, in celebration of the ninth week, Hébé, having been plumbed fore by Curval, from behind by the Duc, shall be turned over to Hercule, who, before the company assembled, shall employ her for purposes to be specified upon the occasion.

On the 4th, Curval shall embugger Zélamir.

On the 6th, the Duc shall embugger Michette; on the 9th, in celebration of the tenth week's festival, the said Michette, who will have been deflowered fore by Curval, and whose ass will have been tried by the Duc, shall be turned over to Bum-Cleaver, that he may enjoy her, etc., etc.

On the 11th, the Bishop shall sodomize Cupidon. On the 13th, Curval shall sodomize Zelmire.

On the 15th, the Bishop shall sodomize Colombe.

On the 16th, for the eleventh week's festival, Colombe, whose cunt will have been deflowered by Curval, her ass by the Bishop, shall be turned over to Antinoüs, who shall enjoy her, etc.

On the 17th, the Duc shall embugger Giton. On the 19th, Curval shall embugger Sophie.

On the 21st, the Bishop shall embugger Narcisse. On the 22nd, the Duc shall embugger Rosette.

On the 23rd, for the twelfth week's festival, Rosette shall be turned over to Invictus.

On the 25th, Curval shall march into Augustine's behind. On the 28th, the Bishop shall enter Fanny's.

On the 30th, for the thirteenth week's festival, the Duc shall take Hercule for his husband and Zéphyr for his wife, and the marriage shall be both accomplished and consummated before the eyes of everyone, as shall be the three others which follow.

On the 6th of February, for the fourteenth week's festival, Bum-Cleaver shall become Curval's husband, Adonis his wife.

On the 13th of February, for the fifteenth week's festival, Antinoüs shall be made husband to the Bishop, to him shall Céladon be made a wife.

On the 20th of February, for the sixteenth week's festival, Invictus shall as a husband be wedded to Durcet, Hyacinthe as a wife.

As for the festival of the seventeenth week, due to fall on the 27th of February, upon the eve of the narrations' conclusion, it shall be celebrated by sacrifices for which Messieurs reserve themselves in petto the choice of victims.

These arrangements provide for the obliteration of all maidenheads by the 30th of January, with the exception of those of the four young boys whom Messieurs are to marry as wives, and whom they are eager to preserve intact until their weddings, in order that their amusement be made to last until the end of the party.

As the objects are progressively depucelated, they shall the place of the wives upon the couches at storytelling time, and, at nighttime, they shall lie with Messieurs, alternately, and at Messieurs' choice, together with the last four fairies Messieurs will take to themselves as wives during the final month.

From the moment a girl or a depucelated boy shall have replaced a wife upon the couch, the said wife shall be repudiated. From this moment onward, she shall be in general discredit, and shall be ranked lower than the servants.

With regard to Hébé, aged twelve, Michette, aged twelve, Colombe, aged thirteen, and Rosette, aged thirteen, as progressively they are surrendered to the fuckers and exercised by the latter, they too shall fall into discredit, shall henceforth be used for none but harsh and brutal purposes, shall rank with the repudiated wives, and shall be treated with utmost rigor. And as of the 24th of January, all four of them will have descended to the same inferior level.

This schedule affirms that unto the Duc shall fall nine pucelages: the first encuntments of Fanny, Sophie, Zelmire, Augustine, the original embuggeries of Hébé, Michette, Giton, Rosette, and Zéphyr.

Unto Curval shall fall the cunt-pucelages of Michette, Hébé, Colombe, Rosette, the ass-pucelages of Zélamir, Zelmire, Sophie, Augustine, and Adonis, being in all nine deflorations.

Unto Durcet, who does not fuck at all, is reserved the ass-pucelage of Hyacinthe, who in the capacity of a wife shall be wedded to him.

And unto the Bishop, who fucks naught but asses, are reserved the sodomistical depucelations of Cupidon, of Colombe, of Narcisse, of Fanny, and of Céladon.

The entire day having been spent preparing this program and chatting about it, and no one having been found at fault, all went uneventfully ahead, the storytelling hour arrived; everyone took his place, the illustrious Duclos mounted the stage. She proceeded in this wise:

A young man, whose mania, although not in my opinion very libertine, is none the less curious enough, appeared at Madame Guérin's shortly after the adventure I spoke of yesterday. He had to have a young and healthy wet nurse; he suckled the good woman's teat and leaked his seed over her thighs while gorging himself on her milk. His prick struck me as paltry and mean, all his person rather puny, and his discharge was as mild as his proceedings were benign.

Another one appeared in the same room the next day; his mania will doubtless prove more entertaining to you. He insisted upon having his woman enveloped in a sheet so that her face and breast would be entirely hidden from him, the single part of her body he wanted to see, and which had to be of the highest degree of excellence, was her ass, all the rest meant nothing to him, and he assured Madame Guérin that a glimpse of anything else would anger him exceedingly. Guérin had a woman brought in from the outside: she was ugly to the point of bitterness and almost fifty years old, but her buttocks were molded like those of Venus, nothing more beautiful could ever bewitch one's gaze.

I was eager to see this operation; the old duenna, well wrapped up, was told at once to lie belly down on the edge of the bed. Our libertine, a man of about thirty and who seemed to me a gentleman of the cloth, lifts her skirts above her loins, is thrilled by what greets his eyes and flatters his tastes. He touches, he spreads this superb breech, showers passionate kisses upon it, and, his imagination fired by what he supposes rather than by what he would actually have seen had the woman been unveiled and even had she been attractive, he fancies he is holding commerce with Aphrodite herself, and at the end of a fairly brief career, his engine hardens thanks to the jerks and jolts, and unlooses a warm rain over the ensemble of the sublime ass exposed to his view. His discharge was sharp and impetuous. He was seated facing the adored idol; one of his hands opened it while with the other he polluted it, and he cried ten times in succession: "Ah, what a beautiful ass! Ah, what a delight to drown such an ass in fuck!" He rose when done, and left without indicating the least desire to find out with whom he had been dealing.

A young abbot called for my sister a short time afterward. He was youthful and handsome, but one could scarcely discern his prick, so minute and soft it was. He stretched his almost naked partner on a couch, knelt down between her thighs, supporting her buttocks with both hands, with one of them tickling the pretty little hole in her behind. Meanwhile, he conveyed his mouth to my sister's cunt. He tickled its clitoris with his tongue, and managed so cunningly, so harmoniously synchronized the two activities, that within the space of three minutes he had plunged her into a delirium; I saw her head toss about, her eyes begin to roll, and heard the rascal cry: "Ah, my dear Reverend Father, you're slaying me with pleasure!"

The abbot's custom was simply to swallow the liquid his libertine dexterity made flow; and this he did not now fail to do, shaking himself the while, agitating himself as he bore down upon my sister: I saw him spatter indubitable evidence of his virility upon the floor. My turn came the next day, and I believe I can assure you, Messieurs, that it was one of the sweetest operations to which in all my life I have ever been exposed: that scoundrel of an abbot had my first fruits, and it was into his mouth I shed my first fuck. More eager than my sister to give him pleasure in return for what he had caused me, I unthinkingly seized his drooping prick, and my little hand replied to what his mouth had made me feel with such delight.

The Duc could not prevent himself from interrupting at this point. To a remarkable degree excited by the pollutions he had undergone that same morning, he had an idea that this species of lubric sport executed with the fascinating Augustine, whose sparkling, roguish eyes announced the most precocious temperament, would deliver him of a charge of fuck that was stinging his balls in a dreadful way. She was a member of his quatrain, he found her likeable, she was destined to be deflowered by him, he summoned her. On this particular evening she had a kerchief tied round her head, was clad in peasant guise, and seemed charming beneath that costume. The duenna hoisted her skirts and established her in the posture Duclos had represented. The Duc first of all lay hands on her buttocks, knelt, brought a finger to the anus and lightly titillated its rim, seized up the clitoris this amiable child already had in considerable growth, and sucked it. The people of Languedoc are high-spirited, they say, and Augustine proved them right; fire leapt into her pretty eyes, she sighed and panted and moaned, her thighs rose mechanically, and the Duc was pleased to sip a gush of young fuck which in all likelihood had never flowed before.

But joy is seldom succeeded by joy. There are libertines so hardened in vice that the simpler, the more delicate and banal be the thing they do, the less effect it has upon their execrable minds. Of their number our beloved Duc was one, he swallowed that delicious child's sperm without his own contriving to flow; all present beheld the moment arrive, for no one is more illogical than a libertine, the moment appeared at hand, I say, when he would blame his unresponse upon the poor little wretch who, all a dither at having yielded to Nature, was hiding her face in her hands and struggling to get free and return to her place.

"Get me another one," thundered the Duc, casting furious glances at Augustine, "I'll suck every last one of them if that's required to lose my fuck."

Zelmire, the second girl in his quatrain, was brought to the fore, she too was the Duc's by escheat. Though equal in years to Augustine, the grief for her plight robbed her of the power to taste a pleasure which, who knows, had it not been for that, Nature might have allowed her to relish.

Up rose her skirts, up above two little thighs whiter than alabaster, a chubby little mons veneris hove into view, it was upholstered by a fluffy down just beginning to appear. She is adjusted, obliged to yield, she obeys automatically, but sweat, strain, suck though he does, nothing happens to the Duc. Fifteen minutes of this and he rises in a fury, and, flinging himself into his closet with Hercule and Narcisse:

"Ah, by fuck!" he roars. "It's very clear to me that's not the game I'm hunting" -- 'tis to the two little girls he alludes -- "and that I'll only have a fair shot at this."

It is not known to what excesses he surrendered himself, but ere an instant had passed screams and shouts declared he had carried the day, and proved that boys are always the far more certain implements to a discharge than the most adorable girls. In the meantime, the Bishop had likewise enchambered himself with Giton, Zélamir, and Invictus, and the outbursts which accompanied his discharge having struck the assembly's ears, the two brothers, who had probably resorted to similar expedients, returned, more calmly to listen to the rest of the story our heroine took up again in these terms.

Nigh unto two years passed by during which time no one of particular interest arrived at Madame Guérin's; the gentleman who called either had tastes too ordinary to warrant description, or had tastes analogous to those I have already described; and then one day I was told to prepare myself, and above all to wash out my mouth. A heavy, thickset man of about fifty stood beside the mistress of the house.

"Well, there she is," said Madame. "She's only twelve, Monsieur, just as clean and tidy as if she'd come this morning out of her mother's belly, and you can take my word for that." The customer inspects me, has me open my mouth, he examines my teeth, sniffs my breath, and evidently satisfied that all is in order, he goes with me into the sanctuary intended for pleasure. We sit down face to face and very near to one another. No one could be more solemn than my gallant nor more phlegmatic. He stares coldly at me, then appraises me with narrowed eyes, I have no idea where all this is leading when, finally breaking his silence, he bids me collect a mouthful of saliva. I obey, and as soon as he fancies my mouth must be full, he throws himself upon my neck, passionately puts his arm around my head, thereby immobilizing it, and gluing his lips to my mouth, he pumps, sucks, eagerly swallows all the bewitching fluid I have collected, and it seems enough to put him in an overwhelming ecstasy. He sucks my tongue into his mouth with identical fervor, and when he senses it is dry, perceives my mouth is empty, he commands me to repeat the operation. He reiterates his, then I do, then he does, and so on eight or ten times over.

He sucked up my saliva with such furious avidity it discomfited my chest and lungs. I thought that at least a few sparks of pleasure were going to climax his transports; I was mistaken. His apathy, whence he emerged only brief instants during his most intense suckings, compassed him again

immediately he had drained me, and when at last I told him I could do
no more, he fell to eyeing me distantly, to staring at me as he had at the
beginning, then got up without a word, paid Guérin, and left..

"Ah, God's prick and balls!" cried Curval, "I'm happier than he, for
I'm coming."

Everyone raised his head, everyone saw the dear Président doing to
Julie, his wife, whom that day he had for couch companion, the same
thing Duclos had just been relating. That this passion appealed admirably
to his tastes was generally well known; Julie by and large procured him
abundant pleasure in this manner, Duclos had no doubt done less well by
her gallant. But that was in all likelihood his own fault; failing to appreciate what certain mouths, in certain conditions, may offer, he got nothing
from Duclos', whereas the Président obtained satisfaction from Julie's.

A month later, said Duclos, who had been invited to continue, I had
dealings with a sucker who assailed what one might term the same fort but
from an entirely different angle. This latter was an elderly abbot who, after
having previously kissed and caressed my bum for above half an hour,
introduced his tongue into its hole, made it penetrate deep, dart to left and
right, turn this way, turn that way, all with such surpassing art I thought
I felt it drive nigh to the depths of my entrails. But this abbot of mine,
much less phlegmatic, as he used one hand to spread my buttocks, used
the other to frig himself very voluptuously, and as he discharged he drew
my anus to his face with such violence and tickled it so lubriciously that
my ecstasy coincided with his. When he was finished, he spent another
moment scrutinizing my buttocks, staring at that hole he'd just reamed
wider, and couldn't prevent himself from gluing his mouth to it one last
time; then he hastened off, assuring me he would be back frequently,
would ask for me, and that he was most content with my ass. He kept
his promise, and for six months he came to visit me three or four times
a week, regularly performing the same operation to which I became so
thoroughly accustomed that each time he executed his little project, I all
but expired with delight -- an aspect of the rite about which he appeared
to care very little, for, as best I could judge, he had no inclination to find
out whether or no my work pleased me; that did not seem to matter to
him. And indeed, who can tell? Men are extraordinary indeed; had he
known of it, my pleasure might even have displeased him.

And now Durcet, whom the story had inflamed, like the old priest
was moved to suck some asshole or other, but would not have a girl's. He
called for Hyacinthe, who of them all pleased him the most. He placed
the little chap, kissed his ass, frigged his prick and sucked it. By the nervous shuddering of his body, by the spasm which ordinarily heralded his
discharge, it was thought the evil little anchovy that Aline was thumping
and pulling as best she could, was finally going to disgorge its seed, but
no, the financier was penurious when it came to parting with his fuck, he

simply could not, or would not, stiffen. It occurs to them all that his object ought to be changed, Céladon is substituted for Hyacinthe, but all's at a standstill, not the least improvement is apparent. The opportune tolling of a bell announcing supper saves the banker's honor.

"Why," says he, laughing with his confreres, "it's not my fault, you saw I was about to win a victory; this damned supper will have to delay it. Well, by God, let's go and have a fling at the table, I'll return all the more ardent to Cupid's tourney after having been crowned by Bacchus."

The evening meal was equally succulent and gay, quite as lubricious as ever, and was followed by orgies in the course of which an abundance of little infamies were perpetrated. Many were the mouths sucked and the asses, but one of the most engaging drolleries of all was the game in which they hid the face and chest of each little girl and gambled upon recognizing her on the basis of a study of her ass. The Duc was occasionally misled, but not so the others, for they were too well accustomed to the use of the bum. The friends retired for the night, and the morrow brought further and new pleasures, and a few reflections.

The Fourth Day

Being full eager to be able to distinguish immediately which of the youngsters in either sex was, in a depucelatory sense, to belong to each of their number, the friends decided to have them wear, regardless of their costume and, in that other extreme, even when undressed, a hair ribbon, which would indicate of whom the individual child was the property. Colors were thereupon chosen: the Duc adopted pink and green: whosoever should wear a pink ribbon to the fore, would be his by the cunt; similarly, whosoever wore a green ribbon to the rear, would be his by the ass. And so Fanny, Zelmire, Sophie, and Augustine straightway affixed a pink ribbon on one side of their coiffures; Rosette, Hébé, Michette, Giton, and Zéphyr attached a green favor to their hair where it fell toward the neck, this clue attesting the rights of the Duc enjoyed to their asses.

Curval chose black for the front, yellow for the rear; thus Michette, Hébé, Colombe, and Rosette were in future constantly to wear a black ribbon forward; Sophie, Zelmire, Augustine, Zélamir, and Adonis pinned a yellow one above their nape.

Durcet identified his Hyacinthe with a lilac ribbon hanging to the rear, and the Bishop, who owned title to but five assholes to be deflowered sodomistically, ordered Cupidon, Narcisse, Céladon, Colombe, and Fanny to wear a violet one in the rear.

Never, regardless of the subject's posture, chore, or dress, were these ribbons to be neglected or improperly worn, and so it was that by this simple arrangement each friend was always able to tell at a glance what property was his, and in what way.

Curval, who had passed the night with Constance, had bitter complaints to lodge against her in the morning. It was not entirely clear what lay at the root of the trouble, nor what precisely the trouble was; so little is needed to displease a libertine. But there was more than enough to the thing to cause him to have her listed for Saturday punishment, and he was formulating charges when that lovely creature declared that she was pregnant; Curval, apart from her husband the only one whom it was possible to suspect as the agent in this affair, had effected no carnal juncture with her save at the beginning of this party, that is to say, four days previously. Our libertines were gladdened by these tidings, seeing in the event much possibility of clandestine delight, and the Duc exulted over this stroke of fortune. In any event, the declaration earned her exemption from the punishment she would otherwise have had to undergo in return for having displeased Curval. She was to be spared: they preferred to leave the fruits on the branch to ripen, a gravid woman diverted them, and what they promised themselves for later on even more lewdly entertained their perfidious imaginations. Constance was dispensed from service at table, from chastisements, and from a few other little odds and ends the accomplishment of which her state no longer rendered voluptuous to observe, but she was still obliged to appear upon the couches and until further orders to share bed of whoever wished to choose her for the night.

It was Durcet who, that morning, contributed his presence to the pollution exercises, and as his prick was extraordinarily small, he gave the pupils rather more a problem than had been posed by the Duc's massive construction. However, they fell earnestly to work. But the little banker, who had been plying a woman's trade all night long, could never bear a man's. He was adamant, intractable, and the skill of these eight charming students combined with that of their deft instructress was unable, when all was said and done, even to get him to raise his nose. He left the classroom in triumph, and as impotence always provokes that kind of mood called a teasing one in the idiom of libertinage, his inspections were astonishingly severe. Rosette amongst the girls, Zélamir amongst the boys were the victims of his thoroughness: one was not as she had been told to be -- this enigma will be explained -- the other, unfortunately, had rid himself of what he had been ordered to keep.

Those present at the public latrines were only seven in number: Duclos, Marie, Aline, and Fanny, two second-class fuckers, and Giton, Curval, who did considerable stiffening that day, grew very excited over Duclos. Dinner, at which his conduct and remarks were very libertine indeed, calmed him not one whit, and the coffee served by Colombe, Sophie, Zéphyr, and his dear friend Adonis, set his brain all afire. He laid hands on this selfsame Adonis, tumbled him onto a sofa, and while spewing forth oaths slid his enormous member between the lad's thighs (approaching him from behind), and as that outsized tool protruded a fair six inches beyond, he commanded Adonis vigorously to frig what emerged, and himself set to frigging the boy above the morsel of flesh upon which Adonis was spitted. Meanwhile, he presented the assembly with an ass no less filthy than broad, whose impure orifice began to exert a potent attraction upon the Duc. Seeing this ass within reach, he trained his vivacious prick on the hole while continuing to suck Zéphyr's mouth, an operation he had begun before this new idea had occurred to him.

Curval, who had not been expecting such an attack, emitted blasphemous paeans of joy. He danced with delight, spread himself wider, braced himself; at the same instant, the fresh young fuck of the charming boy he was frigging started to drip out upon the enormous head of his own aroused instrument. That warm fuck he feels wetting him, the reiterated blows of the Duc who is also beginning to discharge, it all quickens his warrior's soul, the weapon is primed, off goes the gun, floods of foamy sperm splash against Durcet's ass, for the banker has just posted himself there within easy range lest, says he, something be wasted, and Durcet's plump white buttocks are submerged beneath a spellbinding liquor he would have by far preferred as a rinse for his bowels.

Nor was the Bishop idle; he was one after the other sucking clean the divine assholes of Colombe and Sophie. But doubtless fatigued by some nocturnal exercise, he showed not one spark of life, and like all other libertines rendered unjust by caprice and disgust, he lashed out furiously against these two delicious children, blaming them for the only too well merited shortcomings of his debilitated frame. Messieurs nap for a few minutes; then 'tis story-telling time, and in they troop to listen to the amiable Duclos, who resumes her tale in the following manner.

There had been a few changes in Madame Guérin's house, said our heroine. Two very pretty girls had just found dupes who were only too willing to keep them and whom they deceived just the way we all do. To fill the gaps in the ranks, our dear mother had scouted around and set her sights upon a rue Saint-Denis tavern-keeper's daughter, thirteen years old and one of the most fetching creatures in all the wide world. But the little lady, quite as well-behaved as she was pious, was successfully resisting all enticements when Guérin, having one day employed the cleverest stratagem to lure her to her house, immediately put her in the hands of the unusual person whose mania I propose to describe next. He was an ecclesiastic of fifty-five or fifty-six, but so youthful and vigorous you'd have thought him under forty. No man in Europe had such a singular talent for drawing young girls into vice, and as it was his one art, developed to a sublime degree, he had turned it into his one and only pleasure. The whole of his fleshy delight consisted in extirpating childhood prejudices and unnatural terrors, in cultivating scorn for virtue, in decking vice in the most dazzling colors. He neglected nothing: seductive images, flattering promises, delicious examples, he would press everything into service, everything would be brilliantly manipulated, his artistry being faultlessly attuned to the child's age and cast of mind, and never did he miss the mark. Granted a mere two hours of conversation, he was sure to make a whore of the best-behaved and most reasonable little girl; for thirty years he had been conducting his missionary labors in Paris, and, he had once assured Madame Guérin, who counted herself one of his best friends, he had to his credit more than ten thousand girls whom he had personally seduced and plunged into libertinage. He rendered similar services to at least fifteen procuresses, and whenever he was not coping with a particular problem at someone else's behest, he was busy doing research for its own sake and for his professional pleasure, energetically corrupting whatever he came across and then packing it off to his outfitters. Now, the most extraordinary aspect of the entire thing, and the one which, Messieurs, prompts me to cite the example of this uncommon individual, was that he never enjoyed the fruit of his labors. He would encloset himself alone with the child, but, despite his vast understanding, his mind's agility, his eloquent persuasiveness, he used always to emerge from conference greatly inflamed. One could be perfectly certain the operation irritated his senses, but it was impossible to discover where or when or how he satisfied them. Closest scrutiny had never revealed anything but a prodigious blaze in his stare when once he had concluded his speeches, a few twitching movements of his hand upon the front of his breeches, within which one could tell there was a definite erection, produced by the diabolic work he was doing; but that was all.

He came to the house, was accorded a private interview with the young barmaid, I watched the proceedings: the consultation was prolonged, the seducer's language was amazingly pathetic, the child wept, got hot, seemed to enter into a kind of enthusiastic fit; it was at this moment the orator's eyes flamed brightest, and it was now we remarked the gestures in the neighborhood of his fly. Not long afterward, he rose, the child stretched forth her arms as if seeking to embrace him, he kissed her in a grave and fatherly manner, without any trace of lechery. He left, and three hours later the little girl arrived with her baggage at Madame Guérin's.

"And the man?" asked the Duc.

"He disappeared once his sermon was over," Duclos replied. "Without coming back to see the results of his work?"

"No, my Lord, there was no doubt in his mind. He had never once failed."

"Now there is a most extraordinary personage," Curval admitted. "What does your Grace make of it?"

"I suspect," the Duc answered, "that the seduction provided all the heat necessary and that he discharged in his breeches."

"No," quoth the Bishop, "I think you underestimate the man: all this was simply by way of preparation for his debauches, and upon leaving I wager he went off to consummate greater ones."

"Greater ones?" cried Durcet. "And what more delicious, more voluptuous delight could one hope to procure oneself, than that of enjoying the object one creates?".

"I have it!" spoke up the Duc, "I dare say I've found him out: all this, just as you say, was merely preparatory in character, corrupting girls would heat his imagination, the off he'd go to dip his tool in boys. . .. I'll wager he was a bugger, yes, 'tis plain."

Duclos was asked whether she had any evidence to support that conjecture, and did he or did he not also seduce little boys? Our narrator replied that she had no proof of the thing, and despite the Duc's exceedingly likely allegation, everyone remained more or less in suspense as to the character of that strange preacher; after it had been unanimously agreed that his mania was truly delicious, but that one had either to consummate the work or do worse afterward, Duclos went on with her story.

The day after the arrival of our young novice, who was named Henriette, there came to the establishment an eccentric old lecher who put us both, Henriette and I, to work at the same time. This latest libertine had no other pleasure than that of observing through a hole all the voluptuous activities transpiring in an adjoining room, he adored spying on them, thus found in others' pleasures the divine aliment of his own lubricity. He was installed in the room I mentioned to you, the same one to which I and my companions often repaired for the diversion of watching libertines in action. I was assigned the task of amusing him while he looked through the hole, and young Henriette entered the arena together with the asshole-sucker I described you yesterday. The management considered that rascal's very voluptuous antics just the kind of spectacle my onlooker would relish, and in order better to arouse the actor, and in order that he render the scene yet more lascivious and more agreeable to see, he was told he was being given an apprentice and that it was with him she was to make her debut. The little barmaid's air of modesty and childishness speedily convinced him of it; and so he was as hot and as lewd in his nasty stunts as 'twere possible to be; nothing could have been further from his mind than that he was being observed. As for my old buck, his eye glued to the hole, one hand on my bum, the other on his prick, which he gently agitated, he seemed to be keeping the progress of his ecstasy abreast the one he was watching. "Ah, what a sight!" he said now and again; "what a fine ass that little girl has, and how well that bugger in there is tonguing it." At last, Henriette's lover having discharged, mine folded me in his arms and, after a moment's kissing, he turned me over, fondled, kissed, lewdly licked my behind, and squirted evidence of his virility over my cheeks.

"While frigging himself?" the Duc asked.

"Yes, my Lord," answered Duclos, "and frigging a prick whose incredible littleness, I assure you, isn't worth the bother describing..

The gentleman with whom I had to do next, Duclos continued, would not perhaps deserve to be included in my report were it not for one element, a rather unusual one, I should say, which distinguished his otherwise quite routine pleasures, and this little circumstance will illustrate to what point libertinage is able to degrade all a man's feelings of modesty, virtue and decorum. This person did not want to see; he wished to be seen. Knowing that men exist whose whim it is to spy upon the pleasure-takings of others, he bade Guérin find him one such fellow, conceal him, and said he would enact a drama for him. Guérin at once got in touch with the man I had entertained a few days previously behind the partition, and without telling him that the performer he was about to see knew that he was going to be seen -- this would have interfered with his passion's fulfillment -- she gave him to believe he was to observe a very arcane mystery indeed.

The inspector and my sister were put in the room with the hole, the actor and I went into the other one. He was a young man about twenty-eight years old, handsome and strong. Informed of the hole's location, he not too pointedly moved to where he could be perfectly viewed and had me take my place beside him. I frigged him. When his prick held a good slope, he got to his feet, exhibited his tool to the inspector, turned around, displayed his ass, raised my skirts and showed my mine, knelt before me, teased my anus with the tip of his nose, spread heartily, displayed everything with as much thoroughness as delight, and discharged by frigging himself, the while keeping my hinder skirts high and my ass squarely opposite the spy hole, in such wise that he who stood posted on the other side of the wall simultaneously beheld, at this decisive moment, both my bum and my lover's wrathful device. If the latter was in seventh heaven, God knows what was going on in the next room; my sister later told me she had had a madman on her back who had sworn he'd never had as fine a time as this, and after that her buttocks had been washed by a tide no less fierce than the one that had burst over mine.

"If that young man of yours truly had a good prick and pretty ass," Durcet opinioned, "there was ample in the situation to provoke a generous discharge."

"It must then have been delicious," returned Duclos, "for his engine was very long, quite thick, and his ass as soft, as sweetly plump, as attractively formed as the god of love's."

"Did you spread his cheeks?" the Bishop inquired. "Did you show his vent to the inspector?"

"Yes, your Lordship," said Duclos, "he displayed mine, I displayed his, he presented it with incomparable suggestiveness."

"I've been witness to a dozen such scenes," Durcet announced, "which have cost me a fortune in fuck; there is nothing more delicious to see or do. I refer to both: for it is just as pleasant to spy upon someone as to want to be observed..

Another individual, with approximately the same tastes, Duclos went on, took me to the Tuileries some few months later. He wanted me to accost men and frig them six inches from his face while he hid under a pile of folding chairs; and after I had frigged seven or eight passers-by, he settled himself upon a bench by one of the most frequented of the paths, lifted my skirts from behind, and displayed my ass to all and sundry, put his prick in the air and ordered me to frig it well within view of half of Paris, the which, although it was night, created such a scandal that by the time he most cynically unleashed his fuck, more than ten people had gathered around us, and we were obliged to dash away to avoid being publicly covered with shame.

When I related this adventure to Guérin, she laughed approvingly and said she had once known a man in Lyon (where panders enter into the trade at an early age), a man, I say, whose mania was certainly just as unusual. He would disguise himself as a public mercury, himself fetch in visitors to dally with the two girls he paid and maintained for no other purpose, then he would conceal himself in a corner to watch his client go to work; the girl, whose hire depended upon her skill in these moments, would guide the libertine she had in her arms and unfailingly give her employer a view of his prick and ass, the sight of which constituted the one pleasure that agreed with our false pimp's palate, the one that was able to loosen his fuck.

Duclos having brought her recital to an early conclusion that evening, the time that remained until supper was devoted to a few choice lubricities, and as the example of the cynic had fired their four daring brains, the friends did not isolate themselves in their closets, but disported within clear view each of the other. The Duc had Duclos strip off her clothes, had her bend and lean upon the back of a chair and commanded Desgranges to frig him upon her comrade's buttocks, in such wise that the head of his prick might graze Duclos' asshole with each stroke. To that one was added a number of other episodes which the proper presentation of our material forbids us from disclosing at this stage; but the fact remains that the chronicler's inferior vent was completely sprayed and that the Duc, handsomely served and entirely surrounded, discharged to the tune of bellowings and shouts which indicated to what a point his mind has been stimulated. Curval had himself fucked, the Bishop and Durcet for their part did passing strange things with both sexes; then supper was served.

After it, dances were held: the sixteen youngsters, the four fuckers, and the four wives were able to perform three quadrilles, but all the participants at the ball were naked, and our roués, indolently reclining upon sofas, were deliciously amused by all the different beauties one after another offered them by the divers attitudes the dancers were obliged to strike. Messieurs had the storytellers at their side, and these ladies manualized them rapidly or slowly, depending upon the pleasure they were experiencing; but, somewhat fatigued by the day's frolickings, no one discharged, and each went to bed to acquire the strength needed for all the following day's new infamies.

The Fifth Day

That morning it was Curval's duty to lend his presence at the academy of masturbation, and as the little girls were beginning to make tangible progress, he was hard put to resist the multiplying thumps and jerks and the variegated but universally lubricious postures of these eight charming little maids. Wishing to keep his weapon charged, he withdrew without firing it, lunch was announced, and at table the friends decreed that Messieurs' four young lovers, to wit: Zéphyr, the Duc's favorite; Adonis, beloved of Curval; Hyacinthe, friend to Durcet; and Céladon, unto whom the Bishop was plighted, were henceforth to be admitted to all meals, would dine beside their lovers in whose bedchambers they were, as well, regularly to sleep, a favor they would share with the wives and the fuckers; the which eliminated a ceremony customarily performed, as the reader is aware, every morning, this ceremony consisting in the fetching of the four lads by the four off-duty fuckers. They were now to come of their own accord, and when from now on Messieurs were to pass into the little boys' chambers, they were to be received, in accordance with prescribed regulation, by the remaining four only.

The Duc, who for the past two or three days had been head over heels in love with Duclos, whose ass he found superb and language pleasing, demanded that she also sleep in his bedroom, and this precedent having been established, Curval similarly introduced Fanchon, of whom he was passionately fond, into his. The two others decided to wait yet a little longer before deciding who was to fill this fourth post of privilege in their chambers.

It was that same morning ruled that the four young lovers who had just been chosen would have by way of ordinary dress, whenever they were not obliged to wear characterizing costumes, as when formed in quatrains, would have, I say, the clothing and style I am going to describe: it was a little jerkin, tight-fitting, of light cloth, tailored like a Prussian uniform with a slit tail, but much shorter, scarcely reaching to halfway down the thigh; this jacket, like all uniforms buttoned across the chest and at the vent, was of pink satin lined with white taffeta, the cuffs and

trim were white satin, underneath was to be worn a kind of short vest or
waistcoat, also of white satin, and the breeches were to match; but these
breeches were provided with a heart-shaped rear flap under which one
could slip one's hand and grasp the ass without the slightest difficulty; the
flap was held up by a ribbon tied in a big bow, and when one wished to
have the child completely exposed in this part, one had merely to undo the
bow, which was of the color selected by the friend to whom the pucelage
belonged. Their hair, carelessly arranged so that a few curls fell to either
side, floated absolutely free behind, and was simply knotted by a ribbon
of the appropriate color. A highly-scented powder, in color between gray
and pink, tinted their hairdress, their eyebrows were carefully plucked and
emphasized by black pencil, a light touch of rouge applied to the cheeks,
all this heightened their natural beauty; their heads were never covered,
black silk stockings brocaded in rose covered their legs, they were agreeably shod in gray slippers attached by a pink bow. A cream-colored gauze
cravat, very voluptuously tied, blended prettily with a little lace ruffle;
when the four of them were clad in this style, you may rest assured that
nothing in all the world was as charming to behold as these little fellows.

Immediately they were granted their new privileges, a few others
were abolished: all permissions, of the kind they had upon occasion been
accorded in the morning, were absolutely refused now, but they were
given all the rights over the wives the fuckers enjoyed: they could maltreat
the women as they saw fit and not only at mealtime, no, but at any time
of the day, all the time, if they chose, and they could be confident that in
any dispute arising 'twixt the wives and themselves, their side would be
heard with sympathy.

These matters attended to, the usual searches were conducted; the
lovely Fanny, whom Curval had ordered to be in such and such a state,
was found in the contrary one (the sequel will provide elucidation of
this obscure point) : her name was set down in the punishment ledger.
Amongst the young gentlemen, Giton had done what he had been forbidden to do; down went his name. After the chapel functions had been
completed by the very few subjects who were on hand to execute them,
the friends went to dinner.

This was the first meal at which the four lovers joined the friends at
table. They took their places, each sitting to the right of the friend who
doted upon him, the friend's favorite fucker being seated to the friend's
left. These four additional guests lent a further charm to the meal; they
were all four very gentle, very sweet, and were beginning to accommodate
themselves very well to the general tone of the household. The Bishop, in
the liveliest spirits that day, kissed Céladon virtually without interruption
throughout the course of the meal, and as that child was a member of the
quartet chosen to hand around the coffee, he left table a little before dessert. When Monseigneur, who had worked himself into a splendid sweat

over the boy, saw him entirely naked in the salon, he lost all self-control.

"By Jesus!" he cried, his face purple, "since I cannot tup his ass, I can at least do what Curval did to his bardash yesterday."

And so saying he seized the good-natured little rascal, laid him on his belly, and slipped his prick between his thighs. The libertine was lost in the clouds, his weapon's hair rubbed the cute little hole he would fain have perforated: one of his hands fondled this delicious little cupid's buttocks, with the other he frigged Céladon's prick. What was more, he glued his mouth to the lovely child's, pumped the air from his lungs, swallowed his saliva. In order to excite his brother, the Duc created a libertine spectacle by placing himself in front of the Bishop and proceeding to lick out the asshole of Cupidon, the other of the two boys serving coffee that day. Curval moved to within close range and had himself frigged by Michette, and Durcet offered the prelate the sight of Rosette's widespread buttocks. Everyone toiled to procure him the ecstasy to which he plainly aspired; it occurred, his nerves trembled, his teeth chattered, his eyes shone, he would have been a terrifying object for anyone save those three who knew full well the terrible effects joy had upon that man of God. The fuck finally broke forth and flowed over Cupidon's buttocks, for that quick-witted little aide had at the last moment wriggled his way beneath his comrade so as to receive the treasure which might otherwise have gone entirely to waste.

The storytelling hour came, they readied themselves. By an unusual stroke of circumstance, all the fathers found their daughters beside them on their couches. But Messieurs were not alarmed. Duclos began to speak.

In that you have not required me, Messieurs, to give you an exact day by day account of everything that happened to me at Madame Guérin's establishment, but simply to relate the more out of the ordinary events which highlighted some of those days, I shall omit mention of several not very interesting episodes dating from my childhood, for they would be naught but tedious repetitions of what you have heard already. And so I shall tell you that I had just reached the age of sixteen, not without having acquired a wealth of experience in my mtier, when it fell to my lot to have a libertine whose daily caprice merits to be cited. He was a sober, very grave judge of nearly fifty years, a man who, if one is to believe Madame Guérin, who told me she had known him for many years, regularly exercised every morning the whimsicality wherewith I shall entertain you. His ordinary pimp had reached the age of retirement and recommended that the judge put himself in our dear mother's hands; this was his first call at the house, and he began with me.

He stationed himself, alone, in the room with the spy hole, I entered the other with a hod carrier, a Savoyard, I believe; well, he was a common fellow, but a healthy strapping one: those qualifications were enough for the judge, who cared nothing for age or looks. I was, within clear view and as near as possible to the hole, to frig my honest churl, who knew what was expected of him and reckoned this a very pretty way indeed to earn his supper. After having unreservedly complied with all the instructions the good judge had given me, after having done all my sweet country buck could desire of me, I had him discharge into a porcelain dish, and having wrung the last drop from his prick, I dashed into the adjoining room. My man is awaiting me in an ecstasy, he pounces upon the dish, swallows the hot fuck, his own erupts; with one hand I encourage his ejaculation, with the other I collect in my hand every precious dram that falls and, between jets, quickly raising my hand to the old prankster's mouth, with great dexterity and nimbleness I see to it that he swallows his own fuck quite as fast as he squirts it out.

That was all there was to it; no fingerings, no kisses, he didn't even lift my skirts, and rising from his chair with just as much aplomb as a moment before he had been aroused, he took his cane and left, saying that I frigged very skillfully, so he considered, and that I had very well grasped his character. A new workman was brought in the next day, for they had to be changed daily, as had the women. My sister operated for him, he left content, returned again on the morrow, and during my entire stay at Madame Guérin's I never saw a single day go by without him arriving punctually at nine, and never did he raise a single skirt, although he was ministered by some charming girls.

"Had he any inclination to see the commoner's ass?" Curval wanted to know.

"He had indeed, Monsieur le Président," Duclos replied. "While amusing the man whose fuck he ate, one had to take great care to turn him this way and that, and the man had also to turn the girl around in every direction."

"Well, now," said Curval, "that makes sense. But for that I'd not have understood a thing."

Shortly afterward, continued Duclos, the harem's strength was increased by the arrival of a girl of about thirty, attractive enough, but with hair as red as Judas'. At first we though she was a new recruit, but no, she quickly disabused us by explaining that she had come for only one party. The man for whom this latest heroine was intended soon arrived also: he was an important financier of prepossessing appearance, and his singularity of taste, since the girl set aside for him would doubtless not have been wanted by anyone else, this singularity, I say, gave me the greatest desire to observe them come to grips. No sooner had they entered the room than the girl removed every stitch of her clothing and displayed a very fair and very plump body. "Very well, be off, jump about, skip," said the financier, "you know perfectly well I like them in a sweat." And thereupon the redhead falls to cutting capers, running around the room, leaping like a young goat, and our man keeps his eye fixed on her while he frigs himself; these activities continued a great while and there was no telling to what they were leading. When the girl was swimming in perspiration, she approached the libertine, raised an arm, and had him smell her armpit where the sweat was dripping from every hair. "Ah, that's it, that's it!" cried the tycoon, staring with furious approval at that sticky arm she held a centimeter from his nose, "what an odor! ravishing!" Then slipping to his knees before her, he sniffed the interior of her vagina, inhaling deeply, and then breathed in the scent emergent from her asshole, but he returned constantly to her armpits, whether because those parts flattered him the most, or because he found the bouquet superior, it was always there his mouth and nose betook themselves with the greatest fervor. At last a rather lengthy but not very thick device, a device he had been buffeting in vain for about an hour, decided to wake and have a look about. The girl takes her place, the financier comes up from behind and lodges his anchovy under her armpit, she squeezes her arm, exerting what I judged must have been a powerful grip; meanwhile, her posture enables the gentleman to enjoy the sight and odor of her other armpit, he lays hands on it, buries his snout under it and discharges while licking, while devouring this part which affords him such delight.

"And the creature had to have red hair?" asked the Bishop. "That was a sine qua non?"

"Absolutely," Duclos replied. "Those women, as you are not unaware, Monseigneur, exude an infinitely more violent underarm aroma, and his sense of smell once stung, no question of it, by ripe odors, his pleasure organs would be aroused at once."

"Of course," the Bishop agreed. "But, by God, it seems to me I'd have preferred smelling that woman's asshole to sniffing under her arms."

"Ah, ha!" spoke up Curval, "there is much to be said in favor of the one and the other, and let me assure you that if you'll but give the arms a try, you'll find them perfectly delicious."

"Which is to say, I take it," said the Bishop, "that Monsieur le Président finds that stew to his taste?"

"Why yes, I've sampled it," Curval replied, "and apart from a few occasions when I added other episodes to that one, I protest to you that all by itself it has always been able to get some fuck out of me."

"Oh yes, those episodes, I fancy what they were," the Bishop broke in, "you smelled the ass..."

"One moment there," interrupted the Duc. "Don't oblige him to make his confession, Monseigneur, he'd tell us things we are not yet to hear; go on, Duclos, don't let these chatterers encroach upon your domain."

I recall the period, our narrator resumed, when for more than six weeks Guérin absolutely forbade my sister to wash, requiring her, on the contrary, to keep herself in the rankest and most impure state she could contrive to be in; we had no inkling of the Madame's designs until one day there arrived a grog-blossomed old rake who, in a half-drunken and most uncouth tone, asked Guérin whether the whore was ready. "Oh, my goodness, you may be sure she is," Guérin replied. They are brought together, put in the room, I fly to the hole; scarcely am I there than I see my naked sister astride a capacious bidet filled with champagne and there is our man, armed with a great sponge, busily washing her and carefully recovering every bit of dirt that rolls from her body.

It had been so long since she had cleaned any part of herself, for she had been strictly ordered not to wipe her behind, that the wine immediately took on a brown and dirty hue, and probably an odor which could not have been very agreeable. But the more the wine became corrupted by the filth streaming into it, the more delighted our libertine grew. He sipped a little, found it exquisite, provided himself with a glass and, filling it to the brim six or seven times, he downed the putrid and disgusting wine in which he'd just finished washing a body laden for so long with impurities. When he had drunk his fill, he seized my sister, laid her down flat upon the bed, and upon her buttocks and well-opened hole, spewed floods of immodest semen brought to a boil by the unclean details of his unpleasant mania.

But another visitor, a far nastier one, was time and again to attract my regard. We had in the house one of those women who are called street scouts or trotters, to employ the bordello term, and whose function is to run abroad night and day and dig up new recruits. Over forty years old, this creature had, as well as very faded charms which had never been very winning, the dreadful defect that consists in stinking feet. And such, no other, was the fair sort whereof the Marquis de L*** was enamored. He arrives, Dame Louise -- for such was her name -- is introduced to him, he finds her superb, and once he has conducted her into the pleasure sanctuary, "Pray remove your shoes," says he. Louise, who had been explicitly enjoined to wear the same stockings and slippers for a month, offers the Marquis a foot that would have made a man of less fine discrimination puke straight off; but, as I say, that foot's very filth and nauseous quality was precisely what our nobleman cherished most. He catches it up, kisses it with fervor, with his mouth he spreads each toe, one after the other, with his tongue he gathers from each space, and gathers with incomparable enthusiasm, the blackish and fetid scum Nature deposits there and which, with a little encouragement, easily increases by itself. Not only does he draw this unmentionable stuff into his mouth, but he swallows it, savors it, and the fuck he loses while frigging himself stands as unequivocal proof of the excessive pleasure he takes in this fare.

"'Tis beyond me," was the Bishop's simple comment. "Then I suppose I'd best explain it to you," Curval said. "What? You've a taste for that?"

"Observe," the Président replied.

The others rose, came from their niches, surrounded him, and beheld that peerless libertine, in whom were met all the tastes of the most crapulous lewdness, embrace the indescribable foot tendered him by Fanchon, that aged and foul servant we described earlier. Curval was in half a swoon as he sucked.

"There's nothing to be wondered at there," said Durcet, "one need but be mildly jaded, and all these infamies assume a richer meaning: satiety inspires them in the libertinage which executes them unhesitatingly. One grows tired of the commonplace, the imagination becomes vexed, and the slenderness of our means, the weakness of our faculties, the corruption of our souls leads us to these abominations."

Such must surely have been the case, Duclos went on, with the elderly General C***, one of Guérin's most reliable clients. The women he required had to be damaged either by Nature, by libertinage, or by the effects of the law; in a word, he accepted none who were not one-eyed or blind, lame, hunchbacked, legless cripples, or missing an arm or two, or toothless, or mutilated in their limbs, or whipped and branded or clearly marked by some other act of justice, and they always had to be of the ripest old age.

At the scene I witnessed he had been given a woman of about fifty, bearing the brand of a public thief, and who was, in addition, missing an eye. That double degradation figured as a treasure in his view. He closeted himself with her, had her strip away her clothes, ecstatically kissed the indubitable signs of crime on her shoulders, ardently sucked each ridge and furrow of those scars he called honorably won. That accomplished, he transferred his avid attentions to her asshole, he spread open her buttocks, appreciatively kissed the withered hole they defended, sucked it for what seemed an age, and then planting himself astride the old girl's back, he rubbed his prick on the wounds that attested the triumph of justice, and as he rubbed, he praised her for having gone down in exemplary defeat; and then, bending over her bum, he showered further kisses upon the altar at which he had rendered such a lengthy homage, and squirted an abundance of fuck upon the inspiring marks which had so fired his own warrior's spirit.

"Oh, by God!" cried Curval, whose brain was in a lubricious ferment that day, "look my friends, behold by the sign of this risen prick what a flame that passion described ignites in me."

And calling out to Desgranges:

"Hither, impure buggress," he continued in the same strain, "come, you who so resemble what we have just heard described; come, beget me the same pleasure the general got by her."

Desgranges approaches. Durcet, his friend in these excesses, helps the Président strip her. She raises a few objections at first; they are the more certain and pursue their way, scolding her for wishing to hide something whereby she may be cherished all the more by the society. Her branded back comes to light at last, and there are a "T" and a "P" which affirm that she has twice undergone the dishonoring ordeal whose vestiges nevertheless completely ignite our libertines' impudicious urges.

The rest of that worn and wasted body -- that ass of parchment or ancient leather, that ample, noxious hole glistening in its center, this mutilated tit, those three vanished fingers, this short leg that causes her limp, that mouth destitute of teeth -- everything combines to stimulate our libertine pair. Durcet sucks her from in front, Curval posteriorly, and even though objects of the greatest beauty and in the best condition are there before their eyes and ready to brave anything in order to satisfy the least of their desires, even so it is with what Nature and villainy have dishonored, have withered, it is with the filthiest and least appetizing object our two rakes, presently beside themselves, are about to taste the most delicious pleasures Ah, now give me your explanation of man -- here are two men who seem as if they were disputing what is nigh to a cadaver, like two savage mastiffs wrangling over a corpse; here, I say, we have two eminent citizens who, after having given themselves over to the foulest excesses, finally erupt their fuck, and notwithstanding the exhaustion caused by these feats, would very possibly go on to perform other ones of the same crapulous and infamous kind, and perform them without an instant's delay, were it not for the supper bell announcing other pleasures well worth their consideration.

The Président, made desperate by his loss of fuck, and who in such cases could never be revived save by excessive feeding and swilling, flew to work and stuffed himself like a pig. Adonis frigged Invictus and gave him some fuck to drink, but hardly content with this latest outrage, which had been executed at once, Curval rose, said his imagination proposed a few rather more delicious stunts, and without further explanation, led Fanchon, Adonis, and Hercule away with him to the further boudoir and did not reappear until the orgies; but then conducted himself so brilliantly that he was again able to commit a thousand fresh horrors, each more extraordinary than the other, but not, we regret, to be described to the reader, or rather not yet, for the structure of our tale obliges us to defer them.

And then to bed. Curval, the unfathomable Curval to whom that night the divine Adelaide, his daughter, befell, Curval, who could have spent a most delightful night with her, was found the next morning squirming over the body of the disgusting Fanchon, with whom he had performed additional abominations all night long, whilst Adonis and Adelaide, driven from his couch, were, one of them, in a little bed far away, and the other lying on a mattress upon the floor.

The Sixth Day

It was Monseigneur's turn to assist at the masturbations; he presented himself. Had Duclos' disciples been males, Monseigneur would probably not have been able to resist them. But a little crack below the navel was a frightful blemish in his eyes, and had the Graces themselves encircled him, once he had caught sight of that imperfection nothing more would have been needed to calm him. And so he put up an indomitable defense, I even believe his prick remained limp, and the operations were continued. Nothing could be plainer than that Messieurs were extremely eager to find fault with the eight little girls so as to procure themselves the following day, which was the fatal Saturday of retribution, so as, I say, at this time to procure themselves the pleasure of punishing all eight. They had six already on the list; the sweet and beautiful Zelmire made the seventh; did she in all good faith really merit correction? or was it simply that the pleasure of inflicting the proposed penalty won out in a struggle with strict equity? we leave the question to be decided by the wise Durcet's conscience; our task is simply to record events. One very fair dame further swelled the miscreants' ranks: 'twas the gentle Adelaide. Durcet, her husband, appeared anxious to set an example by pardoning less in her than in the others, and it was he himself she happened to disappoint. He had led her to a certain place where the services she had been forced to render him, after certain of his functions, were something less than absolutely clean or palatable; not everyone is as depraved as Curval, and although Adelaide was his daughter, she had none of his tastes. She may have balked. Or she may have managed poorly. Or, again, it might only have been some teasing on Durcet's part. Whatever the cause, she was inscribed upon the punishment list, to the vast satisfaction of nearly all concerned.

The examination of the boys' quarters having unearthed nothing, the friends moved on to the arcane pleasures of the chapel, pleasures all the more piquant and all the more extraordinary in that even those who besought permission to come and procure them, were usually refused admittance. Constance, two subaltern fuckers, and Michette were the only ones to attend that morning's party. At dinner, Zéphyr, of whom they were becoming prouder every day, what for the charms which seemed more and more to embellish him and the voluntary libertinage wherein he was making great strides, Zéphyr, I say, insulted Constance who, although no longer a waitress, nevertheless always appeared at the midday meal. He called her a baby-maker and struck her several blows in the belly to teach her, said he, to lay eggs with her lover, then he kissed the Duc, caressed him, gave his prick a few affectionate tugs, and managed so successfully to fire that hero's brain that Blangis swore the afternoon would not pass without his moistening Zéphyr with fuck; and the little rascal nagged the Duc, daring him to do it at once. As Zéphyr was to serve coffee, he left at dessert time and reappeared naked with the Duc's cup. Instantly they were settled in the salon, the Duc, very animated, began with one or two smutty remarks; then sucked the child's mouth and prick, set him on a chair, his ass at the level of his mouth, and earnestly pumped at his hole for fifteen minutes. His prick rebelled at last, dressed its lofty head, and the Duc saw very clearly that the homage required some incense after all. However, their contract forbade everything save the expedient employed the day before; the Duc resolved therefore to emulate his associates. He had Zéphyr crouch on a sofa, drove his engine between the lad's thighs, but what had befallen Curval happened also to the Duc: his device protruded half a foot beyond. "You'd best do as I did," Curval advised, "frig the child against your prick, water your glans with his fuck." But the Duc found it more pleasant to impale two at the same time. He besought his brother to fit Augustine in place, her buttocks were pressed flush against Zéphyr's thighs and the Duc, thus simultaneously fucking a boy and a girl, as it were, to put yet a little more of the lubricious into the thing, frigged Zéphyr's prick on the pretty, round and fair buttocks of Augustine, and soaked them with that child-fuck which, as may easily be imagined, was mightily warmed by such treatment and soon spattered abundantly out.

Curval, who found the general perspective very inviting, and who spied the Duc's ass, open wide and fairly yawning for a prick -- as does the ass of every bugger at those instants his prick is up -- Curval, I say, drew up to repay him in kind for what he had received the previous evening, and the dear Duc no sooner felt the voluptuous joltings occasioned by this intromission, than his fuck, taking wing at almost the same time Zéphyr's departed him, splashed the lower edges of the temple whose columns Zéphyr was wetting. But Curval did not discharge, and withdrawing his proud and mettlesome engine from the Duc's bum, he menaced the Bishop, who was likewise frigging himself between Giton's thighs, threatening to make him undergo the fate the Duc had just experienced. The Bishop hurls a challenge, 'tis accepted, battle is joined, the Bishop is embuggered and, between the thighs of the pretty child he is caressing, goes on deliciously to lose a draught of libertine fuck most deliciously wheedled out of him. However, a benevolent spectator to it all, Durcet, having no one but Hébé and the duenna to attend to his needs, and although nearly dead drunk, was by no means wasting his opportunities and was quietly perpetrating infamies the proper time has not yet come to disclose. But calm finally descended over the field, the warriors slumbered, and woke again at six, the hour when Duclos' gifted tongue was to lay the foundation for new pleasures. The quatrains that evening featured certain sexual changes: that is to say, all the girls were costumed as sailors, the little boys as tarts; the effect was ravishing, nothing quickens lust like this voluptuous little reversal; adorable to find in a little boy what causes him to resemble a girl, and the girl is far more interesting when for the sake of pleasing she borrows the sex one would like her to have. Each friend had his wife on his couch that day; they exchanged congratulations upon that very religious arrangement, and everyone being ready to listen, Duclos resumed her lewd stories.

There was, at Madame Guérin's, a certain girl of about thirty, blond, rather heavy-set, but unusually fair and healthy; her name was Aurore, she had a charming mouth, fine teeth, and a voluptuous tongue, but -- and who would believe such a thing? --whether because of a faulty education, or owing to a weak stomach, from that adorable mouth there used constantly, incessantly to erupt prodigious quantities of wind, and above all after she had eaten a hearty meal, she was capable, for the space of an hour, of blowing a stream of belches powerful enough to turn a windmill. But they are right who declare no fault exists that is not a little appreciated by someone, and our fine lass, thanks to this one, had one of the most ardent suitors: he was a learned and grave professor of Scholasticism at the Sorbonne who, tired of wasting his time proving the existence of God in his school, would sometimes come to our brothel to convince himself of the existence of his dear God's creatures. He would send prior notice of his intended arrival, and Aurore would feed like one dying of hunger. Curious to see that pious colloquy, I fly to the spy hole: my lovers greet one another, I observe a few preliminary caresses all directed upon the mouth, then most delicately our rhetor seats his companion in a chair, seats himself opposite her and, taking her hands, deposits his relics between them, sad old vestiges they were, in the most deplorable state.

"Act," he enjoins her, "act, my lovely one. Act; you know by what means I may be drawn from this languid condition, I beg you to adopt them with all dispatch, for I feel myself pressed mightily to proceed."

With one hand she fondles the doctor's flabby tool, with the other she draws his head to hers, glues her lips to his mouth and in no time at all she has, one after another, shot sixty great belches down his gullet. Impossible to represent the ecstasy of this servant of God; he was in the clouds, he inhaled, he swallowed everything that came his way, you'd have thought the very idea of losing the least puff of air would have distressed him, and whilst all this was going on, his hands roamed inquiringly over my colleague's breasts and under her petticoat, but these fingerings were no more than episodic; the unique and capital object was that mouth overwhelming him with sighs and digestive rumblings. His prick finally enlarged by the voluptuous vibrations the ceremony caused to be born in him, he discharged into my companion's hand, and ran off to deliver a lecture, protesting as he went that never had he enjoyed himself more.

Some time after this, a rather more extraordinary man came to the house with a particular problem in mind, and it well deserves to be mentioned in this catalogue of natural wonders. Guérin had, that day, urged me to eat, had all but forced me to eat as copiously as, not long before, I had seen Aurora dine. Guérin took care to have me served everything she knew I liked best, and having forewarned me, as we rose from table, of everything I should have to do for the elderly libertine with whom she intended to match me, she had me swallow down three grains of emetic dissolved in a glass of warm water. The old sinner arrived, he was a brothel-hound I had seen dozens of times before without bothering to find out what he came to do. He embraces me, drives a dirty and disgusting tongue into my mouth, and the action of the emetic I'd drunk is complemented by his stinking breath. He sees my stomach's about to rise, he's in ecstasy. "Courage, dearie," he cries, "be brave, never fear, I don't propose to lose a drop of it." Being foreadvised of all he expects of me, I seat him on the couch, lay his head to rest on the edge of it; his thighs are separated, I unbutton his breeches, drag out a slack, stunted instrument that betrays no sign of stiffening, I shake, squeeze, pull it, he opens his mouth: all the while frigging him, all the while receiving the touches of his impudicious hands which stray over my buttocks, at point-blank I launch into his mouth the imperfectly digested dinner that vomitive has fetched up from my stomach. Our man is beside himself, he rolls his eyes, pants, bolts down the spew, goes to my lips to seek more of the impure ejaculation that intoxicates him, he does not indeed miss a drop, and when it seems to him the operation is in danger of ending, he provokes a repetition of it by dexterously inserting his appalling tongue into my mouth, and his prick, that prick I've scarcely been able to touch because of my convulsive retchings, that prick doubtless warmed by nothing but such infamies, grows purple, rises up of itself, and weeps into my fingers the unsuspected proof of the impressions these foul activities have made upon it.

"Ah, by God's balls," said Curval, "that's a very delicious passion indeed, but none the less susceptible of improvement."

"And how?" asked Durcet in a voice broken by signs of lubricity.

"How?" Curval repeated, "why, by the choice of food and of partner."

"Partner? Oh, but of course. You'd prefer a Fanchon."

"To be sure!"

"And the food?" Durcet continued, while Adelaide frigged him.

"Food?" the Président murmured, "why, I think I'd force her to give me back, and in the same manner, what I'd just introduced into her."

"That is to say," stammered the financier, beginning to lose all control of himself, "you'd spew into her mouth, she'd swallow and then have to blow it back at you?"

"Precisely."

And each rushing into his closet, the Président with Fanchon, Augustine, and Zélamir; Durcet with Desgranges, Rosette, and

Invictus: proceedings were halted for roughly thirty minutes. Then
the two lechers returned.

"Ah," the Duc said chidingly to Curval, the first to reappear, "you've
been up to some nastiness or other?"

"Ah, a little of this, a little of that," the Président replied, "it's my life's
happiness, you know. I've not much patience with mild or tidy pleasures."

"But I trust you were also purged of a little fuck?"

"Enough of that nonsense," the Président said, "do you suppose everyone is like you, flinging fuck this way and that every six minutes? Why
no, I leave those efforts and that unconscionable prodigality to you and
to vigorous champions like Durcet," he went on, watching the financier
stagger weakly from his closet.

"Yes," said Durcet, "yes, it's true, there was no resisting the girl. Desgranges is so filthy in word, deed, and body, she is so adroit, so suitable
in every way . . ."

"Well, Duclos," the Duc said, "go on with your story, for if we don't
quiet him down, the indiscreet little fellow will tell us everything he did,
and never once consider what a dreadful breach of good manners it is to
boast of the favors one has received from a pretty woman."

And Duclos obediently returned to her tale.

Since, said our chronicler, these gentlemen are so fond of that kind
of drollery, I greatly regret they were unable to restrain their enthusia-
sism yet another minute, for the effects of what I have still to relate this
evening might, it seems to me, have better found their mark. Precisely
that which Monsieur le Président declared to be lacking to the perfection
of the passion I have just described was entirely present in the one that
follows; what a pity, I repeat, that I was unable to get to it in time. The
example of the elderly Président de Saclanges affords, in every particular
and word for word, all the singularity Monsieur de Curval appeared to
desire. By way of a partner for him, Guérin had chosen the dean of our
chapter: a tall, sturdy lass of about thirty-six, a great and chronic drunk,
loutish, foul-mouthed, rather a fishmonger's wife, although by no means
unattractive; the good Président arrives, they are served supper, both get
blind drunk, both become unreasonable, one vomits in the other's mouth,
the one swallows the stuff, then the other vomits into the mouth of the
first, now he swallows, and so forth and so on, and they finally collapse
into the supper's debris, that is to say, into the filth they've just splashed
all over the floor. And then I am sent into the fray, for my co-worker has
not an ounce of strength left, indeed she has lost consciousness. But this,
however, is the crucial moment from the libertine's point of view: I find
him prone, his prick straight and hard as a crowbar; I seize his instrument,
the Président stammers, swears, draws me to him, sucks my mouth, and

discharges like a bull, the while twisting and turning and continuing to wallow in his ordure.

The same girl, somewhat later, participated in a drama which was surely not much less filthy; a monk of some consequence, who paid her very liberally, threw himself astride her belly after having spread and immobilized my companion's thighs by tying them to heavy articles of furniture. Several kinds of food were brought in and served the monk, who had the dainties placed on the girl's naked belly. The merry fellow then picks up the morsels he is to eat, and dips them one by one in his Dulcinea's open cunt, and only consumes them after they have been completely impregnated with the spices the vagina secretes.

"Ha!" cried the Bishop, "an entirely novel manner of dining." "And one which wouldn't suit you, eh, my Lord?" said Duclos.

"By God's belly, no!" replied the man of the Church, "I'm not that fond of the cunt."

Very well, our storyteller replied, lend an ear to the item with which I am going to close this evening's narrations, I am persuaded it will amuse you more.

I had been with Madame Guérin for eight years -- had just reached the age of seventeen -- and during this period not a day had passed without my seeing a certain farmer-general arrive at the house every morning and be received with the warmest welcome. He was thought very highly of by the management; a man of roughly sixty, rotund, short, he resembled Monsieur Durcet in a good many points. Like Monsieur, he had an air of freshness and youth, and was also plump; he required a different girl every day, and those of the house were never used save in emergencies or when someone contracted abroad failed to meet her appointment. Monsieur Dupont, so was our financier called, was just as discriminating in his choice of girls as he was fastidious in his tastes, he simply would not have a whore to attend to his needs except in the rare and extreme cases I mentioned; he had to have, on the contrary, working women, shopgirls, especially milliners or seamstresses. Their age and coloring also had to meet specification: they had to be between fifteen and eighteen, neither more or less, and, most important of all, they needed to have a sweetly moldered ass, an ass so absolutely clean that the least blemish, a mere grain of matter clinging at the hole was sufficient grounds for rejection. When they were maids, he paid twice as much.

They had made plans for, and were that day actually expecting the arrival of, a young lacemaker of sixteen whose ass was generally acclaimed by connoisseurs as a true model of what an ass should be; Monsieur Dupont did not know the treasure that was to be offered him, and as it turned out the young lady had word sent that on this particular morning she was unable to leave her parents' house and that matters would have to proceed without her. Guérin, knowing Dupont had never set eyes on me, ordered me to dress in a shopgirl's costume at once, to go out, take a cab at the end of the street, and alight again at the brothel, all this fifteen minutes after Dupont entered the house; I was to play my role with care and pass myself for a milliner's apprentice. But the most important consideration of all was the anise water: I was to fill my stomach at once with half a quart of it, and directly afterward I was to drink the large glass of balsamic liqueur she gave me; you shall shortly learn for what its effect was intended. Everything went forward very smoothly; fortunately, we had been given several hours' notice, and in this time were able to make thorough preparations. I arrived at the house with a very silly air, I was presented to the financier who directly scrutinized me very closely, but as I was keeping a sharp eye on my conduct, he could discover nothing about my person which might contradict the story that had been invented for him.

"Is she a maid?" Dupont asks.

"Not in that place," says Guérin, pointing to my belly, "but I will answer for the other side."

And it was a most impudent lie she told. Little does it matter; our man believed her, and that alone was necessary.

"Lift your skirts, hurry it up," says Dupont.

And Guérin raises my skirts from behind, drawing me toward her as she does so and thus entirely exposing the temple at which the libertine performed his worship. He stares, for a moment he fingers my buttocks, he spreads them with both hands, and evidently satisfied, he announces that the ass is suitable for his purposes. Next, he asks me several questions relating to my age, my trade, and content with my feigned innocence and the look of having been born yesterday that I affect, he has me accompany him to his apartment, for there was one reserved exclusively for him at Guérin's: he did not like being observed while at work, he was certain not to be in this place. Both of us having entered, he carefully shuts and secures the door, considers me for a moment, then in a rather brutal fashion -- brutality characterized him throughout the scene -- he inquired me whether it were indeed true that I had never been fucked in the ass. As my role called for total ignorance of the meaning of such an expression, I had him repeat it, declared I still understood nothing, and when by means of the most unambiguous gestures he conveyed what he wished to say, I replied, with a stimulated look of fright and modesty, that I should be a very unhappy girl indeed if ever I had lent myself to such infamies. Whereupon he told me to remove my skirts, but only my skirts, and once I had obeyed him, leaving my blouse down to hide my front, he raised it above my buttocks to the height of my bodice; but while he was undressing me my neckerchief slipped down, revealing my breasts. He became incensed.

"Devil take those damned tits of yours," he cried; "who asked you for tits? That's what I can't bear about these creatures, every single impudent one of them is wild to show you her miserable bubs."

Hastening to cover them over, I approached him to beg his pardon, but observing that I was going to exhibit my cunt thanks to the posture I was about to assume, he lost his temper a second time:

"But, sweet Jesus! Can't you stay put?" he demanded, seizing my haunches and turning me so that there was no danger he would catch a glimpse of anything but my ass, "stay that way, fuck your eyes, I don't care any more of your cunt than I do for your chest, your ass is all you need with me."

So saying, he stood up and guided me to the edge of the bed upon which he installed me in such wise the upper half of my body rested on the bed, then, seating himself on a very low stool, he found himself situated between my wide-flung legs and his head on a level with my ass. He peers at me for another instant, then, deciding I am not yet adjusted as I ought to be, up he gets, fetches a cushion, fits it under my belly, thus arching my ass more sharply; he sits down again, examines, and goes about everything with the sangfroid and confidence of the seasoned and mature libertine. A moment passes, then he grasps my two buttocks, spreads them, poses his open mouth upon the hole, fastens his lips hermetically to it, and immediately, pursuant to the signal he gives me and in obedience to the considerable pressure that has built up within me, I unleash a booming fart, possibly the most explosive one he has received in all his life; it shoots down his gullet and he backs away, furious.

"What the devil!" he cries, "so you are so bold as to fart into my mouth, are you?"

And he straightway claps his mouth to my asshole again.

"Yes, Monsieur," I say as I release a second stifler, "that's how I deal with gentlemen who kiss my ass."

"Very well then! fart, if you must, you little rascal, since you can't help it, fart, I say, fart as hard as you like and as often as you can."

From this moment onward I cast off all restraint, nothing can express the urgency of my desire to give vent to the boisterous winds produced by the potion I had drunk earlier; our man is thrilled by them, he receives some in his mouth, the others in his nostrils. After fifteen minutes of this exercise, he lies down upon the couch, draws me to him, his nose still wedged between my buttocks, orders me to frig him and meanwhile to continue a ceremony which gives rise in him to such exquisite pleasures. I fart, I frig, I manipulate a slack little prick neither much longer nor much thicker than my finger, but by dint of buffets, jerks, and farts the instrument finally stiffens. The augmentation of our gentleman's pleasure, the critical instant's approach is announced by a new iniquity: it is now his tongue that provokes my farts, 'tis his tongue that, like a flail, darts deep into my anus in order to stir up the winds, 'tis against his tongue he wants me to blow those zephyrs, he becomes unreasonable, he is no longer in possession of his wits, 'tis clear, and his wretched little engine sadly sprinkles seven or eight drops of watery, brownish sperm upon my fingers; and now he is restored to his senses. But as his native brutality fomented his distraction, so now it replaces it at once, and he barely gives me enough time to readjust myself. He scolds, he mutters and swears, in one word he offers me the abhorrent image of vice that has slaked its thirst, and I am made the butt of that unthinking indelicacy which, once its glitter has paled, seeks to find revenge in scorn for the worshiped object that latterly captivated the senses.

"Now that's a man I prefer to all the others," said the Bishop. "And do you know if he had his little sixteen-year-old apprentice the next day?"

"Yes, Monseigneur, he did indeed, and the day after that a maid of fifteen far prettier yet. As few men used to pay as much, few were better served."

This passion having stimulated heads so well acquainted with that species of disorder, and having put them in mind of a taste they all relished. Messieurs simply could not bear waiting any longer to make use of it. Each of them plucked what windy fruits there were to be had, neglecting no likely sources, then supper arrived, with their gourmandizing pleasures they blended nearly all the infamies they had just heard described, the Duc got Fanchon tipsy and had the befuddled old thing vomit into his mouth, Durcet had the whole harem fart, and in the course of the evening swallowed at least threescore mouthfuls of unwholesome air. As for Curval, in whose brain all kinds of extravagances danced gaily, he declared he was moved to perform some solitary orgies and went off to the remote boudoir, accompanied by Fanchon, Marie, Desgranges, and thirty bottles of Champagne wine. Later on, all four had to be carried back into society, for they were discovered floating in a very tide of their own ordures, and the Président was found asleep, his mouth fastened to that of Desgranges, who was still wearily retching into it. The three other friends acquitted themselves no less brilliantly, performing feats in like kind or somewhat different; they too had spent their orgy period drinking, they had got the little girls to fart, I truly haven't space to tell you all they did, and had it not been for Duclos, who coolly kept her wits about her, who when it was abandoned by the others assumed the government of the revels, preserved order, and put the merrymakers to bed, I repeat that had it not been for Duclos, it is very probable indeed that rosy-fingered Dawn, opening the gates of Apollo's palace, would have found them lying still plunged in their excrements, rather more after the example of swine than like heroes.

Needful only of rest, each lay by himself that night, and cradled in Morpheus' arms, recovered a little strength for the strenuous new day ahead.

The Seventh Day

The friends had ceased to participate in Duclos' nine o'clock lessons. Wearied from the night's riot, fearing, furthermore, lest some operation might result in loss of fuck at that very early hour, and esteeming, finally, that this ceremony was accelerating their indifference to joys and to objects whose interest and integrity it was surely to their advantage to preserve for a while, they agreed that instead of one of themselves, one of the fuckers would hereafter take his turn at the morning exercises.

The inspection and searches were conducted, only one little girl was wanting to make all eight of them eligible for correction, and she was the lovely and intriguing Sophie, a child accustomed to fulfilling all her duties; however ridiculous they may have seemed to her, she respected them none the less, but Durcet, who had earlier conferred with Louison, her governess, so artfully caused her to tumble into the snare that she was declared to be at fault and was as a consequence added to the fatal register. The sweet Aline, equally subjected to close scrutiny, was also judged guilty, and so it was that the evening's list contained mention of the eight little girls, four of the little boys, and two from among the wives.

These tasks accomplished, Messieurs concentrated their thoughts upon the marriage highlighting the festival that marked the end of the first week. No chapel permissions were granted that day, Monseigneur clad himself pontifically, they betook themselves to the altar. The Duc, representing the bride's father, and Curval, who represented the young groom's, led forth Michette and Giton. Both were extraordinarily arrayed in the most formal dress, but also reversedly, that is to say, the little boy was costumed as a girl, the little girl wore boy's clothes. We regret to say that the sequence we originally established for the treatment of our matter obliges us to postpone yet a little longer the pleasure the reader will doubtless take in learning the details of this religious ceremony; but the appropriate moment for disclosing them will surely arrive, and probably fairly soon.

Messieurs passed into the salon. It was while awaiting the hour of dinner our four libertines, encloseted with that charming little couple, had them remove their clothing, and obliged them mutually to perform everything in the sphere of matrimonial ritual their age permitted, with the single exception of the introduction of the virile member into the little girl's vagina, which introduction could perfectly well have been effected, for the boy stiffened very satisfactorily, but he was held in check in order that nothing might happen to spoil a flower destined for plucking by others. But, apart from that, they were allowed to finger and caress one another; young Michette polluted her little husband and Giton, aided by his masters, frigged his little wife as nicely as you please. However, they were both beginning to realize full well the bondage they were in, and this recognition prevented voluptuous joy, even that joy their young years permitted them to experience, from being born in their little hearts.

They dined, the bride and the groom assisted at the wedding feast, but at coffee, heads having waxed hot over them, they were stripped naked, as were Zélamir, Cupidon, Rosette, and Colombe, who were serving coffee. Thigh-fuckery having become fashionable at this time of day, Curval laid hands on the husband, the Duc captured his bride, and the two men enthighed the couple on the spot. The Bishop, who since coffee had been brought in had taken a liking to him, now fell ravenously upon the charming Zélamir's behind, which he tongued, sucked, and whence he elicited farts, and he soon managed to transpierce the little fellow in the same way, while Durcet committed his preferred little villainies upon Cupidon's charming behind. Our two principal athletes did not discharge; one of them soon had Rosette in his clutches, the other Colombe, they slipped their pricks between the children's legs and, just as they had with Michette and Giton, ordered them to frig, with their pretty little hands and in accordance with the instruction they had been receiving, those monstrous prick ends thrusting beyond their crotches and out into space; and while the youngsters toiled away, the libertines comfortably fingered their helpers' delicious, fresh little assholes. And still no fuck shed; Messieurs knew full well what delicious chores lay ahead that evening, they proceeded circumspectly. The young couple's privileges were abrogated, their marriage, although made in keeping with every formality, became no more than a jest; they each of them returned to their quatrains, and the company established itself in the auditorium. Duclos took up her story.

A man with more or less the same predilections as the financier whose exploits terminated yesterday evening's recital shall be the athlete whom, may it please your Lordships, today's shall begin. He was a crown attorney of some sixty years and not only were his eccentricities unusual, but for practicing them he would have none but women older than he. Guérin gave him one of her friends, an aged procuress whose withered buttocks bore a powerful likeness to a crumple of old parchment being used to keep tobacco moist. Such, notwithstanding, was to be the object employed for our libertine's offerings. He knelt down before that decrepit bum and kissed it lovingly; farts were blown up his nose, he waxed ecstatic, opened his mouth, the lady opened her vent, his tongue went enthusiastically in quest of the mellow winds soughing in that tunnel. He could not resist the delirium into which the operation was plunging him. From his breeches he has brought out an ancient, pale, shriveled little device, an object as ill-favored as the one he deifies. "Ah! Fart, my old sweetie, fart thoughtlessly, fart abundantly," he cries, frigging himself with all his strength. "Fart, my love, for only thy little farts will break the spell binding this slumbering prince." The procuress redoubles her efforts, and, drunk with joy, the libertine surrenders his burden: between his goddess' legs fall two or three unhappy droplets of the sperm responsible for the whole of his delight.

O terrible effect of example! Who would have believed it? At the very same instant, and quite as if they had received a signal, all four of our libertines individually summon the duennas of their quadrilles. They lay eager hands upon those foul and rammy asses, solicit farts, obtain them, and are fully prepared to be just as happy as the crown attorney, but restrain themselves, for they remember the pleasures awaiting them at the orgies; whereupon they dismiss each his Venus, and Duclos continues:

I shall lay little emphasis upon the following passions, said that amiable creature, for I realize that there are not many in your midst, Messieurs, who are its votaries; however, you have commanded me to tell everything, and I obey. A very young man, a young man with a very handsome face, used to find it vastly amusing to lick out my cunt once a month, and at a certain period. I would be lying on my back, my legs flung wide, he used to kneel in front of me and suck, with both hands lifting my flanks so as to bring my cunt to within easy reach. He swallowed both fuck and blood, for he managed so adroitly, worked with such good will, and was such a pretty lad I used to discharge. He would frig himself, would be in seventh heaven, nothing evidently could afford him so much pleasure, and the hottest, the most ardent discharge, performed while in action, used always to convince me of his high humor. The following day he would usually see Aurore, not long afterward it would be my sister, and in the course of the month he would pass us all in review, and he doubtless made the rounds of every other whorehouse in Paris at the same time.

But, Messieurs, I believe you will concur in my judgment when I say that the aforementioned caprice is no more singular than that of another gentleman, an old friend of Guérin, who had been furnishing him for years. She assured us that all his joy consisted in eating expelled ovulations and in lapping up miscarriages; he would be notified whenever a girl found herself in that case, he would rush to the house and swallow the embryo, half swooning with satisfaction.

"I knew that particular man," said Curval. "His existence and his tastes are as authentic as anything else in the world."

"Perhaps," said the Bishop. "And I know something just as certain as your man, and that is I'd not imitate him."

"And why, pray tell?" asked the Président. "I am convinced it would produce a lively discharge, and were Constance to grant me her kind permission, for I hear she's gravid now, why, I can promise her I'll fetch Monsieur her son along before he's fully done, and I'll toss him off like a sardine."

"Oh, all the world knows your horror of pregnant women," cried Constance, "and everyone also knows you only got rid of Adelaide's mother because she conceived a second time, and if Julie were to take my advice, she'd be careful."

"Why yes, 'tis perfectly true that I am not fond of progeny," quoth Curval, "and that when the beast is laden it quickens a furious loathing in me, but to imagine I killed my wife on that account is to be gravely mistaken. Bitch that you are, get it into your head that I have no need of reasons in order to kill a woman, above all a bitch that, were she mine, I'd very surely keep from whelping."

Constance and Adelaide fell to weeping, and this brief dialogue revealed something of the secret hatred the Président bore for the charming wife of the Duc who, for his part, very far from supporting her in discussion, replied to Curval, saying that he ought perfectly well to know that he, Blangis, was equally ill-disposed to offspring, and that although Constance was pregnant, she had not yet given birth. And at this point Constance's tears flowed all the faster; she was on her father's couch, and Durcet, not taxing himself to comfort her, advised her daughter that if she did not cease her blubbering that instant, her state notwithstanding, he was going to boot her ass out of the auditorium. The hapless creature shed inwardly upon her heart the tears wherewith she was reproached, and was content to say: "Alas, Great God! very wretched am I, but 'tis my fate, I must endure it." Adelaide, who had also been weeping away on the Duc's couch and whose distress the Duc had been moving heaven and earth to increase, also managed to dry her tears, and this scene, somewhat tragical although very mirthful to our four libertines' villainous souls, ground to an end, and Duclos resumed her tale:

In Guérin's establishment there was a room most curiously constructed, and it was always used by one man. It had a double floor, and this narrow between-stories area, where there was only space enough to lie down, served to lodge the uncommon breed of libertine in the interests of whose passion I had regular employment. He would take a girl and, descending through a trap door, would lie down and arrange himself in such a manner his head was directly below a hole that had been bored in the floor above; the girl accompanying him had the single chore of frigging him, and I, located above, had simply to do the same thing for a second man. The hole, obscure and seemingly a natural flaw in the planks, remained uncovered as if through negligence, and I, acting at the behest of tidiness, eager to avoid spotting the floor, would while manualizing my man direct his fuck so that it fell through the hole and, consequently, upon the face of the gentleman below. It was all managed with such skill nothing seemed out of place, and the operation would be a success each time: at the moment the fuck frigged from the person above splashed upon the nose of the person being frigged below, the latter would unleash his own, and that was all there was to it.

However, the elderly dame I mentioned not long ago reappeared, but she was to be pitted against a different champion. This new one, a man of about fifty, had her remove her clothes and then licked out every orifice in her old corpse: ass, cunt, mouth, nostrils, armpits, ears, he omitted nothing, and with each sucking the rascal swallowed whatever he obtained. And he went further still, he had her chew slices of pastry which he would then have out of her mouth and into his, and swallow. He would have her keep mouthfuls of wine she had gargled or swished about, he would have them from her, and drink them too; and all the while his prick would be so furiously erected that the fuck seemed ready to fly all unaided. Finally he would sense the crucial instant's arrival and, hurling himself upon the crone, he would thrust his tongue at least six inches into her asshole and discharge like a madman.

"Ah, by God!" said Curval, "will you now say that youth and pretty looks are indispensable to an elicitation of fuck? Why, once again 'tis the filthy act that causes the greatest pleasure: and the filthier it be, the more voluptuously fuck is shed."

"Those are the piquant salts," Durcet concurred, "which as they are exhaled from the object serving our lust, enter us and irritate our animal spirits, put them in a commotion; well now, who is it doubts that everything derelict, maculate, or stinking secretes a greater quantity of these salts and hence has a greater capacity for stimulating and determining our discharge?"

This thesis was soberly discussed for a little while; as there was a quantity of work to be done after supper, it was served earlier than was customary, and at dessert the little girls, every one of them condemned to do penance, departed for the salon where they were to be corrected together with the four boys and the two wives who also lay under sentence. That made fourteen victims: the eight girls, whose names the reader knows, Adelaide and Aline, and four youths: Narcisse, Cupidon, Zélamir, and Giton. Already drunk with anticipation of the particular delight that was awaiting them and of which they were incredibly fond, they completed their intoxication by imbibing a prodigious amount of wine and liqueurs, and then removed to the salon where the patients were awaiting them, and such was Messieurs' common state, so besotted were they, in such lecherous fury did they enter, that there is surely no one in the wide world who would have wished to exchange places with those unlucky culprits.

Attendance at the orgies was that day confined to the delinquents and the four elders who were there as servants; everyone was naked, everyone trembled, everyone was weeping and wondering what to expect when the Président, taking his seat in a tall armchair, bade Durcet announce the name of each criminal, and cite his offense. Durcet's face was as wrath-ful as his colleague's, he took up the register and undertook to read from it, but encountered difficulties and was unable to proceed; the Bishop came to his rescue, and although quite as drunk as the banker, held his wine with greater success and in a loud voice read one after the other the names of the guilty and their faults; and after each citation the Président pronounced sentence in keeping with the physical faculties and age of the criminal, but the punishment decreed was in every instance severe all the same. This ceremony concluded, punishment was inflicted. We are in despair, for here we are once again forced by the design or our history to make a little detour: yes, we must for the time being omit describing those lubricious corrections, but our readers will not hold it against us; they appreciate our inability to give them complete satisfaction at the present moment; but they can be sure of it, their time will come.

The ceremony lasted a very long time. There were fourteen subjects to punish, and some very pleasant episodes interrupted the proceedings. No doubt of it, everything was delicious, for our scoundrels discharged, all four of them, and retired so weary, so drunk with wine and pleasure, that had it not been for the four fuckers who came to fetch them, they might not have reached their chambers where, despite all they had just accomplished, further lewd exploits were performed.

The Duc, who had Adelaide for his bed companion that night, did not want her. She had been one of the delinquents punished, and punished so well by him that he, having poured out every drop of his fuck in her honor, had no more need of her that evening and, relegating her to a mattress on the floor, he gave her place to Duclos, more firmly installed in his good graces than ever.

The Eighth Day

The previous day's examples having made a deep impression, no one was found, no one could be found wanting the next day. The lessons continued, they were executed upon the fuckers, and as the day produced no outstanding event until coffee, we will begin our account with that little rite. Coffee was served by Augustine, Zelmire, Narcisse, and Zéphyr. The thigh-fuckeries began again, Curval laid hands on Zelmire, the Duc on Augustine, and after having admired and kissed their pretty buttocks which, I truly don't know why, that day possessed a charm, an attraction, a blush of vermilion the friends had not hitherto remarked, after, I say, our libertines had thoroughly kissed and caressed those exquisite little asses, farts were elicited from them; the Bishop, who had Narcisse in his grip, had already procured himself some, Zéphyr's could be heard spluttering into Durcet's mouth -- why not imitate them? Zelmire succeeded, but Augustine had striven with might and main, the Duc had threatened her with another Saturday martyrdom, with punishment as severe as what she had just suffered the day before, but strains and struggles, menaces and imprecations were all in vain, nothing emerged from the poor little creature, she was already in tears when a driblet at length appeared and satisfied the Duc who inhaled the aroma and, highly pleased with this mark of docility in the pretty child of whom he was so fond, he camped his enormous engine between her thighs, then withdrew it as he was about to discharge, and totally inundated her two buttocks. Curval had done the same to Zelmire, but the Bishop and Durcet contented themselves with what is known as the little goosing; later, their nap over, they passed into the auditorium, where the splendid Duclos, arrayed that day in everything that could most successfully cause an observer to forget her age, appeared even lovelier under the candlelight, and our libertines, grown very hot with much looking at her, were loath to allow her to ascend to the platform without first having her exhibit her buttocks to the assembly.

"A magnificent ass, upon my soul," said Curval.

"Oh, indeed, my friend," said Durcet, "I warrant there are few better to be seen."

These encomiums heard, our heroine lowered her skirts, took her seat, and resumed her story in such wise as the reader shall observe, if he be pleased to continue, which we advise that he do for the sake of his pleasure.

A reflection and an event were responsible, Messieurs, for the shift in battlefields; the digladiations I shall from now on relate were performed in other surroundings. The reflection was a most simple one: I remarked the lamentable condition of my purse, and straightway was set to thinking. I had been nine years at Madame Guérin's, and although, during that time, I had disbursed very little, I now found myself without even a hundred louis; that woman, extremely clever and never once deaf to the pleading of her own welfare, always found a way to pocket two-thirds of the house's receipts and to impose additional deductions upon the remainder. These practices displeased me and, subject to repeated solicitations from another procuress, Madame Fournier, who wanted nothing more than to have me settle down with her, and knowing that this Fournier received elderly debauchees of a higher tone and greater means than Guérin's clientele, I decided to take my leave of the one and throw in my lot with the other. As for the event which lent support to my ideas, it was the loss of my sister: I had grown very attached to her, and I could no longer remain in a house where everything reminded me of her but whence she was absent.

For nearly six months that dear sister had been receiving visits from a tall, dark, and silent man whose face I found exceedingly disagreeable. They would retire together, and I do not know how they passed their time, for never did my sister want to discuss what they did, and never did they cavort in a place where I could view their commerce. In any event, she came into my room one fine morning, embraced me, and said that her fortune was made, she was to be the mistress of the tall man I disliked, and I learned only that the deciding factor in her conquest was the beauty of her buttocks. And with that she gave me her address, settled her accounts with Guérin, gave each of us a farewell kiss, and left. You may be sure that I did not fail to go the indicated address, for I wished to see her. It was two days after her departure; I arrived, asked for my sister, and my request was answered by shrugs and blank expressions. I saw perfectly clear that my sister had been duped, for I could not imagine she would have deprived me of the pleasure of her company. When I related the thing to Guérin and complained of what had happened, a malign smile crept over her face. She refused to explain herself; hence I concluded she was embroiled in this mysterious adventure but did not want me to become involved in it. It all had a deep effect upon me and brought a swift end to my unresolve; as, Messieurs, I shall have no occasion to speak of that beloved sister in future, I may say now that, notwithstanding the inquiries I had made and the lengths to which I went to find her, I was never able to discover what had become of her.

"I dare say not," Desgranges observed, "for, twenty-four hours after having left you, she was no longer alive. No, she did not deceive you; rather, she was herself deceived. But, as you surmised, Guérin knew what was afoot."

"Merciful Heavens! what are you telling me?" cried Duclos. "Alas! though deprived of the sight of her, I still imagined she was alive."

"Most erroneously," Desgranges replied. "She told you the strict truth: it was indeed the beauty of her buttocks, the astonishing superiority of that memorable ass that procured her the adventure

in which she flattered herself a fortune was to be earned, but wherein she gained death only."

"And the tall silent man?" Duclos asked.

"He was no more than the courtier in the story, he was working for another."

"Yet, I tell you, he saw her assiduously for six months."

"In order to deceive her," Desgranges answered; "but go on with your tale, these clarifications might prove tedious to their Lordships, and should they wish to hear more of the matter, they may rest assured the anecdote will figure in my depositions."

"And spare us any emotional demonstrations, Duclos," said the Duc dryly, upon noticing that it was all she could do to keep back a few involuntary tears, "we don't much care for regrets and grievings, you know; as a matter of fact, all the works of Nature could be blown to hell and we'd not emit so much as a sigh. Leave tears to idiots and children, and may they never soil the cheeks of a clearheaded, clear-thinking woman, the sort we esteem."

With these words, our heroine took herself in hand and resumed her narrative at once.

Owing to the two reasons I have just presented to your Lordships, I made up my mind to leave; Fournier offered me better accommodations, a far more interesting table, much more remunerative although more arduous work, an equal share in the receipts, and service charges. I went to her at once. At that time she occupied an entire house, and five pretty young girls composed her seraglio; I made the sixth. You will allow me to proceed again as earlier I did when describing Guérin's establishment: I will not portray my companions-at-arms until one by one they step into the arena.

On the morrow of my arrival, I was given a project, for Fournier ran a bustling house, people came and went all the time, each of us would often receive five or six clients in the space of a day; but I shall continue, as I have until now, to select none but those who, by dint of singularity or piquancy, are apt to arrest your attention.

The first man I welcomed in my new habitation was a disbursing official, aged about fifty. He had me kneel by the bed with my chin resting on its edge; he established himself on the bed, kneeling also, and above me. He frigged his prick squarely into my mouth, commanding me to keep it wide open; I lost not a drop, and the bawdy fellow was prodigiously amused by the contortions and efforts to vomit this disgusting mouthwash caused in me.

You will perhaps prefer me to group the four other adventures in this category I had at Madame Fournier's, although you understand, Messieurs, that these encounters were separated in time. I am certain the telling will be far from displeasing to Monsieur Durcet, and perhaps very opportune, and for the rest of the evening he will most kindly permit me to entertain him with accounts of a passion for which he has enthusiasm, and which procured me the honor of making his acquaintance.

"What's this?" exclaimed Durcet; "you are going to have me play a role in your story?"

"With your gracious leave, my Lord," Duclos replied. "I shall simply advise Messieurs when I reach the point where you make your entrance."

"But my modesty . . . oh dear, oh dear! Before these little girls, do you mean you intend to disclose all my turpitudes to their innocent hearing?"

And everyone having chuckled over the financier's whimsical fears, Duclos resumed her narrative.

Another libertine, much older and in a different way disgusting, succeeded the one I mentioned a moment ago, and came to give me a second representation of the same mania; he had me stretch out naked upon a bed, stretched out himself, his head to my toe, popped his prick in my mouth and his tongue in my cunt, and having adopted this attitude, bade me make return for the voluptuous titillations he declared his tongue was very certainly going to procure for me. I sucked as best I could; he had my pucelage, he licked, bubbled, splashed about and, without doubt, in all these maneuvers, labored infinitely more in his own behalf than in mine. Whatever may have been the truth, I felt nothing, and was exceedingly happy not to be horribly revolted by the whole affair; there ensued the roué's discharge, an operation which, in accordance with Fournier's earnest wishes, for she had given me foreknowledge of everything, an operation, I say, which I strove to make as lubricious as possible by sucking, by wringing the juice from his prick with my lips, by swishing it about in my mouth, and by running my hand over his buttocks and tickling his anus, which last detail, he indicated, pleased him very much, and which he performed on me in turn as best he could... The business completed, our man beat his retreat, assuring Madame Fournier that never yet had he been outfitted with a girl who gave him more satisfaction than I.

Shortly after this latest of my exploits, an old witch of about seventy came to our house; I was curious to know what brought her to us, she seemed to have an expectant air, and, yes, I was told that she was awaiting a customer. Extremely eager to see to what purpose the old bag of bones was going to be put, I asked my companions whether there were not a room from which one might have a view of the bouts, as had been possible at Guérin's. One of my friends replied that indeed such facilities were available and led me to a chamber equipped with not one, but two holes; we took our posts, and this is what we saw and heard, for the wall was no more than a thin partition, and sound traversed it so easily we lost not a word. The old dame arrived first. She looked at herself in a mirror, primped, made adjustments, as if she fancied her charms were yet capable of conquering. A few minutes later, in walked this Chloë's Daphnis; he was sixty at the most, a tax commissioner, a man who was very comfortably well off and who preferred spending his money upon worn-out sluts, old trash like this, rather than upon pretty girls; and why? 'Twas a singularity of taste you say that you understand, Messieurs, and indeed you explain the thing admirably. He advances, surveying his Dulcinea; she makes him a bow of deepest respect.

"No nonsense, you old bitch," says the rake, "I don't care for elegant manners. Get out of your clothes... But wait just one moment. Have you any teeth?"

"No, Sire, not a one is left in my head," quoth the lady, opening her foul old mouth. "See for yourself, may it please your Lordship."

Whereupon up steps his Lordship and, grasping her head, he deposits upon her lips one of the most passionate kisses I have seen in all my life; not merely did he kiss, but he sucked, he devoured, most amorously he darted his tongue far, far into that putrid gullet, and the dear old grandmother, of whom not so much had been made in many a long year, replied with a tenderness which . . . I should have much difficulty describing to you.

"Very well," said the official, "that will do. Off with your clothes."

Meanwhile, he too undoes his breeches and brings out a little dark and wrinkled member about which there is nothing at all that promises an early erection. However, the old girl is naked, and with unimaginable effrontery comes up to offer her lover the sight of an ancient, yellow, and shriveled body, dry, shapeless, and unfleshed, the full description whereof, irrespective of your particular fancies in such matters, would so fill you with horror it were better for me to say no more; but far from being disgusted, repelled, upset by what greets his eye, our libertine is positively enchanted; ecstatic, he seizes her, draws her to where he is seated in a chair, manualizes her while waiting for her to remove a last stitch of clothing, again darts his tongue into her mouth and, turning her around, for a moment pays his respects to the other side of the coin. I very distinctly saw him fondle her buttocks -- but what am I saying? buttocks? rather, I saw him manipulate the two wrinkled rags which fell in waves and little ripples from her haunches and lay flapping on her thighs. Well, such as they were he drew them apart, voluptuously fastened his lips upon the infamous cloaca they enclosed, drove his tongue repeatedly thereinto, and while he sweated happily over this ruin, she struggled to give some firmness to the moribund device she was rattling.

"Let's get to the heart of the matter," said her beloved; "without my favorite stunts, all your attempts will be useless. You've been told?"

"Yes, Monsieur, I have been told."

"And you know you've got to swallow?"

"Yes, my dearie, I'll swallow, oh yes, my little cabbage, my pet, down it'll go, I'll devour every little drop my duckling makes."

And therewith the libertine deposits her on the bed, her head lying toward its foot, he straightway pops his limp engine between her gums, drives doughtily in up to the balls, wriggles about until, seizing his delight's legs and perching them upon his shoulders, his snout is nicely lodged between the old creature's buttocks. His tongue wanders deep into that exquisite hole; the honeybee going in quest of the rose's nectar sucks not more voluptuously; the lady sucks too, our hero begins to stir. "Ah, fuck!" he cries after a quarter of an hour of this libidinous callisthenic, "suck me, suck me, suck and swallow it, you filthy buggess, swallow, for it's coming, by Jesus' sweet face, it's coming, don't you feel it?" And flinging kisses here and there, scattering kisses upon everything in sight, thighs, vagina, buttocks, anus, everything gets licked, everything is sucked, the old bitch gulps, and the poor old wreck, who withdraws as slack a device as the one he inserted, and who has apparently discharged unerected, goes tottering out all ashamed of his transports, and as promptly as ever he can gains the door in order to avoid the sobering sight of the appalling object which has just seduced him in his weakness.

"And the old bitch?" inquired the Duc.

The old bitch coughed, spat, blew her nose, dressed with all possible dispatch, and left.

A few days later, the same companion thanks to whom I had been able to enjoy witnessing this scene had her turn. She was a blond girl of about sixteen, with the world's most interesting physiognomy; I eagerly seized the opportunity to see her at work. The man with whom she was to hold conference was at least as old as the tax commissioner. He had her kneel between his legs, immobilized her head by catching hold of her ears, and snapped into her startled mouth a prick which looked to me to be dirtier and more unappetizing than a rag left to soak in the gutter. Observing that frightful morsel approaching her clean healthy lips, my poor colleague was moved to back away, but it was not for nothing our gentleman held her like a spaniel by the ears.

"What the devil's this?" he muttered. "Are you going to be difficult?"

And threatening to summon Fournier, who had doubtless recommended the most conciliatory attitude to her, he triumphed over her hesitations. She opens her lips, retreats, opens them again and finally, gagging and spluttering, accepts into that sweetest of mouths that most infamous of relics; from this point onward, the villain's speech was exceedingly rude.

"Ah, you little slut!" he shouted in a rage, "you've got scruples, have you, about sucking the finest prick in France? You suppose, do you, that one's got to wash one's balls just for your sake? Well, fuck you, bitch: suck, do you hear? suck the sweetmeat."

Waxing very hot thanks to these sarcasms and the revulsion he noticed he was inspiring my companion, for true it is, Messieurs, that the loathing you quicken in us becomes the gadfly that arouses your pleasure, stings your lust; waxing most ardent, I say, the libertine plunged into an ecstasy and left in the poor girl's mouth the most definite evidence of his virility. Less complaisant than the old woman, she swallowed nothing, and far more revolted, a moment later she retched her stomach empty, and our libertine, readjusting himself without paying much attention to what she was about, laughed sneeringly between his teeth, amused by his libertinage's cruel consequences.

My turn came next. But more fortunate than my two predecessors, it was to Cupid himself I was turned over, and after having satisfied him I was left with nothing but wonder to find tastes so peculiar in a young man so well framed to please. He arrives, he has me take off what I am wearing and lies down upon the bed, orders me to squat above his face and with my mouth proceed to try to wring a discharge from a very mediocre prick, for which however he has words of praise and whose fuck he entreats me to swallow as soon as I feel it flow.

"But don't waste the occasion to idleness," the little libertine added, "meanwhile, I'd have that cunt of yours flood urine into my mouth, I promise you I'll swallow it as you shall my fuck, and I'd be delighted to sniff a few farts from that splendid ass."

I fell to the task and simultaneously executed my three chores with such skill and grace that the little anchovy soon vomited all its fury into my mouth; I swallowed heartily, my Adonis likewise made short shrift of the piss that poured out of my crack and, while he drank, he inhaled the fragrance that a continual stream of farts bore to his nostrils.

"Forsooth, Mademoiselle," murmured Durcet, "you could surely have dispensed with disclosures that portray all my youthful childishness."

"Ha!" said the Duc with a merry laugh, "well indeed! You who scarcely dare look at a cunt today, do you mean to say you used to have 'em piss in the old days?"

"'Tis true," said Durcet, "I blush to admit it, for what could be more dreadful than to have such turpitudes upon one's conscience? Oh, I presently feel the heavy weight of remorse, my friend... O delicious asses!" he exclaimed, in his enthusiasm kissing Sophie's which he had drawn close for a minute's fondling, "O divine asses! how I reproach myself for the incense I deprived you of! O delicious fundaments, I promise you an expiatory sacrifice, I swear upon your altars never again while I live to stray from the paths of rectitude."

And that splendid behind having heated him somewhat, the libertine placed the novice in what was doubtless an exceedingly indecent posture but one in which he was able, as has been seen above, to give his little anchovy to be sucked while sucking the tidiest, freshest, most voluptuous of asses. But Durcet, become now too blasé, too surfeited with that pleasure, only very rarely found it invigorating; one could suck all one wished, he could do the same till his lips cracked, 'twas always the same: he would withdraw in the same collapsed state and, cursing and swearing at the girl, would regularly postpone until some happier moment the pleasures Nature denied him then.

Not everyone was so unfortunate; the Duc, who had passed into his closet with Zélamir, Bum-Cleaver, and Thérèse, emitted shouts and bellows which attested to his happiness, and Colombe, hawking and spitting in great earnestness, left precious little doubt about the temple at which he had done his worshiping. As for the Bishop, reclining upon his couch in the most natural manner, Adelaide's buttocks pinching his nose and his prick in her mouth, he was in seventh heaven, for he was having a wealth of farts out of the young woman; Curval, in an extremely upright state, plugged Hébé's little mouth with his outsized stopper, and yielded up his fuck as he resorted to other stunts.

Mealtime arrived. The Duc wished to advance the thesis that if happiness consisted in the entire satisfaction of all the senses, it were difficult to be happier than were they.

"The remark is not a libertine's," said Durcet. "How can you be happy if you are able constantly to satisfy yourself? It is not in desire's consummation happiness consists, but in the desire itself, in hurdling the obstacles placed before what one wishes. Well, what is the perspective here? One needs but wish and one has. I swear to you," he continued, "that since my arrival here my fuck has not once flowed because of the objects I find about me in this castle. Every time, I have discharged over what is not here, what is absent from this place, and so it is," the financier declared, "that, according to my belief, there is one essential thing lacking to our happiness. It is the pleasure of comparison, a pleasure which can only be born of the sight of wretched persons, and here one sees none at all. It is from the sight of him who does not in the least enjoy what I enjoy, and who suffers, that comes the charm of being able to say to oneself: 'I am therefore happier than he.' Wherever men may be found equal, and where these differences do not exist, happiness shall never exist either: it is the story of the man who only knows full well what health is worth after he has been ill."

"In that case," said the Bishop, "you would maintain as a real source of pleasure the act of going and contemplating the tears of persons stricken by misery?"

"Most assuredly," Durcet replied. "In all the world there is perhaps no voluptuousness that more flatters the senses than the one you cite."

"What? You would not succor the lowly and wretched?" exclaimed the Bishop who took the most genuine delight in engaging Durcet to expatiate upon a question whose examination was so much to the taste of them all and upon which, they knew, the financier was able to deliver some very sound opinions.

"What is it you term succor?" Durcet responded. "For the voluptuousness I sense and which is the result of this sweet comparison of their condition with mine, would cease to exist were I to succor them: by extricating them from a state of wretchedness, I should cause them to taste an instant's happiness, thus destroying the distinction between them and myself, thus destroying all the pleasure afforded by comparison."

"Well then, following that," reasoned the Duc, "one should in one way or another, so as the better to establish that distinction indispensable to happiness, one should, I say, rather aggravate their plight."

"There is no doubting it," said Durcet, "and that explains the infamies of which I have been accused all my life. Those who are in perfect ignorance of my motives," the banker continued, "call me harsh, ferocious, barbaric, but, laughing at these divers denominations, I go merrily on; I cause, I dare say, what fools describe as atrocities, but thereby I have created pleasure-giving distinctions and have made many a delectable comparison."

"Come now," said the Duc, "confess, my dear fellow: admit that upon more than a score of occasions you have engineered the ruin of some poor folk, simply by that means to serve the perverse tastes you have just acknowledged."

"More than a score?" said Durcet. "More than ten score, my friend, and, without the slightest exaggeration, I could enumerate above four hundred families reduced to beggardom, a state in which they'd not now be languishing had it not been for me."

"And," said Curval, "I fancy you have profited from their ruin?"

"Why yes, that has very frequently been the case, but I must also confess that often enough I have acted not to gain, but purely to undo, at the behest of that certain wickedness which almost always awakens the organs of lubricity in me; my prick positively jumps when I do evil, in evil I discover precisely what is needed to stimulate in me all of pleasure's sensations, and I perform evil for that reason, for it alone, without any ulterior motive."

"Upon my soul," declared the Président, "I own I fancy nothing better than that taste. When I was in Parliament I must have voted at least a hundred times to have some poor devil hanged; they were all innocent, you know, and I would never indulge in that little injustice without experiencing, deep within me, a most voluptuous titillation: no more was needed to inflame my balls, nothing used to heat them more certainly. You can imagine what I felt when I did worse."

"It is certain," said the Duc, whose brain was beginning to warm as he fingered Zéphyr, "that crime has sufficient charm of itself to ignite all the senses, without one having to resort to any other expedient; no one understands better than I that enormities and malpractices, even those at the most extreme remove from libertine misbehavior, are quite as capable of inciting an erection as those which lie directly within the sphere of libertinage. The man who is addressing you at this very instant has owed spasms to stealing, murdering, committing arson, and he is perfectly sure that it is not the object of libertine intentions which fire us, but the idea of evil, and that consequently it is thanks only to evil and only in the name of evil one stiffens, not thanks to the object, and were this object to be divested of the power to cause us to do evil, our prick would droop, 'twould interest us no more."

"What could be more certain than that?" the Bishop demanded. "And thence is born another certitude: the greatest pleasure is derived from the most infamous source. The doctrine which must perpetually govern our conduct is this: the more pleasure you seek in the depths of crime, the more frightful the crime must be; as for myself, Messieurs," added the Bishop, "if I may be permitted to speak personally, I affirm that I have reached the point of no longer being susceptible of this sensation you have been discussing, of no longer experiencing it, I say, as a result of lesser or minor crimes, and if the one I perpetrate does not combine as much of the atrocious, of the base, of the vicious, of the deceitful, of the treacherous as may be possibly imagined, the sensation is not merely faint, there is no sensation at all."

"Very well," said Durcet, "is it possible to commit crimes such as these our minds yearn after, crimes like those you mention? For my part, I must declare that my imagination has always outdistanced my faculties; I lack the means to do what I would do, I have conceived of a thousand times more and better than I have done, and I have ever had complaint against Nature who, while giving me the desire to outrage her, has always deprived me of the means."

"There are," said Curval, "but two or three crimes to perform in this world, and they, once done, there's no more to be said; all the rest is inferior, you cease any longer to feel. Ah, how many times, by God, have I not longed to be able to assail the sun, snatch it out of the universe, make a general darkness, or use that star to burn the world! oh, that would be a crime, oh yes, and not a little misdemeanor such as are all the ones we perform who are limited in a whole year's time to metamorphosing a dozen creatures into lumps of clay."

Whereupon, their minds having waxed gay and hot, as two or three young girls had already had cause to remark, and their pricks beginning to rise, they left the table and went in search of pretty mouths, thereinto to pour the floods of that liquor whose too insistent throbbings promoted the utterance of so many horrors. That evening they confined themselves to mouth pleasures, but invented a hundred manners of varying them, and when they had run, all four of them, each a magnificent race, in a few hours of repose they sought to find the strength necessary to starting out afresh.

The Ninth Day

That morning Duclos expressed her opinion, saying she held it prudent either to offer the little girls new patients to replace the fuckers then being employed in the masturbation exercises, or to terminate their lessons, for she believed their education sufficiently advanced. Duclos very astutely pointed out that by continued use of the young men known by their title of fucker, there might result that species of intrigue Messieurs wished especially to prevent; moreover, she added, for such exercises these young men were worth nothing at all; since they were prone to discharge immediately after they were touched, their skittishness or incontinence ought certainly be better exploited, Messieurs' asses had only to lose if the program remained unchanged. It was therefore decided that the lessons would cease; they had generally succeeded, there were already amongst the little girls a few who frigged masterfully: Augustine, Sophie, and Colombe could easily have been matched, what for skill and nimbleness of wrist, against the capital's most famous friggers. Of them all, Zelmire was least adept: not that she lacked agility or that considerable science was not conspicuous in all her motions, no, but it was her tender and melancholic character which stood in her way, she seemed unable to forget her sorrows, she was sad and pensive at all times. At that morning's breakfast inspection tour, her duenna affirmed she had the previous evening caught the child in a prayerful attitude, flagrantly on her knees before retiring; Zelmire was summoned, questioned, she was asked the subject of her prayers; she at first refused to answer, then, threats having been employed, she fell to weeping and admitted she had besought God to deliver her from the perils wherewith she was beset, and had above all prayed that help would come before her virginity were lost. The Duc thereupon declared she deserved to die, and made her read the articles which dealt specifically with this subject.

"Very well," she sighed, "kill me, at least the God I invoke shall have pity upon me, kill me before you dishonor me, and that soul I have devoted to Him will at least fly in purity to His breast. I shall be delivered of the torment of seeing and hearing so many horrors every day."

A reply wherein reigned such a quantity of virtue, of candid innocence, and of gracious amenity caused our libertines prodigiously to stiffen. There were voices that called out for her instantaneous depucelation, but the Duc, reminding his cohorts of the inviolable contract they had subscribed to, was content to propose -- and his suggestion was unanimously approved -- that she be condemned to punished very violently the following Saturday and that, in the meantime, she kneel and for fifteen minutes take into her mouth and suck each friend's prick, and that she be given by way of warning the assurance that, were she to repeat her error, it would decidedly cost her her life, for she would be judged and punished to the fullest extent of the law. The poor little thing crawled up to accomplish the first part of her penance, but the Duc, whom the ceremony had aroused, and who after having pronounced sentence had prodigiously fondled her ass, like the villain he was, shot all his boiling seed into that pretty little mouth, in so doing threatening to strangle her if she spat out a drop, and the poor little wretch swallowed it all, not without furious repugnances. The three others were similarly sucked one after the other, but yielded nothing, and after the usual visit to the boys' quarters and the excursion to the chapel, which that morning produced little because almost everyone had been refused permission to join the party, the meal was served, and then Messieurs entered the salon for coffee.

It was served by Fanny, Sophie, Hyacinthe, and Zélamir; Curval fancied he might thigh-fuck Hyacinthe, and obliged Sophie to post herself in such a way as to be able to suck that length of his prick which protruded beyond Hyacinthe's tightly squeezed legs. The scene was pleasant and inspiriting, he frigged the little chap he held hugged to his belly, and Hyacinthe discharged upon Sophie's face; the Duc, who owing to the dimensions of his prick was the only other one who could imitate this performance, likewise arranged himself with Zélamir and Fanny, but the lad had not yet reached the discharging age, and thus the nobleman had to do without the very agreeable episode Curval considered so enjoyable. After they had finished, Durcet and the Bishop took charge of the four children and had themselves sucked, but no one discharged, and after a brief nap, the company moved into the auditorium where, everyone having assumed his place, Duclos went on with her disclosures.

Before any other audience, said that amiable girl, I might shrink at broaching the subject of the narratives wherewith this entire week we shall be occupied, but however crapulous that subject, I am too well acquainted with your tastes, Messieurs, to be in any wise apprehensive. No, I believe you'll not be displeased; quite the contrary, I am convinced you will find my anecdotes agreeable. I ought however to advise you that you are about to hear of abominable, filthy goings on; but whose ears could be better made to appreciate them? your hearts love and desire them, hence I enter into the matter without further delay or ambages.

At Madame Fournier's we had a trusty old client who was known as Chevalier, I don't know why, or whence the title came; his custom was to pay us a visit every evening, and the little rite that we regularly performed with him was equally simple and bizarre: he would unbutton his breeches, and we were required to form a queue and one by one drop a turd in them. Once we had all done our duty, he would button up again and go off in great haste, taking that freight with him. While he was being supplied he would frig himself for an instant or two, but he was never seen to discharge, and no one knew where he went or what he did with his breechload of shit.

"Oh, by Jesus!" muttered Curval, who never heard anything he had not a desire to do on the spot, "I'll have someone shit in my breeches, and I'll keep the treasure the whole evening."

And ordering Louison to come render him that service, the old libertine provided the assembly with a full-blown dramatization of the whimsy whereof account had just been delivered.

"Well, go on," he said phlegmatically, nodding to Duclos and settling down on his couch again, "there's nothing to it, and I expect it will only be the lovely Aline, my charming companion for the afternoon, who'll find something inconvenient about it. As for myself, a pound of shit in the vicinity suits me perfectly."

And Duclos resumed her story.

Forewarned, said she, of all that was destined to take place at the home of the libertine to whom I was being sent, I dressed myself as a boy, and as I was only twenty, with pretty hair and a pretty face, that costume very well became me. Before leaving, I took care to do in my breeches what Monsieur le Président has just had done for him in his. My man was awaiting me in bed, I approach him, he kisses me very lewdly two or three times, he tells me I'm the prettiest little boy he's ever set eyes upon, and while praising me he undertakes to unbutton my breeches. I put up a faint resistance with the single purpose of inflaming his desires all the more, he entreats me, urges me, he has his way, but how am I to describe to you the ecstasy that possesses him whe perceives the package I have brought along, and the colorful mess it has made of my two buttocks.

"Why, what's this?" cries he. "You've shit in your breeches, have you? But, my little rascal, 'tis very nasty, you know. How could you have done such a thing?"

And quick as a shot, holding me with my back turned to him and my breeches pulled down, he sets to frigging and rattling himself, presses against me, and spurts his fuck upon my beshitted behind, the while driving his tongue into my mouth.

"Do you mean to say," exclaimed the Duc, "he refrained from touching anything? Didn't he handle it?"

"No, your Lordship," Duclos made him answer, "I recount all that transpired, I conceal no detail; but have a little patience, Sire, and we will gradually reach more entertaining circumstances."

"Come," said one of my companions, "let's go watch a truly humorous fellow. He doesn't need a girl, he amuses himself all alone."

We repaired to the hole, having been informed that in the adjoining room, the one selected for his activities, there was a pierced chair and beneath it a chamber pot we had been busy filling for four days and in which there must have been at least a dozen large turds. Our man arrives. He was an elderly tax-farmer of about seventy years. He shuts the door, goes straight to the pot he knows to be brimming with the goodies he has ordered for his sport. He takes up the vessel and, seating himself in an armchair, passes a full hour gazing lovingly at all the treasure whereof he has been made the proprietor; he sniffs, inhales, he touches, he handles, seems to lift one turd out after another in order to contemplate them the better.

Finally become ecstatic, from his fly he pulls a nasty old black rag which he shakes and beats with all his might; one hand frigs, the other burrows into the pot and scoops out handfuls of divine unction. He anoints his tool, but it remains as limp as before. There are moments, after all, when Nature is so stubborn that even the excesses we most delight in fail to awake a response. He did all in his power, and unavailingly, for nothing resulted or rose gloriously up, but by dint of abuse meted out by the same hand that had just been steeped in the ordure, the ejaculation occurred, he trembled, thrilled, fell backward, smelled, breathed deeply, rubbed his prick, and discharged upon the heap of shit which had just so inspired him.

Another gentleman dined with me one evening. We were alone together, and twelve large plates filled with the same meats were brought in and combined with the remnants of an earlier course. He sniffed these new dishes, sampled their aromas, and after he had finished eating, bade me frig him upon the one that had struck him as the most handsome.

A young crown attorney used to pay according to the number of enemas one was willing to receive at his hands; when I crossed swords with him, I agreed to accept seven, he administered them all himself; thus, seven times over had I to mount a little stepladder, while he, stationed underneath me, frigged himself until I spewed out over his prick the entire charge with which he had lubricated my bowels.

As may be readily imagined, the entire evening was devoted to unclean activities of roughly the same species that had been treated in story, and that Messieurs turned to this kind of sport will be all the more easily understood in the light of their general enthusiasm for this passion; it was of course Curval who carried matters the furthest, but his three colleagues were scarcely less infatuated with the novelties laid out before them. The little girls' eight steaming turds were arranged amidst the supper's dishes, and at the orgies the competition was doubtless even keener for those of the little boys; and thus ended the ninth day whose term they saw arrive with the greatest pleasure, for they had high expectations for the morrow, which was destined to provide them with more amply detailed anecdotes treating a subject they adored.

The Tenth Day

(Remember to be more guarded in the beginning and more gradually to disclose what is to be clarified here.) The farther we advance, the more thoroughly we may inform the reader about certain facts we were obliged to no more than hint at in the earlier part of the story. We are able, for example, presently to advise him of the purpose of the morning visits and searches conducted in the children's quarters, the cause of their punishment when in the course of these inspections delinquents were found, and just what were the delights Messieurs tasted in the chapel: the subjects were expressly forbidden to go to the toilet or in any other place to move their bowels without individual and particular permission, this in order that there be held in reserve matters which could, as the occasion rose, be doled out to those who desired them. The visit served to determine whether anyone had neglected to comply with this order; the officer of the month carefully inspected all the chamber pots and other receptacles, and if he found any that were not empty, the subject concerned was immediately inscribed in the punishment register. However, provision had been made for those who could hold back no longer: they were, a little before the midday meal, to betake themselves to the chapel Messieurs had converted into a privy so designed that our libertines were able to enjoy the pleasure which the satisfaction of these pressing needs had the power to procure them, and the others, who had been allowed, or who had been able, to keep their loads, had the opportunity to be rid of them at some time or another during the day and in that manner which most pleased the friends, and above all in that particular manner upon which full details will subsequently be provided, for these details will compass all the manners of indulging in this voluptuous delight.

And there was yet another cause which led to the distribution of punishment, and it was the following one: what is called in France the bidet ceremony did not exactly please our friends; Curval, for example, could not bear to have the subjects with whom he came to grips wash themselves; Durcet's attitude was identical, and so it was that the one and the other would notify their duennas of the subjects with whom they planned to amuse themselves the next day, and these subjects were forbidden to wipe, rub, or wash themselves in any way and under any circumstances, and the two other friends, who did not share this abhorrence of tidiness and for whom dirt was not by any means essential, nevertheless concurred with Curval and Durcet, aided in maintaining and agreeable state of affairs, and it after having been told to be impure a subject took it into his head to be clean, he was straightway added to the fatal list.

That is what happened that morning to Colombe and Hébé; they had shitted during the previous night's orgies and, knowing that they were listed to serve coffee on the following day, Curval, who planned to amuse himself with both of them and who had even advised them that they would be expected to fart, had recommended that things be left just as they were. The children did nothing to themselves before going to bed. Inspection arrived, and Durcet, aware of the instructions Curval had given, was perfectly amazed to find them as neat as a pin; forgetfulness was the excuse they offered, but their names went down in the register nevertheless.

No chapel permissions were granted that morning. (We should like the reader to make a particular effort to remember what we mean by such an expression; this will dispense us from having to repeat our explanations.) Calculations of what would be required during the storytelling period forbade any prodigality until that time.

Upon this day the boys' masturbation lessons were suspended, for they had entirely served their purpose, and every one of the little lads-frigged as expertly as the cleverest whore in Paris. Zéphyr and Adonis led the pack in skill, speed, and deftness, and there are few pricks which would not ejaculate nigh to bleeding were they to be ministered by little hands as nimble and delicious as theirs.

Nothing worth citing occurred until coffee; it was served by Giton, Adonis, Colombe, and Hébé; these four children had, by way of preparation, been stuffed with every decoction which is best able to provoke winds, and Curval, who had proposed to be treated to farts, received a generous quantity of them. The Duc had himself sucked, or rather licked, by Giton, whose little mouth simply could not manage to engulf the enormous machine tendered him. Durcet performed some choice little horrors with Hébé, the Bishop thigh-fucked Colombe. Six o'clock sounded, they moved into the auditorium where, everyone having taken his post, Duclos began to recount what you shall read:

A new companion had very recently come to Madame Fournier's; owing to the role she is going to play in the account of the passion which follows, I believe I should give you at least a rough sketch of her. She was a young seamstress, debauched by the seducer I earlier mentioned having observed at Guérin's, and she also worked for Fournier. She was fourteen, had chestnut-brown hair, sparkling brown eyes, the most voluptuous little face in all the world, skin lily white and satin smooth, very trimly made she was, although rather inclining to fleshiness, from which slight disadvantage there resulted the sweetest, cutest, the plumpest ass, the fairest, oh 'twas possibly the finest ass in Paris. I was stationed at the hole in the partition and soon beheld the man who was to deflower her, for she was yet a maid on the other side, nothing could be plainer. Such a tidbit could only have been fed to someone very much beloved of the house: he was the venerable Abbé de Fierville, equally renowned for his wealth and his debauchery, and he had the gout to his very fingertips. He arrives swathed to the eyes in a mantle, installs himself in the chamber, examines all the equipment he is about to use, prepares everything, and then the little girl arrives; her name is Eugénie. Somewhat frightened by her first lover's grotesque face, she lowers her gaze and blushes.

"Come hither, come hither," says the libertine, "and show me your behind."

"Oh, Monsieur..." murmurs the shy little thing.

"Come, come," fumes the old roué, "nothing worse than these novices; she just can't imagine anyone should wish to look at an ass. Well, by the Saviour, get your damned skirts up."

And, stepping closer for fear of displeasing Fournier, whom she has promised to be very obedient, she finally pulls her skirt halfway up from behind.

"Higher, do you hear, higher," cries the pleasant old rascal. "Do you suppose I'm going to bother to do it myself?"

And in due time the beautiful ass is completely exposed. The man of God scrutinizes it, has her stand straight, has her bend forward, has her squeeze her legs tight together, has her separate them and, leaning her over the bed, spends a moment crudely, nay, uncouthly rubbing all his frontward privities, which he has brought to light and with which he now prods and pushes Eugénie's matchless bum, as if to electrify himself, as if to attract to himself some of that lovely child's essential heat. From this he passes to kisses, he falls to his knees in order to be more at his ease, and with both hands holding those superb buttocks as far apart as possible, both his tongue and lips rummage about in search of treasure.

"They're right," says he, "you do have a passably fine ass. Have you been shitting recently?"

"Just a little while ago, Father," the little one answers. "Madame had me do that before coming up."

"Why, that's nice... and so there's nothing left in your bowels," says the lecher. "Well, we're going to see."

And catching up the syringe, he fills it with milk, returns to behind his object, brandishes the nozzle, plunges it into the vent, and shoots out the fluid. Having been told what to expect, Eugénie submits to everything; no sooner is the remedy in her entrails than he lies down on the bed and orders Eugénie to come at once and straddle him. "Now," says he, "if you've got anything to do, have the kindness to do it in my mouth." The timid creature has taken her place as she has been told to do, she pushes, the libertine frigs himself, his mouth, sealed hermetically to her asshole, catches every drop of the precious liquid that leaps out of it. He swallows it all, giving evidence of the greatest scrupulousness in this matter, and just when he swills down the final mouthful, his fuck escapes and he is hurled into a delirium. But what is this strange mood, this cloud of loathing which, as in the case of almost every other libertine, comes to darken a mind whence the entire illusion has fled? Brutally casting the little girl far from him once he has done, the saintly man readjusts his cleric's garb, says that he has been cheated, deceived, for this child, he swears, had not priorly shitted, no, they'd lied, she'd come to him full of shit, and he'd swallowed half her turd, fie upon them. It is to be noted that Monsieur l'Abbé wanted milk only, not shit.

He grumbles, he curses, he storms, says he won't pay, won't ever come back, says he'll be damned if he'll stir himself for little snotfaces like this one, and goes off shouting a thousand other invectives I'll surely have occasion to report to you in connection with another passion in which they play a major role rather than, as in this instance, a very subordinate one.

"Well, by God," Curval remarked, "there you have a very fastidious man who'll get upset over swallowing a little shit when there are I don't know how many who feast upon it."

"Patience, Sire, patience," said Duclos, "allow my recitals to succeed each other in the order you yourselves dictated and you shall see the superior libertines you allude to achieve wonders on the stage."

My turn came two days later. Instructions had been given me, and I stayed away from the water closet for thirty-six hours. My hero was an elderly ecclesiastic who served as chaplain to the King; like the aforementioned athlete he too was crippled with gout: he was only to be approached if one were naked, but one's front and breast had to be very thoroughly covered; much emphasis had been placed upon this latter article, and I had been warned that were he to catch the least glimpse of those parts, it would prove a heavy misfortune, I'd never be able to get him to discharge. I approach, he studies my behind with extreme attentiveness, asks my age, asks whether it is true I have a great urge to shit, inquires as to the kind of shit I ordinarily produce, is it soft? is it hard? and a thousand other questions the asking of which, it seems to me, has the effect of animating him, for, as he chatters away his prick gradually lifts its head and leans toward me. That prick, approximately four inches in length by two or three around, had, despite its brilliant sheen, something of so humble and so pitiful an air that one all but needed spectacles to be certain of its existence. Solicited by my man thus to do, I laid firm hands on it, and noticing that my motion were rather well irritating his desires, he made ready to consummate the sacrifice.

"But is it a truly authentic desire, my child," says he, "this desire to shit you mention? For I don't care to be deceived; come, let's see whether you do indeed have shit in your ass."

And so saying, he buries his right hand's longest finger in my fundament, while with his left hand he sustains the erection I have excited in his desire. That plummeting finger had no need to search far, the chaplain was swiftly persuaded I had, quite as I said, the sincerest wish to shit, and when his gropings contacted the object of our mutual concern, he flew into a perfect ecstasy:

"Ah, by God's belly," he cries, "she tells the truth, the chicken is about to lay, and I feel the egg."

Enchanted, the bawdy old priest passes a moment kissing my bum, and observing the haste I am in and that I shall soon be unable to restrain the insurgent turd, he has me climb aboard on apparatus quite similar to the one your Lordships have here in the chapel; once seated, my behind perfectly exposed to his view, I was able to lodge my complaint in a receptacle located two or three inches from his nose. This apparatus had been built expressly for the chaplain, and he employed it frequently, for scarcely a day went by without him coming to Fournier's to assist in delivering either some girl attached to the house or some other from outside it. An armchair drawn close allowed him to observe the process from a point of vantage situated just below the ring supporting my ass.

When we had taken our positions upon our respective thrones, he ordered me to commence the operation. For prelude, I release a series of farts; he inhales them. The turd hoves into sight at last; he begins to pant.

"Shit, my little one, shit away, my angel," he cries, all afire. "Show me the turd coming forth out of your lovely ass."

And he aids the delivery, pressing his fingers about my anus, he facilitates the eruption; he frigs himself, he observes, he is drunk with lust, pleasure's excess finally transports him completely, he loses his head; his cries, his sighs, his fingerings, everything convinces me he is nearing the final stage and, turning my head toward him, I find I have judged correctly, for there is his miniature engine splattering a few drops of sperm into the same pot I have just filled. The chaplain left in a good humor, and even assured me he expected he would honor me with another visit, which promise I knew very well to be false, for it was common knowledge that he never saw the same girl twice.

"Well, I appreciate his feelings in the matter," declared the Président, who was kissing Aline's ass. "One must be in our deplorable situation, one must be reduced to rack and ruin in order to be able to bear having the same ass shit twice."

"Monsieur le Président," spoke up the Bishop, "there is a certain halting tone in your voice which leads me to suspect your prick is in the air."

"Tush," Curval replied, "I'm merely kissing the buttocks of Mademoiselle your daughter, who hasn't even the courtesy to let fly one wretched little fart."

"I am then enjoying better luck than you," the Bishop announced, "for Madame your wife, lo and behold! has just presented me with the most beautiful and the bulkiest turd..."

"Silence, gentlemen, silence, I say!" came from the Duc, whose voice seemed muffled as if by something covering his head. "Silence, by Jesus! we are here to listen, not to act."

"Which is therefore to say, I take it, that you are doing nothing," inquired the Bishop, "and is it in order to listen that you are wallowing under three or four assholes?"

Well, you know, he's right. Go on, Duclos, it were wiser that we hear about foolish acts than commit them. We must save our strength."

And Duclos was on the point of resuming when they all heard the usual shouts and customary blasphemies that accompanied the Duc's discharges; surrounded by his quatrain, his fuck was escaping him as with Sophie, Zéphyr, and Giton he performed countless little wantonries of a kind very analogous to those Duclos had been describing.

"Great God!" Curval exclaimed, "I can't tolerate these bad examples; there's nothing that makes me discharge like a discharge, and would you believe it? here's that little whore," he added, referring to Aline, "who only a moment ago could accomplish nothing at all and who is presently doing everything one could ask for... but no matter, I'll keep my grip. Ah, you bitch, shit away, shit your head off, it will get you nowhere, I don't intend to give up my seed."

"I see very well, Messieurs," said Duclos, "that after having perverted you it is my responsibility to restore you to reason, and to do so I am going to resume my story without waiting for your command."

"No, don't you do it," cried the Bishop, "I am not as continent as Monsieur le Président, not I, my fuck's itching me, and it's got to be shed."

Wherewith, he was seen very publicly to perform things the structure of this very complex fiction prevents us from revealing at this stage, but things whose delightful influence very rapidly brought leaping forth the fuck whose mounting pressure had discomfited the Bishop's thrice-blessed balls. As for Durcet, absorbed in Thérèse's ass, nothing was heard from him, and in all likelihood Nature refused him what she lavishly granted the others, for he was not as a rule mute when accorded her favors. Seeing that now at last calm had been restored, Duclos went on with her lubricious exploits.

A month later, I came to grips with a man whom one had almost to violate in order satisfactorily to carry out an operation somewhat akin to the one I related several minutes ago. I shit upon a dish, I bring it to him and thrust it under his nose while he sits in an armchair quietly reading a book, seemingly unaware of my presence. He looks up, falls to swearing, asks how the devil can the girl have the insolence to do such a thing in his presence, but all the same it's a queer turd she's got there, he contemplates it, handles it; I ask forgiveness for the liberty I have taken, he continues to mumble incoherencies at me, and then discharges with his eyes fixed on the morsel of shit; and in so doing he says he'll find me again someday, that sooner or later he'll see to it that I get what I deserve.

A fourth gentleman employed none but women of seventy or more in practices which were quite similar; I watched him enact his rite with an old creature who could not have been less than eighty. He was reclining upon a sofa, the matron was straddling him; she deposited her strange old package on his belly while frigging a wrinkled, shriveled prick which scarcely discharged at all.

At Fournier's establishment we had another curious article of furniture: a kind of toilet chair, provided with the usual hole and set against the wall; things were so arranged that a man could lie in such a way that while his body extended into the neighboring room, his shoulders passed through an opening and his head occupied the place usually reserved for the chamber pot. I had been appointed to the task, and kneeling between his legs, I sucked his prick as best I could throughout the operation. Well, this extraordinary ceremony consisted in having a workman, who was paid to act a part whose full consequences he neither knew nor divined; in having, I say, a man of the people enter the room containing the chair, climb upon it, and do his business squarely upon the face of the patient over whom I was toiling; but the shit bearer had absolutely to be a poor drudge fetched in from the humblest milieu, he had as well to be old and ugly, he was inspected before being put to work, and were he to lack any of these qualities, our libertine would have nothing to do with him. During all this, I saw nothing but heard rather a lot: the instant of collision was also that of my man's discharge, his fuck sprang down my throat the same moment the turd splashed upon his face, and when he emerged from beneath the chair and got to his feet, I saw by the state he was in that he had been handsomely served. By chance, after the exercise was over, I happened to meet the fellow who had performed so brilliantly; he was from the Auvergne, a good honest chap who earned his livelihood working with stonemasons; he seemed delighted to earn a crown by doing naught but ridding himself of what he would have had one way or another to expel from his bowels, and this little chore struck him as infinitely less arduous than carrying his hod. He was, what for his looks, quite dreadful to behold and must have been over forty.

"Faith," muttered Durcet, "I think that should do it."

And passing into his closet with the eldest of the fuckers, with Thérèse and Desgranges, he was heard braying and whinnying some minutes later; he returned but was disinclined to inform the company of the precise nature of the excesses whereunto he had surrendered himself.

Supper was announced; it proved at least as libertine as ever, and after the meal, the four friends having been moved to spend the evening away from one another instead of frolicking together as they customarily did, the Duc went off to the boudoir at the end of the corridor, taking with him Hercule, Martaine, his daughter Julie, Zelmire, Hébé, Zélamir, Cupidon, and Marie.

Curval commandeered the auditorium, providing himself with what companionship Constance could afford him, for she fell to trembling every time she found herself with him, and he did exceedingly little to allay her fears; he also took Fanchon, Desgranges, Bum-Cleaver, Augustine, Fanny, Narcisse, and Zéphyr.

The Bishop went into the drawing room with Duclos who, that evening, revenged herself upon the fickle Duc, who had led Martaine away from him; Aline, Invictus, Thérèse, Sophie, the charming little Colombe, Céladon, and Adonis completed the prelate's entourage.

Durcet remained in the dining room. It was cleared, rugs and cushions were brought in and strewn all about. He encloseted himself, I say, with Adelaide, his beloved wife, with Antinoüs, Louison, Champville, Michette, Rosette, Hyacinthe, and Giton.

More the redoubling of lecherous appetites than any other reason had doubtless dictated this arrangement, for brains were heated to such a point that evening that it was unanimously agreed no one would go to bed; it was perfectly incredible what was achieved in each room by way of infamies and impurities.

Toward dawn, their Lordships decided to return to table, although they had taken abundant drink throughout the night; everyone trooped into the dining room, there was an indistinct, promiscuous pell-mell, the cooks were awakened and soon sent in scrambled eggs, toast, onion soup, and omelettes. Drinking was resumed, the company grew very merry, all save Constance who was plunged in inconsolable sadness. Curval's hatred was growing just as certainly as was her poor belly; she had that night during the orgies experienced the effects of his hostility, she had suffered everything but blows, for Messieurs had agreed to leave the pear to ripen; she had, I say, blows excepted, undergone every imaginable mistreatment; she though to complain to Durcet and to her husband, the Duc: they both bade her go to the devil and remarked that she must surely have been guilty of some fault which was hidden from their eyes, yes, surely, else how could she thus ever have displeased that most virtuous and most gentle of mortals; they wagged their heads and walked away. And then they all went to bed.

The Eleventh Day

They did not rise till late that day, and dispensing with all the usual ceremonies, went directly to table once they had got up from their beds. Coffee, served by Giton, Hyacinthe, Augustine, and Fanny, was largely uneventful, although Durcet could not do without some farts from Augustine, and the Duc thrust his brave instrument between Fanny's lips. Now, as from the desire to what the desire causes 'tis ever but a single step with personages such as our heroes, they went unswervingly toward satisfying themselves; happily Augustine was prepared, she blew a steady breeze into the little financier's mouth, and he came nigh to stiffening; as for Curval and the Bishop, they confined themselves to fondling the two little boys' behinds, and then our champions moved to the auditorium.

One day little Eugénie, who was becoming more familiar with the rest of us and whom six months in the whorehouse had only rendered all the prettier, Eugénie, I say, one day accosted me and lifting her skirts, bade me look at her ass. "Do you see, Duclos, how Fournier wants me to keep my behind today?"

An inch-thick patch of shit covered her sweet little asshole. "And why does she want you to wear that?" I asked her.

"It's for the sake of an old gentleman who is coming this afternoon," she explained, "and he expects a beshitted ass."

"Well, well," said I, "he'll be very pleased with you I'm sure, for yours couldn't possibly be more thickly encrusted."

And she told me that Fournier's was the hand that had smeared her thus. Curious to witness the impending scene, I flew to the spy hole as soon as dear little Eugénie was summoned. The principal actor was a monk, but one of those monks we call gros bonnets, a Cistercian, tall, heavy, vigorous, and nearing sixty. He caresses the child, kisses her upon the mouth, and demanding to know whether she is neat and clean, he hoists her petticoats personally to verify a constant state of cleanliness whereof Eugénie gives him full assurance, although knowing nothing could be further from the truth; but she had been instructed so to speak to him.

"What's this, my little rascal?" exclaims the monk upon catching sight of that formidable mess. "What? Do you dare tell me you are neat and tidy when your ass is as filthy as this? Why, by the Virgin, I'm sure 'tis a fortnight since this bum's been wiped. 'Tis very troubling indeed, for I like things to be clean, I do, and it truly looks as if I had better look into the situation."

While speaking he had deposited Eugénie upon a bed, knelt behind her buttocks, and begun to pry them apart with both his hands. One would have thought that, at the outset, he purposed simply to observe the state of affairs, which caused him great surprise, but little by little he becomes accustomed to things as they are, sees here a virtue where he had seen only a fault before, sticks out his tongue and moves his head closer, sets to polishing the gem, the clods and spots he removes, the pristine object they conceal inflames his senses, his prick gets up, his nose, mouth, and tongue seem simultaneously to be at work, his ecstasy appears so delicious he is all but deprived of the power to speak, his fuck finally mounts -- he grasps his prick, frigs it, and as he discharges, finishes cleaning that anus, which is now so fresh and pure one would scarcely suppose it had been nasty no more than a minute or two before.

But the libertine was not yet ready to bring the affair to a conclusion, this voluptuous mania of his constituted a mere preliminary; he gets to his feet, bestows further kisses upon his little partner, exposes to her view a great ass of very evil aspect and very unclean, and he orders her to give it a thorough shaking, to socratize it; this brings his prick up furiously again, he now returns to Eugénie's ass, overwhelms it with renewed caresses, lickings, and so forth, but what he did after that it is not for me to relate, nor would it properly figure in these introductory narrations; you will, Messieurs, have the great kindness to allow Madame Martaine to tell you of the behavior of a villain with whom she was only too well acquainted; and in order to avoid all questions, my Lords, which your own regulations forbid me to treat, or resolve, I continue on to another episode.

"Just one word, Duclos," said the Duc, who then queried the story-teller in an indirect language which enabled her to make lawful reply. "Was it big with the monk? Was this Eugénie's first time?..."

"Yes, Sire, the first, and the monk's was about the size of yours."

"Ah, fuck my eyes!" muttered Durcet; "a damned pretty demonstration, I'd like to have seen that."

You would perhaps have been equally curious, Duclos said as she picked up the thread of her narrative, about the individual who, a few days later, passed into my hands. Outfitted with a vessel containing eight or ten great turds gathered from all quarters and whose authors he would have been very distressed to have identified, I was with my own hands to rub him from head to toe with this fragrant pomade. Not an inch on his body was neglected, not even his face, and when I had massaged his prick, which I frigged at the same time, the infamous pig, who all the while stared contentedly at himself in a mirror, left evidence of his humble virility between my palms.

And at last, gentlemen, we have arrived; I can now advise you that the homage is about to be made in the veritable temple. I had been told to hold myself in readiness, I kept my bowels closed for two long days. It was a commander of the Order of the Knights of Malta with whom I was to break a lance; he used to see a different girl every morning for these exercises; the following scene transpired at his home.

"Very fair buttocks," was his opinion as he embraced my behind. "However, my child," he continued, "there's more to it than simply having a comely ass, you know. That comely ass must know how to shit. Tell me, have you the urge?"

"Such an urge I'm dying to satisfy it, Monsieur," I confessed.

"Well, by Jesus, that's delicious!" exclaimed the commander, "that's what is called excellent service to society, but look here, my little duck, would you like to shit in this chamber pot I'm offering you?"

"In faith, Monsieur," I made answer, "what with the need I have to shit, I'd do it anywhere, I'd even shit in your mouth."

"No! In my mouth, you say? Why, bless me, that is delicious, and that's precisely the place I myself had in mind for you," he added, setting the pot aside.

"Well, Monsieur, let's make haste, bring up your mouth," said I, "for indeed I'll not be able to hold back much longer."

He places himself on the couch, I climb astride him, while operating I frig him, he supports my haunches with his hands and receives, piece by piece, everything I deposit in his avid mouth. He is thrilled by it all, nears his ecstasy, my wrist is hardly needed to bring forth the floods of semen which salute my performance; I frig, conclude my shitting, our man loses himself and his seed altogether, and I leave him delighted with me, or at least so he has the kindness to say to Fournier, at the same time requesting the services of another girl for the morrow.

The personage who came next employed more or less the same approach to the problem, but simply kept the morsels in his mouth for a longer period. He reduced them to a fluid, rinsed his mouth with them for a quarter of an hour, and spat out little more than dingy water.

Yet another had, if that is possible, a still more bizarre eccentricity; he liked to find four turds in the pot beneath a pierced chair, but those four turds could not be mixed with so much as a single drop of urine. He would be shut up alone in the room containing this treasure, never did he allow a girl with him, and every precaution had to be taken to insure his solitude, he could not bear the thought he might be observed, and when at last he felt secure he went into action; but I am absolutely unable to tell you what he did, for no one had ever seen him; all that is known is that when he had left the room, the pot was discovered perfectly empty and as tidy as can be. But what he did with his four turds only the devil can tell you, if indeed he knows. He may perhaps have thrown them away somewhere, but, then again, he could also have done something else with them.

However, what would lead one to suspect he did not do that something else with them is that he left the procuring of those four turds entirely up to Fournier, and never made the least inquiry about their origin. One day, in order to observe whether what we were about to say would alarm him -- for his alarm might have provided us with a clue about the fate of those turds -- we told him that the ones he had been served that day had come from several persons suffering from syphilis. He laughed good-naturedly with us, was not in the slightest disturbed, which reaction was not to be expected from someone who had employed rather than cast away the turds. When we sought, upon one or two occasions, to push our questions a little further, he bade us be silent, and never were we to learn more of the matter.

That concludes what I have to tell you this evening, said Duclos; tomorrow I propose to relate my new mode of life, or rather the new turn my same mode of life took, when I met Monsieur d'Aucourt; and as for the charming passion you so heavily favor, I hope to have the honor to entertain you with examples of it for at least another two or three days.

Opinions were divided about the fate of the turds in the episode Duclos had just recounted, and while arguing and reasoning about them, Messieurs had a few produced for themselves; and the Duc, eager to make everyone aware of the taste he was developing for Duclos, exhibited to the entire assembly his libertine manner to amuse himself with her, and the dexterity, aptitude, and promptness, accompanied by the most stirring language, wherewith she knew so artfully how to satisfy him.

Supper and the orgies transpired without any unusual incident, nothing of importance took place before the afternoon of the next day, and so we may move directly to the recitations wherewith Duclos brightened the 12th of November.

The Twelfth Day

The new mode of life I was about to begin, said Duclos, obliges me to draw your attention, Messieurs, to my personal appearance and character at the time; one is better able to figure the pleasures being described if one is first acquainted with the object that procures them. I had just attained my twenty-first year. My hair was brown, but nevertheless my skin was of a most agreeable whiteness. The abundance of hair covering my head fell in floating and perfectly authentic curls to just above my knees. I had the eyes you behold me now to have, and they have always been judged lovely. My figure was rather full although tall, supple, and gracious. With what regards my behind, that part of the anatomy in which libertines today take such a keen interest, it was by common consent superior to the most sublime specimens one is likely ever to see, and there were few women in Paris who had an ass as deliciously molded; it was full, round, very plump, and exceedingly soft, generous, I say, but without its ampleness detracting anything from its elegance, the least gesture immediately discovered that heavenly little rosebud you so cherish, Messieurs, and which, I do indeed like yourselves believe, is a woman's most magical attraction. Although I had been for a long season active in libertinage, my ass could not have been healthier or looked more untried; its splendid condition was in part owing to the good constitution Nature had granted me and in part to the extreme prudence I exercised on the battlefield, scrupulously avoiding encounters capable of damaging my most precious asset. I had very little love for men, I had never had but one attachment; I had a libertine maid, but it was extraordinarily libertine, and after having described my charms it is only fitting that I say a word or two about my vices. I love women, Messieurs, I don't deny it. Not however to the uncommon degree my good colleague, Madame Champville, loves them; she will probably tell you that she has ruined herself for them; I have simply always preferred them to men in my pleasures, and those they have procured me have always exerted a more powerful sway over my senses than masculine delights. Apart from this fault, I have had another of adoring to steal: I have refined this mania to an unbelievable point. Entirely convinced that all possession should be equally distributed in the world and that it is only strength and violence which are opposed to this equality, foremost law of Nature, I have striven to rectify the actual scheme and to do my utmost to re-establish the proper balance. And had it not been for this accursed compulsion I might perhaps still be with the benevolent mortal of whom I shall speak next.

"You say you have done considerable stealing?" said Durcet.

"An astonishing amount, Monsieur; had I not always spent what I filched, I would be wealthy today."

"But was there not more to it than that?" the financier pursued. "Some aggravating detail, such as, for instance, forced entry, abuse of confidence, manifest deceit?"

"Everything under the sun," Duclos assured him. "I did not think it worth dwelling on these matters which would also have disturbed the smooth unfolding of my history, but since it is evident they might amuse you, in future I'll not forget to cite my thefts.

"As well as that fault, I have always been reproached for another: I am said to have a hard heart, a very bad one indeed; but is that fault really mine? or is it not rather from Nature we have our vices as well as our perfections? and is there anything I can do to soften this heart she caused to be insensible? I don't believe I have ever in all my life wept over my troubles, and I can safely assure you I have never dropped a tear for the afflictions of others; I loved my sister, and I lost her without the least twinge of grief, you were witness to the stoic indifference with which I greeted news of her undoing; I would, by God, see the universe perish without a sniffle or a sigh."

"That is how one must be," said the Duc, "compassion is a fool's virtue. Close examination reveals that it is never anything but compassion which costs us delights. But with that toughened heart of yours, you must have committed crimes, for, you know, insensibility leads straight to nothing else."

"My Lord," Duclos replied, "the regulations prescribed for our narrations prevent me from apprising you of a great many things; my companions will supply what you have ordained I omit. I do have one word to say, however: when later on they attempt to represent themselves to you as villains, you may be perfectly sure I have never been any better than they."

"That, I should say, is doing justice to oneself," Blangis observed. "Well, go on with your tales; we'll have to be content with what you tell us, for we have ourselves set bounds to your discourses; but remember that when we, you and I, have a little chat together, I'll insist upon hearing of your various peccadillos."

"And I shall conceal none of them from you, Sire. May it be that after having heard me out you shall have no cause to repent of your indulgence toward one of the King's worst subjects." Wherewith she lifted up her voice and addressed the assembly again:

Despite all these defects, and above all that of being thoroughly unappreciative of the value of the humiliating sentiment of gratitude, which I consider as naught but an injurious burden to humanity and one which completely degrades the pride and self-respect implanted in us by Nature, with all these deficiencies, I say, my companions were nevertheless very fond of me, and of them all I was the most sought after by men.

Such was my situation when a rich landowner named d'Aucourt came to have a party at Fournier's; as he was one of her steadfast clients, but one who preferred girls brought in from outside the house to those residing in it, he was held in the highest esteem, and Madame, who felt I had absolutely to make his acquaintance, gave me notice two days beforehand not to waste an ounce of the precious matter for which he had a greater passion than any of the other men I had met with until then; but from the details you will be able to judge of all this for yourselves. D'Aucourt arrived, and having eyed me up and down, he scolded Madame Fournier for having waited so long to supply him with this pretty creature. I thanked him for his gallantry, and up we went together. D'Aucourt was about fifty years of age, heavy-set, fat, but his face was pleasant to see, there was animation in his features, he was witty and, what pleased me most of all about him, he had a gentleness and honesty of character which enchanted me from the first moment.

"You must have the world's loveliest ass," said he, drawing me to him and burrowing his hand beneath my skirts. His hand went directly to my behind. "I am a connoisseur, and girls of your figure and general look almost invariably possess striking asses. Why, look here, didn't I tell you so?" he continued, after briefly palpating the object, "how fresh and round it is!"

And nimbly turning me around as with one hand he lifted my skirts to my waist and with the other fondled the article, he fell to work examining the altar to which he addressed his prayers.

"Jesus!" he cried, "by the Saviour, 'tis really one of the finest asses I have clapped eyes on in all my days and, believe me, I have studied many.... Spread... Great God, behold that strawberry!... allow me to suck it... devour it... 'tis really a beautiful ass indeed, this one... eh, tell me, dearie, have they given you the instructions?"

"Yes, Monsieur."

"They told you I have them shit?"

"Yes, Monsieur."

"But your health?" went on the capitalist, "there's nothing amiss?"
"Never fear, good sir."

"It's simply, d'ye see, that I carry things rather far," he went on, "and if you have the least illness or symptom, then I run a great risk."

"Sir," said I, "you can do absolutely anything you please, I guarantee you I am as fit and sound and safe as a newborn babe; you may act in confidence."

After this preamble, d'Aucourt had me bend around toward him and, all the while keeping my buttocks spread wide, and gluing his mouth to mine, he sucked my saliva for fifteen minutes or so; he withdrew his mouth in order to expectorate a little "fuck," and then returned to his amorous mouth pumping.

"Spit into my mouth, spit," he repeated, "from time to time, fill it with saliva."

And then I felt his tongue run over my gums, drive as far as possible into my mouth, and I had the impression it was endeavoring to draw everything out of me.

"Excellent," said he, "I'm getting stiff. Let's go to work."

Then he fell to contemplating my buttocks again, ordering me to encourage the rise of his prick. I pulled out a strange little engine three inches thick and only five long; it was as hard as a cobblestone and full of fire.

"Remove your skirts," d'Aucourt told me, "while I take off my breeches; your buttocks and mine too have to be thoroughly at their ease for the ceremony we are about to execute."

Then, once I had obeyed him:

"Lift your blouse further up, that's it, close to your corset," he continued, "and see to it your behind is absolutely disencumbered.... Lie on your stomach upon the bed."

He fetched up a chair and seated himself by the bed, then returned to caressing my bum, the mere sight of which appeared to intoxicate him; he spread my buttocks for a moment and I felt his tongue sound deep into my entrails, this, said he, in order beyond any shadow of equivocation to verify whether indeed the hen were inclined to lay; I report his own expressions to you. All this while, I was not touching him, not at that stage, he was himself lightly stroking the dry little member I had just brought from its lair.

"Are you ready, my child?" he asked. "For it is high time we undertake our task; your shit seems to me as it should be, I've established that, remember to shit gradually, a little at a time, and always wait until I have consumed one morsel before pushing out the next. My operation takes quite a while, so don't be in haste. A light slap on your ass will notify you that I'm ready for more, but see to it that I get no more than a bite."

Having then adopted the most comfortable position, he glued his mouth to the object of his worship, and in less time than it takes to tell I delivered a gobbet of shit the size of a pigeon's egg. He sucked it, turned it a thousand times about in his mouth, chewed it, savored it, at the end of three or four minutes I distinctly saw him swallow it; I push again, the same ceremony is repeated, and as I had a prodigious charge to be rid of, ten times over he filled his mouth and emptied it, and even after all was done he seemed famished still.

"That is all, Monsieur," I said when I had finished, "I'm pushing in vain now."

"It's all over, is it, my little dear? Why, then I believe I'll discharge, yes, discharge while paying my respects to this superb ass. Oh, Great God, what pleasure you give me! I've never eaten more delicious shit,

I'd swear to that before any jury. Give it to me, bring it hither, hither, my angel, bring me your matchless ass to suck, let me devour it."

And thrusting what seemed to be twelve inches of tongue through my anus and while doing so manualizing himself, the libertine spatters his fuck over my legs, not without uttering a host of obscene words and oaths necessary, apparently, to the crowning of his ecstasy.

When at last it was all over, he sat down, invited me to sit beside him and, regarding me with great interest, asked whether I were not tired of the life of the brothel and if I should not be pleased to come across someone who would extricate me from it; seeing he had taken a fancy to me, I began to demur, and to spare you a long story which could not possibly be of any interest to you, after an hour of debating I let myself be won over, and it was decided that on the following day I would take up quarters in his home in return for twenty louis per month and board; that as he was a widower, I could conveniently occupy a large apartment in his town house; that I would have a maid to wait upon me and the society of three of his friends and their mistresses with whom he got together for libertine suppers four times each week, sometimes at his own establishment, sometimes at one of theirs; that my one obligation, and occupation, would be to eat a great deal, and always the fare he had served to me, because, doing what he did, it were essential I be fed on a diet which accorded with his taste -- to eat a great deal, I say, to sleep long and soundly in order that my digestion be good and thorough, to purge myself regularly once a month, and to shit in his mouth twice every day; that this rate of shit consumption, or rather of shit production, ought not to frighten me because, by stuffing me with food, as he planned to do, I would perhaps hear the call not twice but three times a day. The capitalist presented me with a very pretty diamond in token of his eagerness to conclude the bargain; then he embraced me, told me to settle my affairs with Fournier and to be ready the following morning, at which time he would come to fetch me himself. My farewells were quickly said; my heart regretted nothing, for it knew nothing of the art of forming attachments, but my pleasures regretted the loss of Eugénie, with whom for six months I had enjoyed an exceedingly intimate liaison; I left. D'Aucourt received me with wonderful graciousness and himself took me to the very pretty suite which was to be my new habitation; I was soon fully installed. I was expected, indeed condemned, to eat four meals whence were excluded a great number of things I should have adored having: I had to go without fish, oysters, salted meat, eggs, and every kind of dairy product; but on the other hand I was so well recompensed that in truth I had no real grounds for complaint. The basis of an ordinary repast consisted of an immense quantity of breast of chicken, of boned fowl prepared and presented in every imaginable fashion, little beef or other red meat, nothing that contained grease, very little bread or fruit. I had to eat these foods even for breakfast in the morning and, in the afternoon, at tea; at these hours, they were served me without bread, and d'Aucourt gradually induced me entirely to abstain from bread; ever since then I've not eaten it at all, and I've also given up heavy soups. The result of this diet, as my lover had calculated, was two bowel movements per day, and the stools were very soft, very sweet, somewhat small but, so d'Aucourt maintained, of an exquisite taste which could not be obtained by ordinary nourishment; and d'Aucourt was a man whose opinion deserved to be accorded some weight, for he was a connoisseur. Our operations were performed when he awoke and when he retired for the night. Their details were more or less what I have already given you: he would always begin with a prolonged sucking of my mouth, which I had always to present him in its natural state, that is to say, unwashed: I was only allowed to rinse it out afterward. He would not, furthermore, discharge every time he dined, our arrangements did not in any way bind him to fidelity. D'Aucourt kept me as the pièce de résistance, I was the roast beef, as it were, but that did not prevent him from sallying forth every morning for a nibble of lunch somewhere else.

Two days after I had arrived, his comrades in debauch came for an evening at his home, and as each of the three boasted, in the taste we are presently analyzing, a superficially different although fundamentally identical passion, by your leave, Messieurs, every little example adding to our collection, I shall devote a few words to the fantasies in which they indulged themselves.

The guests arrived. The first was an elderly parliamentarian, in his sixties, and named d'Erville; his mistress was a woman of forty, exceedingly handsome, and having no visible defect other than certain excess of flesh: her name was Madame du Cange. The second was a retired military officer of between forty-five and fifty, he was called Després, his mistress was an attractive young person of twenty-six, blond, and having as lovely a body as you may hope to find: her name was Marianne. The third was an abbot, sixty years old, Du Coudrais by name; his mistress was a lad of sixteen, pretty as a star, whom the good ecclesiastic passed off as his nephew.

The table was laid in that part of the house near my chambers; the meal was festive, the fare delicate, and I remarked that the young lady and the youth were on a diet very similar to mine. Characters declared themselves while we dined; it was impossible to be more a libertine than d'Erville; his eyes, his speech, his gestures, everything about him proclaimed debauchery, libertinage was painted in his every line; there was more of the restrained, the deliberate in Després, but lust was none the less the soul of his existence; as for the abbot, he was the world's most arrant, boldest atheist: blasphemies flew from his lips with virtually every word he pronounced; with regard to the ladies, they emulated their lovers, tattled and chattered a blue streak but in a rather agreeable tone; the young boy struck me as being as great a fool as he was a pretty one, and du Cange, who seemed smitten by him, cast a series of tender glances toward him, every one of which he failed even to notice.

All propriety had vanished by the time dessert arrived, and the conversation had become as filthy as the goings on: d'Erville congratulated d'Aucourt upon his latest acquisition and begged to know whether my ass had any merit, and if I shitted pleasantly.

"Oh, by God," my capitalist replied with a smile, "you've only to establish the facts for yourself; we hold our goods in common, you know, and lend one another our mistresses quite as willingly as we do our purses."

"Why," d'Erville murmured, "I believe I will have a peek."

Taking me by the hand at once, he proposed that we repair to a closet together. As I was hesitating, du Cange raised her brows and said in a rude voice:

"Be off with you, Mademoiselle, we don't stand on ceremony here. I'll look after your lover while you're away."

And d'Aucourt, whose eyes I consulted, having made a sign of approbation, I followed the old legislator. 'Tis he, Messieurs, and the other two as well, who are going to offer you the three demonstrations of the taste we are currently studying and which should compose the better part of today's narrations.

As soon as I was closeted with d'Erville, he, very much warmed by the drink he had imbibed, kissed me upon the mouth with extreme enthusiasm, and in so doing belched a few hiccups into my mouth, which nearly made me eject from that orifice what, a few minutes later, he seemed to have the most pressing desire to see emerge from another. He lifted my skirts, examined my behind with all the lubricity of a consummate libertine, then informed me he was not at all surprised at d'Aucourt's choice, for indeed, said he, I had one of the most beautiful asses in Paris. He besought me to commence with a few farts, and after he had absorbed a half dozen of them, he returned to kissing my mouth, the while fondling me and vigorously spreading my buttocks.

"Are you beginning to feel the need?" he asked. "I feel little else," I replied.

"Very well, my pretty child, be so good as to shit upon this dish."

He had brought with him one of white porcelain, he held it while I pushed, and scrupulously examined the turd as it emerged from my behind, a delicious spectacle which, so he maintained, intoxicated him with pleasure. When I had finished, he picked up the plate, ecstatically inhaled the voluptuous product it contained, handled, kissed, sniffed the turd, then telling me he could bear it no longer, and that it was now lust wherewith he was drunk thanks to this, the most sublime piece of shit he had ever seen, he bade me suck his prick; although there was nothing in any way agreeable about this operation, fear of angering d'Aucourt by not co-operating with his friend induced me to accede to everything. He settled himself in an armchair, or rather sprawled sideways in it, having deposited the plate on a neighboring table upon which he also rested half his body, his nose buried in the shit; he extended his legs, and I, having drawn up a low chair and having pulled from his fly a mere suspicion of a very soft prick instead of a real member, despite my repugnance I fell to sucking this miserable relic, hoping that a mouthing would give it at least a little consistency. It did not: once I had taken the wretched object into my mouth, the libertine started his operation and thrust into his the pretty little egg, all bright and new, which I had just laid for him; he did not eat it, he battened upon it: the game lasted three minutes, during which his squirmings, shudderings, contortions, declared a very ardent and a very expressive delight. But it was all in vain, not a trace of solidity appeared in that ugly little stub of a tool which, after having wept tears of chagrin into my mouth, withdrew itself more ashamed than ever and left its master in that prostration, in that abandon, in that exhaustion which is the certain consequence of a potent draught of pleasure.

"Ah," said the parliamentarian, "I forswear my faith; never have I seen anyone shit like that."

Upon returning to the dining room we found only the abbot and his nephew, and as they were operating, I can give you the essential particulars at once. Whereas the others exchanged mistresses in this little society, nothing could induce Du Coudrais to do so: always content with what he had, he never accepted a substitute for it; he would not have been able, I was informed, to amuse himself with a woman; but in every other respect, he and d'Aucourt were alike. He went about his ceremony in the same way, what was more, and when we entered the room the youngster was lying belly down upon the edge of a divan, presenting his ass to his dear uncle who, kneeling down before it, was lovingly receiving into his mouth and steadily consuming all the lad was producing, the while frigging an exceedingly small prick we observed dangling between his thighs. The abbot discharged, our presence notwithstanding, and swore that the boy was shitting better with every day that passed.

Marianne and d'Aucourt, who were amusing themselves together, soon reappeared and were followed by Després and du Cange who, they said, had only been cuddling and volleying while waiting for me.

"Because," said Després, "she and I are old acquaintances, whereas you, my lovely queen, you whom I see for the first time, inspire in me the most ardent desire for a more thorough amusement."

"But," I objected, "Monsieur d'Erville has taken it all; I have nothing more to offer you."

"Why indeed!" he said with a merry laugh, "indeed, I ask nothing from you, I'll furnish all that is needed. I merely require your fingers."

Curious to learn the meaning of this enigma, I accompany him, and as soon as we are alone together, he asks to kiss my ass for a brief minute. I raise it toward him and after two or three licks and sucks at the hole, he unbuttons his breeches and bids me do unto him what he has just done in my behalf. His posture excited my suspicions: he was seated facing the back of a chair, by clinging to which he kept his balance, and beneath him was a pot waiting to be filled; and so, observing he was ready to perform all by himself, I asked why it were necessary for me to kiss his ass.

"Nothing could be more necessary, my heart," he replied; "for my ass, in all of France the most capricious of asses, never shits save when kissed."

I obeyed, but took care to stay clear of danger; perceiving my cautious maneuvering:

"Closer, for God's sake, get closer, sweetie," he said in an imperious tone. "Are you afraid of a little shit?"

And so at last, in order to be friendly, I brought my lips to the vicinity of the hole; but he no sooner felt them there than he tripped the spring, the eruption was so violent one of my cheeks was splashed from temple to chin. He needed but one shot to submerge the plate; never in my life had I seen such a turd: all by itself it would easily have filled a very deep salad bowl. Our man snatches it up, takes it with him, and lies down on the edge of the bed, presents his entirely beshitted ass, and orders me to play with it while he feasts upon what has just darted out of his entrails. Filthy as his bum was, I had to obey. "His mistress doubtless does as much," I said to myself; "I must be as obliging as she." I plunge three fingers into the murky aperture pleading for my attentions; our man is beside himself with joy, he falls upon his own excrements, daubs his face with them, wallows in them, feeds upon them, one of his hands holds the plate, the other jostles his prick rising up majestically between his thighs; I redouble my efforts, they are not in vain, I feel his anus contract around my fingers, this reports that his erector muscles are about to launch the seed, the prospect delights me, the plate is licked clean, and my partner discharges.

Once again back in the salon, I find my inconstant d'Aucourt with the lovely Marianne; the rascal had also made use of her. The only one who remained was the page boy, with whom, I believe, he might also have come to terms had the jealous abbot only consented to relinquish him for half an hour. When everyone had returned, they all spoke of removing their clothes and of performing a few extravagances in front of each other. The idea struck me as excellent, for it would enable me to see Marianne's body, which I had the greatest desire to examine; it proved delicious, firm, fair, splendidly proportioned, and her ass, which I fondled several times in a joking manner, seemed to me a veritable masterpiece.

"What do you want with such a pretty girl?" I asked Desprès. "For the pleasure you appear to cherish places no emphasis upon looks."

"Ah," said he, "you don't know all my mysterious little ways."

I was absolutely unable to learn more about them, and although I lived for more than a year with d'Aucourt, and was present at every get-together, neither Desprès nor Marianne wished to clarify anything to me, and I remained in entire ignorance of their secret intelligences which, of whatever kind they may have been, did not prevent the taste her lover used to satisfy with me from being an authentic and distinct passion worthy in every respect of inclusion in our anthology. Whatever he did with Marianne, I supposed, must have been merely episodic and either has been or certainly will be related at some one of our sessions.

After some rather indecent libertine stunts, some farts, yet a few more little turds or turdlets, we had considerable talk and sounding impieties on the part of the abbot, who seemed to locate one of his most perfect lecheries in ungodly conduct and discourse; after all this, everyone put on his clothes again and went off to bed. The next morning, as usual, I appeared in d'Aucourt's room as he was preparing to arise, and neither of us reprimanded the other for our little infidelities of the evening before. He said that, with the exception of myself, he knew of no girl who shitted better than did Marianne; I put several questions to him, asking what she did with a lover who was so admirably self-sufficient, and d'Aucourt replied that all this was a secret between the two of them and they had never seemed willing to disclose it. And we, my own lover and I, went on with our usual little tricks.

I was not as confined at d'Aucourt's house as I had been before; I sometimes ventured abroad; he had complete faith, he told me, in my honesty, I could very well see what danger I would be exposing him to were I to impair my health, and he left me to my own devices. With what regarded the health in which, most selfishly, he took such a keen interest, I did nothing to betray his trust, but as for the rest, I considered myself free to do just about everything that would earn me any money. And so, being repeatedly solicited by Fournier who was eager to arrange parties for me at her establishment, I lent my talents to every project wherefrom I was assured an honorable profit. I was no longer one of her crew, I was a young lady kept by a farmer-general; would I have the great kindness to give Madame Fournier an hour of my valuable time and pass at her establishment on such and such a day, etc., etc. You may fancy how well that paid. It was in the course of these brief distractions that I encountered the new shit worshiper I'll discuss next.

"Just one instant," put in the Bishop. "I did not want to interrupt you until you reached the end of a chapter; you seem to be at one now. Would you therefore have the kindness to shed some additional light upon two or three essential points in this latest party? When you celebrated the orgies after your interview with Desprès, did the abbot, who until then had been caressing his bardash only, commit acts of infidelity? In a word, did he lay hands upon you? did the others desert their women for the boy?"

"Monseigneur," said Duclos, "the abbot never once left his little boy; he scarcely so much as glanced at us even though we were naked and all but on top of him. But he toyed with d'Aucourt's ass and Desprès' and also d'Erville's: he kissed them, sucked them, d'Aucourt and d'Erville shitted into his mouth and he swallowed the better part of each of those two turds. But he would not touch the women. The same was not true of the three other friends relative to his youthful bardash; they kissed him, licked his asshole, and Desprès went off alone with him for I have no idea what exercise."

"Excellent," said the Bishop. "You observe that you failed to mention everything, and that what you have just recounted forms still another passion, since it figures the taste of a man who has other men shit in his mouth, and quite mature men at that."

"That is true, Monseigneur," Duclos admitted, "I confess my error but am not sorry for it, because the soiree has drawn to a close and has indeed been overlong. The bell we are about to hear struck would have indicated that I did not have sufficient time to end the story I was preparing to begin, and with your gracious leave we will postpone it until tomorrow."

The bell did indeed ring and as no one had discharged during the sitting and as every prick was, however, mightily aloft, they only betook themselves to supper after promising to make good their loss at the orgies. But the impetuous Duc was never able to postpone important business and having ordered Sophie to present her buttocks, he had that lovely child shit, and he swallowed her turd for dessert. Durcet, the Bishop, and Curval, all similarly occupied, concluded the same operation, the first with Hyacinthe, the second with Céladon, the third with Adonis. The last named, having failed to give ample satisfaction, was inscribed in the punishment book, and Curval, swearing like a trooper, revenged himself upon Thérèse's ass, which exploded, at point-blank range, the most ponderous turd imaginable. The orgies were eminently libertine and Durcet, forsaking youthful turds, said that for the evening's games he would have none but what his three old friends could yield him. They humored him with passing fair performances, and the little libertine discharged like a stallion while devouring Curval's shit. Night came at last to restore some measure of calm to so much intemperance, and to restore as well our libertines' desires and faculties.

The Thirteenth Day

The Président, who that night lay with Adelaide, his daughter, having sported with her until he felt sleep about to claim him, had therewith relegated her to the pallet beside his bed in order that Fanchon might have her place, for he was ever eager to have the old duenna by his side when lust awoke him, which occurred almost every night; toward three in the morning, he opened his eyes with a start and fell to swearing and blaspheming like the true rascal he was. He would at such times be gripped by a lubric furor which now and again became dangerous. That is why he was so fond of having that trusty old Fanchon near him, for no one was so skillful at calming him, whether by offering herself or by immediately bringing him one of the objects lying in his bedchamber.

On that particular night, the Président, instantly recollecting some infamies he had perpetrated upon his daughter just before falling asleep, called for her at once with the intention of repeating them; but she was not there. Imagine the consternation and the commotion created by such an incident. Curval springs from bed in a towering rage, asks where his daughter is; candles are lit, everyone hunts about, the place is ransacked, nothing's to be found; the last place searched is the girls' apartments. Every bed is examined, and at last the interesting Adelaide is discovered seated in her nightgown near Sophie's cot. Those two charming girls, united by their similarly tender natures, their piety, virtuous sentiments, candor, and absolutely identical amenity, had been seized by the most beautiful affection for each other and they were exchanging comforting words, consoling one another for the dreadful fate that had been reserved for them. No one had perceived their commerce until then, but what followed proved that this was not the first time they had got together, and it was discovered as well that the elder of the was cultivating the other's finer sentiments, and had especially pleaded with her not to stray from her religion and her duties toward God, Who would one day comfort and console them for all their woes.

I leave it to the reader to picture Curval's fury and stormy reaction when he located the lovely missionary; he seized her by the hair and, overwhelming her with invectives, all very harsh, dragged her to his chamber, where he tied her to his bedpost and left her until the next morning to ponder over her indiscretion. All of the friends having rushed to the scene, it will also be readily imagined with what haste and decision Curval had the two delinquents' names written down in the register. The Duc argued passionately in favor of instantaneous correction, and what he proposed was not by any means mild; but the Bishop having countered with a very reasonable objection to what his brother was urged to do, Durcet was content simply to include them on the agenda. There was no way of attacking the duennas; they were all four bedded in Messieurs' chambers that night. This fact accounted for the imperfect administration of the household, and arrangements were made whereby, in future, there would always be at least one duenna in the girls' quarters and another in the boys'. Their lordships retired to bed again, and Curval, whom anger had rendered more than cruelly impudicious, did things to his daughter we cannot yet describe, but which, by precipitating his discharge, at least put him quietly to sleep.

All the hens in the chicken coop had been so terrified that, on the morrow, no misbehavior was discovered, and amongst the boys, only Narcisse, whom, the evening before, Curval had forbidden to wipe his ass, wishing to have it nicely beshitted at coffee, which this child was scheduled to serve, and who had unfortunately forgot his instructions, only Narcisse, I say, had cleaned his anus and he had done so with extreme care. It was in vain the little chap explained that his mistake could be repaired, since, said he, he wanted to shit there and then; he was told to keep what he had, and that he would be none the less inscribed in the fatal book; which inscriptions the redoubtable Durcet instantly performed before his eyes, thus to make him sense all the enormity of his fault, a veritable sin and possibly by itself capable of upsetting or, who knows? of preventing Monsieur le Président's discharge.

Constance, whom they did not hinder because of her state, Desgranges, and Bum-Cleaver were the only ones who were granted chapel permission; everyone else received the order not to draw the cork until the evening toasts.

The preceding night's events provided the dinner's conversation; they made game of the Président for permitting the bird to fly from its cage, etc.; some champagne restored his gay spirits, and the company sallied forth to coffee. Narcisse, Céladon, and Zelmire distributed it, so did Sophie, who was greatly ashamed of herself; she was asked how often the thing had happened, she replied that it had occurred only twice, and that Madame de Durcet gave her such good counsel that indeed she thought it most unjust to punish them both for it. The Président assured her that what she called good counsel was, in her situation, the very worst, that the devotion wherewith Madame de Durcet had been filling her head would serve no purpose save to get her punished every day, and that, in her present circumstances, she was to have no masters and no gods save his three confreres and himself, no religion save that of blindly serving and obeying them in everything. And, all the while he was delivering this sermon, he had her kneel between his legs and bade her suck his prick, which the poor little thing did all atremble. As always partisan to thigh-fuckery, the Duc, obliged as he was to abstain from the capital practice, impaled Zelmire in this style, meanwhile having the little girl shit in his cupped hand and gobbling it up as quickly as it was received, and all that while Durcet was inducing Céladon to discharge into his mouth, and the Bishop was industriously extracting a turd from Narcisse. A few minutes, no more, were set aside for the nap that they found such an aid to digestion; then, having taken up their posts in the auditorium, Duclos faced the gathering and began the day's narrative.

The gallant octogenarian Fournier had in mind for me, Messieurs, was an official from the auditing bureau, short, pudgy, and with an extremely unpleasant face. He set a pot between us, we squatted down back to back and shitted simultaneously; he seizes up the pot, with his fingers stirs the two turds, mixes them, swallows the batter while I promote his discharge, an eruption which takes place in my mouth. He barely even glanced at my behind. Nor did he do any kissing, but his ecstasy was very sharp and compelling all the same: he pranced all about the room, swearing while he gulped and ejaculated, and then took himself off, giving me four louis for this strange ceremony.

However, my landowner became more fond of me with each passing day, and more trusting too, and this trust, which I lost no time in abusing, soon became the cause of our eternal separation... One day when he had left me alone in his library, I noticed that, before going out for the day, he had filled his purse with money taken from a deep drawer entirely filled with gold. "Ah, what a capture!" I said to myself, and having from that very instant conceived the idea of making off with this sum, I set to watching for the means and opportunity whereby to appropriate it: d'Aucourt never locked the drawer, but he carried with him the key to his library, and having discovered that this door and lock were both very frail, I fancied it would take little effort to break the one and the other. Having adopted the plan, I concentrated upon nothing but taking advantage of the first time d'Aucourt was absent the entire day; that used to be the case twice a week, when he went off for private bacchanals in the company of Després and the abbot; Madame Desgranges will perhaps describe what occurred during these outings, they lie beyond my province.

The favorable moment was soon at hand; d'Aucourt's valets, as libertine as their master, never failed to go with him to these parties, and so I found myself almost alone in the house. Full of impatience to put my project into execution, I go straightway to the door of the library, break the thin panel with a blow of my fist, rush to the drawer, find it unlocked as I knew it would be. I remove everything it contains; my prize amounts to not less than three thousand louis. I fill my pockets, rifle other drawers; a splendid jewel case catches my eye, I pick it up, but what was I not to find in the other drawers of that bountiful secretary!... Fortunate d'Aucourt! What great good luck for you that your imprudence was not discovered by anyone else but me; the secretary contained enough to have had him broken on the wheel, Messieurs, that is all I can tell you. Quite apart from the transparent and expressive notes addressed to him by Després and the abbot pertaining to their secret commerce, there was every kind of furniture needed for the performing of those infamies... But I halt myself here; the boundaries you have prescribed to my depositions prevent me from saying more; Desgranges will treat the whole matter. As for myself, the theft once effected, I left at once, shuddering to think of all the dangers I had perhaps been exposing myself to by frequenting the company of such scoundrels. I crossed over to London and, as my sojourn in that city, where for six months I dwelt in the most comfortable style, offers nothing that could be of any outstanding interest to your Lordships, you will permit me to pass quickly over this part of my story. I had maintained contact with no one in Paris but Fournier; however, she advised me of the hue and cry the landowner had raised over this paltry little robbery, and I finally resolved to put an end to this blathering: I took up pen and paper and very coolly informed him that she who had happened upon his money had also discovered other things, and that if he were determined to continue to search for the culprit, I would as bravely as possible endure my fate and very certainly depose, with the same judge who would question me upon what I had done with the contents of the small drawers, a detailed statement of what I had found in the larger ones. Our man fell as silent as a tomb; and as six months later their three-partied debauchery came broadly to light and as they themselves left France for security abroad, I returned to Paris and, must I avow my misbehavior? I returned, Messieurs, as poor as I had been before dispossessing d'Aucourt, and such were my straits I was obliged to put myself back in Madame Fournier's safekeeping. As I was no more than twenty-three at the time, I did not want for adventures; I am going to ignore those exterior to my domain and recount, with your Lordships' indulgent permission, only the ones wherein I know now that you take some interest.

A week after my return, a barrel brimming with shit was placed in the chamber appointed for pleasures. My Adonis arrives; he proves to be a saintly ecclesiastic, but one so habituated to those pleasures, so blasé, that he was no longer capable of being stirred save by the excesses I shall describe. I was naked when he entered. For a moment he regards my buttocks, then, after having fingered them rather brutally, he tells me to undress him and help him get into the barrel. I remove his garments, aid him to climb in, the old pig slides down into his element; a hole has been specially bored for the purpose and, fifteen seconds after having immersed himself, his prick, almost stiff, pops through the aperture; he orders me to frig it, covered as it is with filth and horrors. I do as I am told, he ducks his head down into the shit, splashes in shit, swallows shit, shouts, discharges, and, clambering out, trots off to immerse himself in a bath, where I leave him in the hands of two house servants who spend a quarter of an hour scrubbing him clean.

Another one appeared shortly afterward. I had shitted and pissed into a pot a week before and had carefully preserved the mixture; this period was necessary before matters reached the stage our latest libertine desired. He was a man of thirty-five, and my guess was that he was connected with finance. Upon entering he asked where the pot was; I handed it to him, he sniffed it experimentally.

"You're perfectly certain that was done a week ago?" he asked.

"Monsieur," I replied, "I am prepared to answer for its age; you will notice the first signs of mildew there, some moldiness near the edge."

"Why, indeed, it looks as if it will do very nicely," he agreed, "it's the mold I adore, you know. Never too moldy to suit me. Show me, if you please," he continued, "the pretty ass that shitted what we have here."

I presented it.

"That's it," said he, "put it right there opposite me so that I can see it while eating its creation."

We arrange ourselves, he samples a little tidbit, is thrilled by the taste, plunges directly ahead, and in no time has devoured that exquisite lunch, only interrupting his chewing to scan my bum; but there was no other episode, he did not even draw his prick from his breeches.

A month passed, another unusual fellow came to our door, and this one would deal with none but Fournier herself. What an object he selected, Great God! she had been sixty-eight summers, an erysipelas was eating every inch of her hide, and the eight rotten teeth decorating her mouth communicated so fetid an odor it was all but impossible to speak with her at a distance of under five yards; but it was these shortcomings and nothing else that enchanted the lover with whom she was to take a tumble. Most eager to observe the contest, I run to the spy hole: the Adonis was an elderly doctor, but younger nevertheless than she. He takes her in his arms, kisses her mouth for a good fifteen minutes, then, having her present an ancient, wrinkled ass such as you see on a very old cow, he kisses and sucks it avidly. A syringe is brought in, three half bottles of liqueur too; Aesculapius' worshiper loads his syringe and pumps the healing drink into the entrails of his Iris; she receives the potion, holds it, the doctor does not cease kissing her, he licks every square of her body.

"Ah, my friend," the old lady cries at last, "I can contain myself no longer, not another second, prepare yourself, dear friend, I'm going to have to give it back."

Salerno's scholar kneels, from his fly pulls forth a dark, wrinkled stub of a device, which he pounds and coaxes with emphasis, Fournier settles her great ugly ass upon his mouth, pushes, the doctor imbibes, a turd or two doubtless emerge with the liquid, he gasps but it all goes down, the libertine discharges and falls backward, dead drunk. 'Twas thus this debauchee satisfied two passions at a single stroke: his wine bibbery and his lewdness.

"One moment," said Durcet. "Those excesses always give me an erection. Desgranges," he pursued, "I fancy you possess an ass closely resembling the one Duclos has just figured; come apply it to my face."

The old procuress obeyed.

"Let it go, release it," Durcet said in a muffled voice, for he was speaking from between that pair of awe-inspiring buttocks. "Give it to me, buggress, never mind if it's not liquid, I am perfectly able to chew, and I always swallow whatever comes my way."

And the operation was concluded while the Bishop was performing a similar one with Antinoüs, Curval with Fanchon, and the Duc with Louison. But our four athletes, fully acquainted with all these extravagances and totally at their ease while committing them, performed with absolute effortlessness and even nonchalance: the four deposits were consumed without a single drop of fuck being shed in any quarter.

"Well, on with your story, Duclos, finish up for the day," the Duc said; "if we are no more tranquil than before, we are at least less impatient and better able to pay attention."

"Alas, Messieurs," our heroine answered, "I fear that the anecdote I have still to relate this evening is far too simple, too mild for the state you are in. 'Tis a pity, but no matter; its turn has come, it must keep its place." And she continued as follows:

The hero of the adventure was an old brigadier in the King's army; he had to be stripped to the skin, then swaddled like an infant; when he was thus prepared, I had to shit while he looked on, bring him the plate and, with the tips of my fingers, feed him my turd as if it were pap. Everything is done according to prescription, our libertine swallows it all and discharges in his swaddling clothes, the while simulating a baby's cry.

"Let us then have recourse to children," said the Duc, "since you leave us with a children's story; Fanny, my dear," he continued, "come to your old friend and shit in his mouth, and remember to suck his prick while you are about it, for it seems to have to discharge again."

"Let thy will be done," murmured the Bishop. "Come hither, Rosette; you have heard the orders given to Fanny. Then do as she."

"May the same orders apply to you," Durcet said to Hébé, who responded to his call.

"When in Rome," said the wise Curval, "do as the Romans do, my little one. Augustine, emulate your companions, cause simultaneously to flow both my fuck into your mouth and your shit into mine."

And all these things were done; upon this occasion, all those worthies came; from everywhere the sounds of farting and falling shit were to be heard, discharges too, and, much lust sated, they betook themselves to the table, their appetite was passing strong. But at the orgies, refinements were employed, the little ones were sent off to bed. Those delicious hours were spent with none but the elite fuckers, the four ladies-in-waiting, the four storytellers. Messieurs became completely drunk and performed horrors of such absolute filthiness that I should not be able to describe them without doing an injustice to the less libertine tableaux I have yet to offer my readers. Curval and Durcet were carried away unconscious, but the Duc and the Bishop, quite as cool as if nothing had happened, were perfectly able to pass the rest of the night indulging in their ordinary riot.

The Fourteenth Day

It was discovered upon that day that the weather had lent its approval to our libertines' infamous enterprises, and had removed them to an even greater distance from the probability they would be spied upon by mortal eyes; an immense blanket of snow had fallen, it filled the surrounding vale, seeming to forbid even to wild beasts access to our scoundrels' retreat; of all human beings, there was not one that existed who could dare hope to reach where they lay fast. Ah, it is not readily to be imagined how much voluptuousness, lust, fierce joy are flattered by those sureties, or what is meant when one is able to say to oneself: "I am alone here, I am at the world's end, withheld from every gaze, here no one can reach me, there is no creature that can come nigh where I am; no limits, hence, no barriers; I am free." Whereupon, thus situate, desires spring forth with an impetuosity which knows no bounds, stops at nothing, and the impunity that electrifies them most deliciously increases all their drunkenness. There, nothing exists save God and one's conscience; well, what weight may the former exert, of what account may God be in the eyes of an atheist in heart and brain? and what sway is the conscience to enjoy, what influence upon him who is so accustomed to vanquishing remorse, routing guilt, that so to do becomes for him a game, nay, a little pleasure? Luckless flock delivered to the murderous tooth of such villains; how would you have trembled had you not still been in ignorance of what lay in store for you!

That day was a festival, the second week had ended, the second marriage was to be celebrated; Messieurs were in a glad humor and thought not but to frolic on that holiday. The marriage to take place was that of Narcisse and Hébé, but, cruel fate it was also decreed that the bride and groom were both doomed to be punished that same evening; and thus, from the warm embrace of hymeneal pleasures they were to move directly to the more bitter lessons taught in this school, how unkind! Little Narcisse, who was not a dull fellow, remarked this irony, but Messieurs none the less proceeded to the usual ceremonies. The Bishop officiated, the couple was conjoined in very holy matrimony, and they were permitted to do to each other, before the public's eyes, all they wanted to do; but, who would have believed it? the order was of a too liberal scope, or too well understood, and the little husband, who had an aptitude for learning, perfectly delighted with the prospect before him but unable to introduce himself into his pretty wife, was however about to deflower her with his fingers, and would have, had he been given his way. Firm hands intervened just in time, and the Duc, making off with Hébé, thigh-fucked her on the spot, while the Bishop did likewise with Narcisse.

Dinner came next, the newly-wedded couple were admitted to the feast, and as they had been given and commanded prodigiously to eat, both upon leaving the table shitted handsomely, one for Durcet's benefit, the other for Curval's, who, after having swallowed those little products of childhood, smacked their lips and declared 'twas delicious.

Coffee was served by Augustine, Fanny, Céladon, and Zéphyr. The Duc bade Augustine frig Zéphyr, and the latter shit in the nobleman's mouth at the same time he discharged; the operation was a stunning success, so much so that the Bishop wanted to duplicate it with Céladon; Fanny attended to the frigging, and the little fellow received orders to shit in Monseigneur's mouth the moment he felt his fuck flow. But the young operatives succeeded less brilliantly than had their companions: Céladon was never able to co-ordinate his shitting with his discharge; however, as this exercise was merely a test of skill, and as the regulations made no mention of the subjects being obliged to excel in it, no punishment was inflicted upon him.

Durcet gleaned shit from Augustine, and the Bishop, firmly erect, had Fanny suck him while she shat in his mouth; he discharged, and as his crisis was violent, he brutalized Fanny somewhat but, unhappily, failed to find adequate grounds for having her punished, great as was his apparent wish to arrange something for her. A greater tease than the Bishop never lived; no sooner would he finish discharging than he would wish for nothing better than to see his pleasure-object gone to the devil; everyone was familiar with his character, and the little girls, the wives, and the little boys dreaded nothing as much as helping him to be rid of his fuck.

The midday nap over, they passed into the auditorium, the company distributed itself, and Duclos resumed the thread of her narrative:

I sometimes used to go into town for parties, said she, and as they were usually more lucrative, Fournier did her best to procure as many of that kind as she could.

She once sent me to the home of an elderly Knight of Malta who opened a kind of wardrobe filled with cubbyholes, each of which housed a porcelain chamber pot containing a turd; the old rake had made arrangements with a sister of his, abbess of one of the most considerable convents in Paris; that obliging girl, upon his request, every morning sent him a crate of fresh shit produced by her prettiest little pensionnaires. He filed away each performance according to a classifying system, and when I arrived he bade me take down such and such a number, and it proved to be the most venerable. I presented the pot to him.

"Oh yes," said he, "that belongs to a girl of sixteen, lovely as the day. Frig me while I eat her gift."

The entire ceremony consisted in twiddling his device and in dressing my bum before his eyes while he ate, then in replenishing the pot he had just emptied. He watched me do it, wiped my asshole clean with his tongue, and discharged while sucking my anus. After that, the wardrobe is closed and locked, I receive my pay, and our man, whom I visited at an early hour in the morning, curls up and goes blissfully back to sleep.

Another, more extraordinary in my opinion, was an elderly monk. He enters, demands eight or ten turds from the first person he sees, girl or boy, it's all the same to him. He mixes them into a paste which he next kneads like dough, bites into the lump and, eating at least half of it, discharges into my mouth.

A third, and of all the men I have met in my life he aroused the greatest disgust in me, a third, I say, ordered me to open my mouth wide. I was naked, lying upon a mattress on the floor, and he was astride me; he popped his stool into my mouth and the villain then lay down beside me, ate what I spat out, and sprayed his fuck over my teats.

"Well, well, that's a pleasant one!" cried Curval; "by Jesus, I do indeed believe I want to shit, I really must try to. Whom shall I take, Monsieur le Duc?"

"Who?" said Blangis. "By my faith, I recommend Julie, my daughter; she is right there under your hand. You are fond of her mouth, put it to use."

"Thank you for the advice," said Julie sullenly. "What have I done to have you say such things?"

"Why, since the idea upsets her," said the Duc, "and since she's a good girl, take Mademoiselle Sophie: she's healthy, pretty, and she's only fourteen, you know."

"Very well, it's to be Sophie, that's decided," said Curval, whose turbulent prick was beginning to gesticulate.

Fanchon approaches the victim, the poor little wretch's tears start to fall at once. Curval laughs lightly, brings up his great, ugly, and dirty behind, pushes it down upon that charming visage, and gives us the image of a toad about to insult a rose. He is frigged, the bomb bursts,

Sophie loses not so much as a crumb, and the crapulous magistrate's tongue and lips reclaim what he has launched; he swallows it all in just four mouthfuls while his prick is being rubbed upon the belly of the poor little creature who, the operation once over, vomits her very guts out, and directly upon the nose of Durcet who has come up posthaste to miss nothing, and who is frigging himself while being covered.

"Off you go, Duclos!" said Curval. "On with your tales, and rejoice at the effect of your discourses; do they not carry the day?"

And therewith Duclos resumed, warmed to the very cockles of her heart by the staggering success which had greeted her anecdote.

The man with whom I held correspondence directly after the one whose example has just seduced you, said Duclos, insisted that the woman he was presented have indigestion; in consequence, Fournier, who had given me no foreknowledge of the thing, had me, during dinner, swallow a certain laxative drug which softened what my bowels contained, indeed rendered it fluid, as if my stool had become transformed into the effect of an enema. Our man arrives and after several preliminary kisses bestowed upon the object of his whole veneration, which, by now, was becoming painfully inflated by gases, I beseech him to start without further delay; the injection is ready to escape, I grasp his prick, he pants, swallows everything, asks for still more; I furnish him with a second deluge, it is soon followed by a third, and the libertine's anchovy finally spits upon my fingers the unequivocal evidence of the sensation he has received.

The next day I treated with a personage whose baroque mania will perhaps find some worshipers amongst yourselves, Messieurs. First of all, he was installed in the room next to the one in which we ordinarily operated and in whose wall was that hole so conveniently placed for observations. He was left alone to arrange himself; a second actor awaited me in the adjoining chamber: he was a cab driver we had picked up at random and who was fully apprised of the situation; as I was too, our cast knew the various roles to perfection. It was a question of having the Phaëthon shit squarely opposite the hole, so that the libertine hidden on the other side of the partition would miss nothing involved in the spectacle. I catch the turd upon a plate, see to it that it lands intact, spread the driver's buttocks, press around his anus, I neglect nothing that can make shitting comfortable; as soon as my man has done all he has to do, I snatch up his prick and get him to discharge over the shit, and all that well within sight of our observer; finally, the package ready, I dash into the other room.

"Here you are, take it quickly, Monsieur," I exclaim, "it's nice and warm."

There is no necessity to repeat the invitation; he grasps the dish, offers me his prick, which I frig, and the rascal bolts everything I tender him while he exhales his fuck in tune with my diligent hand's elastic movements.

"And what was the driver's age?" Curval asked. "About thirty," Duclos answered.

"Why, that's nothing at all," said Curval. "Durcet there will tell you whenever you like that we once knew an individual who did the same thing, and with positively the same attendant circumstances, but with a man of sixty or seventy who had to be found in the lowest sewer of misery and filth."

"And, you know," said Durcet, "it's only pretty that way." The financier's little engine had been gradually lifting its head ever since Sophie's aspersion. "I shall at any given time be happy to do it with the eldest of veterans."

"You're stiff, Durcet," said the Duc, "don't deny it, for I know you: whenever you start that nasty boasting it's because your fuck is coming to a boil. So hold, good friend; though not so seasoned in years as you might like, still, to appease your intemperance, I offer you all I have in my entrails, and I believe you will find it enough to make a meal upon."

"Ah, by God's belly!" cried Durcet, "you always serve your guests well, my dear Duc."

The Duc entering Durcet's alcove, the latter kneels down before the buttocks which are to fill him to overflowing with good cheer; the Duc grunts once, twice, a prodigy tumbles out, the banker swallows and, transported by this crapulous excess, discharges while swearing he has never tasted so much pleasure.

"Duclos," said the Duc, "come do for me what I have done for our good friend."

"My Lord," our storyteller replied, "you will recall that I it this morning, and that you swallowed it."

"Why, yes, 'tis true," the Duc admitted. "Very well then, hither, Martaine, I must have recourse to you, for I want none of those children's asses; I feel my fuck readying to come, but, you know, it comes reluctantly, and so we need something out of the ordinary."

But Martaine's case was that of Duclos, Curval had gobbled her shit that morning.

"What! by fuck," cried the Duc, "am I then to fail to find a turd this evening?"

Whereupon Thérèse advanced and offered the dirtiest, the broadest, and the most stinking possible of asses you, dear reader, may hope to behold.

"Well, that will do, that will do perfectly," said the Duc, assuming the posture, "and if in my present disorder this infamous ass I've got here does not produce its effect, I don't know what I'll have to resort to."

Dramatic moment; Thérèse pushes; the Duc receives! and the incense was quite as dreadful as the temple whence it emerged, but when one is as stiff as the Duc was stiff, 'tis never excess of filth one complains of. Drunk with joy, the scoundrel swallowed every ounce, and directly into Duclos' face, for she was frigging him, shot the most indubitable proof of his male vigor.

Then to table; the ensuing orgies were devoted to the distribution of justice; that week there were seven delinquents: Zelmire, Colombe, Hébé, Adonis, Adelaide, Sophie, and Narcisse; the gentle Adelaide was granted no quarter. Zelmire and Sophie also bore away a few marks of the treatment they had undergone and, without giving further particulars, since circumstances do not permit us to give them yet, everyone retired to bed, and in Morpheus' arms recovered the strength requisite to make further sacrifices to Venus.

The Fifteenth Day

Rarely would the day following correction offer fresh signs of misbehavior. There were none upon this one, but as strict as ever in the
article of permission to shit in the morning, Messieurs granted this favor
to no one but Hercule, Michette, Sophie, and Desgranges, and Curval
came perilously near to discharging while watching the storyteller at
work. Not overmuch was accomplished at coffee, the friends were content
to fondle buttocks and to suck one or two assholes; the hour sounded,
everyone went promptly to establish himself in the amphitheater. Duclos
faced her audience once again and addressed the company in this wise:

There had lately come to Fournier's a little girl of twelve or thirteen,
the age preferred by that singular gentleman I mentioned to you; but I
truly doubt whether in a very long time he had debauched anything so
cunning, so innocent, or so pretty. She had fair hair, was tall for her years
and fit to be painted, her physiognomy was tender and voluptuous, her
eyes the loveliest one could hope to see, and in all her charming person
there was something sweet and intriguing which turned her into a very
enchantress. But what was the degradation to which the such a host of
attractions was about to be subjected! and how shameful was the debut
being prepared for them! She was the daughter of a tradesman in lin-
gerie, purveyor to the Palace and a man of comfortable means, and his
daughter surely had been destined for a happier fate than this of playing
the whore; but the more the man of whom it is a question was able, by
means of his perfidious seductions, to beguile his victims to their ruin,
and the more thorough the depravation into which he guided them, the
greater his pleasure, the fiercer his ecstasy. Little Lucile, directly after her
arrival, was scheduled to satisfy the disgusting and unclean caprices of a
man who, not merely content to have the most crapulous tastes, wished,
still better, to inflict them upon a maid.

He arrives at the house; he proves to be an old notary stuffed with gold
and who, together with his wealth, has all the brutality that avarice and
luxury excite when combined in a seasoned spirit. The child is exhibited
to him; pretty as she may be, his first reaction is disdain; he grumbles, he
grits his teeth, mutters and swears, and says that it damned well seems as
if one can no longer find a pretty girl in Paris; he demands, at last, whether
there is proof positive she is a virgin, he is assured that, yes, the article is
mint, Fournier offers to show it to him.

"What? look at a cunt, I? Madame Fournier! I, look at a cunt! I certainly hope you propose the thing in jest; have you noticed me spending
much time considering those objects since I have been coming to you?

I use them, to be sure, but in a manner which, I believe, attests no great fondness for them."

"Very well, Monsieur," Fournier said, "you will have to take the house's word for it: I declare that she is as much a maid as a child born five minutes ago."

They go upstairs together and, as you may well conceive, curious about the forthcoming tête-à-tête, I go and establish myself at the hole. Poor little Lucile was overcome by a shame only to be described by superlative expressions, hence not to be described at all, for those expressions are needed to represent the impudence, the brutality, and the ill-humor of her sixty-year-old lover.

"Well, what the devil are you doing there, are you a stone?" says he in a harsh voice. "Do I have to tell you to get your skirts up? I should have been looking at your ass two hours ago... Don't stand there like an idiot, move."

"But, Monsieur, what am I to do?"

"Why, Jesus Christ, are such questions still asked? What are you to do? Pick up your skirts and show me that damned ass I'm paying to see."

Lucile obeys, trembling like a leaf, and discloses a little white ass just as darling and sweet as would be that of Venus herself.

"Hum... looks all right," mutters the brute, "bring it nearer..."

Then, getting a firm grip upon the two buttocks and separating them forcefully:

"You're damned certain no one's ever done anything to you here?" "Oh, Monsieur, no one has ever touched me..."

"Very well. Now fart." "But, Monsieur, I can't."

"Well, try, for Christ's sake, make yourself fart."

She struggles, frowns, squints, a little breath of aromatic wind does escape and produces a little echo upon entering the infected mouth of the old libertine, who seems delighted.

"Do you want to shit?" he asks. "No, Monsieur."

"Well, I do, I've something copious to get rid of, if you're interested in the pertinent facts; so prepare yourself to satisfy this particular need of mine... take off your skirts."

They are removed.

"Lie down upon that sofa. Raise your thighs."

Lucile settles herself, the old notary arranges and poses her so that her wide-flung legs display her cunt to the fullest advantage, in which open and prominent position it may be readily employed as a chamber pot. So to use it was his heavenly intention; in order that the container respond more perfectly to what is to be demanded of it, he begins by widening it as much as possible, devoting both hands and all his strength to the task. He takes his place, pushes, a turd lands in the sanctuary Cupid himself would not have disdained having for a temple. He turns around, eyes his work, and with his fingers presses and thrusts the filthy excrement into the vagina and largely out of sight; he establishes himself astride Lucile once again, and ejects a second, then a third stool, and each is succeeded by the same ceremony of burial. Finally, having deposited his last turd, he inserts and tamps it down with such brutal zeal that the little one utters a cry, and by means of this disagreeable operation perhaps loses the precious flower, Nature's ornament, offered the child as a gift to Hymen. This was the moment at which our libertine's pleasure attained its crisis: to have filled the young and pretty cunt to overflowing with shit, to crowd it with shit and stuff it with yet more, that was his supreme delight: all the while in action, he opens his fly and draws out a species of prick, very flaccid it is, and he shakes it, and as he toils away in his disgusting manner, he manages to spatter upon the floor a few drops of thin, discolored sperm, whose loss may be credited solely to the infamies he has been perform-ing. Having concluded his business, he takes himself off, Lucile washes, and that is that.

Some time later, I found myself with another individual whose mania struck me as no less unpleasant: he was an elderly magistrate at the high court. One was obliged not only to watch him shit, no, there was more to it than that: I had to help him, with my fingers, facilitate the matter's emergence by pressing, opening, agitating, compressing his anus, and when once he had been freed of his burden, I had with utmost care to clean the soiled area with my tongue.

"Well, by God! there's a bit of taxing drudgery, I own," said the Bishop. "The four ladies you see here, and they are our wives, or our daughters, or our nieces, these ladies nevertheless have to perform that same chore every day, you know. And what the devil, I ask you, what the devil is a woman's tongue good for if not to wipe assholes? I frankly cannot think of any other use to put it to. Constance," the Bishop pursued, turning to the Duc's lovely wife, who happened to be upon his couch, "give Duclos a little demonstration of your proficiency in the thing; here you are, I'll offer you a very untidy ass, it hasn't been cleaned since this morning, I've been keeping it this way for you. Off you go, display your abilities."

And the poor creature, only too well accustomed to these horrors, executed them as a dutiful, a thoughtful wife should; ah, great God! what will not dread and thralldom produce!

"Oh, by Jesus," said Curval, presenting his ugly, beslimed asshole to the charming Aline, "she'll not be the only one to give examples of excel-lence. Get to work, little whore," said he to that beautiful and virtuous girl, "outdo your companion."

And the thing was accomplished.

"Why, Duclos," said the Bishop, "I think we might proceed now; we only wished to point out that your man's request had nothing of the unusual about it, and that a woman's tongue is fit to nothing if to wipe an ass."

The amiable Duclos fell to laughing and continued:

You will permit me, Messieurs, said she, to interrupt the catalogue of passions for an instant that I may apprise you of an event which has no bearing upon them; it has only to do with me, but as you have ordered me to recount the interesting episodes in my life, even when they are not related to the anthology of tastes we are compiling, I think that the following ought not to be passed by in silence.

I had been a great while at Madame Fournier's, had long since become the first ranked according to seniority, and in her entire entourage was the girl in whom she had the greatest confidence. It was I who most often arranged the parties and received the funds. Fournier had gradually taken the place of the mother I had lost, she had aided me in time of trouble, watched over my welfare, had written faithfully to me when I had been abroad in England, upon my return had as a friend opened her house to me when, in difficult circumstances, I desired to take asylum with her once again. Twenty times over she had lent me money, and often had never asked for it back. The opportunity arrived to show my gratitude and to respond to her limitless faith in me, and you shall judge, Messieurs, with what eagerness my soul opened itself to virtue's entrance and what an easy access it had thereinto: Fournier fell ill, and her first thought was to call me to her bedside.

"Duclos, my child, I love you," said she, "well you know it, and I am going to prove it by the absolute trust I am about to place in you. Despite your mind, which is not a good one, I believe in you incapable of wronging a friend; I am very ill, I am old, I do not know what is to become of me. But I may die soon; I have relatives who will of course be my heirs. I can at least leave them something, and want to: I have a hundred thousand francs in gold in this little coffer; take it, my child," said she, "here, I give it to you, but upon condition you dispose of this money in keeping with my instructions."

"Oh, my dear mother," said I, stretching forth my arms to her, "I beseech you, these precautions distress me; they shall surely prove needless, but if unhappily they were to prove necessary, I take oath and swear exactly to carry out your intentions."

"I believe you, my child," said she, "and that is why my eyes have settled upon you; that little coffer, then, contains one hundred thousand francs in gold; I have scruples, a few scruples, my dear friend, I feel remorseful for the life I have led, the quantity of girls I have cast into crime and snatched away from God. And so I wish to do two things by means of which it is my hope the divinity will be led to deal less severely with me: I think of charity now, and of prayer. You shall take fifteen thousand francs of this money, and you shall give it to the Capuchins on the rue Saint-Honoré, so that those good fathers will say a perpetual mass for the salvation of my soul; another sum, also of fifteen thousand francs, shall be set aside, and when I have closed my eyes, you shall surrender it to the curé of the parish and beg him to distribute it amongst the poor dwelling in this quarter of the city. Charity is a very excellent thing, my child; nothing better repairs in the eyes of God the sins we have committed in this world. The poor are His children, and beloved of Him is he who gives them succor and comfort; never is God more to be pleased than by alms distributed to the needy. There lies the true way of gaining Heaven, my child! As for the remainder, immediately I am dead you shall take sixty thousand francs to one Petignon, a shoemaker's apprentice in the rue du Bouloir: this poor lad is my son, he knows nothing of his origins: he is the bastard issue of adultery. Upon dying, I want the unhappy orphan to benefit from those marks of tenderness I have never shown him while alive. Ten thousand francs are left; I beg you to keep them, my dear Duclos, keep them as a feeble token of my fondness for you, may they be some kind of recompense for the trouble you shall have to take in seeing to the distribution of the rest of my fortune. And may this little sum aid you to resolve to abandon the dreadful trade we follow, a calling wherein there is no salvation, nor any hope. For one is not a whore forever."

Innerly delighted to be entrusted with such a handsome sum, and thoroughly determined, for fear of becoming confused by Fournier's intricate instructions upon sharing it, to keep her fortune intact and for myself alone, I produced a flood of very artificial tears and cast myself into the old matron's arms, reiterated many oaths of fidelity, and turned all my thoughts thenceforth to devising means to prevent the cruel disappointments certain to occur were a return to sound health to bring about a change in her resolutions. The means presented itself the very next day: the doctor prescribed and emetic, and as I was in charge of nursing her, it was to me he handed the medicine, drawing my attention to the fact the package contained two doses, and warning me to be sure to administer only one at a time because, were both given her, death would be the result; were the first to have no effect, or an insufficient one, the second could be employed later, if need be. I promised the doctor to take the greatest possible care, and immediately he had turned his back, banishing from my heart all those futile sentiments which would have stopped a timorous spirit, putting to rout all remorse and all frailty, and thinking exclusively of my gold, of the sweet charm of making it mine, and of the delicious titillation one experiences every time one concerts an evil deed, the certain prognostic of the pleasure it will give, dwelling, I say, upon all that and upon nothing else, I straightway dropped both doses into a glass of water and offered the brew to my dear friend's lips; she swallowed it down without a moment's delay and thereby, just as rapidly, found the death I had sought to procure her.

I cannot describe to you what feelings possessed me when I saw my scheme had succeeded; each of the retchings wherewith she exhaled her life produced a truly delicious sensation throughout my entire being; thrilled, I listened to her, I watched her, I was perfectly intoxicated with joy. She stretched her arms toward me, addressed me a last farewell, I was overwhelmed with pleasurable sensations, I was already forming a thousand plans for spending the gold. I had not long to wait; Fournier expired that same afternoon; the prize belonged to me.

"Duclos," said the Duc, "be truthful: did you frig yourself? did crime's piercingly voluptuous sensation attain your organs of pleasure?"

"Yes, my Lord, I confess it did; thanks to my prank I discharged five times before nightfall."

"It is then true," the Duc intoned in a loud and authoritative voice, "it is then true that crime has of itself such a compelling attractiveness that, unattended by any accessory activity, it may be itself suffice to inflame every passion and to hurl one into the same delirium occasioned by lubricious acts. Well, what say you?"

"Why, my Lord," Duclos answered, "I say I had my employer honorably buried, appropriated the bastard Petignon's inheritance, wasted not a penny on perpetual masses, nor did I bother to make a single charitable distribution, for, as a matter of fact, I have always beheld charity with the most authentic horror, regardless of the speeches, such as Fournier's, that I have heard pronounced in its favor. I maintain that there must be poor in this world, that Nature wishes that such there be, that she requires it, and that it is to fly in the face of her decrees to pretend to restore equilibrium, if it is disorder she wants."

"What's this!" said Durcet. "Do you then have principles, Duclos? I am very pleased to observe this in you; for, as you appear to realize, any relief given to misfortune, any gesture that lightens the load of the distressed, is a real crime against the natural order. The inequality she has created in our persons proves that this discordance pleases Nature, since 'twas she established it, and since she wishes that it exists in fortunes as well as in bodies. And as the weak may always redress matters by means of theft, the strong are equally allowed to restore inequality, or protect it, by refusing to give aid to the wretched. The universe would cease on the spot to subsist were there to be an exact similarity amongst all beings; 'tis of this disparity there is born the order which preserves, contains, directs everything. One must therefore take great care not to disturb it; moreover, in believing that it is a good thing I do for this miserable class of men, I do much ill to another, for indigence is the nursery to which the wealthy and powerful repair in quest of the objects their lust or cruelty needs; I deprive the rich man of that branch of pleasure when, by raising up the downtrodden, I inhibit this class from yielding to him. And thus my charities have done nothing but put one part of humankind very modestly in my debt and done prodigious harm to the other. Hence, I regard charity not only as something evil in itself, but, what is more, I consider it a crime against Nature who, having first made differences apparent to our eyes, has certainly never intended ideas of eliminating them to occupy our heads. And so, far from giving alms to the poor, consoling the widow, succoring the orphan, if it is according to Nature's true intentions I wish to act, not only do I leave these wretches in the state Nature put them into, but I even lend Nature a strong right arm and aid her by prolonging this state and vigorously opposing any efforts they make to change it, and to this end I believe any means may be allowed."

"What!" cried the Duc, "even stealing from and ruining them?"

"Oh my, yes," the financier replied, "even augmenting their number, since this class serves another, and since, by increasing the size of the one, though I may do it a modicum of harm, I shall perform a great service for the other."

"That, my friends, is a very harsh system indeed," said Curval. "Haven't you heard tell of the sweet pleasures of doing good unto others?"

"Abusive pleasures!" Durcet answered at once. "That delight you allude to is nothing like the one I recommend; the first is illusory, a fiction; the second is authentic, real; the first is founded upon vile prejudices, the second upon reason; the first, through the agency of pride, the most false of all our sensations, may provide the heart with a brief instant's titillation; the other is a veritable mental pleasure-taking, and it inflames every other passion by the very fact it runs counter to common opinions. In a word, one of them gets this prick of mine stiff," Durcet concluded, "and I feel practically nothing from the other."

"But must the one criterion for judging everything be our feelings?" asked the Bishop.

"The only one, my friend," said Durcet; "our senses, nothing else, must guide all our actions in life, because only their voice is truly imperious."

"But God knows how many thousand crimes may be the result of such a doctrine," the Bishop observed.

"God knows, yes, and do you suppose that matters?" Durcet demanded; "for it is enjoyable, isn't it? Crime is a natural mode, a manner whereby Nature stirs man, makes him to move. Why would you not have me let myself be moved by Nature in this direction as well as in the direction of virtue? Nature needs virtuous acts, and vicious ones too; I serve Nature as well by performing the one as when I commit the other. But we have entered into a discussion which could lead us far; suppertime is approaching, and Duclos has still ground to cover before completing her task. Go on, charming girl, pursue your way, and believe me when I say you have just acknowledged an act and a doctrine which make you deserving of our eternal esteem and of that of every philosopher."

My first idea when once my good patron had been inhumed was to assume the direction of her house and to maintain it on the same footing she had found so profitable. I announced this project to my colleagues, and they all, Eugénie above the rest, for she was my best beloved, I say, promised to regard me as their new mother. I was not too young to pretend to the title, being then nearly thirty and possessed of all the intelligence and good sense one must have to govern a convent. And so it is, Messieurs, that I shall conclude the story of my adventures not as a public whore, but as an abbess, pretty enough and still youthful enough sometimes, indeed often, to treat directly with our clients; and treat with them I did: I shall in the sequel take care to notify you each time I took personal charge of the problem at hand. All Fournier's customers remained to me, I knew the secret of acquiring additional ones: my apartments were kept very neat and clean, and an excessive submissiveness inculcated in my girls, whom I selected with discrimination, hugely flattered my libertines' caprices.

The first purchaser to arrive was an old treasurer of the Exchequer, a former friend of the departed Fournier; I gave him little Lucile, over whom he waxed very enthusiastic. His habitual mania, quite as filthy as disagreeable for his partner, consisted in shitting upon his Dulcinea's face, of smearing his excrement over all her features, and then of kissing her in this state, and of sucking her. Out of friendship for me, Lucile allowed the old satyr to have his way very completely with her, and he discharged upon her belly as he lay kissing and licking his disgusting performance.

Not long afterward, we had another; Eugénie was also assigned to cope with him. He had a barrel full of shit trundled in, plunged the naked girl into it, and licked every inch of her body, swallowing what he removed, and not finishing until he had rendered her as clean as she had been prior to her immersion. That one was a celebrated lawyer, a rich man and a very well-known one; he possessed, for the enjoyment of women, none but the most modest qualities, which lack he remedied by this species of libertinage he had lovingly cultivated all his life.

The Marquis de R***, one of Fournier's oldest clients, came shortly after her death to express his sorrow upon learning that she was no more; he also assured me he would patronize the house just as faithfully as before and, to convince me of his devotion, wanted to see Eugénie that same evening. This old rake's passion consisted in first bestowing prodigious kisses upon the girl's mouth; he swallowed all the saliva it were possible to drain from her, then kissed her buttocks for a quarter of an hour, called for farts, and finally demanded the major thing. After it had been done, he kept the turd in his mouth and, making the girl bend down over him, he had her embrace him with one hand and frig him with the other; and while he was tasting the pleasure of this masturbation and tickling her beshitted asshole, the girl had to eat the turd she had deposited in his mouth. Although he was prepared to pay very well, he used to find exceedingly few girls who were willing to cooperate in this little abomination, and that is why the Marquis would come regularly to me: he was as eager to remain one of my clients as I was to have him make frequent visits to my establishment...

At this point the Duc, very hot indeed, said that as the supper hour was hard upon them, he would like, before going to table, to execute the last-cited fantasy. And this is how he went about it: he had Sophie come to him, received her turd in his mouth, then obliged Zélamir to run up and eat Sophie's creation. This idiosyncrasy might perhaps have been a delight for anyone else but a child like Zélamir; as yet insufficiently mature, hence unable to appreciate the delicious, he manifested disgust only, and seemed about to misbehave. But the Duc threatened him with everything his anger might produce were the boy to hesitate another instant; the boy obeyed. The stunt struck the others as so engaging that each of them imitated it, more or less, for Durcet held that favors had to be parceled out fairly; was it just, he asked, for the little boys to eat the girls' shit while the girls went hungry? no, surely not, and consequently he had Zéphyr shit in his mouth and ordered up Augustine to eat the marmalade, which that lovely and interesting girl promptly did, her repast being as promptly succeeded by the racking vomitings.

Curval imitated this variation and received his dear Adonis' turd, which Michette consumed, not without a duplication of Augustine's histrionics; as for the Bishop, he was content to emulate his brother, and had the delicate Zelmire excrete a confiture Céladon was induced to gobble up. Accompanying all this were certain unmistakable signs of repugnance which, of course, were of the greatest interest to libertines in whose view the torments they inflict are unexcelled for inspiring satisfaction. The Bishop and the Duc discharged, the two others either could not, or would not, and all four went in to supper, where Duclos' action was the object of the loftiest encomiums.

"A very intelligent creature," observed the Duc, whose regard for the storyteller could not have been more profound. "Intelligent, I say, to have sensed that gratitude is nonsense, an hallucination, and that ties of fondness or of any other sort ought never either to make us pause or even to suspend the effects of crime, because the object which has served us can claim no right to our heart's generosity; that object employs itself only in our behalf, its mere presence humiliates a stout soul, and one must either hate of be rid of it."

"Very true," said Durcet, "so true that you'll never see a man of any wit seek to make others grateful to him. Fully certain that benevolence creates nothing but enemies, he practices only the arts his wisdom approves for his safety."

"One moment," interrupted the Bishop. "It is not at giving you pleasure he who serves you is laboring, but he is rather striving simply to gain an ascendancy over you by putting you in his debt. Well, I ask, what does such a scheme deserve? He does not say, as he serves you: I serve you because I wish to do good for you. No, he simply says: I put you under obligation in order to lower you and to raise myself above you."

"These reflections seem to me," said Durcet, "abundantly to prove how abusive are the services usually rendered, and how absurd is the practice of good. But, they will tell you, one does good for its own sake and for one's own; 'tis all very well for them whose weakness of spirit permits them to enjoy such little delights, but they who are revolted by them, as are we, great God! would be great fools to bother over such tepid stuff."

This doctrine having fired their imaginations, Messieurs drank a great deal, and the orgies were celebrated with vivacity and brio. Our like-thinking libertines sent the children off to bed, chose to spend a part of the night tippling with no one but the four elders and the four storytellers, and in their company to vie with one another in infamies and atrocities. As amongst these twelve individuals there was not one who was not worthy of the noose, the rack, and probably the wheel, I leave it to the reader to picture what was said and done. For from words they passed to deeds, the Duc got hot again, and I don't know just why it happened or how, but they say Thérèse bore the marks of his affection for weeks. However all that may be, let us allow our actors to move from these bacchanals to the chaste bed of the wife that had been prepared for each of the four, and let us see what transpired at the castle on the morrow.

The Sixteenth Day

Our heroes rose as bright and fresh as if they had just arrived from confession; but upon close inspection, one might have noticed that the Duc was beginning to tire a little. Blame for this could have been bestowed upon Duclos; there is no question but that the girl had entirely mastered the art of procuring him delight and that, according to his own words, his discharges were lubricious with no one else, which would corroborate the idea that these matters depend solely upon caprice, upon idiosyncrasy, and that age, looks, virtue, and all the rest have nothing whatever to do with the problem, that it all boils down to a certain tactfulness which is much more often found possessed by beauties in the autumn of life than by those others of no experience whom the springtide yet crowns with all her show.

There was as well another creature in the company who was beginning to make herself very amiable and to attract considerable attention; we are referring to Julie. She was already announcing signs of imagination, debauchery, and of libertinage. Astute enough to sense that she stood in need of protection, clever enough to caress those very persons for whom perhaps she did not at heart have a very great fondness, she contrived to become Duclos' friend, this in order to try to achieve some favor in the eyes of her father upon the others. Every time her turn came to lie with the Duc, she would adopt Duclos' techniques and emulate them so successfully, give proof of such skill, so much consideration, that the Duc was always sure of obtaining delicious discharges whenever he used those two creatures to procure them. Nevertheless, his enthusiasm for his daughter was waning prodigiously, and perhaps without Duclos' assistance, for the narrator consistently spoke well in her behalf, she would never have been able to occupy a place in his good graces. Her husband, Curval, was roughly of the same mind regarding her, and although, by means of her impure mouth and kisses, she still managed to wheedle a few discharges from him, disgust was dangerously near to becoming his predominating attitude toward her: one might even have said that the fires of his hostility were fanned by her impudicious caresses. Durcet held her in no esteem, she had not made him discharge more than twice since the adventures at Silling had started. And so it seemed that no one but the Bishop remained to her, and he indeed was fond of her libertine jargon, and judged hers to be the world's finest ass; and it is certain that Nature had furnished her with one as lovely as that which had been given to Venus. She hence made the most of that part, for she wished absolutely to please at whatever the price; as she felt an extreme need for a protector, she sought to cultivate Duclos.

At the chapel appeared that day no more than three persons: Hébé, Constance, Martaine; no one had been found at fault that morning. After the three subjects had ridded themselves of their freight, Durcet was taken by an impulse to be delivered of his. The Duc, who since early morning had been fluttering and buzzing about the financier's behind, seized the opportunity to satisfy himself and, sending away everyone but Constance, whom they kept as an aide, they encloseted themselves in the chapel. The Duc was appeased by the generous mouthful of shit he had from Durcet; these gentlemen, however, did not limit themselves to that prelude, and afterward Constance reported to the Bishop that they had performed infamies for a good thirty minutes. But what is one to expect? they had been friends, as I have said, since childhood, and since then had never ceased reminding one another of their schoolboy pleasures. As for Constance, she served no great purpose during this tête-à-tête; she wiped asses, sucked and frigged a few pricks, and that was about all.

They retired to the salon, the four friends conversed there for a while, and the midday meal was announced. It was, as usual, splendid and libertine and, after some lewd fingerings and bawdy colling, and a few scandalous remarks which spiced their lascivious byplay, they returned to the salon where Zéphyr and Hyacinthe, Michette and Colombe were waiting to serve coffee. The Duc thigh-fucked Michette, and Curval,

Hyacinthe; Durcet fetched shit out of Colombe, and the Bishop dropped some in Zéphyr's mouth; Curval, recollecting one of the passions Duclos had related the day before, was moved to shit in Colombe's cunt; old Thérèse, who was supervising the day's quartet, placed Colombe in a suitable posture, and Curval performed. But as he produced colossal turds, proportioned by the immense quantity of victuals wherewith he stuffed himself every day, almost all of his creation spilled upon the floor and it was, so to speak, only superficially he beshitified that pretty little virgin cunt which had not, one would have thought, been intended by Nature to be used for such disagreeable pleasures.

Deliciously frigged by Zéphyr, the Bishop yielded his fuck philosophically, joining, to the delights he was feeling, that other offered by the wonderful spectacle being enacted about him. He was furious, he scolded Zéphyr, he scolded Curval, he fumed and grumbled at everyone. He was given a large glass of elixir whereby they hoped his faculties would be restored, Michette and Colombe settled him upon a sofa for his nap and stood by him while he slept. He woke amply refreshed and, in order to give him additional strength, Colombe sucked him for a moment or two; his engine responded by showing some positive signs of life, and they went next into the auditorium. The Bishop had Julie on his couch; as he was rather fond of her, the sight of her improved his mood. The Duc had Aline; Durcet, Constance; the Président, his daughter. Everything being ready, the lovely Duclos installed herself upon her throne and began thus:

There is nothing more untrue than to say money acquired through crime brings no happiness. No greater error, I assure you; my house prospered; never had so many clients come there during Fournier's administration. It was then an idea occurred to me, a rather cruel idea, I admit, but one which, I dare flatter myself in believing, will not be altogether displeasing to your Lordships. It seemed to me that when one had not done unto another the good one ought to have done him, there existed a certain wicked voluptuousness in doing him ill, and my perfidious imagination suggested a little libertine mischief at the expense of that same Petignon, my benefactress' son, and the individual to whom I had been charged to surrender a fortune which, doubtless, would have proven very welcome to that wretch, and which I had already begun to squander upon trifles. The occasion arrived in this way: the poor shoemaker, married to a girl of his own class and sort, had, as the unique fruit of this unfortunate marriage, a daughter of about twelve; I had been to told that, together with all the lovely features of childhood, she possessed all the attributes of the most tender beauty. This child, then being brought up humbly but nevertheless as carefully as the parents' indigence could permit, for she was the joy and light of their life, this child, I say, struck me as a capture well worth making.

Petignon had never come to the house, he knew nothing of the legal rights that were his; immediately after Fournier had mentioned him to me, my first move was to obtain information about him and those around him, and thus I learned that he possessed a treasure in his house. At about the same time the Comte de Mesanges came to me; a famous libertine of whose profession Desgranges will doubtless have at least one occasion to speak, the Comte requested me to provide him with a maid of no more than thirteen at whatever the price. I don't know what he wanted with the article, for he passed for a man with very rigorous scruples when it was a question of women, but his proposal was simple enough: after having, with the help of experts, established her virginity, he said he would buy her from me for a fixed sum and, from this moment on, she would be his, he would be her master, and, he added, the child would be removed, perhaps permanently, from France.

As the Comte was one of my habitués -- you shall see him enter upon the scene very soon -- I set everything in motion in an effort to satisfy him; Petignon's little daughter seemed to me exactly what he needed. But how was I to get my hands upon her? The child never left the house, it was there she received her education; so carefully was she supervised, so circumspectly that I began to despair of the prize. Nor was I able to employ that masterful debaucher of girls I mentioned some time ago; he was away from the city, and the Comte was urging me to hurry. And so I could find only one means, and this means could not have been better designed to serve the secret little wickedness which was impelling me to commit this crime, for the crime was aggravated by it. I resolved to embroil husband and wife in some kind of difficulty, to strive to get both of them imprisoned, and in this way removing some of the obstacles between the child and myself, I fancied I would encounter no trouble in luring her into the snare. Wherewith I consulted one of my friends, a skilled barrister whom I trusted and who was capable of anything; I put him on the scent, he went directly to work: he compiled information, made inquiries, located creditors, aroused them, supported their claims, in brief, it took less than a week to lodge husband and wife behind bars. From then on everything was easy; an adroit scout accosted the little girl, who had been abandoned to the care of some poor neighbors, she was led to me. Her appearance perfectly matched the reports I had received: she had a sweet, a soft, a fair skin, the roundest little ornaments, charms perfectly shaped... In a word, it were difficult to find a prettier child.

As she cost me, all told, about twenty louis, and as the Comte wished to pay a flat price for her and, having once bought her outright, wished neither to hear another word about the transaction nor have further dealings with anyone, I let her go for one hundred louis; it being essential to my interests that no one get wind of my part in the thing, I was content with a net profit of sixty louis, given my attorney another twenty to create just that kind of stir which would prevent her parents from having news of their daughter for a long time. But news did reach them; the girl's disappearance was impossible to conceal. The neighbors who had been guilty of negligence excused themselves at best they were able, and as for the poor shoemaker and his wife, my man-of-law managed matters so well that they were never able to remedy the accident, for both of them died in jail some eleven years after I had made off with my prey. I reaped a twofold advantage from that little mishap, since it simultaneously assured me undisputed ownership of the child I was negotiating to sell and also assured me 60,000 francs for my trouble. As for the child, the Comte was satisfied with her; never did he encounter any difficulties, never did I, no, not a word was said, and it is more than likely Madame Desgranges will finish her story; I know no more about it. But it is high time to return to my own adventures, and to the daily events which may offer you the voluptuous details we have listed.

"Oh by God!" Curval broke in, "I adore your prudence -- there is something in your method which bespeaks a meditated villainy, an orderliness which pleases me more than I can say. And as for that rascality of having given the final stroke to a victim you had until then only scratched...ah, that seems to me a refinement of infamy which deserves a place amongst our own masterpieces."

"I wonder, however," said Durcet, "whether I might not have done worse, for, after all, those parents could have obtained their release from jail: there are God knows how many fools in the world who think of nothing but helping such people. Those eleven years during which they lingered on meant worry for you."

"Monsieur," Duclos answered him, "when one does not enjoy the influence you have in society, when for one's little pranks one is forced to employ second-rate allies, caution often becomes very necessary, and at such times one dares not do all one would like."

"True, true," said the Duc, "she was unable to go any further." And the amiable creature took up the thread of her narrative.

Dreadful it is, my Lords, said that accomplished girl, to have still to relate turpitudes in kind like to those I have been speaking about for several days; but you have required that I cite everything which might bear an even faint resemblance to this great genre of abomination, and insisted too that I suppress nothing. But three more examples of these filthy atrocities and we shall then continue on to other fantasies.

The first I propose to mention is that of an elderly administrator of the demesne, a man of I should say three score and six. He would have the woman remove all her clothes and, after having fondled her buttocks with less delicacy than brutality, he would promptly order her to shit on the floor before his eyes, in the middle of the room. When he had relished this prospect, he would in his turn step up and lay his own turd next to hers, then, combining them with his hands, he would oblige the girl to get down on all fours and eat the hash, and while eating she was to present her behind, which she was to have brought to the party in a most maculated state. While the ceremony was in progress he would manualize himself, and used to discharge as soon as the last bite had vanished. There were few girls, as your Lordships may readily believe, who would consent to submit themselves to such vile use, but all the same the administrator had to have them youthful and healthy... Well, I used somehow to find what he needed, for everything is to be found in Paris; however, the merchandise came dear.

The second example of the three I have left to cite of this species also required what might be termed a furious docility on the girl's part; but as this libertine wished her to be extremely young, I had less trouble supplying him: children lend themselves to these games more readily than do mature women. I located a pretty little shopgirl of twelve or thirteen for the gentleman whom we are about to see in action; he arrives, has the girl take off only the clothing that covers her from the waist down; he toys with her behind for a brief moment, gets her to fart a little, then gives himself four or five copious enemas which, subsequently, he obliges his little partner to receive into her mouth and to swallow as the cascade tumbles out of his rectum. Meanwhile, as he was seated astride her chest, he employed one hand to frig a rather thick device and with the other he kneaded and pinched her mons veneris and, in order that he might do it all as he wished, he had to have a completely hairless cunt to work with. This individual wanted to continue on even after his sixth explosion, for his discharge was not yet achieved. The little girl, convulsed with vomiting, managed to articulate her disinclination to proceed, she begged to be spared, he laughed at her, introduced a seventh draught, expelled it, and his fuck finally did indeed flow.

An elderly banker provides us with the last example of these unclean horrors -- or rather the last example of a man for whom they were the principal element, for I must warn you that we shall have repeated occasion to behold them as accessories to the main endeavor. He had to have a handsome woman, but one aged from forty to forty-five and with an extremely flabby pair of breasts. Immediately they were encloseted together he would have her remove all she was wearing from the waist up, and having brutally handled her teats, would cry: "These damned cow dugs! what good are such tripes, eh? What are they for if not to wipe my ass upon?" Next he would squeeze them, twist them, wring them, twine them together, tug them, pound them, spit upon them, kick and trample them, all the while saying, what a damned infamous thing is a flabby tit, he could not imagine what Nature had intended these bags of skin for, why had Nature spoiled and dishonored woman's body with these things? etc. After all these preposterous remarks he would remove every stitch of his clothing. My God, what a body! how am I to describe it to your

Lordships! 'Twas no more than a disgusting ulcer, a running sore, pus seemed to cover him from head to toe, I could smell his infected odor even in the adjacent room from which I was observing the ritual; such was the relic which, however, the woman had to suck.

"Suck?" said the Duc.

Yes, Messieurs, Duclos affirmed, suck from top to bottom, every square inch of his body had to be sucked, the tongue was to neglect nothing, to explore it all; I had forewarned the girl, but apparently in vain. She'd not expected this; for upon catching sight of that ambulatory corpse she shrank away in horror.

"What's this, bitch?" says he, "do I disgust you? Why, that's a pity, for you're going to have to suck me, your tongue is going to have to lick every part of my body. Come now! Stop playing the shy little girl; others have done the job, see to it that you do it as well as they. That's enough, I tell you, no nonsense."

Ah, they speak true when they say that with money one can accomplish anything; the poor creature I had given him was in the extremest misery, and her was a chance to earn two louis: she did everything she was told, and the podagrous old scoundrel, thrilled by the sensation of a tongue straying softly over his hideous body and sweetening the bitter pungency devouring him, frigged himself voluptuously during the entire operation. When it had been completed, and completed, as you may well suppose, despite the horrible revulsion of the luckless woman, when it was done, I say, he had her lie down upon the floor on her back, he got astride her, shitted all over her bubs, and squeezing his performance between them, he used them, first one, then the other, to wipe his ass. But with what regards his discharge, I saw not so much as a hint, and some time later I learned that it required several such operations before he could be induced to part with his liquor; and as he was a man who seldom twice visited the same place, I saw no more of him and, to tell the truth, was by no means sorry.

"Upon my soul," the Duc observed, "I find the conclusion of that man's operation very reasonable indeed, and I too have never been able to believe that teats were intended for anything but bumwipes."

"One may be certain," said Curval, who at the moment was rather brutally handling those belonging to the sweet and tender Aline, "one may be certain indeed that a tit is a very infamous object. I never catch sight of one without being plunged straightway into a rage. Upon seeing these things I experience a certain disgust, a certain repugnance assails me... only a cunt has a worse and more decided effect upon me."

And so saying, he flung himself into his closet, dragging Aline by the breast and calling out to Sophie and Zelmire, his quatrain's two girls, and Fanchon to follow him. One cannot be sure of precisely what he did, but a loud scream, clearly a woman's, was heard by the others in the auditorium, and shortly afterward came the bellowings that usually indicated the Président had discharged. He returned. Aline was weeping and held a kerchief over her breast, and as these events rarely created any stir, or, at best, a few chuckles, Duclos went on with her story at once.

Several days later I myself took care, said she, of an old monk whose mania, more wearying to the hand, was rather less revolting to the stomach. He presented me with a great ugly behind covered with skin as tough as bull's hide and as wrinkled as a dried leaf; the task here was to knead his ass, to handle it, drub and thump it, squeeze it with all my strength, but when I reached the hole, nothing I did seemed sufficiently violent: I had to catch up the skin, rub it, pinch it, roll it between my fingers, use my nails, and it was thanks only to the vigor of my ministrations his fuck finally emerged. He attended to his own frigging while I abused his bum and vent, and I was not even obliged to show him my ankles. But that man must have made a very fierce and old habit of those manipulations, for his behind, although slack and hanging, was nevertheless upholstered by a skin as horny and as thick as leather.

The next day, doubtless having spoken highly of me and my dexterity to his friends in the monastery, he sent one of his brethren upon whose ass one had to bestow slaps, indeed blows of the hand, and stout ones at that; but this new ecclesiastic, more of a libertine and an examiner, preceded his rite by a meticulous inspection of his woman's buttocks, and my ass was kissed, nuzzled, tongued ten or twelve times over, the intervals being filled by blows aimed at his. When his hide had taken a scarlet hue, his prick got bravely up, and I can certify that it was one of the noblest engines I had palmed and fingered until that day. He put it into my hand, recommending that I frig it while continuing to slap him with the other.

"Unless I am gravely mistaken," said the Bishop, "we have finally reached the article of passive fustigation."

"Yes, Monseigneur," replied Duclos, "we have, and as my task for today has been fulfilled, you will consent to allow me to postpone until tomorrow the beginning of fustigatory tastes; we shall devote several soirees to dealing with them."

As nearly half an hour remained before supper, Durcet said that, to stimulate his appetite, he wished to give his entrails a few rinses; his announcement made something of an impression upon the women, who began to tremble; but sentence had been decreed, there was no revoking it. Thérèse, his servant that day, assured him she introduced the tube with wonderful skill; from the assertion she passed to the proof, and as soon as the little financier felt his bowels loaded, he singled out Rosette, beckoned her to him, and bade her open her mouth. There was some balking, a few complaints and a word or two of pleading, but the capital thing was obedience and, sure enough, the poor little girl swallowed two eruptions, having been granted the option or regurgitating them afterward. And regurgitate them she did, and soon. Happily, the supper bell sounded, for the financier was getting ready to begin again. But the prospect of a meal changed the disposition of their Lordships' minds, they went to taste different pleasures. A few turds were lodged on a few bubs at the orgies, and a great deal of shit was gleaned from asses; within the assembly's full view, the Duc consumed Duclos' turd, while that splendid girl sucked him, and while the bawdy fellow's hands roamed here and there, his fuck came out in a thick spray; Curval having imitated him with Champville, the friends began to speak of retiring for the night.

The Seventeenth Day

The terrible antipathy the Président had for Constance was manifest in daily outbursts: he had spent the night with her, having made a bilateral arrangement with Durcet, to whom he returned her the following morning with the most bitter complaints about her behavior.

"Since because of her condition," said he, "the society seems loath to expose her to the customary punishments for fear she be brought to bed before the time we have appointed to pluck her fruit, at least, by Jesus," said he, "we should find some means or other to punish the whore when she chooses to play the fool."

Ah, but what is that spirit of evil that inhabits libertines? Some glimmer of it may be obtained by analyzing Constance's prodigious fault. O reader, what do you suppose it was had waked Curval's wrath? Even worse than you may have dreamt: she had most unfortunately turned her front toward her master when he had called for her behind, ah yes, and such sins are not to be forgiven. But the worst part of her error was her denial of the fact; she declared, and there seemed some basis to her contention, that the Président was calumniating her, that he was seeking naught but her downfall, that she never lay with him but he would invent some such untruth; but as the law was precise and formal on this point, and as women's speeches were given no credence whatever in that society, but one question remained posed: how in future was this female to be chastised without risking the spoilage of the fruit ripening in her? It was decided that for each misdemeanor she would be obliged to eat a turd and, consequently, Curval insisted that she begin there and then. Approbation greeted his demand. They were at the time breakfasting in the girls' quarters, word was dispatched, Constance was summoned, the Président shitted in the center of the room, and she was enjoined to approach his creation on hands and knees and to devour what the cruel man had just wrought. She cast herself upon her knees, yes, but in this posture begged pardon, and her solicitations went unheeded; Nature had put bronze in those breasts where hearts are commonly to be found. Nothing more entertaining than the grimaces and affected airs to which the poor woman resorted before capitulating, and God knows how amused Messieurs were by the scene. At last, however, decisive action had to be taken, Constance's very soul seemed to burst before she was half done, but it had all to be done nevertheless, and every ounce disappeared from the tiles on the floor.

Excited by what he was witnessing, each of our friends, while watching, had himself frigged by a small girl; Curval, singularly aroused by the operation and benefiting from the wondrous skill of Augustine's enchanted fingers, feeling himself nigh to overflowing, called to Constance, who had scarcely finished eating her mournful breakfast.

"Hither, come to me, whore," said he, "after having bolted some fish one needs a little sauce, good white sauce. Come get a mouthful."

Well, there was no escaping that ordeal either, and Curval, who, while operating, was having Augustine shit, opened the sluices and let fly into the mouth of the Duc's miserable wife, and at the same time swallowed the fresh and delicate little turd the interesting Augustine had hatched for him.

The inspection tours were conducted, Durcet found shit in Sophie's chamber pot. The young lady sought to excuse her error by maintaining that she had been suffering from indigestion.

"Not at all," Durcet observed as expertly he handled the turd, "that is not true: indigestion produces diarrhea, soup, my dear, and this article looks very sound to me."

And straightway taking up his baneful notebook, he wrote down the name of that charming creature, who did her best to hide her tears and refrained, at Durcet's request, from deploring her situation. Everyone else had abided by the regulations, but in the boys' chamber, Zélamir, who had shitted the previous evening during the orgies and who had been told not to wipe his little bum, had tidied it up none the less, disobeying the orders. These were the crimes of the first magnitude: Zélamir's name was inscribed. Notwithstanding the boy's delinquency, Durcet kissed his ass and had himself sucked for a brief moment, then Messieurs passed on to the chapel, where they beheld the shitting of two subaltern fuckers, Aline, Fanny, Thérèse, and Champville. The Duc received Fanny's performance in his mouth, and he ate it, the Bishop's mouth caught the two fuckers' turds, one of which the prelate devoured, Durcet made Champville's his own, and the Président, despite his discharge, gulped down Aline's with all the avidity he had exhibited while consuming what Augustine had done for him.

Constance's scene had heated the company's imagination, for it had been a long time since Messieurs had indulged themselves in such extravagances so early in the morning. Dinner conversation dealt with moral science. The Duc declared he could not understand why in France the law smote so heavily against libertinage, since libertinage, by keeping the citizens busy, kept them clear of cabals and plots and revolutions; the Bishop observed that, no, the laws did not exactly aim at the suppression of libertinage, but at its excesses. Whereupon the latter were analyzed, and the Duc proved that there was nothing dangerous in excess, no excess which could justly arouse the government's suspicion, and that, these facts being clear, the official attitude was not only cruel but absurd; what other word was there to describe bringing artillery to bear upon mosquitoes?

From remarks they progressed to effects, the Duc, half-drunk, abandoned himself in Zephyr's arms, and for thirty long minutes sucked that lovely child's mouth while Hercule, exploiting the situation, buried his enormous engine in the Duc's anus. Blangis was all complacency, and without stirring, without the flicker of an eyelash, went on with his kissing as, virtually without noticing it, he changed sex. His companions all gave themselves over to other infamies, and then they sallied forth to coffee. As they had just played a multitude of silly little pranks, the atmosphere was calm, and this was perhaps the one coffee hour during the entire four months' outing when no fuck was shed. Duclos was already upon the tribune, awaiting the company; when everyone had taken his place, she addressed her auditors in this wise:

I had recently suffered a loss in my house, and it had a deep effect upon me in every sense. Eugénie, whom I loved with a passion and who, thanks to her most extraordinary complaisance in whatever was connected with the possibility of earning me money, had been especially useful to me, Eugénie, I say, had just been spirited away. It happened in the strangest fashion: a domestic, having first paid the price settled upon, came to conduct her, so he said, to a supper that was to be held outside the city; her participation in the affair would be worth seven or eight louis. I was not at the house at the time the transaction took place, for I should never have allowed her to leave with someone I didn't know, but the domestic applied directly to her and she agreed to go... I have never seen her since.

"Nor shall you ever again," said Desgranges. "The party proposed was her last one, and it will be my agreeable task to add the denouement to that lovely girl's history."

"Great God!" cried Duclos. "She was so beautiful, that girl... only twenty, her face was so sweet, she was so delicate..."

"And, one might add, her body was the most superb in Paris," Desgranges said. "All those charms conspired to her undoing, but go on with what you were saying, let's not become mired down in circumstances."

Lucile was the girl who took her place, Duclos continued, both in my heart and in my bed, but not in the household's activities, for she had not by any means Eugénie's submissive temper nor her great understanding.

All the same, it was to her hands I entrusted, not long afterward, that certain Benedictine prior who used to pay me a visit now and again, and who had in past times been wont to frolic with Eugénie. After the good father had warmed her cunt with his tongue and thoroughly sucked her mouth, the major phase of the process began: Lucile took the whip and plied it lightly over his prick and balls, and he discharged from a limp machine; the gentle rubbing, the mere application of the lash produced his orgasm. His greatest pleasure used to consist in watching the girl slash with her whip at the drops of fuck as they spattered from his prick.

The next day, I myself took charge of a gentleman upon whose bare behind one had to lay one hundred carefully counted whip strokes; before his beating he prepared himself by kissing one's behind and while being lashed he frigged himself.

A third, with whom I had dealings some time later, had even heavier demands to satisfy; he also gilded each detail with additional ceremony: I received notice of his intended arrival a week in advance, and during that time I had to avoid washing any part of my body, and above all was to spare my cunt, my ass, my mouth; and furthermore, as soon as I learned he was to come, I selected three cat-o'-nine-tails and immersed them in a pot full of mixed urine and shit, and kept the whips soaking there until he presented himself. He was an elderly collector of the salt tax, a man of considerable means, a widower, without children, and he treated himself to such parties all the time. The first thing that interested him was to determine whether I had scrupulously abstained from ablutions, as he had enjoined me; I assured him I had followed his instructions to the letter; he wished proof, and began by applying a kiss to my lips. This experience must have convinced him, for he then suggested we go up to the room, and I realized that had he, upon kissing me, discovered I had cleansed my mouth in any way at all, he would not have wished to continue with the party. We go up together, as I say, he regards the whips steeping in the pot, then, bidding me undress, he sets to sniffing every part of my body, above all the orifices he had expressly forbidden me to wash; as I had honored his prescription in perfect faith and in every article, he doubtless discovered the aroma he desired to be there, for I saw him grow restless, appear anxious to be off, and heard him exclaim: "Ah, by fuck, that's what I want, that's just what I want!" I proceeded to fondle his ass: it was sheathed in what positively resembled boiled leather in color, texture, and toughness. After having spent a minute caressing, handling, poking about those gnarled, storm-beaten hindquarters, I seized a cat-o'-nine-tails and, without drying it, I gave him ten stinging cuts, putting all my strength into the blows; but this beginning produced not a tremor, he not only remained impassive, but my blows put not so much as the faintest scratch upon that unshakable citadel. Having opened with this prologue, I sank three of my fingers into his anus, took firm hold, and began to rattle him with might and main, but our man was insensible to the same degree here as elsewhere; my struggles failed to be acknowledged by so much as a sigh. These two initial ceremonies completed, his turn came to act; I lay belly down upon the bed, he knelt, spread my buttocks, and alternately shot his pilgrim tongue into this hole and into the other, and they, one may be sure, were, in keeping with his instructions, not entirely unaromatic. After he had done considerable sucking, I took up another whip, laid on a second time and socratized him again, he knelt as before and returned to his licking, and so it went, each of us doing his part at least fifteen times over. Finally, giving me further instructions and bidding me guide my movements in consonance with the state of his prick, which I was to observe carefully but which I was not to touch, when next he knelt I unleashed my turd. It shot squarely into his face, he fell back, exclaimed that I was an insolent creature, and discharged while frigging himself and while uttering cries that might have been heard in the street had I not taken the precaution of drawing the shutters. But the turd fell to the floor, he did naught but stare at and smell it, neither putting it in his mouth nor even touching it; he had received at least two hundred lashes, and I may assure you... his body bore not a trace of what it had sustained, his horny ass, fortified by years of rude usage, betrayed not the least mark.

"Well, by God's bum button!" chortled the Duc, "there's an ass, Président, worth as much as the curiosity you drag about."

"Oh yes, yes," said Curval, a stammer in his voice, for Aline was frigging him, "yes indeed, that fellow seems to have both my buttocks and my tastes, for, you know, I am infinitely opposed to the use of the bidet, but I prefer a longer abstinence: I usually set the period at a minimum of three months."

"Président, your prick's stiff," the Duc said.

"Do you think so?" Curval replied. "Faith, you'd best consult Aline here, she'll be able to tell you what's what, as for myself, you know, I'm so accustomed to that particular state of affairs that I rarely notice when it ends or when it begins. There is only one thing I can tell you with complete confidence, and that is that at this very moment I'd hugely like to have my hands upon a very impure whore; I'd like her to present me with a bucketful of shit, fill a bowl to above the rim, I'd like her ass to stink from shit, I'd like her cunt to smell like a beach covered with dead fish. But hold! Thérèse, O thou whose filth is as old as the hills, thou who since baptism hast not wiped thine ass, and whose infamous cunt breeds a pestilence three leagues on every side, come bring all that to my nose's delectation, I beg thee, and to that put a fine wet turd, if 'twould please thee."

Thérèse approaches, with foul and evil charms, with parts disgusting and withered and wounded she rubs the magistrate's face, upon his nose she excretes the desired turd, Aline does frig amain, the libertine discharges, and Duclos therewith resumes the story she has to tell.

An elderly rascal, who used to receive a new girl every day for the operation I am going to describe, besought one of my friends to persuade me to visit him, and at the same time I was given information about the ceremony regularly performed at the lecher's home. I arrive, he examines me with a phlegmatic glance, the kind of glance one encounters among habitual libertines, and which in an instant arrives at an infallible estimate of the object under scrutiny.

"I have been told you have a fine ass," said he in a drawling tone, "and as for the past sixty years I have had a decided weakness for fine cheeks, I should like to see whether there is any foundation to your reputation... lift your skirts."

That last phrase, energetically spoken, sufficed as an order; not only did I offer a view of the treasure, but I moved it as near as possible to his connoisseur's nose. At first I stand erect, then little by little I bend forward and exhibit the object of his devotion in every form and aspect most apt to please him. With each movement, I feel the old scoundrel's hands wander over the surface, scouting the terrain, probing the geography, sometimes creating a more consolidated effect, sometimes attempting to give it a more generous cast, compressing here, broadening there.

"The hole is ample, very ample," says he, "appearances attest a furious sodomistical prostitution."

"Alas, Monsieur," I concede, "we are living in an age when men are so capricious that in order to please them, one must indeed be prepared for virtually anything, and consent to it all."

Whereupon I feel his mouth glue itself hermetically to my asshole, and his tongue strive to penetrate into the chasm; I seize my opportunity, as I have been advised, and profiting from my situation, slide out, directly upon his probing tongue, the warmest, most humid, densest eructation. The maneuver displeases him not at all, but on the other hand does little to animate him; finally, after I have unleashed half a dozen winds, he gets to his feet, leads me to his bed, and points to an earthenware crock in which four cat-o'-nine-tails are marinating. Above the crock hang several whips suspended from gilded hooks.

"Arm yourself," murmurs the roué, "take a cat-o'-nine-tails and one of those other weapons, here is my ass. As you observe, it is dry, lean, and exceedingly well seasoned. Touch it."

I do so; he continues:

"You notice," says he, "that it's old, toughened by severe treatment, and it's not to be warmed save by the most incredibly excessive attacks. I am going to keep myself in this posture," and while speaking he stretched out upon the bed and rested his knees on the floor. "Employ those instruments, first one, then the other, now the cat-o'-nine-tails, now the whip. This is going to take a little time, but you will receive an unequivocal sign when the climax approaches. As soon as you see something out of the ordinary happening to this ass of mine, hold yourself in readiness to imitate what you see it doing; we will then exchange places, I shall kneel down before your splendid buttocks, you shall do what you shall have observed me do, and I'll discharge. But above all do not become impatient; I warn you once again: this business is not to be accomplished in haste."

I begin, I alternate weapons in accordance with the prescription. But, my God! what nonchalance, what stoicism! I was drenched in sweat; that my strokes be more freely applied he had suggested I roll my sleeves to above the elbow. Three-quarters of an hour went by and I was still beating him, putting every ounce of strength into my blows, sometimes tearing at his stubborn flesh with the cat-o'-nine-tails, sometimes with the steel-tipped thongs, three-quarters of an hour, I say, and it seemed as if I had got nowhere. Still, silent, our lecher was as quiet as death; one might say he was mutely savoring the interior stirrings of delight quickened by this ordeal, but there was no outward sign of pleasure, not a single indication of pleasure's influence even upon his skin. I proceeded. By and by I heard a clock strike two and realized I had been at work three whole hours; then all of a sudden I see his rump rise, his buttocks part, I slash and send my thongs whistling between certain crevices; a turd emerges, falls, I whip away, my blows send the shit flying to the floor.

"Courage," I say to him, "we're within sight of port."

And then my man gets up in a rage; his prick, hard and in fierce revolt, is glued to his belly.

"Do what I did," says he, "imitate me, I need nothing now but shit and you'll have my fuck."

I promptly adopt the position he has just abandoned, he kneels as he said he would, and into his mouth I lay an egg which I have been holding in store for him for three days. As he receives it his fuck leaps, and he flings himself backward, shouting with joy, but without swallowing, and indeed without keeping the turd in his mouth for more than a second. In conclusion let me say, Messieurs, that, your Lordships excepted, for you are without doubt superior examples of this species, I have seen few men convulse more frantically, few who have manifested a more trenchant delight; he came nigh to swooning as he gave vent to his fuck. That séance was worth two louis.

But no sooner did I return to the house than I found Lucile come to grips with another old chap who, without having laid a finger upon her, without any preliminaries, had simply ordered her to fustigate him from the small of the back to just above the knees; Lucile was using a cat-o'-nine-tails soaked in vinegar, was endowing her blows with all the force she could muster, and this individual ended his ritual by having her suck him. The girl knelt before him when he gave her the signal and, adjusting his old weary balls so that they dangled upon her teats, she took the flabby engine in her mouth whereinto the chastened sinner hastened to weep for his transgressions.

And Duclos having therewith put a period to what she had to relate that day, and the supper hour not yet having arrived, Messieurs delivered themselves of a few smutty comments while waiting.

"You must be done up, Président," gibed the Duc. "I've seen you discharge twice today, and you're hardly accustomed to such feats of liberality."

"Let's wager on a third," replied Curval, who was pawing Duclos' buttocks.

"Why, certainly, as much as you like and as often," the Duc returned.

"And I ask for only one condition," Curval said, "and that is to be allowed to do whatever I like."

"Oh, I'm afraid not," the Duc answered, "for you know very well that there are certain things we have mutually promised not to do before the appointed time indicated on our schedules: having ourselves fucked was one of them -- before proceeding to that we were, according to prior agreement, to wait until some example of that passion were cited to us, but by your common request, gentlemen, we ceded on that point and suspended the restriction. There are many other pleasures and modes of taking them we ought to have forbidden ourselves until the moment they were embodied in story, and which we have instead tolerated, provided the experiments are conducted in privacy -- in, that is to say, either our closets or our bedchambers. You, Président, surrendered yourself to one with Aline just a short while ago; did she utter that piercing scream for no reason at all? and has she no motive for keeping her breast covered now? Very well then, choose from amongst those mysterious modes, or from one of those we permit in public, and I'll wager one hundred louis you'll not be able to derive your third from one of those legitimate sources."

The Président then asked whether he might be allowed to repair to the boudoir at the end of the corridor and to take along the subjects he deemed necessary to success; his request was granted, although it was stipulated that Duclos would have to be witness to the goings on, and that her word would be accepted upon the existence of the discharge or upon Curval's failure to produce it.

"Agreed," said the Président, "I accept the conditions."

And by way of a preliminary, he had Duclos give him five hundred lashes within view of the assembly; that accomplished, he led away his dear and devoted friend Constance, in whose behalf his colleagues besought Curval to do nothing which might damage her pregnancy; the Président also took with him his daughter Adelaide, Augustine, Zelmire, Céladon, Zéphyr, Thérèse, Fanchon, Champville, Desgranges, Duclos, of course, and three fuckers besides.

"Why fuck my eyes!" exclaimed the Duc, "there was nothing in the bargain that said he could recruit an army."

But the Bishop and Durcet took the Président's side in the matter of manpower and firmly reminded Blangis that the terms of the wager included no limitation upon numbers. The Président led his band away, and at the end of thirty minutes, an interval the Bishop, Durcet, and the Duc, with the few subjects remaining to them, did not pass in holy orison, thirty minutes later, I say, Constance and Zelmire returned in tears, and the Président reappeared soon afterward with the rest of his force; Duclos then related the mighty things he had done, paid homage to his vigor, and certified that in all fairness and justice he merited the crown of myrtle. The reader will kindly allow us to suppress the text of Duclos' report, for the architecture of our novel bids us conceal the precise circumstances of what transpired in that remote boudoir; but Curval had won his wager, and that, we consider, is the essential point.

"These hundred louis," he remarked upon receiving them from the Duc, "will be useful in paying a fine which, I fear, shall soon be levied upon me."

And here is still another thing the explanation of which we pray the reader will permit us to postpone until the appropriate moment arrives; for the time being he need but observe how that rascal Curval would anticipate his misdeeds well in advance, and how, with unruffled calm, he would accept the fact that they would bring down upon him certain and merited punishment, a fatal necessity he faced unflinchingly and with a proud smile.

Between that time and the opening of the next day's narrations absolutely nothing out of the ordinary transpired, and therefore we propose to conduct the reader to the auditorium at once.

The Eighteenth Day

Beautiful, radiant, bejeweled, grown more brilliant with each passing day, Duclos thus started the eighteenth session's stories:

A tall and stoutly constructed creature named Justine had just been added to my entourage; she was twenty-five, five feet six inches tall, with the husky arms and solid legs of a barmaid, but her features were fine all the same, her skin was clear and smooth, and she had as splendid a body as one might wish. As my establishment used to be swarming with a crowd of those old rakehells who are incapable of experiencing the faintest pleasure save when heated by the lash or torture, I thought that a pensionnaire like Justine, furnished as she was with the forearm of a blacksmith, could be nothing but a very real asset. The day following her arrival, I decided to put her fustigatory talents to the test; I had been given to understand she wielded a whip with prodigious skill, and hence matched her against an old commissar of the quarter whom she was to flog from chest to shin and then, on the other side, from the middle of his back to his calves. The operation over with, the libertine simply hoisted the girl's skirts and planted his load upon her buttocks. Justine comported herself like a true heroine of Cythera, and our good old martyr avowed to me afterward that I had got my hands on a treasure, and that in all his days no one had ever whipped him as that rascal had.

To demonstrate how much I counted upon her contribution to our little community, a few days later I arranged a meeting between Justine and an old veteran of many a campaign on the fields of love; her required a round thousand strokes all over his body, he would have no part of himself spared, and when he was afire and nicely bloodied, the girl had to piss into her cupped hand and smear her urine over those areas of his body which looked to be most seriously molested. This lotion rubbed on, the heavy labor had to be begun again, then he would discharge, the girl would carefully collect his fuck, once again using her cupped hand, and she would give him a second massage, this time employing the balm wrung from his prick. Another triumph for my new colleague, and every succeeding day brought her further and more impassioned acclaim; but it was impossible to exercise her arm on the champion who presented himself this time.

This extraordinary man would have nothing of the feminine but womanish dress: the wearer of the costume had to be a man; in other words, the roué wanted to be spanked by a man got up as a girl. And what was the instrument she had to use on him? Don't think for a moment he was content with a birch ferule or even a cat, no, he demanded a bundle of osier switches wherewith very barbarously one had to tear his buttocks. Actually, this particular affair seeming to have somewhat of the flavor of sodomy, I felt I ought not become too deeply involved in it; but as he was one of Fournier's former and most reliable clients, a man who had been truly attached to our house in fair weather and in foul, and who, further-more, might, thanks to his position, be able to render us some service, I raised no objections and, having prettily disguised a young lad of eighteen who sometimes availed us of his services and who had a very attractive face, I presented him, armed with a handful of switches, to his opponent.

And a very entertaining contest it was -- you may well imagine how eager I was to observe it. He began with a careful study of his pretended maiden, and having found him, evidently, much to his liking, he opened with five or six kisses upon the youth's mouth: those kisses would have looked peculiar from three miles away; next, he exhibited his cheeks, and in all his behavior and words seeming to take the young man for a girl, he told him to fondle his buttocks and knead them just a little rigorously; the lad, whom I had told exactly what to expect, did everything asked of him.

"Well, let's be off," said the bawd, "ply those switches, spare not to strike hard."

The youth catches up the bundle of withes and therewith, swinging right merrily, lays fifty slashing blows upon a pair of buttocks which seem only to thirst for more; already definitely marked by those two score and ten stripes, the libertine hurls himself upon his masculine flagellatrice, draws up her petticoats, one hand verifies her sex, the other fervently clutches her buttocks, he knows not which altar to bow down before first, the ass finally captures his primary attentions, he glues his mouth to its hole, much ardor in his expression. Ah, what a difference between the worship Nature is said to prescribe and that other which is said to outrage her! O God of certain justice, were this truly an outrage, would the homage be paid with such great emotion? Never was woman's ass kissed as was that lad's; three or four times over his lover's tongue entirely disappeared into the anus; returning to his former position at last, "O dear child," cried he, "resume your operation."

Further flagellation ensued, but as it was livelier, the patient met this new assault with far more courage and intrepidity. Blood makes its appearance, another stroke brings his prick bounding up, and he engages the young object of his transports to seize it without an instant's delay. While the latter manipulates him, he wishes to render the youth the same service, lifts up the boy's skirts again, but it's a prick he's now gone in quest of; he touches it, grasps, shakes, pulls it, and soon introduces it into his mouth. After these initial caresses, he calls for a third round of blows and receives a storm of them. This latest experience puts him in a perfect tumult; he flings his Adonis upon the bed, lies down upon him, simultaneously toys with his own prick and his companion's, then presses one upon the other, glues his lips to the boy's mouth and, having succeeded in warming him by means of these caresses, he procures him the divine pleasure at the same moment he is overwhelmed himself: both discharge in harmony. Enchanted by the scene, our libertine sought to placate my risen indignation, and at last coaxed a promise from me to arrange for further delights in the same kind, both with that young fellow and with any others I could find for him. I attempted to work at his conversion, I assured him I had some charming girls who would be happy to flog him and who could do so quite as well; no, said he, none of that, he would not so much as look at what I had to offer him.

"Oh, I can readily believe it," said the Bishop. "When one has a decided taste for men, there's no changing, the difference between boy and girl is so extreme that one's not apt to be tempted to try what is patently inferior."

"Monseigneur," said the Président, "you have broached a thesis which merits a two-hour dissertation."

"And which will always conclude by giving further support to my contention," said the Bishop, "because the fact that a boy is superior to a girl is beyond doubt or dispute."

"Beyond contradiction too," Curval agreed, "but nevertheless one might still inform you that a few objections have been here and there raised to your doctrine and that, for a certain order of pleasures, such as Martaine and Desgranges shall discuss, a girl is to be preferred to a boy."

"That I deny," said the Bishop with emphasis, "and even for such pleasures as you allude to the boy is worth more than the girl. Consider the problem from the point of view of evil, evil almost always being pleasure's true and major charm; considered thus, the crime must appear greater when perpetrated upon a being of your identical sort than when inflicted upon one which is not, and this once established, the delight automatically doubles."

"Yes," said Curval, "but that despotism, that empire, that delirium born of the abuse of one's power over the weak..."

"But the same is no less true in the other case," the Bishop insisted. "If the victim is yours, thoroughly in your power, that supremacy which when using women you think better established than when using men, is based upon pure prejudice, upon nothing, and results merely from the custom whereby females are more ordinarily submitted to your caprices than are males. But give up that popular superstition for a moment, view the thing equitably and, provided the man is bound absolutely by your chains and by the same authority you exert over women, you will obtain the idea of a greater crime; your lubricity ought hence to increase at least twofold."

"I am of the Bishop's mind," Durcet joined in, "and once it is certain that sovereignty is fully established, I believe the abuse of power more delicious when exercised at the expense of one's peer than at a woman's."

"Gentlemen," said the Duc, "I should greatly prefer you to postpone your discussions until mealtime. I believe these hours have been reserved for listening to the narrations, and it would seem to me proper were you to refrain from employing them upon philosophical exchanges."

"He is right," said Curval. "Go on with your story, Duclos."

And that agreeable directress of Cytherean sport plunged again into the matter she had to relate.

Another elderly man, said she, this one a clerk at parliament, paid me a call one morning, and as during Fournier's administration he had been accustomed to dealing exclusively with me, tradition bade him solicit an interview with me now. Our conference consisted in slapping his face with gradually increasing force, and in frigging him the while; that is to say, one had at first to slap him gently, then, as his prick assumed consistency, one slowly augmented the force of one's blows, and finally a series of truly bone-shattering cuffs would provoke his ejaculation. I had so well apprehended the precise nature of his eccentricity that my twentieth slap brought his fuck springing out.

"The twentieth, you say? Why, by Jesus," exclaimed the Bishop, "my prick would have gone dead limp by the third."

"There you are, my friend," the Duc declared, "to each his own peculiar mania, we ought never blame nor wonder at another's; tolerance, I say. Say on, Duclos, give us one more and have done."

My last example for the evening, said Duclos, originally was told to me by one of my friends; she had been living for two years with a man whose prick never stiffened until one had first bestowed a score of fillips upon his nose and tweaked it, pulled his ears till they bled, and bitten his buttocks, chewed his prick, nipped his balls. Aroused by these potent preliminary titillations, his prick would shoot aloft like a stallion's, and while swearing like a demon he'd almost always discharge upon the visage of the girl at whose hands he had been receiving this exhilarating treatment.

Of all that had been recounted during that afternoon's sitting, only the masculine fustigations had affected their Lordships' brains which, now passing hot, were only cooled after prolonged use of the fantasy which had fired their enthusiasm; thus it was the Duc had Hercule flog him until blood seeped from his pores, Durcet employed Invictus to the same effect, the Bishop made use of Antinoüs, and Bum-Cleaver ministered to Curval.

The Bishop, who had done nothing that day, did finally discharge at the orgies, they say, while eating the turd Zélamir had been preparing for forty-eight hours. And then they went to bed.

The Nineteenth Day

That morning, after having made some observations upon the shit the subjects were producing for lubricious purposes, the friends decided that the society ought to try something Duclos had spoken of in her narrations: I am referring to the suppression of bread and soup from all the tables save Messieurs'. These two articles were withdrawn, and replaced by twice the former quantity of fowl and game. They hoped to remark some improvement, and in less than a week an essential difference in the community's excrements was indeed perceived: they were more mellow, softer, dissolved more readily, had an infinitely more subtle flavor, and the friends discovered that d'Aucourt's advice to Duclos had been that of a consummate libertine thoroughly penetrated with an appreciation of such matters. It was pointed out, however, that this new diet might have some effect upon breaths:

"Well, what does that matter?" asked Curval, to whom the Duc had addressed his objection; "'tis very faulty reasoning to maintain that, to give pleasure, a woman's mouth or a youth's must be absolutely clean and sweet smelling. Setting aside all idiosyncrasy for a moment, I most willingly grant you that he who requires stinking breath and a foul mouth is moved by depravation only, but for your part you must grant me that a mouth entirely bereft of odor gives not the slightest pleasure when kissed. There must always be some kind of spice to the thing, some flavor there, for where's the joy if it's not stung alive? the joy's asleep, I say, and it's only waked by a little filth. However clean may be the mouth, the lover who sucks it assuredly does an unclean thing, and there is no doubt at all in his mind that it is that very uncleanness that pleases him. Give a somewhat greater degree of strength to the impulse and you'll want that mouth to be impure. If it fall short of smelling of rot or the cadaver, well, be patient, the taste will develop, but that it have nothing but an odor of milk and honey or infancy, that, I tell you, is insufferable. And so the diet we're going to subject them to will, at the worst, lead not at all to corruption, but only to a certain alteration, and that is all that's necessary."

The morning searches brought nothing to light... the youngsters were keeping strict watch over their conduct. No one requested toilet permission, and the company sat down at table. Adelaide, one of the servants at the meal, having been enjoined by Durcet to fart in a champagne glass, and having been unable to comply, was directly entered in the fatal book by her unfeeling husband who, since the beginning of the week, had been continually endeavoring to find her at fault.

Coffee came next; it was handed round by Cupidon, Giton, Michette, and Sophie. The Duc thigh-fucked Sophie, and while so doing had her shit upon his hand; the nobleman took that pretty little packet and smeared it over his face, the Bishop did precisely the same thing with Giton and Curval with Michette, but as for Durcet, he popped his little device into Cupidon's mouth as that charming boy squeezed out his turd. There were, notwithstanding, no discharges and, having risen from their nap, Messieurs went to hear Duclos.

A man we had never seen previously, said that amiable whore, came to the house and proposed a rather unusual ceremony: he wished to be tied to one side of a stepladder; we secured his thighs and waist to the third rung and, raising his arms above his head, tied his wrists to the uppermost step. He was naked. Once firmly bound, he had to be exposed to the most ferocious beating, clubbed with the cat's handle when the knots at the tips of the cords were worn out. He was naked, I repeat, there was no need to lay a finger upon him, nor did he even touch himself, but after having received a savage pounding his monstrous instrument rose like a rocket, it was seen to sway and bounce between the ladder's rungs, hovering like a pendulum and, soon after, impetuously launch its fuck into the middle of the room. He was unbound, he paid, and that was all.

The following day he sent us one of his friends whose buttocks and thighs, member and balls had to be pricked with a golden needle. Not until he was covered with blood did he discharge. I handled that commission myself, and as he constantly shouted to me to thrust deeper, I had almost to bury the needle in his glans before seeing his fuck squirt into my palm. As he unleashed it, he thrust his face against mine, sucked my mouth prodigiously, and that was all there was to it.

A third -- and he too was an acquaintance of his two predecessors -- ordered me to flail every bit of his body with nettles. I soon had him-streaming blood, he eyed himself in a mirror, and it was not before he saw his body reduced to a scarlet shambles that he let fly his fuck, without touching anything, fondling anything, without requiring anything else of me.

Those excesses entertained me hugely, I took a secret delight in participating in them; and all my whimsical clients were equally delighted with me. It was at about the period of those three scenes that a Danish nobleman, having been sent to me for pleasure parties of a very different character, which others have been designated to discuss, had the imprudence to arrive at my establishment with ten thousand francs in diamonds, as much in other gems, and five hundred louis in cash. The prize was too handsome to be allowed to get away; between the two of us, Lucile and I managed to rob the Dane of his last sou. He thought to lodge a complaint, but as I used to pay a heavy bribe to the police, and as in those days one did just about whatever one pleased with gold, the gentleman was ordered to put a stop to his wailing, and his belongings became mine, or rather most of them did, for, in order to assure myself of little clear title to that treasure, I had to yield a few precious stones to the minions of the law. Never have I committed a theft, and I would have you remark this interesting fact, without encountering some stroke of good fortune the next day; this latest windfall was a new client, but one of those daily clients one may truly consider a brothel's bread and butter.

This individual was an old courtier who, weary of the homages he used unendingly to receive in the palaces of kings, like to visit whores and enjoy a change of role. He wanted to start with me; very well, said I, and we began without further ado. I had to make him recite his lessons and recite his little speeches, and every time he made a mistake, he had to get down on his knees and receive, sometimes on his knuckles, sometimes on his behind, vigorous blows of a leathern ferule such as the regents use in schoolrooms. It was also my task to keep a sharp eye out for signs of emotion; once the fire had been lit, I would snatch up his prick and shake it skillfully, scolding him all the while, calling him a little libertine, a very scurvy fellow, a worry to His Majesty, and other childish names which would cause him to come very voluptuously. The identical ceremony was to be executed five times each week at my establishment, but always with a different and properly instructed girl, and for this service I received a stipend of twenty-five louis per month. I knew so many women in Paris I had no trouble promising him what he asked and keeping my word; I had that charming pupil in my house for a decade, toward the end of which period he decided to pack his bags and go off to pursue his studies in hell.

However, I too was aging with the passing years, and although I had the kind of face which retains its beauty, I was beginning to notice that my visitors were men more and more often conveyed to me by whim and accident. I still had some staunch and dependable suitors even at thirty-six, and the rest of the adventures in which I took a hand belong to the period between that time and my fortieth year.

Though thirty-six years old, as I say, the libertine, whose mania I am going to relate in closing today's session, would have nothing to do with anyone else. He was an abbot of sixty or thereabouts, for I received no one but gentlemen of a certain age, and every woman who would like to seek her fortune in our trade will doubtless see fit to impose the same rules barring irresponsible youth from her house. The holy man arrives, and as soon as we are closeted together he begs to see my bum.

"Ah, yes, there's the world's finest ass," he says admiringly. "But, unfortunately, that is not the apparatus which is to provide me with the pittance I intend to consume. Here, take hold," says he, putting his buttocks into my hands, "that's the source whence all good things do come... Be so kind as to help me shit."

I bring up a porcelain pot and place it upon my knees, the abbot backs toward me, stoops, I press his anus, pry it open, and, to be brief, agitate it in every way I think likely to hasten his evacuation. It takes place, an enormous turd fills the bowl, I offer it to its author, he seizes it, precipitates himself upon it, devours it, and discharges after fifteen minutes of the most violent flogging which I administer upon the same behind that shortly before laid such a splendid egg for his breakfast. He swallowed it all; he had so nicely judged the situation that his sperm did not appear until the last mouthful vanished. All the while I plied my whip, I excited him with steady stream of comments such as: "Well, then, little rascal, what's this?" and, "Why, here's a nasty little chap, can you really eat shit that way?" and, "I'll teach you, you funny little whoreson bastard; perform such disgraceful things, will you?"

And it was by dint of these actions and speeches that the libertine attained the summit of joy.

At this point, Curval was moved to give the company a before-supper demonstration in fact of what Duclos had described in words. He summoned Fanchon, she extracted shit from him, and the libertine devoured it while the old sorceress drubbed him with all the strength of her skinny but sinewed arm. That lubric exhibition having inspired his confreres, they began hunting for shit wherever any might be found, and then Curval, who had not discharged, mixed the rest of his turd with Thérèse's, whom he had excrete without further ado.

The Bishop, accustomed to making use of his brother's delights, did the same thing with Duclos, the Duc with Marie, little Durcet with Louison. It was atrocious, why, it was unthinkable to employ such decrepit old horrors when such pretty objects stood ready at one's beck and call; but, oh how well 'tis known, satiety is born in the arms of abundance, and when in the very thick of voluptuous delights one takes an even keener pleasure in torments.

These unclean stunts over and done with, and the doing having cost only one discharge, and 'twas the Bishop who produced it, the friends went to table. Having involved themselves in a series of foul activities, they thought best not to change horses in midstream, and for the orgies would have only the four old duennas and the four storytellers; everyone else was packed off to bed. Their Lordships said so many things, did so many more, that all four came like geysers, and our libertine quartet did not retire until overcome with drink and exhaustion.

The Twentieth Day

Something very humorous indeed had occurred the night before: absolutely drunk, the Duc, instead of gaining his bedchamber, had installed himself in young Sophie's bed, and despite all the child could say, for she knew perfectly well what he was doing violated the rules, he would not be budged, and continued with great heat to maintain he was damned well where he belonged, namely, in his bed with Aline, who was listed as his wife for the night. But as he was allowed certain privileges with Aline which were still forbidden with the little girls, when he sought to put Sophie in the posture that favored the amusements of his choice, and when the poor child, to whom no one had as yet ever done such a thing, felt the massive head of the Duc's prick hammer at her young behind's narrow gate and contrive to batter a thoroughfare, the poor little creature fell to uttering dreadful screeches, and, leaping up, fled naked about the room. The Duc followed hard on her heels, swearing like a demon, still mistaking her for Aline. "Buggress!" he roared, "dost think it the first time?" And fancying he has overtaken her and has her at last, he falls upon Zelmire's bed, thinking it his own, and embraces that little girl, supposing Aline has decided to behave reasonably. The same proceedings with Zelmire as a moment ago with Sophie, because the Duc most decidedly wishes to attain his objective; but immediately Zelmire perceives what he is about, she imitates her companion and duplicates her resistance, pronounces a terrible scream, and leaps away.

However, Sophie, the first to take to flight, collects her wits and, seeing full well that there is but one way to put an end to this quid pro quo, sets off in search of light and some cool-headed individual capable of restoring order, and consequently she thinks to look for Duclos. But

Duclos had behaved like a pig at the orgies and got herself blind drunk, Sophie comes upon her stretched out unconscious in the middle of the Duc's bed, and fails absolutely to bring her to her senses. Desperate, knowing not to whom under such circumstances she may apply, hearing all her comrades calling for help, she gathers up courage and enters Durcet's apartment; the financier is lying with his daughter, Constance, and Sophie blurts out what has been happening. Constance at any rate did rise from the bed, despite the efforts the drunken Durcet made to restrain her by saying he wanted to discharge; she took a candle and accompanied Sophie to the girls' chamber: she discovered the poor little dears, all in their nightgowns, clustered in the center of the room, and the Duc pursuing now one of them, now another, still persuaded he was dealing with no one but Aline, whom he swore was become a witch that night and had many shapes. Constance finally showed him his error, and entreating him to allow her to guide him back to his room, where, she assured him, he would find a very submissive Aline only too eager to do all he chose to demand of her, the Duc who, thoroughly besotted and acting as always in the very best of faith, really had no other design than to plant his staff in Aline's ass, let himself be taken to her; that lovely girl was there to greet him, and he went to bed; Constance withdrew from the room, and calm was restored generally.

They laughed very heartily all the next day over that nocturnal adventure, and the Duc declared that if, by great misfortune, he were in such a case to happen all accidentally to obliterate a maidenhead, he would not, so it seemed to him, be liable or justly subject to a fine because, intoxicated, he could not be held accountable for his actions; but, oh no, the others assured him, he was mistaken in that, he would indeed have to pay.

They breakfasted amidst their sultanas as usual, and all the little girls avowed they'd been furiously afraid. Not one, however, was found at fault despite the night's alarms; similarly, everything was in order in the boys' quarters, and coffee, like dinner, offering nothing extraordinary, they passed into the auditorium where Duclos, entirely set to rights after the previous evening's riot, amused the company with the following five episodes:

It was once again I, Messieurs, who went on the stage in the play I am about to describe to you. The other person in the drama was a medical man; the doctor's first act was to examine my buttocks, and as he came to the conclusion they were superb, he spent more than an hour doing nothing but kissing them. He at last confessed his little foibles: they were all connected with shit and shitting, as I had surmised, and knowing what was expected of me, I adopted the appropriate posture. I filled the white porcelain pot I used to employ for this sort of enterprise. Immediately he is the master of my turd, he raises it to his mouth and begins tucking it away; he has no sooner taken a bite than I pick up a bull's pizzle -- that was the instrument wherewith I was to caress his bum -- I shout threats and imprecations at him, then strike, scold him for the dreadful things he is wont to do, the infamous things, and without heeding me, the libertine swallows the last mouthful, discharges, and is off with the speed of light, having tossed a louis onto the table.

Shortly afterward another came to the house, and I entrusted him to Lucile, who had truly to struggle to make him discharge. He had first of all to be sure the turd that was to be served up to him originated with an old beggar woman, and to convince him, I had to have the old crone operate before his own eyes. I gave him a venerable dame of seventy, covered with ulcers and wens and other signs of erysipelas, and whose last tooth had fallen from her gums fifteen years before. "Good, that's excellent," said he, "precisely the sort I need." Then, enclosing himself with Lucile and the turd, that equally skillful, complacent, and determined girl had to excite him to the point at which he would eat that very mature lump. He sniffed it, stared at it, even touched it, but that was all, he could not seem to make himself go further. Whereupon Lucile, having to resort to something more persuasive than rhetoric, thrust the fire tongs into the fire and, drawing them out red-hot, announced she proposed to burn his buttocks if he did not obey her on the spot and eat his luncheon. Our man trembles, has another try: the same disgust, he recoils. As good as her word, Lucile lowers his breeches and, bringing to light an ass of very evil aspect and scarred all over, discolored and withered by operations in this same kind, she deftly singes his cheeks. The lecher swears, Lucile applies her iron again, now scorches and finally produces a very definite and sufficiently profound burn in the middle of his ass; pain screws him up to resolution at last, he bites off a mouthful, additional burnings excite him further, and little by little the work is completed. The downing of the last nibble of shit coincided with his discharge, and I have seen exceedingly few as violent; he emitted loud cries and screams, howled like a wolf and rolled on the floor; I thought he had been seized by a frenzy or an attack of epilepsy. Delighted with the patient understanding he had encountered in our house, the libertine promised to be my regular customer, provided I would give him the same girl but a different old woman each time.

"The more repulsive the source," said he, "the better you'll be paid for the yield. You have simply no idea," he added, "to what lengths my depravity carries me; I hardly dare acknowledge it to myself."

Upon his recommendation, one of his friends visited us the next day, and this individual's depravity carried him, in my opinion, a great deal further, for instead of a relatively mild branding, he had to be soundly beaten with red-hot tongs, and the author of the turd offered him had to be the oldest, filthiest, most disgusting thief we could find. A degenerate old valet of eighty, whom we had had in the house for ages, pleased him wonderfully well for his operation, and, rolling his eyes, smacking his lips, he gobbled up the old devil's turd while it was still warm and while the good Justine, using tongs heated to such a temperature they could hardly be held, thrashed his bum. And she was furthermore obliged to snatch up great bits of his flesh with the instrument, and all but roast them.

Another had his buttocks, belly, balls, and prick stabbed with a heavy cobbler's awl, and all this with more or less the same circumstances, that is to say, until he would eat a turd I presented to him in a chamber pot. He was not, however, curious about the turd's origins.

Messieurs, it is not easy to imagine to what lengths men are driven in the delirium of their inflamed imaginations. Have I not beheld one who, acting according to the same principles, required me to shower bone-breaking blows of a cane upon him as he ate a turd which, before his own eyes, he had us fish up out of the depths of the house's privy? and his perfidious discharge did not flow into my mouth until he had devoured the last spoonful of that foul muck.

"Well, you know, everything's imaginable and even possible," said Curval as he pensively fondled Desgranges' buttocks. "I am convinced one can go still further than that."

"Further?" said the Duc who at that moment was mauling the bare behind of Adelaide, his wife for the day. "And what the devil would you have one do?"

"Worse!" replied Curval, something of a hiss in his voice. "It seems to me one never sufficiently exploits the possible."

"I entirely agree with the Président," spoke up Durcet, then in the act of embuggering Antinoüs, "and I have the feeling my mind is capable of further improvements upon all those piggish stunts."

"I think I know what Durcet means," said the Bishop who, for the time being, was idle, or who rather had not yet begun to operate.

"Well, what the devil does he mean?" the Duc demanded to know.

Whereupon the Bishop stood up and went to Durcet's alcove; the two men whispered together, the Bishop then moved on to where Curval was, and the latter said, "That's it, exactly!" And then the Bishop spoke in the Duc's ear.

"By fuck!" His Highness exclaimed, "I'd never have thought of that one."

As these gentlemen said no more that might shed light on the thing, we have no way of knowing just what Durcet did mean or what the Duc declared he would never have thought of. And even were it that we knew, I believe we would be well advised to keep knowledge of the thing strictly to ourselves, at least in the interest of modesty, for there are an infinite number of things one ought merely to indicate, prudent circumspection requires that one keep a bridle on one's tongue; there are such things, are there not, as chaste ears? one may now and again encounter them, and I am absolutely convinced the reader has already had occasion to be grateful for the discretion we have employed in his regard; the further he reads on more secure shall be our claim to his sincerest praise upon this head, why, yes, we feel we may almost assure him of it even at this early stage. Well, whatever one may say, each one has his own soul to save, and of what punishment, both in this world and in the next, is he not deserving who all immoderately were to be pleased to divulge all the caprices, all the whims and tastes, all the clandestine horrors whereunto men are subject when their fancy is free and afire? 'twould be to reveal secrets which ought to be sunk in obscurity for humanity's sake, 'twould be to undertake the general corruption of manners and to precipitate his brethren in Jesus Christ into all the extravagances such tableaux might feature in very lively color and profusion; and God, Who seeth even unto the depths of our hearts, this puissant God Who hath made heaven and earth and Who must one day judge us, God alone knoweth whether we have any desire to hear ourselves reproached by Him for such crimes.

Messieurs put the finishing touches on several horrors they had begun; Curval, to cite one example, had Desgranges shit, the others occupied themselves with either that same distraction, or with some others not much more improving, and their Lordships then went to supper. At the orgies, Duclos having overheard the friends discussing the new diet we alluded to earlier, whose purpose was to render shit more abundant and more delicate, at the orgies, I say, Duclos noted that she was truly astonished to find connoisseurs like themselves unaware of the true secret whereby turds are made both very abundant and very tasty. Questioned about the measures which ought to be adopted, she said that there was but one: the subject should be given a mild indigestion; there was no need to make him eat what he did not like or what was unwholesome, but, by obliging him to eat hurriedly and between meals, the desired results could be obtained at once. The experiment was performed that same evening: Fanny was waked -- no one had paid any attention to her, and she had gone to bed after supper -- she was immediately required to eat four large plain cakes, and the next morning she furnished one of the biggest and most beautiful turds they had been able to procure from her up until that time. Duclos' suggested system was therefore approved, although they upheld their decision to do away with bread; Duclos said they were well advised to be rid of it; the fruits produced by her method, said she, would only be better. From that time on not a day passed but they'd gently upset those pretty youngsters' digestions in one way or another, and the results were simply beyond anything you could imagine. I mention this in passing so that, should any amateur be disposed to make use of the formula, he may be firmly persuaded there is none superior.

The remainder of the evening having brought nothing extraordinary, everyone retired in order to be freshly rested for the following day's wedding: the brilliant match to be made was destined to unite Colombe and

Zélamir, and this ceremony was to be the basis for celebrating the third week's festival.

The Twenty-First Day

Preparations for that ceremony were started early in the morning; they were of the usual sort but, and I have no idea whether or not it was by a stroke of chance, the inspection uncovered signs of the young bride's misbehavior. Durcet declared he had found shit in her chamber pot; she denied having put it there, asserting that, to cause her to be punished, the duenna had come and done the thing during the night, and that governesses often planted such evidence when they wished to embroil the children in difficulties. Well, she defended herself very eloquently and to no purpose whatever, for she was not carefully heard, and as her little husband-to-be was already on the list, the prospect of correcting both of them was the cause of great amusement.

Nevertheless, the young bride and groom, once the mass had been said, were conducted with much pomp to the salon where the ceremony was to be completed before mealtime; they were both of the same age, and the little girl was delivered naked to her husband, who was permitted to do whatever he wanted. Is there any voice so compelling as example's? And where if not in Silling were it possible to receive very bad examples and the most contagious ones? The young man sped like an arrow to its mark, hopped upon his little wife, and as his prick was greatly stiff, although not yet capable of a discharge, he would inevitably have got his spear in her... but mild as would have been the damage done her, the source of all Messieurs' glory lay in preventing anything from harming the tender flower they wished alone to pluck. And so it was the Bishop checked the lad's impetuous career, and profiting from his erection, straightway thrust into his ass the very pretty and already very well-formed engine wherewith Zélamir was about to plumb his young spouse. What a disappointment for that young man, and what a discrepancy between the old Bishop's slack-sprung vent and the strait and tidy cunt of a little thirteen-year-old virgin! But Zélamir was having to deal with people who were deaf to common-sense arguments.

Curval laid hands on Colombe and thigh-fucked her from in front while licking her eyes, her mouth, her nostrils, in a word, her entire face. Meanwhile, he must surely have been rendered some kind of service, for he discharged, and Curval was not a man to lose his fuck over silly trifles.

They dined, the wedded couple appeared at the meal and again in the salon for coffee, which that day was served by the very cream of the subjects, by, I wish to say, Augustine, Zelmire, Adonis, and Zéphyr. Curval wished to stiffen afresh, had absolutely to have some shit, and Augustine shot him as fine an artifact as it were in human power to create. The Duc had himself sucked by Zelmire, Durcet by Colombe, the Bishop by Adonis. The last named shitted into Durcet's mouth after having dispatched the Bishop. But no sign of fuck; it was becoming rare, they had failed to exercise any restraint at the outset of the holiday, and as they realized the extreme need of seed they would have toward the end, Messieurs were growing more frugal. They went next to the auditorium where the majestic Duclos, invited to display her ass before starting, exposed that matchless ensemble most libertinely to the eyes of the assembly, and then began to speak:

Here is still another trait of my character, Messieurs, said that sublime woman; after having made you well enough acquainted with it, you will be so kind as to judge what I intend to omit from what I am going to tell you... and you will, I trust, dispense me from having to say more about myself.

Lucile's mother had just fallen into a state of the most wretched poverty, and it was only by the most extraordinary stroke of chance that this charming girl, who had received no news at all of her mother since having fled her house, now learned of her extreme distress: one of our street scouts -- hard in pursuit of some young girl for a client who shared the tastes and designs of the Marquis de

Mesanges, for a client, that is to say, who was eager to make an outright and final purchase -- one of our scouts came in to report to me, as I was lying in bed with Lucile, that she had chanced upon a little fifteen-year-old, without question a maid, extremely pretty, and, she said, closely resembling Mademoiselle Lucile; yes, she went on, they were like two peas in a pod, but this little girl she'd found was in such bedraggled condition that she'd have to be kept and fattened for several days before she'd be fit to market. And thereupon she gave a description of the aged woman with whom the child had been discovered, and of the frightful indigence wherein that mother lay; from certain traits, details of age and appearance, from all she heard concerning the daughter, Lucile had a secret feeling the persons being discussed might well be her own mother and sister. She knew she had left home when the latter was still very young, hence it was hard to be sure of the thing, and she asked my permission to go and verify her suspicions.

At this point my infernal mind conceived a little horror; its effect was to set my body afire. Telling the street scout to leave the room, and being unable to resist the fury raging in my blood, I began by entreating Lucile to frig me. Then, halting halfway through the operation:

"Why do you want to go to see that old woman?" I asked Lucile; "what do you propose to do?"

"Why, but don't you see," said Lucile, whose heart was still undeveloped, "there are certain things that one is expected to do... I ought to help her if I can, and above all if she turns out to be my mother."

"Idiot," I muttered, thrusting her away from me, "go sacrifice alone to your disgusting popular prejudices, and for not daring to brave them, go lose the most incredibly fine opportunity to irritate your senses by a horror that would make you discharge for a decade."

Bewildered by my words, Lucile stared at me, and I saw I had to explain this philosophy to her, for she apparently had not the vaguest understanding of it. I therefore did lecture her, I made her comprehend the vileness, the baseness of the ties wherewith they seek to bind us to the author of our days; I demonstrated to her that for having carried us in her womb, instead of deserving some gratitude, a mother merits naught but hate, since 'twas for her pleasure alone and at the risk of exposing us to all the ills and sorrows the world holds in store for us that she brought us into the light, with the sole object of satisfying her brutal lubricity. To this I added roughly everything one might deem helpful in supporting the doctrine which same right-thinking dictates, and which the heart urges when it is not cluttered up with stupidities imbibed in the nursery.

"And what matters it to you," I added, "whether that creature be happy or wretched? Does her situation have anything to do with yours? does it affect you? Get rid of those demeaning ties whose absurdity I've just proven to you, and thereby entirely isolating this creature, sundering her utterly from yourself, you will not only recognize that her misfortune must be a matter of indifference to you, but that it might even be exceedingly voluptuous to worsen her plight. For, after all, you do owe her your hatred, that has been made clear, and thus you would be taking your revenge: you would be performing what fools term an evil deed, and you know the immense influence crime exerts upon the senses. And so here are two sources of pleasure in the outrages I'd like to have you inflict upon her: both the sweet delights of vengeance, and those one always tastes whenever one does evil."

Whether it was that I employed a greater eloquence in exhorting Lucile than I do in recounting the fact to you now, or whether it was because her already very libertine and very corrupt spirit instantly notified her heart of the voluptuous promise contained in my principles, she tasted them, and I saw her lovely cheeks flush in response to that libertine flame which never fails to appear every time one violates some prohibition, abolishes some restraint.

"All right," she murmured, "what are we to do?"

"Amuse ourselves with her," said I, "and make some money at the same time; as for pleasure, you can be sure to have some if you adopt my principles. And as for the money, the same thing applies, for I can make use of both your old gray-haired mother and your young sister; I'll arrange two different parties which will prove very lucrative."

Lucile accepts, I frig her the better to excite her to commit the crime, and we turn all our thoughts to devising plans. Let me first undertake to outline the first of them, since it deserves to be included in the category of passions I have to discuss, although I shall have to alter the exact chronology in order to fit it into the sequence of events, and when I shall have informed you of this first part of my scheme, I shall enlighten you upon the second.

There was a man, well placed in society and exceedingly wealthy, exceedingly influential and having a disorder of the mind which surpasses all that words are able to convey; as I was acquainted with him only as the Comte, you will allow me, however well advised of his full name I may be, simply to designate him by his title. The Comte was somewhat above thirty-five years of age, and all his passions had reached their maximum strength; he had neither faith nor law, no god and no religion, and was above all else endowed, like yourselves, Messieurs, with an invincible horror of what is called the charitable sentiment; he used to say that to understand this impulse was totally beyond his powers, and that he would not for an instant assent to the notion that one dare outrage Nature to the point of upsetting the order she had imposed when she created different classes of individuals; the very idea of elevating one such class through the bestowing of alms or aid, and thus of overthrowing another, the idea of devoting sums of money, not upon agreeable things which might afford one pleasure, but rather upon these absurd and revolting relief enterprises, all this he considered an insult to his intelligence or a mystery his intelligence could not possibly grasp. Thoroughly instilled, nay, penetrated though he was with these opinions, he reasoned still further; not only did he derive the keenest delight from refusing aid to the needy, but he ameliorated what was already an ecstasy by outrageously persecuting the humble and injured. One of his higher pleasures, for example, consisted in having meticulous searches made of those dark, shadowy regions where starving indigence gnaws whatever crust it has earned by terrible toil, and sprinkles tears upon its meager portion. He would stiffen at the thought of going abroad not only to enjoy the bitterness of those tears, but even... but even to aggravate their cause and, if 'twere possible, to snatch away the wretched substance that kept the damned yet amongst the living. And this taste of his was no whim, no light fantasy, 'twas a fury; he used to say that he knew no more piercing delight, nothing that could more successfully arouse him, inflame his soul, than these excesses I speak of. Nor was this rage of his, he one day assured me, the fruit of depravation; no, he had been possessed by this mania since his youngest years, and his heart, perpetually toughened against misery's plaintive accents, had never conceived any gentler, milder feelings for it.

As it is of the greatest importance you be familiar with the subject, you must first of all know that the same man had three different passions:

the one I am going to relate to you, another, which
Martaine will explain to you later when she refers to this same personage, and a third, yet more atrocious, which Desgranges will doubtless reserve for the end of her contribution as doubtless one of the most
impressive upon her list. But we'll begin with the one on mine.

Straightway I had informed the Comte of the nest of misery I had
discovered for him, of the inhabitants of that nest, he was transported
with joy. But it so happened that business intimately connected with his
fortune and having an important bearing upon his advancement, which
he took much care not to neglect, in that he held them vital to his misconduct, business, I say, was going to occupy his attention for the next
two weeks, and as he did not want to let the little girl slip through his
fingers, he preferred sacrificing the pleasure the first scene promised him,
and to be certain of enjoying the second. And so he ordered me to have
the child kidnapped at whatever cost, but without delay, and to have her
deposited at the address he indicated to me. And in order to keep you in
suspense no longer, my Lords, that address was Madame Desgranges', for
she was the agent who furnished him with material for his third class of
secret parties. And now to return to the objects of all our maneuvering.

So far, we had done little but locate Lucile's mother, both to set the
stage for the recognition scene between mother and daughter and to study
the problems associated with the kidnapping of the little girl. Lucile, well
coached in her part, only greeted her mother in order to insult her, to
say that it was thanks to her she had been hurled into libertinage, and
to these she added a thousand other similarly unkind remarks, which
broke the poor woman's heart and ruined the pleasure of rediscover-
ing her daughter. During this first interview, I thought I glimpsed the
appropriate way to talk with the woman, and pointed out to her that,
having rescued her elder child from an impure existence, I was willing
to do as much for the younger one. But the stratagem did not succeed,
the poor wretch fell to weeping and said that nothing in the world would
induce her to part with the one treasure she had left, that the little girl
was her one resource, she herself was old, infirm, that the child cared
for her, and that to be deprived of her would be to lose life itself. At this
juncture, Messieurs, I must confess, and I do so with shame, that I felt a
faint stirring in the depths of my heart; it advised me that my voluptuous
pleasure was bound only to be increased by the horrible refinements I was
about to give to my meditated crime, and having informed the old lady
that shortly thereafter her daughter would come to pay her a visit with a
man of great influence, who could perhaps render her great services, we
left, and I bent all my efforts to employing the lures and devices I usually
relied upon to snare game. I had carefully examined the little girl, she
was worth my going to some trouble: fifteen years of age, a pretty figure,
a very lovely skin, and very pretty features. She arrived three days later,

and after having examined every part of her body and found nothing but what was very charming, dimpled, and very neat despite the poor nourishment she had for so long had to put up with, I passed her along to Madame Desgranges: this transaction marked the beginning of our commercial relations.

His private affairs attended to, our Comte reappeared; Lucile conducts him to her mother's home, and 'tis at this point begins the scene I wish to describe. The old mother was found in bed, the room was without heat although we were then in the midst of a bitterly cold winter; beside her bed sat a wooden crock containing milk. The Comte pissed into the crock as soon as he had entered. To prevent any possible trouble, and in order to feel himself the undisputed master of the fort, the Comte had posted two of his minions, a pair of strapping lads, on the stairway, and they were to offer a stubborn obstacle to any undesirable coming up or going down.

"My dear old buggress," intoned the Comte, "we have come here with your daughter, you see her there, and a damned pretty whore she is, upon my soul; we have come here, I say, to relieve what ails you, wretched old leper that you are, but before we can help you, you must tell us what's amiss. Well, go on, speak," he said, seating himself and beginning to palpate Lucile's buttocks, "go on, I say, itemize your sufferings."

"Alas!" said the good woman, "you come with that vixen not to help me but to insult me."

"Vixen? How's this," said the Comte, "you dare use insults with your daughter? By God," he went on, rising to his feet and dragging the old thing from her litter, "get out of that bed, get down on your knees, and ask to be forgiven for the language you have just employed."

There was no resist.

"And you, Lucile, lift your skirts and have your mother kiss your cheeks, and I am damned certain she wants nothing more than to kiss them, eager as she must be for some kind of reconciliation."

The insolent Lucile rubs her ass upon the seamed and wrinkled visage of her dear old mother; overwhelming her with a tirade of playful epithets, the Comte permits the poor woman to crawl back into bed, and then resumes the conversation. "I tell you once again," he says, "that if you recite all your troubles to me, I'll take the best care of you."

The woe-ridden are credulous; and they love to lament. The old woman made them privy to all her sufferings, and complained especially, with great bitterness, of the theft of her daughter; she sharply accused Lucile of having had a hand in it and of knowing where the child presently was, since the lady with whom she had come a little while ago had proposed to take her under her wing; that was the basis for her supposition (and there was considerable logic in the way she argued) that this same lady had taken her away. Meanwhile, the Comte, directly facing Lucile's ass, for by this time he had got her to step out of her skirts, the

Comte, I say, now and again kissing that handsome ass and frigging himself uninterruptedly, listened, put questions to her, requested details, and regulated all the titillations of his perfidious lust according to the old woman's replies. But when she said that the absence of her daughter, thanks to whose work she was procure her wherewithal, was going to lead her gradually but inexorably to the grave, since she had nothing and for four days had been kept barely alive by that small quantity of milk he had just spoiled:

"Why, then, bitch," said the Comte, aiming his prick at the old creature and continuing to explore Lucile's buttocks, "why, then go ahead and croak, you foul old whore, do you suppose the world will be any worse off without you?"

And as he concluded his question he loosed his sperm.

"Were that to happen," he observed, "I believe I'd have only one regret, and that would be not having myself hastened the event."

But there was more to it than that, the Comte was not the sort of a man to be appeased by a mere discharge; Lucile, fully aware of the role she was to play, now that he had been relieved, busied herself preventing the old woman from noticing what he was about, and the Comte, rummaging through every corner of the room, came upon a silver goblet, the last vestige of the material well-being that had once upon a time been this poor wretch's; he put the goblet in his pocket. This fresh outrage having put new hardness into his prick, he again dragged the old woman from her bed, stripped her naked, and bade Lucile frig him upon the matron's withered old frame. Once again nothing could be done to stop him, and the villain darted his fuck over that ancient flesh, redoubled his insults, and said that the poor wretch could rest perfectly assured he was not yet done with her, and that she would soon have news of himself and of her little girl who, he wished to have her know, was in his power. He then proceeded to that last discharge, his transports of lust were ignited by the horrors wherewith his perfidious imagination was already in a ferment, by the ruin of the entire family he was contemplating, and he left. But in order not to have to return to this affair, hear, Messieurs, how I surpassed myself in villainy. Seeing that he might have confidence in me, the Comte informed me of the second scene he was preparing for the benefit of the old woman and her little daughter; he told me he wanted the child brought to him without delay and, as he wanted to reunite the whole family, he wished to have me cede Lucile to him too, for he had been deeply moved by her lovely ass; he made no effort to conceal that his purpose was to ruin Lucile as well as her ass, together with her mother and sister.

I loved Lucile. But I loved money even more. He offered me an unheard-of price for these three creatures, I agreed to everything. Four days later, Lucile, her little sister and her aged mother were brought together; Madame Desgranges will tell you about that meeting. As for your faithful Duclos, she continues and resumes the thread of her story this anecdote has interrupted; indeed, she wonders whether she ought not have recited it at some later time, for, esteeming it a very stirring episode, she considers it would have proven a fitting climax to her contribution.

"One moment," said Durcet, "I cannot hear such stories without being affected, their influence upon me would be difficult to describe. I have been restraining my fuck since the middle of the tale, kindly allow me to unburden myself now."

And he dashed into his closet with Michette, Zélamir, Cupidon, Fanny, Thérèse, and Adelaide; several minutes later his shouts began to ring out, and soon after the uproar started, Adelaide emerged in tears, saying that all this made her very unhappy, and wondering why they had to excite her husband with such dreadful stories; she who told them, Adelaide declared, not others, ought by rights to be the victim. During the interim the Duc and the Bishop had not wasted an instant, but the manner in which they operated belonging to the class of procedures circumstances compel us still to mask from the reader's view, we beg him to suffer the curtain to remain down, and to allow us to move on to the four tales Duclos had yet to relate before bringing this twenty-first meeting of the assembly to a close.

A week after Lucile's departure, I handled a rascal blessed with a rather curious mania. Warned several days in advance of his intended arrival, I had let a great number of turds accumulate in my one-holed chair, and I had induced one of my young ladies to add a few more to the collection. Our man appeared costumed as a Savoyard rustic; 'twas in the morning, he swept out my room, removed the pot from beneath the chair, and went out to empty it (this emptying, I might note in parentheses, took a considerable length of time); when he returned he showed me how carefully he'd cleaned it out and asked for his payment. But, and this of course was all stipulated in our prior agreement, instead of giving him a coin, I seize the broom and fall to belaboring him with the handle.

"Your payment, villain?" I cry, "why, here's what you deserve."

And I bestow at least a dozen blows upon him. He seeks to escape me, I pursue him, and the libertine, whose critical moment has arrived, discharges all the way down the stairs, bawling out at the top of his voice that they're cracking his skull, that they want to kill him, and that he's got himself into the house of a scoundrel, she's not by any means the honest woman he at first took her for, etc.

Another carried, in a small pocket case, a little knotty stick which he kept for an unusual purpose; he wanted me to insert the stick into his urethral canal, and, having plunged it in to a depth of three inches, to rattle it with utmost vigor, and with my other hand to pull back his foreskin and frig his poor device. At the very instant he discharged, one had to pull out the stick, raise one's skirts in front, and he would discharge upon one's mound.

Six months later I had to do with an abbot who wanted me to take a burning candle and direct the drops of molten tallow so that they fell upon his penis and balls; it required nothing more than the sensation this ceremony produced to bring about his discharge. His machine required no touching, but it remained limp throughout; before they would yield fuck, his genitals had to be given such a heavy coating of wax that toward the end there was no recognizing this strange object as a part of the human anatomy.

That ecclesiastic had a friend who loved nothing so much as to offer his bum to be perforated by a multitude of gold pins, and when thus decorated, his hindquarter far more resembling a pincushion than an ordinary ass, he would sit down, the better to savor the effect he cherished, and, presenting one's very wide-spread buttocks to him, he would twiddle his member and discharge into one's vent.

"Durcet," said the Duc, "I should very much like to see that sweet chubby ass of yours studded all over with golden pins, ah yes, I'm persuaded 'twould thus appear more interesting than ever."

"Your Grace," quoth the financier, "you know that for forty years it has been my glory and my honor to imitate you in all things; I but ask you to have the kindness to set me an example, and you have my word that I will follow it."

"God's loin-scum!" exclaimed the good Curval, who had not until now been heard from, "by His sacred seed, I do declare that story about Lucile has made me stiff! I've held my peace, but my head's been at work none the less. Look here," said he, exhibiting his prick standing high, "see whether I do not say true. I've a furious impatience to hear the denouement of the story of those three buggresses; I have the highest hope they'll meet one another in a common grave."

"Softly there, softly," said the Duc, "let's not anticipate events. Were you not stiff, Monsieur le Président, you'd not be in such a hurry to hear talk of wheels and gibbets. You resemble a great many other of Justice's servitors, whose pricks, they say, rise up every time they pronounce the sentence of death."

"Never mind the magistrature," Curval replied, "the fact remains that I am enchanted by Duclos' doings, that I find her a charming girl, and that her story of the Comte has put me in a dreadful state, and in this state, I say, I could be easily persuaded to go abroad, stop a carriage on the highway, and rob its occupants."

"Ah, Président, take care," said the Bishop; "keep a hand upon yourself, my dear fellow, else we'll cease to be in safety here. One such slip, and the least we could expect would be the noose for all of us."

"The noose? Ah, the noose, yes... but not for us. However, I don't for a minute deny I'd myself gladly condemn these young ladies here to be hanged, and especially Madame la Duchesse, who's lying like a cow upon my sofa and who, merely because she's got a spoonful of modified fuck in the womb, fancies no one dares touch her any more."

"Oh," said Constance, "'tis surely not with you I count upon being respected because of my state. Your loathing for pregnant women is only too notorious."

"A prodigious loathing, isn't it?" said Curval with a chuckle, "why, indeed it is prodigious."

And, transported by enthusiasm, he was, I believe, on the verge of committing some sacrilege against that superb belly, when Duclos intervened.

"Come, Sire, come with me," said she; "since 'tis I who have caused the hurt, I'd like to repair it."

And together they passed into the secluded boudoir, followed by Augustine, Hébé, Cupidon, and Thérèse. It was not long before the Président's braying resounded through the castle, and despite all Duclos' attentions, little Hébé returned weeping from the hurly-burly; there was even more to it than tears, but we dare not yet disclose just what it was had set her to trembling. A little patience, friend reader, and we shall soon hide nothing from your inquisitive gaze.

And now Curval himself returns, grumbling between his teeth and swearing that all those dratted laws prevent a man from discharging at his ease, etc.; their Lordships sit down at table. After supper they withdrew to mete out punishment for the misbehavior that had accrued during the week, but the guilty were not that evening in great number: only Sophie, Colombe, Adelaide, and Zélamir merited correction, and received it. Durcet, who since the beginning of the evening had waxed very hot, and who had been particularly inspired by Adelaide, granted her no quarter; Sophie, whom they had detected shedding tears during the story of the Comte, was punished for that misdemeanor as well as for her former one, and the Duc and Curval, we understand, treated the day's little newlyweds, Zélamir and Colombe, with a severity that almost bordered upon barbarity.

The Duc and Curval, in splendid form and singularly wrought up, said they had no wish to retire, and having had a quantity of beverages fetched in, they passed the night drinking with the four storytellers and Julie, whose libertinage, increasing every day, gave her the air of a very amiable creature who deserved to be ranked among these objects for whom Messieurs had some regard.

The following morning, while making his rounds, Durcet found all seven of them dead drunk. The naked girl was discovered lodged between her father and her husband and in a posture which gave evidence of neither virtue nor decency in libertinage; it was plain enough to the financier that (to hold the reader in suspense no longer) they had both enjoyed her simultaneously.

Duclos, who, from all appearances, had functioned as an instrument to this crime, lay sprawled near the compact trio, and the others were strewn in a confused heap in the corner opposite the fire, which someone had taken care to keep burning throughout the night.

The Twenty-Second Day

As a result of these all-night bacchanals, exceedingly little was accomplished on the twenty-second day of November; half the customary exercises were forgot, at dinner Messieurs appeared to be in a daze, and it was not until coffee they began to come somewhat to their senses. The coffee was served them by Rosette and Sophie, Zélamir and Giton. In an effort to return to his usual old self, Curval had Giton shit, and the Duc swallowed Rosette's turd; the Bishop had himself sucked by Sophie, Durcet by Zélamir, but no one discharged. They moved dutifully into the auditorium; the matchless Duclos, weak and queasy after the preceding day's excesses, took her place with drooping eyelids, and her tales were so brief, they contained so few episodes, were recounted so listlessly, that we have taken it upon ourselves to supply them, and in the reader's behalf to clarify the somewhat confused speech she made to our friends.

In keeping with prescription, she recounted five passions: the first was that of a man who used to have his ass frigged with a tin dildo priorly charged with warm water, the which liquid was pumped into his fundament at the same instant he ejaculated; nothing else was required to obtain that effect, he needed no one else's ministry.

The second man had the same mania, but was wont to use a far greater number of instruments; initially, he called for a very minute one, then gradually increased the caliber, ascending the scale by small fractions of an inch until he reached a weapon with the dimensions of a veritable fieldpiece, and only discharged upon receiving a torrent from its muzzle.

Far more of the mysterious was required to please the third one's palate: at the outset of the game, he had an enormous instrument introduced into his ass, then it was withdrawn, he would shit, would eat what he had just rendered, and next he had to be flogged. The flogging administered, it was time to reinsert the formidable device in his rectum, then once again it was removed, and it was the whore's turn to shit, and after that she picked up the whip again and lashed him while he munched what she had done; a third time, yes, a third time the instrument was driven home, and that, plus the girl's turd he finished eating, was sufficient to complete his happiness.

In her fourth tale, Duclos made mention of a man who would have all his joints bound with strings; in order to make his discharge even more delicious, his neck itself was compressed, and, half choking, he would shoot his fuck squarely at the whore's asshole.

And in her fifth, she referred to that individual who used to tie a slender cord tightly to his glans; the girl, naked, would pass the other end of the cord between her thighs, and walk away from him, drawing the cord taut and offering the patient a full view of her ass; he would then discharge.

Truly exhausted after having fulfilled her task, the storyteller begged to leave to retire, and she was allowed to. A few moments were devoted to uttering smutty comments upon this and that, and then the four libertines went to supper, but everyone felt the effects of our two principal actors' disorderliness. At the orgies they were also as prudent and restrained as 'twere possible for such debauchees to be, and the entire household went more or less quietly to bed.

The Twenty-Third Day

But how is it possible to shout and roar the way you do when you discharge? the Duc demanded of Curval upon bidding him good morning on the 23rd. "Why the devil must you scream that way? I've never seen such violent discharges."

"Why, by God," Curval replied, "is it for you, whom one can hear a league away, to address such a reproach to a modest man like myself? Those little murmurs you hear, my good friend, are caused by my extremely sensitive nervous system; the objects which excite our passions create such a lively commotion in the electrically charged fluid that flows in our nerves, the shock received by the animal spirits composing this fluid is of such a degree of violence, that the entire mechanism is rattled by these effects, and one is just as powerless to suppress one's cries when overwhelmed by the terrible blows imparted by pleasure, as one would be when assailed by the powerful emotions of pain."

"Well, you define the thing very well, Président, but what was the delicate object that could have produced such a vibration in your animal spirits?"

"I was very energetically sucking Adonis' prick, his mouth, and his asshole, for I was cast down with despair at not being able to do more to my couch companion; all the while I made the best of my hard situation, Antinoüs, seconded by your dear daughter Julie, labored, each in his own way, to evacuate the liquor whose eventual outpouring occasioned the musical sounds which, you say, struck your ears."

"And it all worked so well that now, today," said the Duc, "you're as weak as a baby."

"No, your Grace, not at all," Curval declared; "deign but to observe my career, my motions today, and but do me the honor of judging my style and vehemence in sport, and you shall see me conduct myself quite as ever, and assuredly as well as you yourself."

They were at this point in the conversation when Durcet arrived to say breakfast was being served. They passed into the qirls' quarters, where those eight charming little houris were distributing cups of coffee and hot water; the Duc therewith demanded to know of Durcet, the month's steward and presiding officer, why was it the coffee was being served with water?

"You'll have it with milk whenever you wish," said the financier. "Would you prefer it thus now?"

The Duc said that yes, he would.

"Augustine, my dear," Durcet said, "a little milk in Monsieur le Duc's cup, if you please."

Thereupon the little girl, prepared for any eventuality, placed Blangis' cup beneath her ass, and through her anus squeezed three or four spoonfuls of milk, very clear and perfectly fresh. This cunning feat produced much pleasant laughter, everyone requested milk in his coffee. All the asses were charged in the same way Augustine's was: 'twas an agreeable little surprise the month's director of games had thought to give his colleagues. Fanny poured some into the Bishop's cup, Zelmire into Curval's, and Michette into the financier's; the friends took a second round of coffee, and the four other girls performed over these new cups the same ceremony their comrades had over the first cups; and so on and on; the whole thing entertained their Lordships immoderately. It heated the Bishop's brain; he affirmed he wanted something beside milk, and the lovely Sophie stepped forth to satisfy him. Although all eight definitely wished to shit, they had been strongly urged to exercise self-restraint while dispensing the milk, and this first time to yield absolutely nothing else.

Next, they paid the little boys a good-morning visit; Curval induced Zélamir to shit from him, the Duc applauded what Giton brought to light. Two subaltern fuckers, Constance, and Rosette provided the spectacle in the chapel latrine. Rosette was one of those upon whom the old formula for promoting indigestion had been tried out; at coffee, she had had the world's worst time keeping her milk free of foreign ingredients, and now, seated upon the throne, she released the most superb turd you could hope to lay eyes upon. Duclos was congratulated, they said her system was a resounding success, and from then on they used it every day; never once did it fail them. The conversation at the dinner was enlivened by the breakfast's pleasantry, and a number of other things of the same kind were invented and proposed; we shall perhaps have occasion to mention them in the sequel.

After-dinner coffee was served by four subjects of the same age: to wit, Zelmire, Augustine, Zéphyr, and Adonis. The Duc thigh-fucked Augustine while tickling her anus with his thumb, Curval did the same thing with Zelmire, but may or may not have used his thumb, his hand was not in clear view; the Bishop toiled between Zéphyr's tightly squeezed legs, and the financier fucked Adonis' mouth. Augustine announced that she was ready to shit, how would they like her to do a little shit? The poor dear could not wait another moment, she too had been exposed to the indigestion-producing experiments. Curval beckoned her to him, opened his mouth, and the delightful little girl dropped a monstrous turd into it; the Président gobbled it up in a trice, not without unleashing a veritable stream of fuck into Fanchon's hands.

"There you are," he said to the Duc, "you see that night-time merriment has no damaging effect upon the following day's pleasures; you're lagging behind, Monsieur le Duc."

"I'll not be behind for long," said the latter, to whom Zelmire, inspired by an urge no less imperious, was rendering the same service Augustine had a moment before rendered Curval. And, yes, as he pronounces those words, the Duc topples over, utters piercing shrieks, swallows shit, and discharges like a madman.

"Enough of this," said the stern, austere voice of the Bishop, moderation's exponent; "at least two of us must preserve our strength for the stories."

Durcet, who, unlike the Duc and Curval, had no surfeit of fuck to fling carelessly about, assented wholeheartedly, and after the shortest possible nap, they installed themselves in the auditorium, where, in the following terms, the spellbinding Duclos resumed her brilliant and lascivious history:

Why is it, Messieurs, the radiant creature inquired, that in this world there are men whose hearts have been so numbed, whose sentiments of honor and delicacy have been so deadened, that one sees them pleased and amused by what degrades and soils them?

One is even led to suppose their joy can be mined nowhere save from the depths of opprobrium, that, for such men, delights cannot exist elsewhere save in what brings them into consort with dishonor and infamy. To what I am going now to recount to you, my Lords, to the various instances I shall lay before you in order to prove my assertion, do not reply, saying that 'tis physical sensation which is the foundation of these subsequent pleasures; I know, to be sure, physical sensation is involved herein, but be perfectly certain that it does not exist in some sort save thanks to the powerful support given it by moral sensation, and be sure as well that, were you to provide these individuals with the same physical sensation and to omit to join to it all that the moral may yield, you'd fail entirely to stir them.

There very often came to me a man of whose name and quality I was ignorant, but who, however, I knew most certainly to be a man of circumstance. The kind of woman with whom I married him made no difference at all: beautiful or ugly, old or young, it was all the same to him; his partner had only to play her role competently, and that role was as follows: ordinarily, he would come to the house in the morning, he would enter, as though by accident, into a room where a girl lay upon a bed, her skirts raised to above her waist and in the attitude of a woman frigging herself. Immediately his entrance was noticed, the woman, as if surprised, would spring from the bed.

"What are you doing here, villain?" she would ask very crossly; "who gave you permission to disturb me?"

He would beg forgiveness, his apologies would go unheeded, and all the while showering him with a renewed deluge of the harshest and most biting invectives, she would fall to giving him furious kicks upon the posterior, and she would become all the more certain of her aim as the patient, far from dodging or shielding his behind, would unfailingly turn himself and present the target within easy range, although looking for all the world as if he wished only to escape this punishment and flee the room. The kicking is redoubled, he cries to be spared, blows and curses are the only replies he receives, and as soon as he feels he is sufficiently excited, he promptly draws his prick from his breeches, which he has hitherto kept tightly buttoned, and lightly giving his device three or four flicks of the wrist, he discharges while rushing away under an unremitting storm of kicks and abuses.

A second personage, either tougher or more accustomed to this sort of exercise, would not enter the lists save with a street porter or some other stout rascal willing to sweat for his hire. The libertine enters furtively while his opponent is busily counting his money; the churl cries thief; whereupon the hard language and blows begin. Whereas with the former debauchee, the blows were scattered somewhat over his body, this one, keeping his breeches down about his ankles, wishes to receive everything squarely in the center of his unclothed bum, and that bum has to be buffeted by a good heavy boot, amply studded with hobnails and well coated with mud. At the moment he felt himself about to discharge, our gentleman ceased to parry the blows; planted firmly in the middle of the room, his breeches still lowered, and agitating his prick with all his strength, he braved his enemy's assaults, and, at this crucial juncture, dared him do his worst, insulting him in his own turn, and swearing he was about to die of pleasure. The more vile, the more lowly the man I found for this stalwart libertine, the more scurvy his antagonist, the heavier and the more filthy his boot, the more overpowering would be my client's ecstasy; I had to employ the same tact and discrimination in selecting his assailant that I would have had to devote to embellishing and beautifying another man's woman.

A third wished to find himself in what in a whorehouse is called the harem, at the same instant two other men, paid so to do and on hand for no other purpose, began a dispute. Both would turn upon our libertine, he would ask to be spared, would throw himself upon his knees, would not be listened to, and one of the two champions would directly snatch up a cane and fall to belaboring him all the while he crept to the entrance of another room where he would take refuge. There he would be received by a girl, she would console him, caress him as one might a child who has come to be comforted, she would raise her skirts, display her ass, and the libertine, all smiles, would spray his fuck upon it.

A fourth required the same preliminaries, but as soon as the strokes of the cane began to rain down upon his back, he would frig himself within sight of all. Then this last operation would be suspended for a moment; there would, however, be no interruption in the dual attack of blows and oaths; then he'd get hot again, frig some more, and when they saw his fuck was about to fly, they'd open a window, pick him up by the waist, and fling him out; he would land upon a specially prepared dung heap after a fall of no more than six feet. And that was the critical moment; he had been morally aroused by the foregoing preliminaries, and his physical self only became so thanks to his fall; 'twas never but upon that dung heap he loosed his fuck. When one went to look from the window, he was gone; there was an obscure little door below (he had a key to it), and he'd disappear through it at once.

A man paid for the purpose and dressed like a rowdy would abruptly enter the chamber in which the man who furnishes us with the fifth example would be lying with a girl, kissing her ass while awaiting developments. Accosting the expectant libertine, the bully, having forced the door, would insolently ask what right he had thus to meddle with his mistress and then, laying his hands upon his sword, he would tell the usurper to defend himself. All confused, the latter would fall to his knees, ask pardon, grovel on the floor, kiss his rival's feet too, and swear he was ready to relinquish the lady at once, for he had no desire to fight over a woman. The bully, whom his adversary's pliability rendered all the more insolent, now called his enemy a coward, a contemptible fellow, a whoreson ass-fucker, and a dog, and threatened to carve up his face with the edge of his sword. And the more ugly became the one's behavior, the more humble and fawning became the other's. Finally, after a few minutes of debate, the assailant offered to make a settlement with his enemy:

"I see damned well that you've got no guts at all," said he, "and so I'll let you go, but upon condition you kiss my ass."

"Oh, Monsieur, I'll do whatever you like," said the other, enchanted by this solution, "I'd even kiss it if 'twere all beshitted, if you wish, provided you do me no harm."

Sheathing his sword, the bully directly pulled down his breeches, the libertine, only too delighted, leapt enthusiastically to work, and while the young man let fly half a dozen farts at his nose, the old rake, having attained the summit of ecstasy, loosed his fuck and swooned with pleasure.

"Every one of those excesses makes sense to me," Durcet said in a faltering tone, for the little libertine was stiff after hearing tell of these turpitudes. "Nothing more logical than to adore degradation and to reap delight from scorn. He who ardently loves the things which dishonor, finds pleasure in being dishonored and must necessarily stiffen when told that he is. Turpitude is, to certain spirits, a very sound cause of joy. One loves to hear oneself called what one wishes only to merit being, and it is truly impossible to guess how far a man may go in this direction, provided he be ashamed of nothing. 'Tis once again the story of certain sick persons whom nothing delights like the disintegration of their body."

"'Tis all a question of cynicism," was Curval's deliberated opinion, pronounced while toying with Fanchon's buttocks. "Who is unaware that even punishment produces enthusiasms, and have we not seen certain individual's pricks stiffen into clubs at the same instant they find themselves publicly disgraced? Everyone knows the story of the brave Marquis de S*** who, when informed of the magistrates' decision to burn him in effigy, pulled his prick from his breeches and exclaimed: 'God be fucked, it has taken them years to do it, but it's achieved at last; covered with opprobrium and infamy, am I? Oh, leave me, for I've got absolutely to discharge'; and he did so in less time than it takes to tell."

"Those are undisputed facts," the Duc commented, nodding gravely. "But can you explain to me their cause?"

"It resides in our heart," Curval replied. "Once a man has degraded himself, debased himself through excesses, he has imparted something of a vicious cast to his soul, and nothing can rectify that situation. In any other case, shame would act as a deterrent and incline him away from the vices to which his mind advises him to surrender, but here that possibility has been eliminated altogether: 'tis the first token of shame he has obliterated, the initial call he has definitively silenced, and from the state in which one is when one has ceased to blush, to that other state wherein one adores everything that causes others to blush, there is no more, nor less, than a single step. All that before affected one disagreeably, now encountering an otherwise prepared soul, in metamorphosed into pleasure, and from this moment onward, whatever recalls the new state one has adopted can henceforth only be voluptuous."

"But what a distance one must first have ventured along the road of vice to arrive at that point!" said the Bishop.

"Yes, yes, 'tis so," Curval acknowledged; "but little by little one makes one's way along, and the path one treads is strewn with flowers; one excess leads to another, the imagination, never sated, soon brings us to our destination, and as the traveler's heart has only hardened as he has pursued his career, immediately he reaches his goal, that heart which of old contained some virtues, no longer recognizes a single one. Accustomed to livelier things, it promptly shrugs off those early impressions, those soft and unsweet, those tasteless ones which till then had made it drunk, and as it strongly senses that infamy and dishonor are going surely to be the consequences of its new impulsions, in order to have nothing to fear of them, it begins by making itself familiar with them. It no sooner caresses than it is seized with a fondness for them, because they are of the same nature as its new conquests; and now that heart is fixed unalterably, forever."

"And that," the Bishop observed, "is what makes mending one's way so difficult."

"Say rather that it is impossible, my friend. And how are the punishments inflicted upon him you wish to reform ever to succeed, since, with the exception of one or two privations, the state of degradation which characterizes the situation in which you place him when you punish him, pleases him, amuses him, delights him, and inwardly he relishes the self that has gone so far as to merit being treated in this way?"

"Oh, what is this glory, jest, and riddle of the world!" sighed the Duc.

"Yes, my friend, an enigma above all else," said the grave Curval. "And that perhaps is what led a very witty individual to say that better every time to fuck a man than to seek to comprehend him."

And the arrival of supper interrupting our interlocutors, they seated themselves at table without having achieved a thing during the soiree. Natheless, at dessert, Curval, his prick as hard as a demon's, declared he'd be damned if it wasn't a pucelage he wanted to pop, even if he had twenty fines to pay, and instantly laying rude hands upon Zelmire, who had been reserved for him, he was about to drag her off to the boudoir when his three colleagues, casting themselves in his path, besought him to reconsider and submit to the law he had himself prescribed; and, said they, since they too had equally powerful urges to breach the contract, but held themselves somehow in check all the same, he should imitate them, at least out of a feeling of comradeship. And as they had straightway sent word to have Julie fetched in, for Curval was fond of her, she, upon arriving, took him directly in hand, and, together with Champville and Bum-Cleaver, they all four went into the salon; the other three friends soon joined them there, for the orgies were scheduled to begin. Upon entering, they found Curval close at grips with his aides, who, adopting the most lubricious postures and providing the most libertine exhortations, finally caused him to yield up his fuck.

In the course of the orgies, Durcet had the duennas give him two or three hundred kicks in the ass; not to be outdone, his peers had the fuckers serve them identically, and before retiring for the night, no one was exempted from shedding more or less fuck, depending upon the faculties wherewith by Nature he had been endowed. Fearing some fresh return of the defloratory whim Curval had just announced, the duennas were, through precaution, assigned to sleep in the boys' and girls' chambers. But this measure was unnecessary, and Julie, who looked after the Président all night long, the following morning turned him over to the society as limp as an empty glove.

The Twenty-Fourth Day

Piety is indeed a true disease of the soul. Apply whatever remedies you please, the fever will not subside, the patient never heals; finding readier entry into the souls of the woebegone and downtrodden, because to be devout consoles them for their other ills, it is far more difficult to cure in such persons than in others. Such was the case with Adelaide: the more that vista of debauchery and of libertinage unfolded before her eyes, the more she recoiled and sought sanctuary in the arms of that comfort-giving God she hoped one day would come and deliver her from the evils which, she saw only too well, her dreadful situation was going to bring down upon her head. No one had a more profound appreciation of her circumstances than she; her mind could not more clearly have foreseen everything that was necessarily to follow the fatal beginning of which already she had been a victim, however mildly; she wonderfully well understood that, as the stories grew progressively stronger, the men's use of her and of her companions, evolving sympathetically, would also grow more ferocious. All that, despite everything she was told, made her avidly seek out, as often and for as long as she could, the society of her beloved Sophie. No longer did she dare go in quest of her at night; her overseers were sharp-eyed, wary, and drastic steps had been taken to thwart any more of those escapades, but whenever she found herself free for an instant, she would fly to her soul mate, and upon this very morning of the day we are presently chronicling, having risen early from the Bishop's bed, where she had lain that night, she went into the young girls' quarters to chat with her dearest correspondent. Durcet, who because of his duties that month used also to rise earlier than the others, found her there and declared to her there was nothing for it, he could not both carry out his functions and overlook this infraction of the rules; the society would have to decide the matter according to its pleasure. Adelaide wept, tears were her sole weapon, and she resorted to them.

The only favor she dared beg from her husband was to try to prevent Sophie from being punished; for Sophie, she argued, could not be guilty, since it had been she, Adelaide, who had come looking for her, not Sophie who had gone in search of Adelaide. Durcet said he would report the fact as he had observed it, would disguise nothing; no one is less apt to be melted than a punisher whose keenest interest lies in punishing.

And such was the case here, of course; was there anything prettier to punish than Sophie? Surely not, and what cause might Durcet have for sparing her?

Their Lordships assembled, the financier made his report. Here was an habitual offender; the Président recollected that, when he had been at the Palais de Justice, his ingenious confreres used to contend that recidivism in a man proves Nature is acting more strongly in him than education or principles; hence, by repeated errors, he attests, so to speak, that he is not his own master; hence, he must be doubly punished -- the Président now reasoned just as logically and with the same inspired verve that, as had won him his schoolmates' admiration, and he declared that, as he viewed the thing, one had no choice but to invoke the law and punish the incurable Adelaide and her companion with all permissible rigor. But as the law fixed the death penalty for this offense, and as Messieurs were disposed to amuse themselves yet a little longer with these ladies before taking the final step, they were content to summon them, to make them kneel, and to read them the article out of the ordinances applying to their case, drawing their attention to the grave risk they had just run in committing such a transgression. That done, their judges pronounced a sentence thrice as severe as the one which had been executed upon them the previous Saturday, they were forced to swear they would not repeat their crime, they were advised that, should the same thing occur again, they would have to endure the extreme penalty, and their names were inscribed in the register.

Durcet's inspection added three more names to the page; two from amongst the little girls, one of the boys rounded out the morning's capture. All this was the result of the experimenting with minor indigestions; it was succeeding extremely well, but those poor children, unable to restrain themselves another moment, were beginning to tumble one after another into states of culpability: such had been the experience of Fanny and of Hébé amongst the girls, and of Hyacinthe amongst the boys. The evidence found in their pots was enormous, and Durcet frolicked about with it for a long time. Never had so many permissions been requested on any given morning, and certain subordinate personages were heard to curse Duclos for having imparted her secret. Notwithstanding the multitude of requests, leave to shit was granted only to Constance, Hercule, two second-rank fuckers, Augustine,

Zéphyr, and Desgranges; they provided a few minutes' entertainment, and Messieurs sat down to dine.

"Well, now you see your mistake in allowing your daughter to receive religious instruction," Durcet said to Curval; "there's nothing to be done about her now. Those imbecilities have taken root in her head. And I told you they would, ages ago."

"In faith," said Curval, "I thought that acquaintance with them would be just one more reason she'd have for despising them, and that as she grew up she would convince herself of the stupidity of those infamous dogmas."

"What you say is all very well for reasoning minds," said the Bishop, "but one simply must not expect it to succeed with a child."

"I'm afraid we're going to be forced to resort to violent measures," said the Duc, who knew very well Adelaide could overhear him.

"Oh yes, in good time," Durcet nodded. "I can assure her that if she has no one but me for her advocate, she'll be poorly defended in court."

"Oh, I know that, Monsieur!" Adelaide stammered through her tears; "everyone is aware of your feelings toward me."

"My feelings?" protested Durcet. "But, my dear wife, I ought perhaps to begin by informing you I have never had any feelings whatsoever for a woman, and assuredly fewer for you, who belong to me, than for any other. I hate religion, as well as those who practice it, and I warn you that, from the indifference I have in your regard, I shall pass damned quickly to the most violent aversion if you continue to revere infamous and execrable illusions, phantoms which have ever been the object of my contemptuous scorn. One must first have lost one's mind to be able to acknowledge a god, and to have gone completely mad to worship such a thing. In short, I declare to you before your father and these other gentlemen that there are no lengths to which I shall not go if I ever again find you guilty of such a sin. You should have been sent to a nunnery if you wanted to pray to your fuck-in-the-ass God; there you'd have been able to worship the bugger to your heart's content."

"Ah!" put in Adelaide, groaning, "a nun, Great God, a nun, would to heaven that I were such."

And Durcet, who at the time was sitting opposite her, annoyed by her response, hurled a silver plate at her face; it would have killed her had it struck her head, for the shock was so violent the missile bent double upon crashing against the wall.

"You're an insolent creature," Curval said to his daughter, who, to avoid plate, had leapt between her father and Antinoüs. "You deserve to have your belly kicked in."

And driving her away from him with a blow of his fist:

"Go crawl on your knees and beg your husband's forgiveness," said he, "or we'll expose you to the severest ordeal you've ever dreamt of."

In tears, she cast herself at Durcet's feet, but he, having got a very solid erection from hurling the plate, and declaring he'd have given a thousand louis to have hit his mark, Durcet said that he felt an immediate, a general, and an exemplary punishment was in order; another would of course be executed on Saturday, but he proposed that this one time they do without the children's services at coffee and devote that period to amusing themselves with Adelaide. Everyone consented to the proposal; Adelaide, Louison, and Fanchon, the most wicked of the four elders and the most dreaded by the women, moved into the salon; certain considerations obliged us to draw a curtain over what transpired there. But of one thing we may be perfectly certain: our four heroes discharged during that set-to, and Adelaide was allowed to take to her bed. 'Tis for the reader to invent the combinations and scene he'd like best, and kindly consent to be conveyed, if 'twould please him to accompany us, directly to the throne room where Duclos is about to resume her narrative. All of the friends have taken their places near their wives, all, that is to say, save the Duc, who was to have Adelaide that afternoon, and who has replaced her with Augustine; everyone then being ready, Duclos begins to speak.

One day, said that talented orator, while I was maintaining before one of my fellow procuresses that I had surely seen all it were possible to see of the most furious by way of passive flagellation, in that I had flogged and witnessed others flog men with thorns and the bull's pizzle:

"Oh, by God," my colleague answered, "you still have a great deal to see, my dear, and to persuade you that you've by no means observed the worst, I'll send one of my clients around tomorrow."

And having given me notice of the hour of the visit, and advised me of the ritual expected by that elderly post-office commissioner whose name, I remember, was Monsieur de Grancourt, I made full preparations and awaited for our man; I was to give him my personal attention, the thing was so arranged. He arrives at the house, and after we have retired to a room together:

"Monsieur," I say, "I deeply regret having to make the following disclosure, but I am bound to inform you that you are a prisoner and cannot leave this place. I further regret to say that Parliament has delegated me to arrest and punish you, and the Legislature has so willed it, and I have its order in my pocket. The person who sent you to me set a trap for you, for she knew full well the implications of your coming here, and she could most assuredly have enabled you to avoid this scene. As for the rest, you know the facts in the case: 'tis not with impunity one perpetrates the black and dreadful crimes you have committed, and I consider you exceedingly fortunate to get off with so little."

Our man had listened with the keenest attention to my harangue, and immediately I had done, he burst into tears and fell down on his knees before me, imploring me to deal leniently with him.

"Well I know," said he, "that I have greatly misbehaved. I know I have affronted God and justice; but since 'tis you, my sweet lady, who are appointed to chasten me, I most earnestly entreat your indulgence in my regard."

"Monsieur," I replied, "I shall do my duty. How can you be sure I am not myself being closely watched? What makes you suppose I have it in my power to respond to your pleas for merciful compassion? Remove your clothes and adopt a docile attitude, that is all I can say to you."

Grancourt obeyed; in a trice he was as naked as the palm of your hand. But, great God! what was this body he offered to my sight! I can only compare its skin to a ruffled taffeta. Upon that whole body, marked everywhere, there was not a single spot which did not bear terrible evidence of the lash.

However, into the fire I had thrust an iron scourge garnished with pointed steel tips; I had received the weapon that morning together with the final instructions. This murderous instrument had reached a bright-red color about the same moment Grancourt had removed his last stitch. I snatched the scourge from the coals and, starting to beat him with it, gently at first, then with increasing severity, then with all my strength, and that heedless of where my blows fell, rending him from the nape of his neck to his heels, I had my man streaming blood in an instant.

"You are a villain," I told him as I brought the scourge whistling down upon his body, "you're a villain and you've committed all sorts of crimes. Nothing is sacred to you, and I've lately heard that you've poisoned your own mother."

"'Tis true, Madame, oh, 'tis only too true. I'm a monster, I'm a criminal," said he as he frigged himself. "There's no infamy I've not perpetrated and am not prepared to do again. Come now, your blows are utterly in vain, I'll never mend my ways, I find too much delight in crime. You'd have to kill me to put a stop to my joy; crime is my element, 'tis my life, I've lived in crime, I'll die in it."

And you may well imagine how, these remarks of his inspiring my arm and tongue, I redoubled my blows and invectives. The word "fuck" escaped his lips, however: that was the signal: I lay on with all my might and endeavor to strike his most sensitive parts. He skips, hops, jumps, and capers, he eludes me and, discharging, he scampers into a tub of warm water specially prepared to purify him after this bloody ceremonial. Ah, upon my soul, yes! I ceded to my friend the honor of having seen more of this sort of thing than I, and I believe we two were able to say at the time that we had seen more than all the rest of Paris, for our Grancourt's needs never varied, and for above twenty years he had been going every day to that woman's establishment for the same treatment.

Shortly afterward, that same woman arranged to have me meet another libertine whose idiosyncrasy, I fancy, will seem at least unusual to you. The scene transpired in his little house at Roule. I am introduced into a rather obscurely lit room, where I find a man lying in bed, and, posed in the center of the room, a coffin.

"You see before you," our libertine said to me, "a man reclining upon his deathbed, one who would not close his eyes without rendering a last homage to the object he worships. I adore asses, and if I am to perish, I want to die while kissing one. When life shall have fled this frame, you yourself shall lift me into that coffin, draw round the shrouds, and nail down the lid. It is my design thus to die in pleasure's embrace, and at this last moment to be served by the very object of my lubricious heats. Come... come," he continued in a broken, weak, gasping voice, "make haste, for I am nigh to the threshold."

I draw near to him, turn around, I exhibit my buttocks.

"Ah, wondrous ass!" he cries. "'Tis well, I am easy thus to be able to take with me to the grave the idea of a behind as pretty as that one!"

And he fondled it, opened it, nuzzled and kissed it just the way the healthiest man in the world might have done.

"Oh, indeed!" said he a moment later as he left off his task and rolled toward the wall, "well I knew 'twould not be for long I'd savor this pleasure; I do now expire, remember what I have enjoined you to do."

And so saying, he uttered a profound sigh, grew rigid, and played his part with such skill that damn me if I didn't think he was dead. I kept my wits about me; eager to see the end of this droll ceremony, I wrapped him in the shroud. He had ceased to stir, and whether it was that he knew some secret for feigning death, or whether my imagination had been affected, he felt as rigid and cold as a bar of iron; only his prick gave some hints of life: it too was rigid, but not cold, and glued to his belly, and drops of fuck seemed to come oozing from it despite his moribund condition. Directly I have him swathed in the sheet, I take him up in my arms, and it wasn't easy, for the way he'd become rigid made him as heavy as a steer. I succeeded nevertheless in transporting him to the coffin. As soon as I have laid him out, I start reciting the prayer for the dead, and finally I nail the coffin shut; that was the critical instant for him: no sooner have I driven the last nail home than he sets to screeching like a madman:

"Holy name of God, I'm coming! Get out, whore, get out, for if I catch you, you're done for!"

I'm seized by fear, I dart to the stairs, upon which I meet a tactful manservant who is thoroughly acquainted with his master's manias and who gives me two louis; I proceed to the door, while the valet hastens into the patient's bedchamber to free him from the sealed coffin.

"Now there's a quaint taste," said Durcet. "Well, Curval, what do you think of that one?"

"Marvelous," the Président replied; "there you have an individual who wishes to make himself familiar with the idea of death, and hence unafraid of it, and who to that end has found no better means than to associate it with a libertine idea. There is absolutely no doubt about it: that man will die fondling an ass."

"Nor any doubt," said Champville, "that he is proudly impious; I know him, and I shall have occasion to describe the use he makes of religion's holiest mysteries."

"I don't wonder he is an unbeliever," said the Duc. "He's clearly a man who laughs at the whole business and who wishes to accustom himself to acting and thinking the same way during his last minutes."

"For my part," the Bishop said, "I find something very piquant in that passion, and I'll not hide the fact I'm stiff from hearing about it. Continue, Duclos, go on, for I have the feeling I might do something silly, and I'd prefer to leave well enough alone for the rest of the day."

Very well, said that splendid raconteur, here's one less complex; 'tis the story of a man who for five years regularly applied at my door for the single pleasure of getting me to sew up his asshole. He used to stretch out belly down upon a bed, I would seat myself between his legs and, equipped with a stout needle and half a spool of heavy cobbler's thread, I'd sew his anus completely closed, and this fellow's skin in that area was so toughened and so used to needle thrusts that my operation would not draw a single drop of blood from his hide. While I worked, he would frig himself, and he used to discharge like a mule when I'd taken the last stitch. His ecstasy dissipated, I'd promptly undo my work, and that would be that.

Another used to have brandy rubbed over every part of his body where Nature had placed hair, then I'd put a match to those areas I'd rubbed with alcohol, and all the hair would go up in flames. He would discharge upon finding himself afire, meanwhile I'd shown him my belly, my cunt, and so forth, for that fellow had the bad taste never to want to see anything but fronts.

"But, tell me, Messieurs, did any of you know Mirecourt, today président in the upper chamber, and in those days attorney to the Crown?"

"I knew him," said Curval.

"Well, my Lord, do you know what used to be, and what I dare say still is, his passion?"

"No; and he passes, or wishes to pass, for a devout and good subject, I'd be most pleased to know."

"My Lord," Duclos said, "he likes also to be taken for an ass..."

"Ah! by God! said the Duc; and turning to Curval: "what do you think of that, my friend? Damned strange taste, don't you think, for a judge? I'll wager that once he's an ass he thinks he's going to pronounce judgment. Well, what next?" he asked of Duclos.

"Next, your Grace, one must lead him by the halter, walk him about the room for an hour, he brays, one mounts astride him, and when one's in the saddle, one whips his entire body with a switch, as if to quicken his gait. He breaks into a trot, and as he's started by now to frig himself, he soon discharges and, while he does so, makes loud noises, bucks, rears, and throws the rider."

"That, I'd say, is more diverting than lubricious. And pray tell me, Duclos," the Duc went on, "did that man ever tell you he had some comrade who shared his taste?"

"Why, indeed, he did tell me so," said the amiable Duclos, entering into the joke with a merry laugh and descending from her platform, for her day's stint was over; "Yes, Sire, he told me he had a quantity of comrades, but that not all of them would allow themselves to be mounted."

The séance had come to an end, Messieurs were disposed to perform a few stunts before supper; the Duc hugged Augustine in close embrace.

"You know," he said dreamily, frigging her clitoris and directing her to grasp his prick, "you know, I'm not at all surprised that Curval is sometimes tempted to violate the pact and pop a pucelage or two, for I feel at this very moment, for example, that I could willingly send Augustine's to the devil."

"Which one?" Curval inquired.

"Both of them, bless my soul," answered the Duc; "but one must behave oneself during this sojourn; in having thus to wait a little while for our pleasures, we make them far more delicious. Well, little girl," he continued, "show me your buttocks, perhaps 'twill change the character of my ideas.... Bleeding Christ! look at that little whore's ass! Curval, what do you advise me to do with this thing?"

"Put some vinegar sauce on it," said Curval.

"Mercy!" exclaimed the Duc, "what a notion. But patience, patience... everything will come in good time."

"My very dear brother," said the Bishop in a halting voice, "there's something in your words that smells of fuck."

"Really? For indeed I have the greatest desire to lose some." "And what prevents you?" the Bishop wanted to know.

"Oh, many things, many things," the Duc replied. "First of all, I see no shit in the pipe, and I'd like shit, and then... I don't know -- there are so many things I'd like..."

"What?" asked Durcet just before Antinoüs' turd cascaded into his mouth.

"What?" echoed the Duc. "There's, to begin with, a little infamy I simply must perform."

And retiring to the distant boudoir with Augustine, Zélamir, Cupidon, Duclos, Desgranges, and Hercule, he was heard, a minute later, to utter ringing cries and oaths which proved the Duc had finally managed to calm his brain and soothe his balls. Little precise information exists upon what he did to Augustine, but, notwithstanding his love for her, she was seen to return in tears and, ominous sign! one of her fingers had been twisted. We deeply regret not yet to be able to explain all this to the reader, but it is quite certain that these gentlemen, on the sly and before the arrival of the day heralding open season, were giving themselves over to tricks which have not so far been embodied in story, hence to unsanctioned deeds, and in so doing they were acting in formal violation of the regulations they had sworn in honor to observe; but, you know, when an entire society commits the same faults, they are commonly pardoned. The Duc came back and was pleased to see that Durcet and the Bishop had not been wasting their time, and that Curval, in Bum-Cleaver's arms, was deliciously doing everything one may possibly do with all the voluptuous objects one may possibly assemble around oneself.

Supper was served, orgies followed as usual, the household retired to bed. Lame and aching as Adelaide was, the Duc, who was scheduled to have her by him that night, wanted her there, and as he had come from the orgies rather drunk, as was his wont, it is said that he did not deal tenderly with her. But by and large the night was passed just like all the preceding nights, that is to say, in the depths of delirium and debauchery, and fair-haired Aurora having come, as the poets say, to fling open the gates of the palace where dwelt Apollo, that god, somewhat a libertine himself, only mounted his azure chariot in order to bring light to shed upon new lecheries.

The Twenty-Fifth Day

However, a new intrigue was quietly taking form within the impenetrable walls of the Château of Silling; but it did not have the dangerous significance that had been attributed to Adelaide's league with Sophie. This latest association was being hatched between Aline and Zelmire; those two young girls' conformity of character contributed greatly to their attachment to each other: both were mild-natured and sensitive, no more than thirty months separated them in age, they were both very childlike, very simple, very good-hearted: they had, in brief, almost all of the same virtues, and almost all the same vices, for Zelmire, sweet and tender, was also, like Aline, careless and lazy. They suited one another so admirably that, on the morning of the 25th, they were discovered in the same bed, and this is how it happened: being destined for Curval, Zelmire slept, as we know, in his bedchamber. Aline was Curval's bedwife that same night. But Curval, having returned dead drunk from the orgies, wished to sleep with no one but Invictus, and thus it fell out that these two little doves, abandoned and brought together by fortune, from dread of the cold both camped in the same bed and, in bed, 'twas maintained, their little fingers itched more than their dear little elbows.

Upon opening his eyes in the morning and seeing these two birds sharing the same nest, Curval demanded to know what they were doing there, and ordering them both to come instantly into his bed, he sniffed about just below each one's clitoris, and clearly recognized that both of them were still full of fuck. The case was grave: Messieurs did indeed wish the young ladies to be victims of impudicity, but they insisted that, amongst themselves, they behave decently -- oh, for what will libertinage, perpetually inconsistent libertinage, not insist upon! -- and if they sometimes consented to permit the ladies to indulge in a little reciprocal impurity, it all had to be both upon Messieurs' express instructions and before their eyes. And thus it was the case was brought before the council, and the two delinquents, who neither could nor dared deny the thing, were ordered to demonstrate what they had been up to, and before a crowd of spectators to display just what their individual talents were. They did as they were told, with much blushing and not a little weeping, and asked to be forgiven their mistakes. But too attractive was the prospect of having that pretty couple amongst the culprits to be punished the following Saturday; consequently, they were not forgiven, but were speedily included in Durcet's book of sorrows which, incidentally, was being very agreeably filled up that week.

This chore completed, breakfast was finished, and Durcet conducted his searches. The fatal indigestions yielded still another miscreant: 'twas the little Michette, she'd been unable to hold the bridge, she said they'd made her eat too much the night before, and these were followed by a thousand other infantile excuses which did not prevent her name from being written down. Curval, his prick jumping like a young colt, seized the chamber pot and devoured its contents. And then bringing his angry eyes to bear upon her:

"Oh yes, by Jesus," said he, "yes, by the Saviour's fuck, you shall be spanked, my little rascal, my own hand will see to that. There are rules against shitting that way; you should at least have given us notice; you know damned well that we are prepared to receive shit at any hour of the day or night."

And he fondled her buttocks very vivaciously while repeating the rules to her.

The boys were found intact, no chapel permissions were distributed to them, and Messieurs repaired to table. During the meal, there was plentiful and penetrating discussion of Aline's deed; they ascribed a holier-than-thou attitude to her, said she appeared a little hypocrite, and behold! here was proof of her real temperament at last come to light.

"How now, my friend," Durcet said to the Bishop, "is one still to lay any store by appearances, above all those that girls parade?"

'Twas unanimously agreed nothing was more deceitful than a girl, and that, as they were every one of them false, they never made use of their wits save to be more skillfully false. These observations brought the table talk around to women, and the Bishop who abhorred them, gave vent to all the hatred they inspired in him. He reduced them to the state of the vilest animals, and proved their existence so perfectly useless in this world that one could extirpate them from the face of the earth without in the slightest countercarrying the designs of Nature who, having in times past very surely found the means to create without women, would find it again when only men were left.

They proceeded to coffee; it was presented them by Augustine, Michette, Hyacinthe, and Narcisse. The Bishop, one of whose greatest uncomplex pleasures was to suck little boys' pricks, had been spending a few minutes playing this game with Hyacinthe, when all of a sudden he reared back and let out, not a shout, but a bubbling noise, for his mouth was full; his exclamation was interpreted thus: "Ah, by God's balls, my friends, a pucelage! That's the first time this little rascal has discharged, I'm sure of it!" And, truth to tell, no one had so far observed Hyacinthe carry things to that point; he was indeed thought still too young to bring it off. But he was well advanced in his fourteenth year, 'tis the age when Nature customarily heaps her favors upon us, and nothing could have been more real than the victory the Bishop thought he had achieved. None the less, the others were anxious to verify the thing, and each wishing to be witness to the adventure, they drew up their chairs in a semicircle around the young man. Augustine, the most accomplished frigger in the seraglio, received permission to manualize the lad within clear sight of the assembly, and Hyacinthe was given leave to fondle and caress her in whatsoever part of her body he desired. There's no spectacle more voluptuous than that offered by a young maid of fifteen, lovely as the day, lending herself to the caresses of a boy of fourteen and provoking, by means of the most delicious pollutions, his springtide discharge.

Hyacinthe, aided perhaps by Nature, but yet more certainly by the examples he had before his nose, fondled, handled, kissed naught but his frigger's pretty little buttocks, and it required little more than an instant of this to bring color to his cheeks, to fetch two or three sighs from his lips, to induce his pretty little prick to shoot, to a distance of one yard, five or six jets of sweet fuck white as cream, which emissions happened to land on Durcet's thigh, for the banker was seated nearest the boy and was having himself frigged by Narcisse while watching the operation. The fact once indubitably established, they caressed and kissed the child rather universally, each swore he'd love to receive a small portion of that youthful sperm, and as it appeared that, at his age and for a beginning, six discharges were not too many, in that he had after all just delivered himself of two without the least difficulty, our libertines induced him to shed another in each of their mouths.

Much heated by this performance, the Duc laid hands on Augustine and frigged her clitoris with his tongue until he had elicited several solid discharges from her; full of fire and blessed with a mettlesome spirit, that little minx shot them off in short order. While the Duc was thus polluting Augustine, nothing was more engaging than to see Durcet, come up to gather symptoms of the pleasure he was not provoking, kiss that beautiful child's mouth a thousand times over, and swallow, so to speak, the voluptuousness another was causing to circulate throughout her senses. The hour was advanced, they were obliged to omit the midday nap and to pass directly into the auditorium where Duclos had been awaiting them for a long time; as soon as everyone had arranged himself, she took up the thread of her adventures and spoke as hereafter you may read:

I have already had the honor to remark in your Lordships' presence, that it is most difficult to fathom all the tortures man invents for himself in order to find, in the degradation they produce, or the agonies, those sparks of pleasure which age or satiety have made to grow faint in him. Hard it is to credit the assertion that one such gentleman of this sort, a person of sixty years and to a singular degree jaded by all the pleasures of lubricity, used only to be able to restore his senses to life by having the flames of burning candles applied to every part of his body, and principally to the ones Nature has intended for those selfsame pleasures. He would have his thighs seared, his prick, his balls roasted, and above all else his asshole: while all this was going forward, he would be kissing an ass, and after the grievous operation had been repeated for the fifteenth or twentieth time, he would discharge while sucking the anus of the girl who'd been burning him.

Soon after that one, I had dealings with another who obliged me to use a horse's currycomb on him, to rub down his entire body with that instrument, quite as one does to the animal I have just named. Directly his body was all an open wound, I'd next rub him with alcohol, and this second torture would cause him abundantly to discharge upon my breasts -- that was the battlefield he chose to spray with his fuck. I would kneel before him, squeeze his prick between my bubs, and he'd quietly wash them with his balls' acrid humor.

A third would have would have every hair on his ass plucked out one by one. While that lengthy operation was advancing, he would frig himself upon a warm turd I'd just done for him. Then, at the crisis' approach, I had, to give it the necessary encouragement, to drive the point of a scissors deep enough into each of his buttocks to draw a jet of blood. His ass was a maze of wounds and scars, I was scarce able to find an open space for my two gashes; immediately the steel entered him, he'd plunge his nose into the shit, smear it upon his face, and floods of sperm would crown his ecstasy.

A fourth put his prick in my mouth and bade me bite it as hard as I could; in the meantime, as I chewed his poor device, I was expected to lacerate his buttocks with an iron comb whose teeth were ground to sharp points; and then, at the moment I sensed his prick ready to melt -- a very faint, a barely perceptible erection would tell me so --and then, I say, I'd spread his buttocks prodigiously wide, ease them close to a burning candle I'd kept in readiness on the floor, and I'd braise his asshole with it. 'Twas the burning sensation of that candle under his anus decided his emission;

I'd therewith redouble my bitings, and would soon find my mouth full.

"One moment, if you please," said the Bishop. "Every time I hear of someone discharging into a mouth I am reminded of the good fortune I had earlier today, and my spirits are disposed to tasting further pleasures of the same sort."

Saying which, he draws Invictus near, for that champion was on duty in the Bishop's alcove that afternoon, and falls to sucking the brave fellow's prick with all the energetic lustiness of a true bugger. Fuck explodes, the prelate gobbles it up, and straightway goes to repeat the operation upon Zéphyr. The Bishop was brandishing his knobkerrie, and 'twas seldom that women would feel completely at their ease when he was in this critical state and they were near him. Unfortunately, it was his niece Aline who happened to be within range.

"What are you doing there, bitch?" he rasped; "I want men for my fun."

Aline seeks to elude him, he seizes her by the hair and, dragging her into his closet along with Zelmire and Hébé, the two girls in his quartet:

"You'll see," says he to his friends, "you'll see how I'm going to teach these wenches to slip cunts under my hand when I'm doing my best to find some pricks."

Upon his order, Fanchon accompanied the three maidens, and an instant later Aline was heard to utter very shrill cries; then came tidings of Monseigneur's discharge, reverberating howls which blended with his dear niece's dolorous accents. Everyone returned... Aline was weeping, squeezing and clutching her behind.

"Come show me what he did to you," said the Duc; "I love nothing better than to see traces of my distinguished brother's brutality."

Aline displayed I've no idea what, for I have never been able to discover what went on in those infernal closets, but the Duc exclaimed: "By fuck, 'tis delicious, I think I'll go off and do the same." But Curval having pointed out to him that time was growing short, and having added that he had an amusing enterprise in mind for the orgies, which scheme would demand a clear head and all his fuck, Duclos was asked to go ahead with the fifth story in order that the sitting be brought to a proper conclusion; the storyteller therewith addressed the convocation once again:

Belonging to that group of extraordinary individuals, said she, whose mania consists in wallowing in degradation and in insulting their own dignity, was a certain judge of the circuit court whose name was Foucolet. There's truly no believing the point to which that fellow would carry his furor; he had to be given a sample of almost every torture. I used to hang him, but the rope would break just in time and he would fall upon a mattress; the next instant, I would strap him to a St. Andrew's cross and make as if to break his limbs with a bar, but it was only a roll of pasteboard; I used to brand him upon the shoulder, the iron I used was warm and left a faint imprint, no more; I would flog his back in precise imitation of the public servant who performs those noble feats, and whilst I was doing all this I had to overwhelm him with a stream of atrocious invectives, bitter reproaches for various crimes, for which, during each successive operation, he would demand, a candle in his hand and wearing only his shirt, God's forgiveness and the law's, pronouncing his entreaties in a very humble and contrite tone; finally, the meeting would be brought to a close on my ass, where the libertine would yield up his fuck when his head had reached the ultimate degree of distraction.

"Well now, are you going to let me discharge in peace now that Duclos has finished?" the Duc asked Curval.

"No, not a bit of it," the Président replied; "preserve your fuck, I tell you I need it for the orgies."

"Oh, so you take me for your valet, do you?" the Duc exclaimed. "You take me for a worn-out bugger? Do you suppose that the small quantity of fuck I'm going to lose in a moment will prevent me from joining in all the infamies which are going to pop into your head four hours from now? Come now, Président, you know me better than that; banish your fears, I'll be fit again for anything inside fifteen minutes, but my good and holy brother has been pleased to give me a little example of an atrocity I'd be grief-stricken not to execute with Adelaide, your dear and estimable daughter."

And pushing her forthwith into his closet, along with Thérèse, Colombe, and Fanny, the female elements of his quatrain, he probably did there, with them, what the Bishop had done to his niece, and discharged with the same episodes, for, as not long before they heard Aline's terrible scream, so now their ears were treated to another from the lips of Adelaide and the bawdy Duc's yells of lust. Curval wished to learn which of the two brothers had been the better behaved; he summoned the two women, and having pored at length over their two behinds, he decided that the Duc had not merely imitated, but surpassed the Bishop.

They sat down at table, and having by means of some drug or other stuffed the bowels of all the subjects, men and women, with an abundance of wind, after supper they played the game of fart-in-the-face:

Messieurs, all four of them, lay back upon couches, their heads raised, and one by one the members of the household stepped up to deliver their farts into the waiting mouths. Duclos was requested to do the counting and mark down the scores; there were thirty-six farters against only four swallowers: hence there were certain persons who received as many as one hundred and fifty farts. It had been for this rousing ceremony Curval had wanted the Duc to keep himself fit, but such precautions, as Blangis had made perfectly clear, were quite unnecessary; he was too great a friend of libertinage to allow some new excess to find him unprepared; to the contrary, any new excess always had the greatest effect upon him, his situation notwithstanding, and he did not fail to produce a second discharge thanks to the humid mistral Fanchon wafted into his mouth.

As for Curval, they were Antinoüs' farts which cost him his fuck, whereas Durcet bent before the gale that swept out of Martaine's asshole, and the Bishop lost all control in the face of what Desgranges offered him. The youthful beauties' efforts, 'twill be remarked, came to naught; but is it not true that it is always the crapulous individual who best executes the infamous deed?

The Twenty-Sixth Day

In that nothing was more delicious than meting out punishments, in that nothing prepared the way for so many pleasures, and those very sorts of pleasures Messieurs had mutually promised not to taste until in the stories mention thereof should permit fullest indulgence in them, the libertines sought by every imaginable means to trip the subjects into states of delinquency, and so procure themselves the joy of chastising their hapless victims; to this end, the friends, having convoked an extraordinary assembly that morning, their purpose being to deliberate upon this problem, they added several articles to the household regulations, infraction of which was necessarily to occasion punishment. Firstly, the wives, the small boys, and the girls were expressly forbidden to fart anywhere save in the friends' mouths. Instantly they were seized by the desire to break wind, they were without delay to go and find one of the friends and administer unto him what required to be set at large; a severe afflictive penalty would be the reward for disobedience. Secondly, the use of bidets and ass-wipings of any kind were absolutely outlawed; it was generally proclaimed that all subjects without exception would hereafter never wash themselves, and never under any circumstances wipe the ass after having shitted; that, whenever an ass were found clean, upon the subject concerned would lie the burden of proving it had been licked clean by one of the friends, and that friend would have to be mentioned by name. In response to which citation, the friend would be questioned, and, being in a position to procure himself two pleasures, instead of only one, to wit: that of having cleaned the ass with his tongue, and that of having punished the subject who had afforded him this first pleasure...

Examples of this will be provided.

Thirdly, a new ceremony was introduced: at the time of the morning coffee, at the time of their entry into the girls' quarters, and also when, after that, they passed into the boys', each of the subjects would hereafter, one by one, step forth and, in a loud and clear voice, say to each of the friends: "I don't care a fuck for God; there's shit in my ass, would you like some?" and those who should fail in an intelligible voice to pronounce both the blasphemy and the invitation, would instantly be inscribed in the dread book. The reader will readily imagine what difficulties the pious Adelaide and her young pupil Sophie had to surmount before being able to utter such infamies, and their inner struggles procured Messieurs some excellent entertainment.

The foregoing once framed in law, they turned to consider delations and decided to admit them; this barbarous means of multiplying vexations, accepted by every tyrant, was warmly embraced by these. It was decided, fourthly, that every subject who should lodge complaint against some other, would thereby earn a one-half reduction of the punishment he was to suffer for the next fault he committed. Messieurs were in no way deprived by this system, because the subject who had just accused another subject could never know the extent of the punishment a half of which, he was promised, would be suppressed; and so it was a simple matter indeed to give him precisely what one wished to give him, and still to persuade him he had got off more lightly than otherwise he might. Messieurs agreed upon and published their decision, that no delation required substantiating proof in order to be believed, and that, to be inscribed, accusation brought by anyone would suffice. The duennas' authority, furthermore, was increased, and upon the basis of their slightest complaint, whether true or false, the subject would be condemned immediately. In a word, over this small population they established all the vexation, all the injustice one could imagine, certain in the belief that the more harshly their tyranny was exercised, the greater the sum of pleasures they would derive from their privileged situation.

All this legislation composed and voted, they visited the chamber pots. Colombe was found guilty; her excuses hinged upon the food they had made her eat between meals the day before; she had, said she, been unable to resist, she was dreadfully unhappy about the whole thing, and this was the fourth successive week she had been punished. The statement was true, and she had only to blame her ass, which was the freshest, the sweetest, the best-made and most endearing little ass you could hope to see. She pointed out she'd not wiped herself, and that, she supposed, should be regarded as a point in her favor. Durcet examined her, and having indeed discovered a very thick and very broad patch of shit, he assured her that, in the light of this, she'd be treated a little less rigorously. Curval, stiff at the time, laid hands on her, and having completely cleaned her anus, he had her produce her turd and ate it while having her frig him, periodically interrupting his chewing to kiss her upon the mouth and to order her to swallow, in her turn, what of her own creation he brought to her lips. They next inspected Augustine and Sophie, who had been solemnly enjoined, after the stools they had yielded up the night before, to remain in the most impure state. Sophie's appearance conformed with her instructions, even though she had slept in the Bishop's chamber, but Augustine was as neat as a pin. Sure of her reply, she advanced proudly and said that they knew very well she had, as was her custom, lain the night in Monsieur le Duc's bedchamber, and that before going to sleep he had summoned her to his bed, where he had licked her asshole while she had frigged his prick in her mouth. When interrogated, the Duc said that he had no remembrance of the thing (although the story was completely true), that he had fallen asleep with his prick in Duclos' ass, that they could substantiate the fact. They went about the matter with all possible seriousness and gravity, they sent for Duclos who, seeing clearly what was afoot, lent her support to everything the Duc advanced, and maintained that Augustine had been called to Monsieur's bed only for a brief instant, that Monsieur had shitted into Augustine's mouth and then, upon second thought, had bade her return to the bed in order that he might eat his turd. Augustine sought to defend her thesis and dispute Duclos' contentions, but silence was imposed upon her and, although perfectly innocent, her name was written down.

Amongst the boys, whose chambers they visited next, Cupidon was found guilty; he had done the world's most gorgeous turd in his chamber pot. The Duc snatched it up and gobbled it up while the young malefactor sucked his member.

All requests for chapel permissions were refused; they then went to dine. The beautiful Constance, whom they sometimes dispensed from serving at table because of her state, was however feeling fit that day, and made her appearance naked; the sight of her belly, which was beginning somewhat to swell, made Curval's head very hot; the others, seeing his treatment of the poor creature's buttocks and breasts growing rather rough -- Curval's horror for her was doubling every day, that was plain -- were swayed by her entreaties and their common desire to preserve her fruit, at least until a certain date, and she was allowed to absent herself from all the day's functions, save for the narrations, wherefrom she was never excused. Curval started in again with his frightful speeches about child-breeders, he declared that if he had government of the country he would borrow their law from the inhabitants of Formosa, where pregnant women under thirty are, together with their fruit, ground in a large mortar; should that law, he protested, be introduced into France, the population would still be twice what it ought to be.

Coffee came next; it was presented by Sophie, Fanny, Zélamir, and Adonis, but served in a passing strange manner: 'twas in the children's mouths, one had to sip it therefrom. Sophie served hers to the Duc, Fanny Curval's, Zélamir the Bishop's, and Durcet got his out of Adonis. They extracted a mouthful, gargled it a moment, and returned it into the mouths of those who'd served them. Curval, who had risen from the table in a great ferment, got stiff all over again thanks to this ceremony, and when it had been completed, he laid hands on Fanny and discharged into her mouth, ordering her to swallow the whey; the threats accompanying his instructions succeeded in making the poor wretch obey without the flutter of an eyelash. The Duc and his two other confreres collected shit or farts; having finished their nap, they all trooped in to listen to Duclos, who spoke to them in this wise:

I will move with dispatch, said that amiable girl, through my last two adventures concerning these unusual men who find their delight only in the pain they are made to undergo, and then with your leave we will pass on to a different variety.

The first, while he had me frig him, naked and standing up, wanted floods of hot water poured down on us through an opening in the ceiling; our bodies were to be showered during the entire operation. It was quite in vain I argued that, while not sharing in this passion of his, I was nevertheless, like himself, to be a victim of it; he replied, assuring me I would suffer no hurt from the experience, and that these showers were good for one's health. I believed him and let him have his way; as this scene transpired in his house, the temperature of the water, a critical detail, was something lying beyond my control. It was indeed nearly boiling. Messieurs, there is no conceiving the pleasure he felt upon being drenched by it. As for myself, all the while operating with all possible speed, I screeched, yes, I confess it, I screeched like a drowning tomcat; my skin came peeling off, and I made myself the firm promise never to return to that man's house.

"Ah, buggerfuck!" exclaimed the Duc, "I have the strongest inclination to give the beauteous Aline a comparable scalding."

"Your Grace," the latter replied in a humble but decided tone, "I am not a tomcat."

And the naive candor in her childlike reply having fetched a chuckle from everyone, Duclos was asked to give the second and final example of the same genre.

It was a great deal less painful for me, said Duclos; I had simply to don a stout glove, then with this protected hand to take burning grit from a frying pan I'd been heating on a stove, and, my hand filled, to rub that fiery sand over my man's body, from head to toe. His body was so inured to this exercise that he seemed to be covered not with skin, but with leather. When one reached his prick, one had to seize it and massage it in a handful of that same sand; he'd be up like a shot. Then, with the other hand, I placed a small fire shovel, heated red-hot for this purpose, under his balls. This rubbing with one hand, the consuming heat which rose to bake his testicles, perhaps a little touching of my two buttocks, which I had to keep well exposed and within reach during the operation, this combination of elements melted him altogether and he discharged, being very careful to spill his seed upon the hot shovel where, to his unutterable delight, he watched it sizzle and evaporate in steam.

"Curval," said the Duc, "there's a man who, 'twould appear to me, has no greater fondness than have you for population."

"It looks that way to me," Curval assented; "I make no bones about the fact I love the idea of watching fuck burn."

"Oh, I know all the ideas fuck inspires in you," said the Duc with a hearty laugh. "And even were the seed to ripen, the egg to hatch, you'd perform a combustion with the same pleasure, wouldn't you?"

"Upon my soul, I do fear I would," said Curval, as he did I know not what to Adelaide that brought a loud scream from her lips.

"And who the devil do you think you are dealing with, whore?" Curval demanded of his daughter. "What are these chirpings and squallings all about? Remember the company you are in. Can't you see that the Duc's trying to talk to me of burning, provoking, instilling good manners into hatched fuck, and what are you, pray tell me, but a little something hatched out of my balls' fuck? Duclos, I say, continue, if you please," Curval added, "for I have the feeling this bitch's tears might make me discharge. And I'd prefer not to."

And here we are, said our heroine, come to details which, bringing with them characters of a more singular piquancy, will perhaps please you more. You know of course that in Paris we have the custom of exposing the dead before the doors of houses. There was a particular gentleman, well placed in society, who used to pay me twelve francs for every one of these lugubrious objects to which, in a given evening, I could lead him; his whole delight consisted in going up with me as near to them as possible, to the very edge of the coffin if we were able, and once we had posted ourselves there, I had to frig him in such wise his fuck would shoot out upon the coffin. We used to run from one to another, would often pay our respects to three or four in an evening; it all depended upon the number I had located for him in advance, and we performed the same operation beside each of them; he never touched anything but my behind while I toiled over his prick. He was a man of about thirty, and I had his trade for at least ten years. I'm sure that, during the period of our collaboration, I made him discharge upon more than two thousand coffins.

"But would he not say something during the rite?" inquired the Duc. "Did he not speak either to you or to the corpse?"

"He would shower invectives upon the deceased," Duclos replied; for example: 'Here, you rascal, here, take it, you villain, you bugger, take my fuck along with you to hell.'"

"A very unusual mania, that one," Curval commented.

"My friend," said the Duc, "you can be certain that man was one of our own sort, and that he surely did not stop at that."

"You are quite right, my Lord," spoke up Martaine, "and I shall have occasion to bring that actor back upon the stage."

Taking advantage of the silence which succeeded Martaine's interjection, Duclos went on.

Another one, said she, carrying a more or less similar fantasy a good deal further, wanted me to keep spies on the watch near the cemeteries and to bring in word every time there was a burial of some young girl whose death had been caused by anything but a dangerous disease -- he was very emphatic upon that point. As soon as I had got wind of something suitable, and he always paid me very handsomely for those discoveries, we would set off after sundown, enter the cemetery by one means or another, and heading at once for the grave our informant had indicated, above which the earth had only recently been broken, we would both fall to work, dig down to the cadaver, and when once we'd uncovered it, I'd frig him over it while he spent his time handling it and, above all, if 'twere possible, its buttocks. If perchance, and it frequently occurred, he stiffened a second time, he'd therewith shit, and have me shit also, upon the corpse, and discharge thereupon, all the while palpating whatever parts of the body he could lay his hands on.

"Oh, my, but that one does strike a response in me," said Curval, "and if I have to make my confession to you here and now, I'll assure you I've done the same thing from time to time. To be sure, I added a few little episodes I dare say our rules prevent me from describing at this point. Be that as it may, my prick's got monstrously fat; spread your thighs, Adelaide..."

And I've not the faintest idea what happened next; all we know is that the couch groaned beneath its burden, unmistakable sounds of a discharge pealed from the Président niche, and I am led to suppose that, very simply and very virtuously, his honor the judge had just committed incest.

"Président," the Duc called over, "I'll wager you thought she was dead."

"Why, indeed, that's true," said Curval, "else how in the world could I have discharged?"

And hearing not another word from the several alcoves, Duclos brought that evening's stories to a close with the following one:

Lest I leave you, Messieurs, with dark images and sad thoughts, I am going to conclude the soiree with the story of the Duc de Bonnefort's passion. That young lord, whom I amused five or six times, and who used frequently to see one of my close friends for the same operation, required a woman, armed with a dildo, to frig herself naked in his presence -- to frig herself, I say, both before and behind and to keep it up for three hours without a moment's interruption. He has a clock there to guide you, and if you drop the work before having completed the third hour, no payment for you. He sits opposite you, he observes you, makes you turn this way, that way, some other way, exhorts you to ply the dildo more energetically, he would have you go out of your mind with pleasure, and if indeed transported by the effects of the operation, you should really swoon away with delight, 'tis very certain you will hasten his. But if you keep your head, at the precise instant the clock strikes the third hour, up he gets, approaches you, and discharges in your face.

"Truly," quoth the Bishop, "I fail to understand, Duclos, why you didn't prefer to leave us with those other images and thoughts rather than with this innocuous picture. They had some spice to them, some color, and excited us powerfully, whereas here we have some sort of milksop business which, now that the session is over, leaves us with nothing at all in our heads."

"No, she did the right thing, insofar as I'm concerned," said Julie, who was lying with Durcet, "and I give her my warmest thanks. We'll all be allowed to go to bed more peacefully now that they don't have all those frightful ideas in their heads."

"Ah, lovely Julie, you may be very gravely mistaken," said Durcet, "for I never remember anything but the earlier one when the later one displeases me; you doubt my word? why, then pray have the kindness to follow me."

And, together with Sophie and Michette, Durcet fled into his closet to discharge I don't know how, but none the less in a manner which must not have suited Sophie, for she uttered a piercing scream and emerged from the sanctuary as red as a cockscomb.

"Well," drawled the Duc, "you surely could not have wanted to confuse her with a corpse for that stunt; for you've just made her give out the most furious sign of life."

"She was afraid, that's all," Durcet explained; "ask her what I did to her and make her tell you in a whisper."

He sent Sophie to speak to the Duc.

"Ah," said the latter aloud, "there's nothing in that either to warrant screams, or, for that matter, a discharge."

And because the supper call sounded, they suspended their conversation and their pleasures in order to go and enjoy those of the table. The orgies were celebrated rather quietly, and Messieurs retired to bed in good order; not one of them had even the appearance of being drunk; and that was extremely unusual.

The Twenty-Seventh Day

The denunciations, authorized on the previous day, began early that morning; the sultanas, having remarked that, save for Rosette, they were all listed for correction, decided that all eight of themselves ought to be included in the game and promptly went to level accusations against her. They reported she had spent the whole night farting, and as this was really only a teasing they were giving her, she had the entire harem against whom to pit her denials; her name was straightway inscribed. Everything else moved along splendidly and, except for Sophie and Zelmire, who stuttered just a little, the friends were thrilled by the new compliment they had from these brazen little hussies: "God's fuck, I've an assful of shit, wouldst care for some?" And, as a matter of fact, there was shit everywhere to be had indeed, for, from fear of some temptation to wash, the governesses had removed every pot, every receptacle, every towel, and all water. The diet of meat but no bread was beginning to warm all those little unwashed mouths, Messieurs noticed that there was already a very appreciable difference in the little girls' breaths.

"Damn my eyes!" exclaimed Curval as he withdrew his tongue from Augustine's gullet; "that now signifies at least something; kissing this one makes me stiff."

Everyone agreed there had been a distinct improvement.

As there was nothing new or out of the ordinary until coffee, we are going to transport the reader directly to the salon. Coffee was served by Sophie, Zelmire, Giton, and Narcisse. The Duc said he was perfectly sure Sophie was the sort of girl who could discharge; the experiment, in his view, had absolutely to be made. He asked Durcet to keep a close eye on her and, laying her upon a divan, he simultaneously polluted the edges of her vagina, her clitoris, and her asshole, at first with his fingers, next with his tongue; and Nature triumphed: after fifteen minutes of this, the lovely girl became uneasy, troubled, she flushed crimson, she sighed, she panted, Durcet drew Curval's and the Bishop's attention to all these manifestations, for 'twas they who'd doubted her discharging capacities; the Duc suggested that, since he had always been confident of them, it was for the others to convince themselves, and so they all fell to imbibing that young fuck, and the little rascal's cunt left all their lips moist. The Duc could not resist the experiment's lubricious appeal; he got up and, squatting over the child, discharged upon her half-opened fur, then used his fingers to work as much as possible of his seed into the interior of her cunt. His head inspired by what he was watching, Curval seized the little one and demanded something other than fuck of her; she tendered her cunning little ass, the Président glued his mouth to it, the intelligent reader will have no trouble guessing what he received therefrom. Zelmire was meanwhile amusing the Bishop: she first frigged, then sucked his fundament. And all that while, Curval was having himself frigged by Narcisse, whose ass he kissed ardently. However, no one but the Duc lost his fuck; Duclos had announced some pretty stories for that afternoon which, she promised, would outdo what she had served up the day before, and Messieurs were disposed to save their forces for the auditorium. The hour having come, they passed to their alcoves, and that interesting girl expressed herself in the following manner:

A man of whose circumstances and existence I had not previously
known anything, she said, and about whom I was later to learn only a little,
and, therefore, a man about whom I can give you no better than an imperfect portrait, sent me a note, and in it besought me to come to his house,
in the rue Blanche-du-Rempart, at nine o'clock in the evening. I had no
reason to be suspicious, his note said; although I had no acquaintance
of him, I could be certain that neither would I have cause to complain
were I to come as he bade me do. Two louis accompanied the letter, and
despite my usual cautiousness, which ought certainly to have opposed
my accepting the invitation of a man of whom I knew nothing, despite
all that, I took the risk, trusting to I know not what intuition which, in a
very low voice, told me I had nothing to fear. And so I went; and I arrived
at the given address. I am greeted by a valet who informs me that I am
to undress entirely, for, he explains, it is only if I am naked that he can
introduce me into his master's apartment; I execute the order, and directly
he sees me in the state desired, he takes me by the hand, and having led
me through several intervening chambers, finally knocks upon a door.

It opens, I enter, the valet withdraws, the door closes again; but, with
what regards the amount of light in the room, there was precious little
difference between that place and the inside of a hat, neither light nor air
penetrated into that room from any opening whatever. No sooner am I in
than a naked man comes up to me and seizes me without a word; I keep
my wits about me, persuaded that the whole thing surely boiled down
to nothing more than a little fuck to be shed by one means or another;
that job once over with, I say to myself, I'll be quits with this whole nocturnal ceremony. And so I waste not a moment placing my hand upon
his groin, with the intention of draining the venom from the monster as
rapidly as possible. I discover a very large prick, very hard and also very
rebellious, but scarcely have I touched it than my fingers are forced away:
my opponent seems not to want me to find out anything about him; I
am edged toward a stool and made to sit down. The unknown libertine
plumps himself down near me, and grasping my tits one after the other,
he squeezes and wrings them so violently that I protest that he is hurting
me. Wherewith his brutalities cease, he leads me to an elevated sofa, and
has me stretch out flat upon it; then seating himself between my parted
legs, he falls to doing to my buttocks what he has just left off doing to my
breasts: he palpates and squeezes them with unparalleled violence, he
spreads them, compresses them again, kneads them, mauls, kisses, and
bites them, he sucks my asshole, and as these reiterated attacks were less
dangerous on that side than they might have been on the other, I held my
peace and put up no resistance, and as I let him toil over my hindquarters I wondered what could be the purpose of this mysteriousness when,
after all, the things he was doing were perfectly ordinary. I was trying to
guess what he was driving at when all of a sudden my man began to utter

bloodcurdling shrieks:

"Run for it, you damned whore, run for it, I tell you," he shouted, "get out of here, you bitch, for I'm discharging and won't be held responsible for your life!"

As you may readily imagine, my first movement was to leap to my feet; I spied a feeble glimmer of light -- it was coming through the doorway I had entered -- I dashed toward it -- ran into the valet who had received me at the door -- flung myself into his arms... He gave me back my clothes, also gave me two louis, I left the place at once, very pleased to have got off so cheaply.

"And you had excellent cause to congratulate yourself," said Martaine, "for what you were exposed to was merely a diminutive version of his ordinary passion. I shall present the man to you again, Messieurs," that worldly dame continued, "but in a more dangerous aspect."

"I expect my characterization of him will be even darker," said Desgranges, "and I wish to join Madame Martaine in assuring you that you were exceedingly fortunate to have had to put up with no more than you did, for the same gentleman has far more unusual passions."

"But let us wait and hear his entire story before arguing the point," the Duc suggested, "and, Duclos, make haste to tell us another so as to remove from our minds the image of an individual who will unfailingly arouse us if we dwell any longer on him."

The libertine with whom next I came into contact, Duclos went on, wished to have a woman who had a very handsome bust, and as that is one of my beauties, after having exposed it to his scrutiny, he preferred me to any of my girls. But what use did that wretched libertine design to make of both my breasts and my face? He had me lie down, entirely naked, upon a divan, straddled my chest, deposited his prick between my dugs, ordered me to squeeze them together as tightly as I was able, and after a brief career, the wicked fellow inundated them with fuck while expectorating at least twenty mouthfuls of thick spittle, all of which landed on my face.

"Well," grumbled Adelaide, in whose face the Duc had just been spitting, "I fail to see any necessity for imitating that infamy. Are you done now?" she continued as she wiped her face. But the Duc had not discharged.

"I'll finish when it suits my convenience, sweet child," the Duc replied to her; "bear well in mind that, alive though you may be, you are only so in order to obey and to let be done to you what we please. Proceed with your story, Duclos, for I might do something worse and, adoring this beautiful creature as I do," he said, resorting to a bit of persiflage, "I'd hardly wish entirely to outrage her."

I know not, Messieurs, Duclos said as she resumed her discourse, whether you have ever heard tell of the Commander de Saint-Elme's passion. He had a gaming house where all who came to risk their money were deftly fleeced; but the most extraordinary part of it all was that cheating his visitors used to make the Commander's prick stiffen: every time he'd pick someone's pocket he'd discharge in his breeches, and a woman with whom I used to be on the very best terms, and whom he had been keeping for a long time, once told me that sometimes the thing would heat him to such a point that he would be obliged to go to her to seek some relief from the ardor devouring him. He did not confine himself to robbing customers at roulette; every other kind of theft was just as attractive in his eyes, and no article was safe when he was in the vicinity. Were he to dine at your table, he would make off with the silverware; when he entered your study, he'd pilfer your jewels; if near your pocket, he'd appropriate your snuffbox or your handkerchief. Everything was subject to seizure: he took a keen interest in anything provided he could get his hands on it, and everything gave him a stout erection, and would even cause him to discharge once he had made it his own.

But in that eccentricity of his he was certainly less outstanding than the parliamentary judge with whom I had to cope shortly after my arrival at Fournier's establishment, and whom I had as a client for many years: his being a rather ticklish case, he would deal with no one but me.

The jurisconsult had a little apartment, which he rented the year around, looking out upon the place de Grève; an old servant lived as a caretaker in the apartment, and her only duties were these two: to keep the premises in good order and to send word to her employer whenever preparations for an execution were visible upon the square. The judge would immediately get in touch with me, tell me to hold myself in readiness; he would disguise himself and come to fetch me in a cab, and we would repair to his little apartment.

In the salon the casement window was placed in such a manner it commanded a direct view of, and was situated near, the scaffold; we would post ourselves there, the judge and I, behind a latticework screen upon one of whose horizontal slats he rested an excellent pair of opera glasses, and while waiting for the patient to make his appearance, Themis' wise henchman would amuse himself upon a bed which had been drawn close to the window; while waiting, I say, he would kiss my ass, an episode which, by the by, pleased him enormously. Finally, the crowd's hubbub would announce the victim's arrival, the man of the gown would return to his place at the window and would have me take mine beside him, with the injunction to frig his prick gently, proportioning my strokes to the progress of the execution he was about to watch, in such sort that the sperm would not escape until the moment the patient rendered up his soul unto God. Everything was arranged, the criminal mounted upon the platform, the jurist contemplated him; the nearer the patient approached to death, the more furious became the villain's prick in my hands. The axe was raised, the axe was brought down, 'twas the instant he discharged: "Ah, gentle Jesus!" he'd say, "double-fucked Christ! How I'd like to be the executioner myself, and how much better than that I'd swing the blade!"

Moreover, his pleasures' impressions would be measured by the method of execution, a hanging produced in him little more than an exceedingly mild sensation, a man being broken on the wheel threw him into a delirium, but were the criminal to be either burned alive or quartered, my client would swoon away from pleasure. Man or woman, it made no difference to him.

"I dare say," he once remarked, "that only a pregnant woman would have a stronger effect upon me, and, unfortunately, the thing cannot be brought about."

"But, your honor," I said to him upon another occasion, "through your public function you have cooperated in the destruction of this luckless victim."

"Assuredly, yes," he replied, "and that precisely is what creates all the diversion for me; I have been judging for a good thirty years and have never pronounced any but the death sentence."

"And do you suppose," I said, "that you have not, if only a little, to reproach yourself for the death of these people, which so resembles murder?"

"Splendid," he murmured; "must one, however, look at the matter so closely?"

"But in society such a thing is called a horror," I protested.

"Oh," said he, "one has got to learn how to make the best of the horror; there is in horror matter to produce an erection, you see, and the reason therefor is quite simple: this thing, however frightful you wish to imagine it, ceases to be horrible for you immediately it acquires the power to make you discharge; it is, hence, no longer horrible save in the eyes of others, but who is to assure me that the opinion of others, almost always erroneous or faulty in every other connection, is not equally so in this instance? There is nothing," he pursued, "either fundamentally good, nor anything fundamentally evil; everything is relative, relative to our point of view, that is to say, to our manners, to our opinions, to our prejudices. This point once established, it is extremely possible that something, perfectly indifferent in itself, may indeed be distasteful in your eyes, but may be most delicious in mine; and immediately I find it pleasing, immediately I find it amusing, regardless of our inability to agree in assigning a character to it, should I not be a fool to deprive myself of it merely because you condemn it? Come, come, my dear Duclos, a man's life is something of such slight importance that one may sport with it as much as one likes, just as one might with a cat's life or with that of a dog; 'tis up to the feeble and weak to defend themselves, they have virtually the same weapons we possess. And since you are so scrupulous," my man added, "my stars!

what would you think of the fantasy of one of my friends!"

And, with your Lordships' leave, I shall terminate the evening by giving, as my fifth story, the account of the taste the judge related me.

This philosophical jurist told me that his friend would deal only with women scheduled to be executed. The nearer the moment that they are delivered to him borders on the moment they are going to perish, the better he pays for them. But he insists that the conference be held after they have been notified of their sentence. Thanks to his position in society within easy reach of this sort of prize, he never lets one slip through his fingers and," my informant went on, "I have seen him pay up to one hundred louis for this kind of tête-à-tête. However, he does not carnally enjoy them, or rather he requires nothing of them but that they exhibit their buttocks and shit before his eyes; for taste of shit, he maintains, there is nothing to equal what one gets from a woman who has just heard the death penalty pronounced against her. He will go to any lengths to obtain these private interviews, and of course, as you may well suppose, he does not wish to be known by the victim. He sometimes passes himself off as the confessor, or at other times as a friend of the family, and his proposals are always fortified by the promise that, if they indulge his little whimsies, he may very possibly be able to be of help to them.

"And when he has finished, when he has satisfied himself, by what, my dear Duclos," said the judge, "do you fancy he concludes his operation? Just as I do, my worthy friend; he reserves his fuck for the climax, and releases it at last when before his delighted gaze the condemned person expires."

"Ah, that's true villainy," I told him.

"Villainy?" he interrupted. "My dear child, all that's mere verbiage, prattle. Nothing's villainous if it causes an erection, and the single crime that exists in this world is to refuse oneself anything that might produce a discharge."

"And so it was he refused himself nothing," said Martaine; "Madame Desgranges and I shall have, or so I hope, occasion to entertain the company with several lubricious and criminal anecdotes relating to the same personage."

"Excellent," said Curval, "for there's a man I'm already hugely fond of. That's just the way one should reason about one's pleasures, and his philosophy pleases me infinitely. It is truly incredible the way man, already restricted in all his amusements, in all his faculties, seeks further to narrow the scope of his existence through his contemptible prejudices. For example, it is not commonly suspected what limitations he who has raised up murder as a crime has imposed upon all his delights; he has deprived himself of a hundred joys, each more delicious than the other, by daring to adopt the odious illusion which founds that particular nonsense. What the devil difference can it make to Nature whether there are one, ten, twenty, five hundred more or fewer human beings on earth? Conquerors, heroes, tyrants -- do they inhibit themselves by that absurd law? Do you hear them saying that we ought not do unto others that which onto ourselves we would not have done? Forsooth, my friends, I tell you frankly that I tremble, I groan when I hear fools dare to tell me that such is the law of Nature, etc... Merciful Heaven! all athirst for crimes and murders, 'tis to see to it they are committed, to inspire them Nature has wrought her law, and the one commandment she graves deep in our hearts is to satisfy ourselves at no matter whose expense. But

patience; I shall perhaps soon have a better occasion to expand upon these questions, I have made the profoundest study of them, and, in communicating my conclusions to you, I hope to convince you, as convinced am I, that the single way of serving Nature is blindly to respond to her desires, of whatever kind they may be, because, for the sake of maintaining the divine balance she has struck universally, vice being quite as necessary to the general scheme as virtue, she is wont to urge us to do this, now to do that, depending upon what is at the moment necessary to her design. Yes, my friends, I shall someday discuss all that before you, but for the moment I must be still, for I have fuck that needs spilling, that devilish fellow at the executions has made my poor balls swell dreadfully."

And the Président departed for the boudoir at the end of the corridor, with him went Desgranges and Fanchon, his two dear friends, for they were as great scoundrels as he; and with him also went Aline, Sophie, Hébé, Antinoüs, and Zéphyr. I have little definite information upon what the libertine took it into his head to do in the midst of those seven persons, but his absence was prolonged and he was heard to shout: "Come, damn it, turn this way, do you hear? But that's not what I told you to do" and other ill-humored remarks interspersed with oaths to which he was known to be greatly addicted while enacting scenes of debauchery; the women finally returned, their faces very red, their hair very untidy, and with the air of having been furiously mauled and pawed in every sense. Meanwhile, the Duc and his two friends had scarcely been marking time, but of their number only the Bishop had discharged, and in a manner so extraordinary that we had better say nothing about it at present.

They went to the supper table, where Curval philosophized a little more, for, with that man, passions had not the least influence upon doctrines; firm in his principles, he was just as much an atheist, an iconoclast, a criminal after having shed his fuck as when, before, he had been in a lubricious ferment, and that precisely is how all wise, level-headed people should be. Never ought fuck be allowed to dictate or affect one's principles; 'tis for one's principles to regulate one's manner of shedding it. And whether one is stiff, or whether one is not, one's philosophy, acting independently of passions, should always remain the same.

The amusement at the orgies consisted in a verification which had not until then been undertaken, but which was interesting none the less: Messieurs were moved to decide who amongst the boys, who amongst the girls had the most beautiful ass. And so, first of all, they had the eight boys form a line: they were standing erect... yes, but, on the other hand, they were made to bend forward just a little, for that is the only way properly to judge an ass. The examination was both very long and very severe, opinions clashed, opinions were reversed, rectified, each ass was inspected fifteen times, and the apple was generally accorded to Zéphyr; it was unanimously agreed that it was physically impossible to find anything more perfect, better molded, better cleft.

Next they turned to the girls, who adopted the same posture. Deliberation was at first very slow, very prolonged, it proved all but impossible to decide from amongst Augustine, Zelmire, and Sophie. Augustine, taller, better made than the other two, would doubtless have triumphed had the jury been composed of painters; but libertines call rather for grace than exactitude, for fullness sooner than regularity. There was in her disfavor a shade too much of the slender and of the delicate; the two other contestants offered a carnation so fresh, so healthy, so plump, buttocks so fair and so round, a back whose line descended so voluptuously, that Augustine was eliminated from further consideration. But how were they to decide between the two who remained? After ten rounds of balloting, opinion was still equally divided.

At last, Zelmire won the prize; the two charming winners were assembled, were kissed, handled, frigged for the rest of the evening, Zelmire was ordered to frig Zéphyr who, discharging like a musket, afforded, in the throes of pleasure, the most entrancing spectacle; then, in his turn, he frigged the young lady who all but fainted away in his arms, and all these scenes, of unspeakable lubricity, brought about the loss of the Duc's fuck and of his brother's, but only mildly stirred Curval and Durcet, who agreed that what they needed were scenes far less Arcadian, far less ethereal if their weary old souls were to be cheered, and that all these winsome frolickings were only good for youngsters.

They went to bed, and Curval, plunged into the thick of fresh infamies, compensated himself for the tender pastorals he had been obliged to witness.

The Twenty-Eighth Day

It was a wedding day, and the turn of Cupidon and Rosette to be united in holy matrimony, and by still another fateful combination of accidents, both were listed for punishment that evening. As no one was found at fault that morning, that entire part of the day was devoted to the wedding ceremony, and when it was over, the newlyweds were brought into the salon to see what they would do together. The mysteries of Venus were, as we know, often celebrated in these children's presence; although none of them had so far taken an active part in them, they were well enough grounded in the theory of the thing to be able to execute about everything that there is to do. Cupidon, his prick very rigidly aloft, insinuated his little peg between Rosette's thighs, and she lent herself to his maneuvers with all the candor of the most thorough innocence; the young lad was managing so nicely that he was probably well on the way to success when the Bishop, taking him in his arms, had put in himself what, I fancy, the child would greatly have liked to put into his little wife; all the while he perforated the Bishop's ample hole, he regarded her with eyes which declared his regrets, but she was herself soon occupied: the Duc thigh-fucked her. Curval stepped up in the lewdest fashion to fondle the ass of the Bishop's little fucker, and as that pretty little ass was found, in keeping with instructions, in the desired state, he licked it and began to stiffen. Durcet was up to the same tricks with the little girl the Duc was holding with her chest pressed to his.

However, no one discharged, and Messieurs went in to dine; the young bride and groom, who had been admitted to the table, also appeared to serve coffee, together with Augustine and Zélamir. And the voluptuous Augustine, deeply distressed over not having won the prize for beauty the night before, had, as though sulking, left her hair in just that kind of disarray which rendered her a thousand times more intriguing to see. Curval was stirred by the sight, and, examining her buttocks:

"I fail to understand how it happened that this little rascal did not win the palm," said he, "for devil take me if in all the world there exists a finer ass than this one here."

So saying, he pried it open, and inquired of Augustine whether she were ready to do her old friend a great kindness. "Oh, yes," she replied, "a very great one indeed, for I really have to get rid of what I have there." Curval rests her upon a sofa and, kneeling before that radiant behind, he devours its turd in a flash.

"Sacred name of God," says he, licking his lips, turning toward his colleagues, and pointing to the prick straining against his abdomen, "I'm in a state for furiously undertaking something or other."

"And what would it be?" asked the Duc, who was very fond of making the Président utter horrors when he was in that particular state.

"What?" said Curval. "Why, whatever infamy you wish to propose, even were it to dismember Nature and unhinge the universe."

"Come along now," said Durcet, upon seeing him cast furious glances in the direction of Augustine, "come along, let's go listen to Duclos, it's story time. I'm persuaded," he went on, addressing the others, "that if he gets the bit in his teeth, that poor little duckling is going to spend a trying quarter of an hour."

"Oh, yes!" said the inflamed Président, "a very trying one, I can vouch for that."

"Curval," said the Duc, whose prick was nodding in the air like a vengeful lance, and who had just finished eliciting some shit from Rosette, "let the others entrust the harem to the two of us, and two hours from now we'll have turned in a capital performance."

Durcet and the Bishop, at the moment calmer than their copropri-etors, each took one of them by the arm, and it was thus, that is to say, breeches about their ankles and pricks aloft, that those libertines made their solemn entrance into the auditorium, where the assembly was already gathered and ready to hear Duclos' latest offerings; she, having anticipated, from those two gentlemen's state, that she would soon be interrupted, began in these terms:

A nobleman at the court, aged about fifty-five, came and asked me for one of the prettiest girls I could lay my hands on. He said nothing to indicate his favorite mania, and to satisfy any need he might have, I gave him a young dressmaker who had never yet attended a party and who was incontestably one of the loveliest creatures France could boast. I introduce them to each other and, curious to observe what is about to transpire, I quickly repair to my post at the spy hole.

"Now where in the devil has Madame Duclos been," he opened by saying, "to find an ugly chit like yourself? Has she been raking over someone's dung heap? You must have been servicing a couple of soldiers when they came to fetch you here."

And the young lady, blushing to the ears with shame, for she had been forewarned of nothing, was at a loss to know what tack to take.

"Well, get your clothes off then," the courtier continued. "My God, but you're a clumsy slut! I've seen ugly whores in my life, but never one the likes of you, nor so stupid. Well, then? Are we going to be able to get this over with today? Ah, yes, there's that body they've been praising to the skies. Sacred Mother, what are those dugs! you'd think they'd been grafted from an old cow."

And he fell to handling them brutally.

"And this belly! What could have caused those wrinkles? You surely haven't whelped twenty children at your age?"

"Not one, Monsieur, I assure you."

"Oh, I see, not one, eh! That's how all these bitches talk; listen to them a while and they'll be trying to convince you they're all virgins... Well, move about, will you, turn around... infamous ass you've got drag-ging there. Flabby, disgusting buttocks -- I understand now why they described you as unusual. It must have taken a lot of kicks in the ass to have arranged things this way."

And you will allow me, Messieurs, to remind you that the ass he

was referring to was as beautiful an ass as one could find anywhere. Be
that as it may, the girl began to grow upset; I could almost make out the
flutterings of her little heart, and I saw her lovely eyes become worried,
then misty. And the more troubled she became, the more energetically
the scoundrel sought to mortify her. I cannot possibly remember all the
ungenerous things he said to her; one would not dare say anything more
stinging, more biting, to the vilest, most infamous of creatures. Finally,
a lump welled up in her throat and her tears began to flow; 'twas for this
last development the libertine, who had been polluting himself with might
and main, had reserved the bouquet of his litanies. 'Tis impossible, once
again, to render for you all the horrible observations he made upon her
skin, her figure, her features, the sickening odor he declared she exhaled,
how he criticized her bearing, her mind; in brief, he hunted up everything,
he invented everything to humiliate her pride, and discharged all over
her while vomiting atrocities a street sweeper would never dare utter.
This scene had a most amusing outcome: the girl seemed to have taken
it as a lesson, and it prompted her to take an oath; she swore never again
to expose herself to such an adventure, and a week later I learned she
had entered a convent for the rest of her life. I related this to the young
man, who found it all prodigiously funny, and who later asked me for
someone else to convert.

Another, Duclos continued, requested me to find him extremely
sensitive girls who were awaiting news of an event whose unfavorable
outcome might cause them an access of profoundest grief. I had unending
difficulty finding anything to answer this description, and it was virtually
impossible to pawn off a makeshift upon the connoisseur. He knew what
he was about, had been playing the game for ages, and one glance was
sufficient to tell him whether the blow he was to strike would reach the
mark. And so I made no effort to deceive him, and managed somehow
always to get him girls who were in the mental state he desired. I one
day produced a maid who was expecting word from Dijon of a young
man she idolized and whose name was Valcourt. I presented the girl to
the libertine.

"Where do you come from, Mademoiselle?" he asked her in a decent
and respectful tone.

"From Dijon, Monsieur."

"From Dijon? Why, that's a strange coincidence, for I have just this
instant had a letter from Dijon containing tidings which have sore distressed me."

"And what is the trouble?" the girl asked with great interest; "I know
everyone in the town, this news you have heard may be of some importance to me."

"Oh, not at all," our man replied, "it relates only to me; it has to do
with the death of a young man -- I was keenly fond of him, he had just

married a girl whom my brother, who also lives in Dijon, had found for him, a girl to whom he was passionately attached, and the day after the wedding, he suddenly died."

"His name, Monsieur, if you please?"

"His name was Valcourt; he was originally from Paris," and the libertine named the street and the number at which Valcourt had lived. "You cannot possibly have known him, though."

But the young girl had collapsed in a faint.

Therewith our libertine, beside himself with delight, muttered a string of oaths, unbuttoned his breeches, and set to frigging himself upon her supine body. "Ah, by Christ! that's what I want. Make haste now, hurry," he said to himself, "the buttocks, I only need the buttocks to discharge."

And turning her over, and pulling up her skirts, he darts seven or eight jets of fuck upon the motionless girl's ass, and then takes himself off without a thought either for the consequences of what he has said, or for what will become of the unhappy creature.

"And did she croak as a result?" inquired Curval, who was being fucked at a great rate.

"No," Duclos admitted, "but she fell ill and lay six weeks at death's door."

"Very fine stunt, oh my, yes!" said the Duc. "But," that scoundrel went on, "I should have preferred it had your man chosen the period of her menstruation for his disclosure."

"Yes," Curval said, "quite. But, Monsieur le Duc, tell us all the truth: your prick's in the air, I can sense it from here: you would have preferred that she drop dead on the spot."

"Well, have it your own way," called back the Duc. "Since you'd wish it so, I consent, for, you know, I've not many scruples over a girl's death."

"Durcet," said the Bishop, "if you don't send those two rascals out to discharge, there'll be a merry to-do this evening."

"Ah, by the Almighty's balls," Curval shouted toward the Bishop's niche, "you're afraid for your flock. But what difference would two more or two less make? Well, Monsieur le Duc, you've heard Monseigneur the Bishop's suggestion, let's go to the boudoir, but we'll go together, for it's all too evident these other gentlemen wish to avoid a scandal tonight."

No sooner said than done; and our two libertines had themselves followed by Zelmire, Augustine, Sophie, Colombe, Cupidon, Narcisse, Zélamir, Adonis, escorted by Bum-Cleaver, Invictus, Thérèse, Fanchon, Constance, and Julie. A brief interval ensued, then two or three women's screams were heard, then the bellowings of our two lechers, who were disgorging their fuck simultaneously. Augustine reappeared dabbing at her bleeding nose, Adelaide's breast was covered by a scarf. As for Julie, always libertine enough and clever enough to get through any ordeal unscathed, she was laughing like one in hysterics and saying that had it not been for her they'd never have been able to discharge. The rest of the troupe returned; Zélamir and Adonis still had their buttocks smeared with fuck. Having assured their confreres they had conducted themselves with all possible decency and modesty, that they might have nothing to be reproached for, and that now, perfectly calm, they were in a fit state to listen, Messieurs gave Duclos the signal to proceed and she did so in the following terms:

I sincerely regret Monsieur de Curval's precipitate haste to relieve his needs, said that superb creature, for I had two pregnant-woman stories to tell him, and they would perhaps have afforded him some real pleasure. I know his taste for the fruit-laden, and I am certain that, had he a flicker of warmth left in his bowels, these two tales would divert him.

"Tell them all the same," said Curval. "You are aware, I trust, that fucking has not the least effect upon my sentiments, and that the moment when I am most infatuated with evil is always the moment after I have performed it."

Very well, said Duclos, I have seen a man whose mania was straitly connected with observing a woman give birth; he would frig himself when seeing her labor pains begin, and used to discharge squarely upon the infant's head directly it hove into view.

A second would perch a seven-month-pregnant woman upon an isolated pedestal at least fifteen feet high. She was obliged to keep her balance, and her mind on what she was about, for if by mischance she were to have grown dizzy, she and her issue would have been definitively ruined. The libertine I speak of, very little affected by the situation of the poor creature he paid for her acrobatic skill, kept her where she was until he had discharged, and frigged himself before her while exclaiming: "Ah, the lovely statue, the beautiful ornament, the empress upon her dais!"

"Well, Curval, you'd have shaken that column, wouldn't you, eh?" said the Duc.

"Ah, not at all, you're mistaken; I have too much respect for Nature and her works. Is not the most interesting of them all the propagation of our species? is it not a kind of miracle we ought to adore incessantly, and ought we not to have the warmest interest in those who perform it? For my part, I never see a pregnant woman without being melted; think for a moment what a marvelous thing is a woman who, just like an oven, can make a little snot hatch deep in her vagina. Is there anything more beautiful, anything quite as fetching as that? Constance, dear girl, come hither, I beseech you, come let me kiss the sanctuary wherein, at this very moment, such a profound mystery is in progress."

And as he found her right there in his alcove, he was not long searching after the temple he wished to minister to. But there is reason to suppose Constance took a somewhat different view of his intentions, or, at least, that she only half believed his professions, for an instant later she was heard to vent a scream which bore no relationship at all to the consequences of a reverence or an homage. Then silence closed again; observing that all lay quiet, Duclos concluded her narrations with the following little tale:

I knew a man, said she, whose passion consisted in hearing children wail and cry; he had to have a mother with a child of no more than three or four. He required this mother to give her offspring a sound thrashing; it had to be done before him, and when the little creature, aroused by this treatment, began to bawl, the mother had next to catch hold of the rogue's prick and frig it industriously, directing the glans at the child, in whose face he would discharge when the little one was singing his loudest.

"Now, I wager," the Bishop said to Curval, "that fellow was no more a friend of increase than you are."

"I dare say not," Curval conceded. "He must be, according to the argument of a lady reputed to possess a great fund of wit, he must be, I say, a great scoundrel; for, in keeping with the development of her thought, any man who loves neither animals, nor children, nor swollen-bellied women, is a monster fit to be put on the rack. Well, by that agreeable old fool's judgment, my case is heard and decided and writ off the agenda," said the Président, "for I certainly have no affection for any one of those three things."

And as it was late, and as interruptions had consumed a sizable portion of the séance, they went straight to supper. At table, they debated the following questions: what need has man for sensibility? and is it or is it not useful to his happiness? Curval proved that it was nothing if not dangerous, and that it was the first sentiment, this one of human kindness, one had to extirpate from children, by early making them grow accustomed to the most ferocious spectacles. Each of them having differently approached the problem, by many and long detours they all finally ended up agreeing with Curval. Supper over, the Duc and he were of the opinion the women and youngsters should be sent to bed, and they proposed the orgies be made an entirely masculine tournament; everyone concurred, the idea was adopted, Messieurs enchambered themselves with the eight

fuckers and spent almost all the night having themselves fucked and drinking liqueurs. They stumbled to bed two hours before dawn, and the morrow brought with it both events and stories the reader will perhaps find entertaining if he will give himself the trouble to read what follows.

The Twenty-Ninth Day

There is a proverb -- and what splendid things proverbs are --there is one, I say, which maintains that the appetite is restored by eating.

This proverb, coarse, nay, vulgar though it be, has none the less a very extensive significance: to wit, that, by dint of performing horrors, one's desire to commit additional ones is whetted, and that the more of them one commits, the more of them one desires.

Well, such exactly was the case with our insatiable libertines. Through unpardonable harshness, through a detestable refinement of debauchery, they, as we know, had condemned their wives to render them the vilest and most unclean services upon their emergence from the privy. They were not content with that, and on the 29th of November they proclaimed a new (which appeared to have been inspired by the previous night's sodomistical libertinage), a new law, I say, which ruled that, as of the 1st of December, those wives would serve as the only pots to their masters' needs, and that the said needs, both the greater and the lesser, would never be executed anywhere save in their wives' mouths; that whenever Messieurs were moved to satisfy these fundamental urges, they would be followed about by four sultanas who would, once the urge had been satisfied, render them the service which heretofore the wives had rendered them and which the said wives would hereafter be unable to render them, since they were going to have graver employment; that the four officiating sultanas would be Colombe for Curval, Hébé for the Duc, Rosette for the Bishop, and Michette for Durcet; and that the least error or failure committed in the course of either of these operations, whether in the course of that involving the wives or in that other involving the four little girls, would be punished with prodigious severity.

The poor women had no sooner learned of this new regulation than they wept and wrung their hands, unfortunately, it was all but in vain. It was however ordained that each wife would serve her husband, and Aline the Bishop, and that for this one operation Messieurs would not be allowed to exchange them. Two of the duennas were ordered to take turns presenting themselves for the same service, and the time for their rendering it was unalterably fixed at the hour Messieurs would depart the evening orgies; it was decided that Messieurs would at all times proceed to this ritual in each other's company, that while the elders were operating, the four sultanas, while waiting to give the service required of them, would make conspicuous display of their asses, and that the elders would move from one anus to the next, to press it, open it, and encourage it generally to function. This regulation promulgated, the friends proceeded that morning to administer the punishments which had not been distributed the night before because of the decision to perform the orgies with the assistance of men only.

The operation was undertaken in the sultanas' quarters; they were all eight taken care of, and after them came Adelaide, Aline, and Cupidon, who also were included upon the fatal list; the ceremony, with the details and all the protocol observed under such circumstances, dragged on for nearly four hours, at the end of which their Lordships descended to dinner, their heads swimming, especially Curval's head, for he, prodigiously cherishing these exercises, never took part in them without the most definite erection. As for the Duc, he had discharged in the thick of the fray, and so had Durcet. This latter, who was beginning to develop a very mischievous libertine testiness toward his wife Adelaide, was unable to discipline her without shudders of pleasure which ultimately loosened his seed.

Dinner was, as usual, followed by coffee; Messieurs, disposed to have some neat little asses on hand, had appointed Zéphyr and Giton to serve the cups, and to these two might have added a large number of others; but there was not one sultana whose ass was in anything like an appropriate state. In accordance with schedule, the coffee-serving team was rounded out by Colombe and Michette. Curval, examining Colombe's ass, the bedaubed condition whereof, in part the Président's own work, generated some singular desires in him, thrust his prick between her thighs from behind, while so doing fondling her buttocks vivaciously; now and again, as it moved to and fro, his engine, as if through maladdress, nudged up against the dear little hole he would have given a kingdom to perforate. For a moment he studied it attentively.

"O sacred God," he said, turning to his friends, "I'll pay the society two hundred louis on the spot for leave to fuck this ass."

Reason prevailed, however, he kept a grip upon himself and did not even discharge. But the Bishop had Zéphyr discharge into his mouth and yielded up his own sanctified fuck as he swallowed that delicious child's; Durcet had himself kicked in the ass by Giton, then had Giton shit, and remained chaste. Messieurs removed to the auditorium, where each father, by an arrangement which was encountered rather frequently, had his daughter on his couch beside him; breeches lowered, they listened to our talented storyteller's five tales.

It seemed as though, since the day I had so exactly executed Fournier's pious will, happiness smiled ever more warmly upon my house, said that distinguished whore. Never had I had so many wealthy acquaintances.

The Benedictine prior, among my most faithful clients, one day came to tell me that, having heard of a quite remarkable fantasy and having subsequently observed it performed by one of his friends who was wild about it, he had a powerful desire to enact it himself, and hence he asked me for a girl well fledged with hair. I gave him a big creature of twenty-eight years who had veritable thickets both under the arms and upon her mound. "Splendid," said the prior upon beholding the goods, "that's just what I need." And as he and I were very closely attached to each other, as we had taken many a gay tumble together, he made no objections when I requested leave to watch him at work. He had the girl undress and half recline upon a couch, her arms extended above her head, and, armed with a sharp pair of scissors he set to cropping the hear beneath her arms. Once he had clipped away every bit of it, he turned to her mound, and barbered it also, but so thoroughly that when he was done one would never have believed the least vestige of hair had ever grown on any of the areas he had worked over. The job done, he kissed the parts he'd shorn and spurted his fuck upon that hairless mound, in a perfect ecstasy over the fruit of his labor.

Another required a doubtless much more bizarre ceremony: I am thinking now of the Duc de Florville; I was advised to bring him one of the most beautiful women I could find. A manservant welcomed us at the Duc's mansion, and we entered by a side door.

"We will now prepare this attractive creature," the valet said to me; "for there are several adjustments to be made in order that she be in a state to amuse my Lord the Duc... come with me."

By way of detours and corridors equally somber and immense, we finally reached a lugubrious suite of rooms, lighted only by six tapers placed on the floor around a mattress covered with black satin; the entire room was hung in funereal stuffs, and the sight, as we entered, woke the worst apprehensions in us.

"Calm your fears," said our guide, "you will not suffer the least hurt; but be ready for anything," he added, speaking to the girl, "and above all see to it that you do everything I tell you."

He had her remove all her clothes, loosened her coiffure, and indicated she was to leave her hair, which was superb, to hang free. Next, he bade her lie down upon the mattress surrounded by tall candles, enjoined her to feign death and to be exceedingly careful, throughout the whole of the scene to follow, neither to stir nor breathe more deeply than she had to.

"For if unhappily my master, who is going to imagine you are really dead, perceives you are only pretending, he'll be furious, will leave you at once, and surely will not pay you a sou."

Directly he had placed the girl upon the pallet in the attitude of a corpse, he had her twist her mouth in such a way as to give the impression of pain, her eyes too were to suggest she had died in agony; he scattered her tresses over her naked breast, lay a dagger beside her, and near her heart smeared chicken's blood, painting a wound the size of one's hand.

"I repeat to you," he said to the girl, "be not afraid, you have nothing to say, nothing to do, you have simply to remain absolutely still and to draw your breath at the moments when you see he is farthest from you. And now, Madame," the valet said to me, "we may withdraw from the room. Come with me, please; that you not be worried about your girl, I am going to place you where you will be able to hear and watch the entire scene."

We quit the room, leaving the girl, who was not without her misgivings, but whom the manservant's speeches had reassured somewhat. He conducts me to a small chamber adjoining the apartment where the mystery is to be celebrated, and through a crack between two panels, over which the black material was hung, I could hear everything. To see was still easier, for the material was only crepe, I could distinguish objects on the other side quite as clearly as if I had been in the room itself.

The valet drew the cord that rang a bell, that was the signal, and a few minutes later we saw a tall, thin, wasted man of about sixty enter upon the stage. Beneath a loose-flowing dressing robe of India taffeta he was completely naked. He halted upon coming through the doorway; I had best tell you now that the Duc, supposing he was absolutely alone, had not the faintest idea his actions were being observed.

"Ah, what a beautiful corpse!" he exclaimed at once. "Death... 'tis beautiful to behold.... But, my God, what's this!" said he upon catching sight of the blood, the knife. "It must have been an assassin... only a moment ago... ah, Great God, how stiff he must be now, the person who did that."

And, frigging himself:

"How I would have loved to see him strike that blow!" And fondling the corpse, moving his hand over its belly: "Pregnant?... No, apparently not. What a pity."

And continuing to explore with his hands:

"Superb flesh! It's still warm... a lovely breast."

Wherewith he bent over her and kissed her mouth with incredible emotion:

"Still drooling," he said; "how I adore this saliva!"

And once again he drove his tongue almost into her gullet; no one could possibly have played the role more convincingly than did that girl, she lay stock-still, and whenever the Duc drew near she ceased entirely to breathe. Finally, he rolled her over upon her stomach:

"I must have a look at this lovely ass," he murmured. And after having scanned it:

"Jesus Christ! What matchless buttocks!"

And then he opened them, kissed them, and we distinctly saw him place his tongue in that cunning little hole.

"Oh, upon my word!" he cried, sweating with admiration, "this is certainly one of the most superb corpses I have ever seen in my life; happy he who took this girl's life, oh, enviable person, what pleasure he must have known!"

The very idea made him discharge; he was lying beside her, squeezing her, his thighs glued against her buttocks, and he discharged upon her asshole, giving out unbelievable signs of pleasure, and, as he yielded his sperm, crying like a demon:

"Ah fuck, fuck, ah good God, if only I had killed her, if only I had been the one!"

Thus the operation ended, the libertine rose and disappeared; we entered the room to resurrect our brave little friend. She was exhausted, unable to budge: constraint, fright, everything had numbed her senses, she was about ready in all earnestness to become the character she had just personified so expertly. We departed with four louis the valet gave us; as you may well imagine, he doubtless surrendered no more than half of our pay.

"Ye living gods!" cried Curval, "now that is a passion! To say the least, the thing has flavor, aroma."

"I'm as stiff as a mule," said the Duc; "I'll stake my fortune on it, that fellow had other tricks up his sleeve."

"Right you are, my Lord," said Martaine; "he now and again employed a greater realism. I think Madame Desgranges and I have evidence to prove it to you."

"And what the devil are you going to do while waiting?" Curval asked the Duc.

"Don't disturb me, don't disturb me," the Duc shouted, "I'm fucking my daughter, I'm pretending she's dead."

"Rascal," Curval rejoined, "that makes two crimes in your head."

"Ah, by fuck," said the Duc, "would that they were more real..." And his impure seed burst into Julie's vagina.

"Well now, Duclos, what comes next? Go on with your stories," said he as soon as he had finished his affair, "go on, my dear friend, don't allow the Président to discharge, for I can hear him over there effecting an incestuous connection with his daughter; the funny little fellow is working up some evil ideas in his head; his parents have made me his tutor, they expect me to keep an eye on his behavior and I'd be distressed were it to become perverted."

"Too late," said Curval, "too late, old man, I'm discharging; ah, Christ be doublefucked, 'tis a pretty death."

And while encunting Adelaide, the scoundrel fancied to himself, as had the Duc, that he was fucking his murdered daughter; O incredible distraction of the mind of a libertine, who can naught hear, naught see, but he would imitate it that instant!

"Duclos, you must indeed continue," said the Bishop, "else I'll be seduced by those bawdy fellows' example, and in my present state I might carry things a good deal further than they."

Some time after that last adventure I went alone to the home of another libertine, said Duclos, whose mania, more humiliating perhaps, was not however so saturnine. He receives me in a drawing room whose floor was covered with a very handsome rug. He bids me remove all I am wearing and then, having me get down on my hands and knees:

"Let's see," says he, stroking and patting the heads of two great Danes lying on either side of his chair, "let's see whether you are as nimble and quick as my dogs. Ready? Go get it!"

And with that he tosses some large roasted chestnuts on the floor; speaking to me as if I were an animal, he says:

"Go fetch them!"

I run on all fours after a chestnut, thinking it best to play the game with good humor and enter into the spirit of his eccentricity; I run along, I say, I endeavor to bring back the chestnuts, but the two dogs, also springing forward, outrun me, seize the chestnuts, and take them back to their master.

"Well, you're clearly in need of some practice before you'll be in good form," said the gentleman; "it's not, by chance, that you are afraid my dogs might bite you? Don't worry yourself about them, my dear, they'll do you no harm, but inwardly, you know, they'll look down upon you if they see that you're a clumsy creature. So let's try again -- try harder. Here's your chance to get even... bring it back!"

Another chestnut thrown, another victory carried off by the dogs, another defeat for me; well, to make a long story short, the game lasted two hours, during which I managed to get the chestnut only once and to bring it back in my mouth to him who had thrown it. But whether triumphant or bested, never did the dogs do me any harm; on the contrary, they seemed to be having a good time playing and to be amused by me, quite as though I were a dog too.

"That's enough," said the gentleman. "You've worked hard enough; it's time to eat."

He rang, a servant entered.

"Bring some food for my animals," he said.

And a moment later the servant returned, carrying an ebony feeding trough which was filled with a kind of very delicate chopped meat. He set the trough on the floor.

"Very well," my gentlemen said to me, "get down and eat with my dogs, and try to put on a better show while eating than you did while playing."

There was nothing for me to reply; I had to obey. Still on all fours, I plunged my head into the trough; the trough was very clean, the food very good, I fell to munching away beside the dogs, which very politely moved over, leaving me peacefully to my share. And that was the critical instant for our libertine; the humiliation of a woman, the degradation to which he reduced her, wonderfully stimulated his spirits.

"Oh, the buggress!" said he, frigging himself assiduously, "the tramp, look at her there, gorging herself with the dogs, that's how one should deal with all women, and if they were to be handled thus, we'd have no more sauciness from them, ah no! Domestic animals like those dogs, why should they not be treated in the same way? Ah! impudent bitch that you are, whore, slime, scum!" he cried, stepping near and spraying his fuck over my bum, "buggress, I'll have you eat with my dogs."

And that was the end of that; our man vanished, I dressed promptly, and lying by my mantelet I found two louis, the current price and doubtless the one the rogue was accustomed to paying for his pleasures.

At this point, Messieurs, Duclos continued, I am obliged to retrace my steps and, by way of conclusion to the evening's narrations, to recount two adventures I had during my youth. As they are somewhat on the strong side, they would have been out of place amidst the mild escapades with which you had me start at the beginning of the month; and so I set them aside and kept them for the end of my contribution.

I was only sixteen at the time, and was still with Madame Guérin; I had been sent to the home of a man of unchallenged distinction, and, upon arriving there, was simply told to wait in a small antechamber, told to be at my ease, told to be sure to obey the lord who would soon be coming to sport with me; but they were careful not to tell me anything else: I'd not have had such a fright if I'd been forewarned, and our libertine would certainly not have had as much pleasure. I had been in the room for about an hour when the door opened at last. It was the master of the house himself.

"What the devil are you doing here," he demanded with an air of surprise, "at this time of day?... What about it, whore!" he cries, seizing me by the throat and all but choking the breath out of me, "what about it! Has the slut come here to rob me?"

He calls to someone, a trustworthy servant immediately appears.

"La Fleur," says his angry master, "I've got a thief here; she was hiding when I came in. Strip her and prepare to carry out the orders I give you."

La Fleur does as he is told, I am despoiled of my clothes in a trice, they are tossed aside as they are peeled off my body.

"Very well," the libertine says to his servant, "go find a sack, then sew this creature up inside it and toss her into the river."

The valet goes to find the sack. I leave it to you to wonder whether I did not take advantage of these few moments to cast myself at the nobleman's feet and beg him to spare me, assuring him that it was Madame Guérin, his usual procuress, who had herself sent me to his house. But the lewd gentleman will have none of it, he grasps my two buttocks, and kneading them brutally between his fists:

"Why, fuck my eyes," says he, "I think I'll feed this pretty ass to the fish."

That was the single lubricious action he seemed inclined to permit himself, and until then he had exposed nothing which might have led me to suppose libertinage had something to do with the scene. The valet returns, bringing a sack with him; despite all my protests, and they were heated, I am dumped into it, the mouth of the sack is sewn up, and La Fleur lifts me upon his shoulders. It was then I heard the effects of our libertine's mounting crisis; he had probably begun to frig himself as soon as I had been put in the sack. At the same instant La Fleur raised me to his shoulders, the villain's fuck departed him.

"Into the river, into the river, do you hear me, La Fleur?" he said, stammering with pleasure. "Yes, into the river with her, and you'll slip a stone into the sack, so that the whore will drown all the more quickly."

And that was all he had to say, I was borne out, we went into the adjacent room where La Fleur, having ripped open the sack, returned me my clothes, gave me two louis, and also gave me some unequivocal proof of the manner, radically unlike his master's, in which he conducted himself in the pursuit of happiness; then I returned to Guérin's. I severely scolded Guérin for having sent me there so poorly prepared; to placate me, she arranged another party: it took place two days later, and I was even less well prepared for the battle I was to wage with this new foe.

More or less as in the adventure I have just related, I was to go and wait in an antechamber of the apartment belonging to a farmer-general, but this time I waited in the company of the valet who, sent thither by his master, had come to fetch me at Guérin's. To while away the time before my gentleman's arrival, the valet diverted me by bringing out and displaying several precious stones kept in a desk drawer in the room.

"Bless me," said the good pander, "were you to take one or two of them I don't fancy it would make much difference; the old Croesus is so damned rich I wager he doesn't even know how many of 'em or what kind he's got here in his desk. Go right ahead, if you like, don't bother yourself about me, I'm not the sort of fellow to betray a little friend."

Alas! I was only too well disposed to follow this perfidious advice; you know my predilections, I've told you about them; and so, without his having to say another word, I put my hand upon a little gold box worth seven or eight louis, not daring to make off with any more valuable object. That was all that rascal of a valet desired, and to avoid having to return to the matter later on, I afterward learned that, had I refused to take something, he would, without my being aware of it, have slipped a jewel or two into my pocket. The master arrives, greets me with kindness and courtesy, the valet leaves the room, we two remain there together. This man, unlike the other, amused himself in a very real sense; he scattered a profusion of kisses over my ass, had me flog him, fart in his mouth, he put his prick in mine, and in one word had his fill of every kind and shape of lubricity save for that sometimes sought in the cunt; but 'twas all to no purpose, he did not discharge. The propitious moment for that had not yet come, all this he had been doing was secondary, preparatory; you will soon see to what it was leading.

"Why, my stars!" he suddenly exclaimed, "it had entirely slipped my mind. There's a domestic still waiting in the other room for a gem I just a moment ago promised to give him for his master. Excuse me, my dear, but I really must keep my word to him; then we'll get back to work."

Guilty of the little larceny I'd just committed at the instigation of that accursed valet, you may well suppose that this remark made me tremble. I thought for an instant to stop him, confess to the theft, then I decided it would be better to play innocent and run the risk. He opens the desk, looks through first one drawer then the next, rummages about, and failing to find what he is after, he darts furious glances at me.

"You slut, you alone," says he, "apart from a valet in whom I have entire confidence, you have been the only person to enter this room during the past three hours; the article is missing; you must have taken it."

"Oh, Monsieur," I say, shaking in every limb, "you may be sure I am incapable..."

"Damn your eyes," he roars (now, you will remark that his breeches were still unbuttoned, that his prick was protruding from them, that this prick held a vertical slope; all this, you would suppose, ought to have enlightened me and dispelled my fears, but I had all but lost my head, and noticed nothing), "come along, buggress, my valuable has got to be found."

He ordered me to strip; twenty times I besought him on bended knee to spare me the humiliation of such a search, he would be moved by nothing, nothing melted him, he himself angrily tore off my clothes, and as soon as I was naked, he went through my pockets and, of course, it was not long before he came across the box.

"Ah, you bitch!" he cried, "I need no more than that to be convinced. So, buggress, you come to a man's house to steal from him?"

And immediately summoning his lieutenant:

"Go bring an officer of the police at once," he said.

"Oh, Monsieur!" I cried, "have pity upon my youthful truancy, I have been beguiled into this, 'twas not done of my own will, I was told to..."

"Well," the lecherous gentleman interrupted, "you will explain all that to the officer, for I'll be damned if I don't mean to put a stop to all this crime."

The valet leaves again; the libertine, still wearing a blinding erection, flings himself into an armchair and while he fumbles about his crotch, he showers a thousand invectives upon me.

"This tramp, this monster," said he, "she comes to my house to rob me, I who wanted to give her the reward her services deserve... ah, by God, we shall see."

As he utters these words a knock is heard at the door, and I see a gendarme enter.

"Officer," says the master of the premises, "I have a thieving wench here I wish to put in your safekeeping, and I turn her over to you naked, for I put her in that state in order to search her clothing; there is the girl, over there are her garments, and here is the stolen article; I urge you to have her hanged, officer, and good night to you."

Whereupon he reeled backward, sat down in his chair, and discharged.

"Yes, hang the bitch, by sweet Jesus, I want to see her hanged, offi-cer, do you understand me? Hang her, that's all I ask of you!" he fairly screamed.

The pretended gendarme leads me away with my clothes and the damning box, takes me into a nearby room, removes his uniform, and reveals himself to be the same valet who received me and incited me to steal; so upset had I been, I'd not recognized him hitherto.

"Well, well!" said he, "were you frightened?"

"Alas," I murmur, hardly able to speak, "out of my very wits." "It's all over," he said, "and here is your money."

So saying, he presents me with the same box I had stolen, 'tis a gift from his master, he restores my clothes to me, hands me a glass of brandy, and escorts me back to Madame Guérin's.

"That's an odd and pleasant mania," the Bishop observed; "the major part of it can be extracted for use in other connections. My one criticism is that it contains an excess of delicacy; you know, of course, that I don't greatly favor mixing fine feelings with libertinage. Leave that element out of it, I say, and from that story one may learn the infallible method of preventing a whore from complaining, regardless of the iniquitous ways one might be disposed to take with her. One has only to proffer the bait, draw her into the trap, and when you've caught her red-handed, why then you are at liberty to do what you wish with her, there's nothing more to fear, she won't dare emit a peep for fear either of being accused or the object of your recriminations."

"It is indeed," said Curval, "and I am sure that had I been in that gentleman's place, I would have permitted myself to go somewhat further, and you, my dear Duclos, might not have got off so lightly."

The stories having been long that evening, the supper hour arrived before Messieurs had the opportunity to indulge in any frolicking. They thus repaired to table firmly resolved to make the most of the period following the meal. It was then that, having assembled the entire house-hold, they decided to determine which of the little girls and boys could be justifiably ranked as mature men and women. To establish the critical facts, Messieurs thought best to frig everyone of the one sex and of the other about whom they had any doubts, or rather suspicions; amongst the women, they were sure of Augustine, Fanny, and Zelmire: these three charming little creatures, aged between fourteen and fifteen, all discharged in response to the lightest touch; Hébé and Michette, each being only twelve, were hardly worth considering, and so it was simply a question of experimenting with Sophie, Colombe, and Rosette, the first of whom was fourteen, the latter two being thirteen years old.

Amongst the boys, it was a matter of common knowledge that Zéphyr, Adonis, and Céladon shot their fuck like grown men; Giton and Narcisse were too young to bother putting through their paces; the abilities of Zélamir, Cupidon, and Hyacinthe remained to be ascertained. The friends formed a circle about a pile of well-stuffed pillows arranged on the floor, Champville and Duclos were nominated for the pollutions; one, owing to her qualities as a tribade, was to act as the young girls' fricatrice, the other, absolute mistress of the art of frigging the male member, was to pollute the three little lads. They entered the ring formed by the friends' chairs and filled with pillows, and there Sophie, Colombe, Rosette, Zélamir, Cupidon, and Hyacinthe were turned over to Champville and Duclos; and each friend, the better to appreciate the spectacle, took a child between his thighs: the Duc appropriated Augustine, Curval had Zelmire to do his bidding, Durcet entrusted himself to Zéphyr's skill, the Bishop favored Adonis to supply his needs.

The ceremony began with the boys; Duclos, her breasts and ass uncovered, her sleeve rolled to the elbow, mobilized all her many talents and set to polluting each of those delicious Ganymedes one after the other. The human hand could not possibly have wandered and tugged, squeezed and patted more voluptuously; her wrist, her fingers flew with a deftness... her movements were of a delicacy and of a willfulness... she offered those little boys her mouth, her breast, her ass, made all of herself available with such art that there could be no question but that they who were not finally to discharge had not yet the power to do so. Zélamir and Cupidon hardened, but all Duclos' lore, all her agility, was quite in vain. With Hyacinthe, however, the storm burst after the sixth flick of the wrist: fuck leapt over Duclos' breast, and the child went half out of his mind while fondling her ass. Messieurs were careful to observe that throughout the entire operation it had never once occurred to the lad to touch her in front.

The girls' turn came next; virtually naked, her hair very elegantly arranged and equally stylish in every other part of herself, Champville did not look thirty years old, although she was fifty if a day. The lubricity of this operation, whence, as a thoroughgoing tribade, she expected to mine the greatest pleasure, animated her large dark-brown eyes which, since her youth, had always been extremely handsome. She put at least as much verve, daring, and brilliance into her actions as Duclos had into hers, she simultaneously polluted the clitoris, the entrance to the vagina, and the asshole, but Nature developed nothing worthy of notice in Colombe and Rosette; there was not even the faintest appearance of pleasure in their expressions. But things were not thus with the beautiful Sophie: the tenth digital foray brought her fainting upon Champville's breast; little broken sighs, little panting sounds, the tender shade of crimson which sprang into her lovely cheeks, her parted lips which grew moist, everything manifested the delirium whereinto Nature had hurled her, and she was declared a woman. The Duc, his device as solid as a mace, ordered

Champville to frig her a second time, and when she discharged afresh, the villain chose that moment to mix his impure fuck with that young virgin's. As for Curval, he had wrought his fell deed between Zelmire's thighs, and the two others theirs with the young boys they held locked between their legs.

The company retired for the night, and the following morning having furnished no event which deserves to be cited in this catalogue of exceptional feats, and dinner having furnished nothing, nor coffee, we shall remove at once to the auditorium, where the magnificently arrayed Duclos appears once again upon the platform, this time to end, with five new stories, the one hundred and fifty narrations which have been entrusted to her for the thirty days of the month of November.

The Thirtieth Day

I am not sure, Messieurs, said the beauteous storyteller, whether you have heard of the caprice, quite as unusual as dangerous, for which the Comte de Lernos is celebrated, but my several liaisons with him having afforded me a thorough acquaintance of his maneuvers, and as I found them most extraordinary indeed, I believe they ought to be included amongst the delights you have ordered me to detail. The Comte de Lernos' passion to lead into evil as many girls and married women as he is able, and apart from the books he employs to seduce them, there is truly no sort of device he will not invent to deliver them up to men; he either exploits their secret yearnings by uniting them with the object upon whom they only think longingly, or he finds them lovers if such they are lacking. He has a house devoted to nothing else, and in it all the matches he made are tested when the individuals concerned come to grips. He unites them, guarantees them freedom from intrusion, provides them with all the facilities needed for recreation, and then goes into an adjoining chamber to enjoy the pleasure of spying upon them while they are in action. But the point to which he multiplies these disorders simply defies belief, nor would one credit an account of the immense number of obstacles he is willing to surmount in order to form these little marriages. He has associates in nearly every convent in Paris and amongst a vast quantity of married women, and this army is led by a general of such great skill that not a day passes but at least three or four little skirmishes are fought in his house. Never does he fail to watch the voluptuous jousts -- without the participants suspecting his presence -- but once he has gone to take up his observation post at the hole, as he stands watch all alone, no one knows how he proceeds to his discharge, nor what its character is; nothing but the fact is known, and that is all; I thought none the less that it was worthy of being mentioned to you.

The fantasy of the elderly Président Desportes will perhaps prove more amusing to you. Fully informed of the etiquette observed at the home of this habitual debauchee, I arrive at his house toward ten o'clock in the morning and, perfectly naked, I present my buttocks to be kissed; he is seated in an armchair, very grave, very solemn, and the first thing I do is fart in his face. My président is irritated, he gets to his feet, seizes a bundle of switches he has close at hand, and falls to pursuing me; my first impulse is to get out of his way.

"Impudent hussy," says he, chasing after me all the while, "I'll teach you to come to my home to behave in this outrageous fashion."

I'm to flee, he's to follow on my heels; I finally gain a narrow alley, I take cover in an impregnable retreat, but, lo! there he is, he's somehow managed to get at me. The président's threats and imprecations redouble as he sees he has me trapped; he brandishes the switches, threatens to use them upon me: I creep into a corner, cower there, put on a terrified air, I shrink to the size of a mouse; this terrified, groveling attitude of mine finally awakes his fuck, and the roué squirts it over my breasts while shouting with pleasure.

"What! Do you mean to say he didn't give you a single lick with the switches?" the Duc demanded.

"He didn't bring them within a yard of me," Duclos replied.

"A very patient individual, that one," Curval remarked; "my friends, I believe we all agree that we are somewhat less so when we have in our hands the instrument Duclos mentions."

"But you need only a small amount of patience, Messieurs," said Champville, "for I shall shortly present to you other samples of the same breed, but they'll be rather less mild tempered than Madame Duclos' président."

And Duclos, observing that silence had succeeded these comments, saw she could continue with her stories, and proceeded in the following manner:

Soon after this adventure had befallen me, I went to the town house of the Marquis de Saint-Giraud, whose fantasy consisted in seating a naked woman upon a children's swing and having her swing to a great height, back and forth. Each time you pass by his nose, he's waiting for you, and you've got either to let fly a fart at him or expect a slap upon your ass. I did my best to satisfy him; I received several slaps, but also gave him some overpowering farts. And the Marquis having finally discharged after an hour of this monotonous and fatiguing ceremony, the swing was brought to a halt, and my audience came to an end.

About three years after I had become the mistress of Fournier's establishment, a man came to make an unusual proposal to me: he wished me to find libertines who would amuse themselves with his wife and daughter, the only condition being that he be hidden in a place whence he could observe everything that transpired. Not only would whatever money I might earn from their employment be mine, but, he went on, he planned to give me an additional two louis for every encounter I could arrange for them; and there was only one final condition to the bargain: for his wife's partners he wished none but men of a certain taste, and for his daughter, men addicted to another kind of whimsy: his wife's men were all to shit upon her breasts, and the procedure to be observed with his daughter involved having the men raise her skirts, broadly expose her behind in front of the hole through which he would be doing his spying, and then discharge into her mouth. He would surrender the merchandise for the said passions, but for no others. After having made this gentleman promise to accept all responsibility in the event his wife and daughter brought complaint for having been made to come to my house, I agreed to all he wanted and in my turn promised that the two ladies would be furnished in strict accordance with his instructions. He arrived with his wares the very next day: madame was a woman of thirty-six, not very pretty, but tall and majestically formed, with a great air of sweet mildness and of modesty; her daughter was fifteen years old, blond, rather inclining toward heaviness, with the most tender, most winning countenance in all the world...

"Indeed, Monsieur," quoth his wife, "you have us do strange things..."

"I know, my dear, I know," said the lecher, "and it mortifies me, but so it must be. Accept your lot, do as you're told, there's nothing for it, I shall not give over. And if you balk in the slightest way at the propositions and the actions we are going to submit you to -- you, Madame, and you, Mademoiselle -- I shall tomorrow convey you to a place I know, and it is highly unlikely you'll ever return alive from it."

Wherewith the wife shed a tear or two; as the man for whom I intended her was waiting, I requested her to pass without further delay into the chamber I had set aside for their bout; mademoiselle would remain in another room with one of my girls, she would be perfectly safe there and would be notified when her turn had come. At this cruel moment there were a few more tears, and it seemed clear to me that this was the first time the brutal husband had required such a thing of his wife; unhappily, her debut was arduous, for aside from the baroque taste of the individual to whom I was surrendering her, he was an imperious and brusque old libertine who would surely not treat her with any excess of courtesy or consideration.

"That will do, no more tears," said the husband. "Bear in mind that I am watching your conduct, and that if you do not give ample satisfaction to the thoughtful gentleman who is going to take you in hand, I will come in myself and force you to do his bidding."

She enters the arena, the husband and I go into the neighboring room from which we are to watch it all. It is difficult to imagine the point to which this old scoundrel's imagination was excited by contemplating his miserable wife being made a victim of some stranger's brutality; he was thrilled by each thing she was forced to do; that poor humiliated woman's modesty and candor beneath the atrocious assaults of the libertine engaged to exercise her, composed a delicious spectacle for her husband. But when he saw her thrown brutally to the floor, and when the old ape to whom I had delivered her shit upon her chest, and her husband saw the tears, beheld the horrified shudders of his wife as she first heard proposed and then saw this infamy executed, he could restrain himself no longer, and the hand with which I was frigging him was straightway soaked with fuck. This first scene ended at last, and if it had afforded him pleasure, it was as nothing compared to the climax produced by the second. It was only with great difficulty, and above all with numerous and grave threats, that we succeeded in getting the young lady to enter the ring; she had witnessed her mother's tears but knew nothing of what had been done to her. The poor little girl raised all kinds of objections; we finally helped her make up her mind. The man to whom I turned her over was fully instructed of all that was required to be done: he was one of my regular clients whom I delighted with this windfall and who, to express his gratitude, consented to all I prescribed.

"Oh, the lovely ass!" cried the libertine father once his daughter's stud displayed her entirely naked. "Oh, sacred Jesus, what adorable buttocks!"

"Gracious!" I exclaimed, "am I to take it that this is the first time you have set eyes on them?"

"Yes, indeed it is," said he, "I required this expedient to enjoy the spectacle; but if 'tis the first time I see that superb ass, you may rest assured it shall not be the last."

I frigged him at a lively pace, he grew ecstatic; but when he saw the appalling things that young virgin was being forced to submit to, when he saw a consummate libertine's hands straying over that extraordinary body which had never before suffered such fondlings, when he saw her compelled to sink to her knees, open her mouth, when he saw a fat prick introduced into it, and saw that engine discharge inside, he tottered backward and, swearing like one possessed, shouting that he'd never in his life tasted any pleasure as keen as this, he left certain proof of his statements between my fingers. Their adventure had drawn to a conclusion, the two poor women retreated, weeping abundant tears, and the husband, but too enthusiastic over the drama they had enacted for him, doubtless found the means to persuade them to provide him with additional performances, for I received that family at my house for more than six years and, always following the orders the husband gave me, I made those two unlucky creatures acquainted with practically all the different passions I have mentioned in the course of my thirty days of storytelling; there were, to be sure, ten or twelve of the passions they had no opportunity to satisfy, because we did not practice them in my house.

"Oh, yes," said Curval, "there are many ways to prostitute a wife and a daughter. As if these bitches were made for anything else! Are they not born for our pleasures, and from that moment onward, must they not satisfy them at no matter what price? I've had a quantity of wives," said the Président, "and three or four daughters of whom, thank God, I've only one left, and if I'm not mistaken Monsieur le Duc is fucking Mademoiselle Adelaide at this very instant; but had any one of those creatures ever balked at being prostituted, in any of the numerous manners of prostitution I regularly submitted them to, may I be damned alive or condemned never to fuck anything but cunts for the rest of my life -- which is worse -- if I'd not have blown their bloody brains out."

"Président, your prick is in the air again," said the Duc; "your fucking remarks always betray you."

"My prick in the air? No," the Président said, "but I am on the verge of getting some shit from our dear little Sophie, and I have high hopes her delicious turd will precipitate something. Oh, upon my soul, even more than I'd suspected," said Curval, after he'd gobbled up the hash; "by the good God I'd like to fuck, I believe that my prick is taking on some consistency. Who from amongst you, Messieurs, would like to accompany me into the boudoir?"

"I'd be honored," said Durcet, dragging along Aline, whom he had been pawing steadily for an hour.

And our two libertines, having summoned Augustine, Fanny, Colombe, Hébé, Zélamir, Adonis, Hyacinthe, and Cupidon, and enlisted Julie and two duennas, Martaine and Champville, Antinoüs and Hercule, absented themselves for half an hour, at the end of which they returned triumphant, each having yielded up their vital liquor to the sweetest excesses of crapulence and debauchery.

"Move on," Curval said to Duclos, "give us your final tale, dear friend. And if it manages to make this prick of mine dance up again, you shall be able to congratulate yourself upon having wrought a miracle, for in faith, it is at least a year since I've lost so much fuck at a single sitting. On the other hand, it is true that..."

"Very well," the Bishop interrupted, "that will do; if we listen to you, we will hear something much worse than the passion Duclos is likely to describe to us. And so, since that would be to retreat from the stronger to the weaker, permit us to bid you be silent and listen instead to our storyteller."

That gifted whore thereupon terminated her recitations with the following passion:

The time has finally arrived, my Lords, to relate the passion of the Marquis de Mesanges to whom, you will recall, I sold the daughter of the unfortunate shoemaker, Petignon, who perished in jail with his wife while I enjoyed the inheritance his mother had left for him. As 'twas Lucile who satisfied him, you will allow me to place the story in her mouth.

"I arrive at the Marquis' mansion," that charming girl told me, "at about ten o'clock in the morning. As soon as I enter, all the doors are shut.

"'What are you doing here, little bitch?' says the Marquis, all afire. 'Who gave you permission to disturb me?'

"And since you gave me no prior warning of what was to happen, you may readily imagine how terrified I was by this reception.

"'Well, take off your clothes, be quick about it,' the Marquis continues. 'Since I've got my hands on you, whore, you'll not get out of here with your skin intact... indeed, you're going to perish -- your last minutes have arrived.'

"I burst into tears, I fall down at the Marquis' feet, but nothing would bend him. And as I was not quick enough in undressing, he himself tore my clothes off, ripping them away by sheer force. But what truly petrified me was to see him thrown them one after another into the fire.

"'You'll have no further use for these,' he muttered, casting each article into a large grate. 'No further need for this mantelet, this dress, these stockings, this bodice, no,' said he when all had been consumed, 'all you'll need now is a coffin.'

"And there I was, naked; the Marquis, who had never before seen me, contemplated my ass for a brief space, he uttered oaths as he fondled it, but he did not bring his lips near it.

"'Very well, whore' said he, 'enough of this, you're going to follow your clothes, I'm going to bind you to those andirons; yes, by fuck, yes indeed, by sweet Jesus, I'm going to burn you alive, you bitch, I'm going to have the pleasure of inhaling the aroma of your burning flesh.'

"And so saying he falls half-unconscious into an armchair and discharges, darting his fuck upon the remnants of my burning clothes. He rings, a valet enters and then leads me out, and in another room I find a complete new outfit, clothes twice as fine as those he has incinerated."

That is the account of it I had from Lucile; it remains now to discover whether 'twas for that or for worse he employed the girl I sold him.

"For something far worse," said Desgranges; "I am glad you have introduced the Marquis to their Lordships, for I believe I too shall have something to say about him."

"May it be, Madame," Duclos said to Desgranges, "and you, my amiable companions," she added, speaking to her two other colleagues, "may it be that you speak with greater energy than have I, with livelier images, brighter diction, superior wit, and more persuasive eloquence. 'Tis now your turn, I have done, and I would but beseech Messieurs to have the kindness to forgive me if I have perchance bored them in any wise, for there is an almost unavoidable monotony in the recital of such anecdotes;

all compounded, fitted into the same framework, they lose the luster that is theirs as independent happenings."

With these words, the superb Duclos respectfully saluted the company, bowed, and descended from her throne; she next went from alcove to alcove and was generally applauded and caressed by all the friends. Supper was served, Duclos was invited to sit at the table, a favor which had never before been accorded to a woman. Her conversation was quite as agreeable as her storytelling had been, and by way of recompense for the pleasure she had given them, Messieurs named her to be the governor-general of the two harems, and the four friends also made the promise, in an aside, that no matter what the extreme treatment to which they might expose the women in the course of the sojourn, she would always be dealt with gently, and very certainly taken back with them to Paris, where the society would amply reward her for the trouble she had gone to in order to help Messieurs procure themselves a little good cheer. She, Curval, and the Duc so completely besotted themselves at supper that they were practically incapacitated and barely managed, with the expense of much effort, to reach the orgies, which they soon left, allowing Durcet and the Bishop to carry on alone, and betook themselves to the remote boudoir; Champville, Antinoüs, Bum-Cleaver, Thérèse, and Louison accompanied them, and one may be perfectly confident that they uttered and had done to them at least as many horrors and infamies as, at their end, their two more sober friends were able to invent.

Everyone repaired to his bed at two in the morning, and 'twas thus the month of November ended, thus came to a close the first phase of this lubricious and interesting holiday, for whose second part we will not keep the public waiting if to our consideration it has kindly received what we have chronicled so far.

MISTAKES I HAVE MADE

I have been too explicit, not sufficiently reticent, about the chapel activities at the beginning; must not elaborate upon them until after the stories in which they are mentioned.

Said too much about active and passive sodomy; conceal that until the stories have discussed it.

I was wrong to have made Duclos react strongly to the death of her sister; that doesn't sort with the rest of her character; change it.

If I said Aline was a virgin upon arrival at the château, that was an error: she isn't, and could not be. The Bishop has depucelated her in every sector.

And not having been able to reread all this, there must be a swarm of other mistakes.

When later I put the text in final order, I must be particularly careful to have a notebook beside me at all times; I'll have to put down very exact mention of each happening and each portrait as I write it; otherwise, I'll get horribly confused because of the multitude of characters.

For the Second Part, begin with the assumption Augustine and Zéphyr are already sleeping in the Duc's bedchamber in the First Part; likewise Adonis and Zelmire in Curval's, Hyacinthe and Fanny in Durcet's, Céladon and Sophie in the Bishop's, even though none of them has been deflowered yet.

Part The Second

HE 150 COMPLEX PASSIONS, OR THOSE BELONGING TO THE SECOND CLASS, COMPOSING THE THIRTY-ONE DAYS OF DECEMBER SPENT IN HEARING THE NARRATIONS OF MADAME CHAMPVILLE; INTERSPERSED AMONGST WHICH ARE THE SCANDALOUS DOINGS AT THE CHÂTEAU DURING THAT MONTH; ALL BEING SET DOWN IN THE FORM OF A JOURNAL.

(DRAFT)

THE 1ST OF DECEMBER: Champville assumes the task of storytelling and relates the one hundred and fifty following tales (the number of each precedes the tale).

Won't depucelate any save those aged between three and seven, but only cuntishly. 'Tis he who deflowers Champville at the age of five.

He ties a girl of nine in a curled-up position and depucelates her from behind.

He wishes to rape a girl of twelve or thirteen, and depucelates her while holding a pistol against her heart.

He likes to frig a man upon a maiden's cunt, he uses the fuck for pomade, and next encunts the maid while she is held by the man.

He wishes to depucelate three girls in succession, one in the cradle, one at the age of five, the other at seven.

THE 2ND. 6. He'll not depucelate anyone who is not between nine years old and thirteen. His prick is enormous; four women are needed to hold the virgin. The same individual Martaine speaks of, who only embuggers three-year-olds, the same hell-inspired individual.

He has his valet depucelate the maid, aged ten to twelve, before his eyes, and during the operation touches them nowhere save upon the ass. He now fondles the girl's, now the valet's. Discharges upon the valet's ass.

He wishes to depucelate a girl destined to be married the following day.

He wishes the marriage to be performed, and to depucelate the bride at some time between the hour of the mass and the moment the couple retires to bed.

He would have his valet, a very ingenious personage, go about marrying girls left and right and bring them to his master, who therewith fucks them, and next sells them to procuresses.

THE 3RD. 11. He must be provided with two sisters; he depucelates them.

He marries the girl, depucelates her, but 'tis all a fraud, the marriage is a fraud, once he's fucked her, he leaves her.

He will only fuck a maid, and then only immediately after another man has deflowered her while he has watched. He must have her cunt muddied up with sperm.

This one depucelates with an artificial engine, very large, and, without introducing himself, discharges upon the hole he has cleared.

He will have none but maids of rank and distinction and pays for them in accordance with their wealth. This individual proves to be the Duc, who will admit having depucelated more than fifteen hundred of them over a period of thirty years.

THE 4TH. 16. He forces a brother to fuck his sister in his presence, then fucks her afterward; he obliges both to shit before-hand.

He forces a father to fuck his daughter after he has himself had her maidenhead.

He brings his nine-year-old daughter to the brothel, and while she is held by a procuress, depucelates her. He has had twelve daughters; has had all twelve maidenheads.

Must have virgins between the ages of thirty and forty to fuck.

He will depucelate no one but nuns, and spends immense sums of money to get them; he fucks several.

'Tis the evening of the 4th of December, at the orgies, the Duc depucelates Fanny, who is held by the four governesses and ministered by Duclos. He fucks her twice in a row, she faints, the second time he fucks her while she is unconscious.

THE 5TH. To celebrate the fifth week's festival, Hyacinthe and Fanny are joined in matrimony, the marriage is consummated very publicly.

He would have the mother hold her daughter, he first fucks the mother, then depucelates the daughter while she is held by the mother. The same one Desgranges mentions on the 20th of February.

He likes adultery only; one must locate women for him who are generally known to be virtuous and well behaved, he makes them disgusted with their husbands.

He enjoys having the husband come himself to prostitute his wife and hold her while he fucks her. (Messieurs imitate that passion forthwith.)

He places a married woman upon a bed, encunts her while that woman's daughter, suspended above, presents him with her cunt to be licked; the next instant he effects a reversal and encunts the daughter while kissing the mother's asshole. When he has done licking the daughter's cunt, he has her piss; then he kisses the mother's asshole and has her shit.

He has four daughters, legitimate and wedded; he wishes to fuck all four: he makes all four of them conceive and bear children so as some-day to have the pleasure of depucelating the children he has had by his daughters and whom their husbands suppose to be their own.

Apropos of which the Duc recounts -- but his anecdote cannot be numbered amongst the stories because, Messieurs being unable to duplicate it, it does not compose a passion -- the Duc recounts, I say, that he once knew a man who fucked three children he had by his mother, amongst whom there was a daughter whom he had marry his son, so that in fucking her he fucked his sister, his daughter and his daughter-in-law, and thus he also constrained his son to fuck his own sister and mother-in-law. Curval recounts another unusual history, that of a brother and a sister who reached an agreement whereby each would surrender his children to the other: the sister had a boy and a girl, so did the brother. They mixed the pudding in such wise that sometimes they fucked their nephews, sometimes their own children, and sometimes their first cousins, or else the brothers and sister would fuck while the father and mother, that is to say, the brother and sister, fucked one another also.

That evening, Fanny is surrendered cuntwardly to the assembly, but as the Bishop and Monsieur Durcet do not fuck cunts, she is only fucked by Curval and the Duc. Henceforth, she wears a small ribbon aslant, like a baldric, and after the loss of both her pucelages she will wear a very wide pink ribbon.

THE 6TH. 26. He has himself frigged while a woman is being frigged about the clitoris, and he wishes to discharge at the same time the girl does, but he discharges upon the buttocks of the man who frigs the girl.

He kisses the asshole of one girl while a second girl frigs his ass and a third his prick; they then exchange tasks, so that, when all is said and done, each of the three has her ass kissed, each frigs his prick, each frigs his ass. Farts are required of them all.

He licks the cunt of one girl while fucking a second in the mouth and while his asshole is being licked by a third; then exchange of positions as above. The cunts must discharge, he swallows their balm.

He sucks a beshitted ass, has a tongue frig his own beshitted asshole, and frigs himself upon a beshitted ass; the three girls then exchange positions.

He has two girls frigged before his eyes, and alternately fucks the friggeresses from the rear, but in the cunt, while they continue with their sapphotizings.

Zéphyr and Cupidon are upon that day discovered in the act of frigging each other, but they have not yet had recourse to reciprocal embuggery; they are punished. Fanny is much encunted at the orgies.

THE 7TH. 31. He would have an older girl introduce a younger girl to bad habits; the older must frig her, give her wicked advice, and end up by holding her while he fucks her, whether virgin or not.

He calls for four women; he fucks two of them orally, two cuntwardly, taking great care not to insert his prick in a mouth until having first had it in a cunt. While all this is going on, he is closely followed by a fifth woman, who throughout frigs his asshole with a dildo.

This libertine requires a dozen women, six young, six old and, if 'tis possible, six of them should be mothers and the other six their daughters. He pumps out their cunts, asses and mouths; when applying his lips to the cunt, he wants copious urine; when at the mouth, much saliva; when at the ass, abundant farts.

He employs eight women to frig him; each of the eight must be situated in a different posture. (This had better be illustrated by a drawing.)

Wishes to have three men and three women fucking each other in divers attitudes.

THE 8TH. 36. He forms twelve groups of two girls each; they are so arranged only their asses are visible to him; all the rest of their bodies must be concealed from his sight. He frigs himself while studying all those buttocks.

He has six couples simultaneously frig themselves in a room paneled with mirrors; each couple is composed of two girls frigging each other in various and equally lubricious postures. He is in the middle of the room, he regards both the couples and their reflections, and discharges in the middle of it all, having been frigged by an old woman. He has kissed the buttocks of every participant in this drama.

He has four streetwalkers besot themselves with wine and then fight with each other while he looks on; and when they are thoroughly drunk, they one after another vomit into his mouth. He favors the oldest and ugliest women possible.

He has a girl shit in his mouth, but does not eat her turd, and while the first girl is in action, a second sucks his prick and frigs his ass; while discharging, he shits into the hand of the girl who is socratizing him. The girls exchange places.

He has a man shit into his mouth and eats while a little boy frigs him, then the man frigs him and he has the boy shit.

That evening, at the orgies, Curval depucelates Michette, in front: she is held by the four duennas and ministered by Duclos; this arrangement is the conventional one and is observed upon all occasions; therefore we will not allude to it again.

THE 9TH. 41. He fucks one girl in her mouth just after having shitted into the same receptacle; a second girl is lying on top of the first, with the first girl's head between her thighs, and upon the face of the second girl a third girl drops a turd, and he, while thus fucking his own turd in the first girl's mouth, eats the shit deposited by the third girl upon the second girl's face, and then they alternate roles, in such wise that each girl enacts all three of them.

Thirty girls pass through his hands during a given day, and he has them all shit into his mouth, consumes the turds of the three or four prettiest. He repeats this party five times a week, which means that he sees 7800 girls a year. When Champville first encounters him, he is seventy years old and has been in business for fifty.

He sees twelve girls every morning and swallows their dozen turds; he sees them all at the same time.

He places himself in a bathtub; thirty women come up one after another and piss and shit into it till it is full; he discharges while paddling about in all that.

He shits in the presence of four women, requires them to watch and indeed help deliver him of his turd; next, he wishes them to divide it into equal parts and eat it; then each woman does a turd of her own. He mixes them and swallows the entire batter, but his shit-furnishers have got to be women of at least sixty.

That evening Michette's cunt is put at the disposal of the assembly; thereafter she wears the little sash.

THE 10TH. 46. He has girls A and B shit. Then he forces B to eat A's turd, and A to eat B's. Then both A and B shit a second time; he eats both their turds.

He requires a mother and her three daughters, and he eats the girls' shit upon the mother's ass, and the mother's shit upon one daughter's ass.

He obliges a daughter to shit into her mother's mouth and to wipe her ass with her mother's teats; next, he eats the turd in the mother's mouth, and afterward has the mother shit into her daughter's mouth, whence, as before, he eats the turd.

(It would perhaps be advisable to substitute a son and a mother, in order to create a contrast with 47.)

He wishes a father to eat his son's turd, then he eats the father's.

He would have the brother shit in his sister's cunt, and he eats the turd; the sister then must shit in her brother's mouth. He eats this second turd, too.

THE 11TH. 51. Champville announces she is now going to speak of impieties, and makes mention of a man who wishes the whore, while frigging him, to pronounce dreadful blasphemies; in his turn he utters terrible ones. His amusement during their dialogue consists in kissing her ass; he does no more than that.

He would have a girl come with him to a church, and frig him there, especially at the time the holy sacrament is exposed. He situates himself as near to the altar as possible, and fondles her ass while she performs her task.

He goes to confession for the sole purpose of making his confessor's prick rise aloft; he lists a quantity of infamous misdeeds, and frigs himself in the confessional all the while he speaks.

He wishes the girl to go and make her confession, then fucks her orally the moment she emerges from the confessional.

He fucks a whore throughout a mass being said in his private chapel, and discharges when the Host is raised.

That evening, the Duc depucelates Sophie cuntwardly, and while doing so blasphemes considerably.

THE 12TH. 56. He buys a confessor, who yields him his place; thus he is able to hear the young pensionnaires' confessions and to give them the worst possible advice while pardoning them their sins.

He would have his daughter go to confess to a monk he has previously bribed, and he is placed where he can overhear everything; but the monk demands that the penitent keep her skirts raised high while she catalogues her faults, and her ass posted within plain sight of the father: thus he is able to hear his daughter's confession and contemplate her ass at the same time.

Has mass celebrated for completely naked whores; while observing the spectacle, he frigs his prick upon another girl's ass.

He has his wife go to confess to a monk he has bought: the monk seduces the wife and fucks her in front of her husband, who is hidden. If the wife refuses, he emerges from hiding and helps the monk force her.

On that day they celebrate the sixth week's festival with the marriage of Céladon and Sophie, which union is consummated, and in the evening Sophie's cunt is put generally to use, and she dons the sash. Because of this event only four passions are recounted on the 12th.

THE 13TH. 60. Fucks whores on the altar at the same moment mass is about to be said; they have their naked asses on the sacred stone.

He has a naked girl sit astride and bend forward over a large crucifix; he fucks her cunt from behind while she is thus crouched down in such wise the head of Christ frigs her clitoris.

He farts and has the whore fart in the chalice, he pisses thereinto and has her piss thereinto, he shits thereinto and has her shit thereinto, and finally he discharges into the chalice.

He has a small boy shit upon the paten, and he eats this while the boy sucks him.

He has two girls shit upon a crucifix, he shits thereupon when they have finished, and he is frigged against the three turds covering the idol's face.

THE 14TH. 65. He breaks up a crucifix, smashes several images of the Virgin and the Eternal Father, shits upon the debris and burns the whole mess. The same man has the mania of bringing a whore to hear the sermon and having himself frigged while listening to the word of God.

He takes communion and, the wafer still in his mouth, has four whores shit upon it.

He has her go to communion and fucks her in the mouth when she returns.

He interrupts a priest in the midst of saying mass in his private chapel, interrupts him, I say, in order to frig himself into the chalice, obliges the whore to frig the priest thereinto, and forces the latter to quaff the mead.

(Passion Number 69 omitted by Sade. -- Tr.)

70. He intervenes directly the Host is consecrated and forces the priest to fuck the whore with the Host.

Upon this day Augustine and Zelmire are found frigging together; they are both rigorously punished.

THE 15TH. 71. He has the girl fart upon the Host, himself farts thereupon, and then swallows the Host while fucking the whore.

The same man who had himself nailed into a coffin -- Duclos mentioned him -- compels the whore to shit upon the Host; he also shits upon it and flings the whole affair into a privy.

Frigs the whore's clitoris with the Host, has her discharge upon it, then buries it in her cunt and fucks her, discharging upon it in his turn.

Chops it up with a knife and has the crumbs rammed into his asshole.

Has himself frigged and then discharges upon the Host and finally, when he is restored to perfect calm and after his fuck has flowed, feeds biscuit and all to a dog.

The same evening, the Bishop consecrates a Host and Curval destroys Hébé's maidenhead with it, he drives it into her cunt and discharges thereupon. Several others are consecrated, and the already depucelated sultanas are all fucked with Hosts.

THE 16TH. Profanation, Champville announces, lately the principal element in her stories, will from now on be no more accessory, and what, to borrow the brothel term, are known as little ceremonies are going to provide the main ingredient in the following complex passions. She asks her auditors to remember that everything connected with that will be presented merely as secondary matter, but that the difference subsisting between her stories and the examples Duclos has given, is that Duclos always pictured a man with one woman, whereas she, Champville, will always show several women administering to a single man.

He has himself flogged by one girl during mass, he fucks a second girl orally, and he discharges when the Host is elevated.

He has two women gently flog his ass with a martinet; each woman bestows ten stripes, alternating them with asshole friggery.

He has himself whipped by four different girls while farts are being launched into his mouth: the girls take turns, so that each will have had a chance both to whip and to fart.

He has himself whipped by his wife while he fucks his daughter, next by his daughter while he fucks his wife; this is the same individual Duclos spoke of, the same man who prostituted his wife and daughter in her whorehouse.

He has himself whipped simultaneously by two girls, one flogs the front of him, the other his rear, and when at last he has been well stimulated, he fucks one of them while the other plies the lash, then the second while the first flogs him.

That same evening Hébé's cunt is made available to the public, and she wears the little sash, not being entitled to the large one until she has lost both her pucelages.

THE 17TH. 81. He has himself flogged while kissing a boy's ass and while fucking a girl in the mouth, then he fucks the boy in the mouth while kissing the girl's asshole, the while constantly receiving the lash from another girl, then he has the boy flog him, orally fucks the whore who'd been whipping him, and then has himself flogged by the girl whose ass he had been kissing.

He has himself whipped by an old woman, fucks an old man in the mouth, and has the daughter of this aged couple shit into his own mouth, then changes so that, ultimately, everyone takes his turn in each role.

He has himself whipped while frigging himself and while discharging upon a crucifix propped up by a girl's buttocks.

He has himself whipped while fucking a whore from the rear, using his prick to tamp a Host into her fundament.

He passes an entire brothel in review; he receives the lash from all the whores while kissing the madame's asshole and receiving therefrom into his mouth both wind and rain and hailstones.

THE 18TH. 86. He has himself whipped by teams of cab drivers and chimney sweeps who pass two at a time, one plying the lash, the other farting in his mouth; he employs ten or twelve in a morning.

He has himself held by three girls, he gets down on hands and knees, a fourth girl mounts astride him and thrashes him; each member of the quartet takes her turn mounting and flogging him.

Naked, he puts himself in the midst of six girls; he is conscience-stricken, asks to be forgiven, casts himself down upon his knees. Each girl decrees a penance, and he is given one hundred strokes for each penance he refuses to do: 'tis the girl he refuses who whips him. Well, these penances are all exceedingly unpleasant: one would like to shit into his mouth; another have him lick up her spittle from the floor; a third is menstruating and would have him lick her cunt clean; the fourth hasn't washed her feet, will he kindly lick between her toes; the fifth has snot awaiting his tongue, etc.

Fifteen girls arrive in teams of three: one whips him, one sucks him, the other shits; then she who shitted, whips; she who sucked, shits; she who whipped, sucks. And so he proceeds till he has had done with all fifteen; he sees nothing, heeds nothing, is wild with joy: a procuress is in charge of the game. He renews this party six times each week.

(This one is truly charming and has my infinite recommendation; the thing has got to move very briskly along, each girl must bestow twenty-give strokes of the whip, and it is between whippings that the first sucks and the third shits. If you would prefer fifty strokes from each girl, that will total up to seven hundred fifty, a very agreeable figure, not by any means excessive.)

Twenty-five whores soften up his ass with a quantity of slaps and fondlings; he is not sent away until his ass has become completely insensible.

That evening the Duc is flogged while culling Zelmire's forward maidenhead.

THE 19TH. 91. He has himself tried by a jury of six whores; each knows the role she is to play. He is sentenced to be hanged. And hanged he is; but the cord snaps: 'tis the instant he discharges. (Relate this to similar ones Duclos described.)

He arranges six old women in a semicircle; while three young whores lash him, the six crones spit in his face.

A girl frigs his asshole with the handle of a cat-o'-nine-tails, a second girl whips his thighs and prick from the front; 'tis thus he is made eventually to discharge over the tits of the whipper posted before him.

Two women flay him with bulls' pizzles while a third, kneeling before him, causes him to discharge upon her breasts.

She recounts only four that day because of the marriage of Zelmire and Adonis which marks the seventh week's conclusion, and which is consummated, Zelmire having been depucelated, with what regards the cunt, the night before.

THE 20TH. 95. He struggles with six women, the cuts of whose whips he pretends to wish to avoid; he strives to snatch the whips from their hands, but they are too strong for him and fustigate him none the less. He is naked.

He runs the gauntlet between two ranks of twelve girls who are wielding switches; he is whipped all about the body and discharges after the ninth race.

He has the soles of his feet whipped, then his prick, then his thighs while, as he lies upon a couch, three women successively mount astride him and shit in his mouth.

Three girls alternately flog him, one with a martinet, one with a bull's pizzle, the other with a cat-o'-nine-tails. A fourth, kneeling before him and whose asshole the lecher's lackey is frigging, sucks the master's prick while frigging the lackey's, which he has discharge upon his sucker's buttocks.

He is amidst six girls: one pricks him with a needle, the second uses pincers on him, the third burns him, the fourth bites him, the fifth scratches him, the sixth flagellates him. All that everywhere upon his body, indiscriminately. He discharges in the thick of this activity.

That evening Zelmire, depucelated on 18th of December, is surrendered cuntwardly to the assembly -- to, that is to say, Curval and the

Duc, who alone of the four friends fuck cunts. Once Curval has fucked Zelmire, his hatred for Adelaide and Constance redoubles; he wishes to have Constance minister to Zelmire.

THE 21ST. 100. He has himself frigged by his lackey while the girl, naked, balances upon a narrow pedestal; all the while he is being frigged, she may neither budge nor lose her equilibrium.

He has the procuress frig him while he fondles her buttocks; and meanwhile, between her fingers, the girl holds a very short candle which she must not drop until the roué has spat out his fuck; he is very careful not to discharge before the girl's fingers have been seared.

He sups at an immense table; for light, he has six burning candles, each inserted in the ass of a naked girl lying upon the dining table.

While he takes his supper he has a girl kneel on sharp pebbles, and if in the course of the entire meal she stirs, she is not paid. Above her are two tilted candles whence hot tallow spills upon her bare back and breasts. She need but make the slightest movement and she is packed off without being paid a sou.

He obliges her to remain four days in a very narrow iron cage, wherein she can neither sit nor lie down; he feeds her through the bars.

He is the one Desgranges will mention in connection with the turkey's ballet.

That same evening, Curval depucelates Colombe's cunt.

THE 22ND. 105. He wraps a girl and a cat in a large blanket, has her stand and dance about; the cat bites, scratches her as she falls to the floor; but, come what may, she must skip and leap, and continue her antics until the man discharges.

He massages a woman with a certain substance which causes her skin to itch so violently that she scratches herself till her blood flows; he watches her at work, frigging himself the while.

He gives a woman a potion to drink, it halts her menstruating, and thus he makes her run the risk of grave illness.

He makes her swallow a medicine intended for horses, it causes her horrible gripes and colics; he watches her suffer and shit all day long.

He rubs a naked girl with honey, then binds her to a column and releases upon her a swarm of large flies.

That same evening, Colombe's cunt is put at the free disposition of the company.

THE 23RD. 110. He places the girl upon a pivot which revolves with prodigious speed. She is naked and bound and turns until he discharges.

He keeps a girl suspended head downward until he discharges.

Makes her swallow a heavy dose of emetic, persuades her she has been poisoned, and frigs himself while watching her vomit.

Kneads and mauls her breasts until they are entirely black and blue.

Kneads and maltreats her ass for three hours; he repeats this rite for nine days in succession.

THE 24TH. 115. He has a girl climb a tall ladder until she is at least twenty feet above the ground, at which point a rung cracks and she falls, but upon mattresses prepared in advance; he walks up to her and discharges upon her body the very moment she lands, and sometimes he chooses this instant to fuck her.

He slaps a girl's face with all his strength and discharges while so doing; he is seated in a comfortable chair and the girl is upon her knees, facing him.

Beats her knuckles with hickory ferrules.

Powerful slaps upon her buttocks until her behind is scarlet.

Inserts the nozzle of a bellows in her asshole; he inflates her.

He introduces an enema of almost boiling water into her bowels, then amuses himself observing her writhe, and discharges upon her ass.

That evening, Aline's ass is soundly slapped by the four colleagues, who keep it up until her ass is crimson; a duenna holds her by the shoulders. A few slaps are bestowed upon Augustine's ass, too.

THE 25TH. 121. He has some pious women recruited for his pleasure, beats them with a crucifix and rosaries, and then has each of them pose as a statue of the Virgin upon an altar, but pose in a cramped position from which they are not to budge. They must remain thus throughout an exceedingly long mass; when at last the Elevation occurs, each woman is to shit upon the Host.

Has her run naked about a garden at night, the season is winter, the weather freezing; here and there are stretched cords upon which she trips and falls.

When she has removed all her clothes, he casts her, as if by accident, into a vat of nearly boiling water and prevents her from climbing out until he has first discharged upon her body.

Naked, on a wintry day she is secured to a post in the middle of a garden and there she remains until she has repeated five Pater Nosters and five Hail Marys, or until he has yielded his fuck, which another girl excites to flow as he contemplates the spectacle.

He spreads a powerful glue upon the rim of a privy seat and sends the girl in to shit; directly she sits down, her ass is caught fast. Meanwhile, from the other side a small charcoal brazier is introduced beneath her ass. Scorched, she leaps up, leaving an almost perfect circle of skin behind her.

That evening profane tricks are played at the expense of Adelaide and Sophie, the two believers, and the Duc depucelates Augustine, of whom he has been passionately fond for weeks; thrice he discharges into her cunt. And that same evening the idea enters his head to have her run naked through the courtyard, dreadful though the weather be. He proposes the idea with great energy and in forceful language, but his confreres regretfully reject it, saying that Augustine is very pretty and that the program calls for her further use; and, the Bishop points out, she still has not been depucelated aft. The Duc offers to pay two hundred louis into the common fund if the society will allow him to take her down into the cellars at once; he is again refused. He wishes at least that she have her ass spanked; she receives twenty-five blows from each friend. But the Duc applies his with his fist and discharges a fourth time between the eighteenth and nineteenth. He requisitions her for his bed and that night encunts her thrice again.

THE 26TH. 126. He gets the girl thoroughly drunk, she lies down to sleep. While asleep, her bed is raised. Toward the middle of the night, she reaches down for her chamber pot; not finding it within reach, she gropes further and tumbles out upon a mattress; the man awaits her there and fucks her as soon as she has fallen.

He has her run naked about the garden, he follows after her, brandishing a cabman's whip, but only threatens her with it. She is obliged to run until she falls from weariness; at which instant he springs upon her and fucks her.

He bestows one hundred strokes, ten at a time, with a martinet of black silk; between each series of blows, he kisses the girl's ass with great fervor.

He flogs her with a cat-o'-nine-tails whose thongs have been steeped in brandy, and does not discharge until the girl's blood is flowing. Then he discharges upon her buttocks.

Champville recounts only four passions on the 26th of December because it is the day of the eight week's festival. It is celebrated by the marriage of Zéphyr and Augustine, both of whom belong to the Duc and lie at night in his chamber; but prior to the ceremony, His Grace would have Curval flog the boy while he, Blangis, flogs the girl; and 'tis done.

Each receives a hundred lashes, but the Duc, more than ever aroused by Augustine because she has made him discharge frequently, lays on very emphatically and is content with nothing short of much blood.

In connection with that evening's entertainments, we must fully explain the character of the Saturday punishments -- how they are meted out and how many lashes are distributed. You might draw up a list itemizing the crimes and, to the right, the appropriate number of lashes.

THE 27TH. 130. He likes to whip none but little girls between the ages of five and seven, and always finds a pretext so as to make it appear as if he were punishing them.

A woman comes to confess to him, he is a priest; she recites all her sins, and by way of penance, he gives her five hundred lashes.

He receives four women and gives each six hundred lashes.

He has the same ceremony performed in his presence by two valets, one relieving the other when his arm is fatigued by the whipping; twenty women are dealt with, each merits six hundred strokes: the women are not bound. He frigs himself while the work is in progress.

He flogs only boys aged from fourteen to sixteen, and he has them discharge into his mouth afterward. Each is warmed by one hundred lashes; he always sees two at a sitting.

Augustine's cunt is surrendered that evening; Curval encunts her twice and, like the Duc, wishes to whip her when he has had done with her. Both gentlemen fall upon that charming girl like ravenous beasts; they propose a contribution of four hundred louis to the common fund in exchange for permission to take her in hand together that same evening; their offer is rejected.

THE 28TH. 135. He has a naked girl enter a chamber; whereupon two men fall upon her and each whips one of her buttocks until it is raw. She is bound. When 'tis over, he frigs the men's pricks upon the whore's bleeding ass, and frigs himself thereupon also.

She is bound hand and foot to the wall. Facing her, and also attached to the wall, is a blade of steel adjusted to the height of her belly. If she strives to avoid a blow, it is forward she must lunge; she cuts herself. If she wishes to avoid the blade, she must fling herself backward toward the lash.

He flogs a girl, giving her one hundred lashes the first day, two hundred the second, four hundred the third, etc., etc., and ceases on the ninth day.

He has the whore descend on all fours, climbs upon her back and faces her buttocks; he squeezes his legs tight about her ribs. Once in the saddle, he brings his lash down upon her ass and curls the thongs round to her cunt, and as for this operation he employs a martinet, he has no trouble directing his blows so that they carry into the vagina's interior, and that is just what he does.

He must have a pregnant woman, he has her bend backward over a cylinder which supports her back. Her head, on the other side of the cylinder, rests upon the seat of a chair and is secured to it; her hair is strewn about, her legs tied as far apart as possible and her swollen belly appears stretched exceedingly taut; her cunt fairly yawns in his face. 'Tis upon her belly he beats a tattoo, and when his whip has brought a profusion of blood into sight, he walks round to the other side of the cylinder and discharges upon her face.

N.B. -- According to my notes, the adoptions do not occur until after defloration, hence say that the Duc adopts Augustine at this point. Verify whether or not this is true, and whether the adoption of the four sultanas does not occur at the very beginning, and whether at the beginning it is not said that they sleep in the bedrooms of the friends who have adopted them.

That evening, the Duc repudiates Constance, who therewith falls into the greatest discredit; however, they treat her with some consideration, because of her pregnancy, in connection with which Messieurs have certain plans. Augustine now passes for the Duc's wife, and hereafter performs none but a wife's functions upon the sofa and in the chapel. Constance descends in rank to below that of the governesses.

THE 29TH. 140. He works exclusively with girls of fifteen, and he flogs them with sting nettles and holly until they are bleeding; his taste in asses is highly developed, he is not easy to please.

Flogs only with a bull's pizzle, continuing until the buttocks are in tatters; he uses four women one after another.

Flogs only with steel-tipped martinets, discharges only when blood is flowing generally.

The same man of whom Desgranges will speak on the 20th of February requires pregnant women; he flogs with a bullwhip, by means of which he is able to remove respectable chunks of flesh from the buttocks; from time to time he aims a blow or two at her belly.

Rosette is flogged that evening, and Curval has her forward maidenhead. The intrigue between Hercule and Julie is brought to light; she has been having herself fucked. When scolded for her misbehavior, she replies libertinely; she is therewith whipped extraordinarily. Then, because Messieurs are fond of her, and also of Hercule, who has given yeoman service so far, they are pardoned and frolicked with.

THE 30TH. 144. He places a candle at a certain height. Attached to the middle finger of her right hand is a piece of bread soaked in wax and set afire; if she does not make haste, she'll be burned. Her task is, with this bit of ignited bread, to light the other candle set high upon the shelf; she is obliged to leap in order to reach it; the libertine, armed with a leathern-thonged whip, lashes her with all his strength, to encourage her to leap higher and to light the candle more quickly. If she succeeds, there's an end to the game; if not, she is flogged till she falls unconscious.

He flogs first his wife, then his daughter, and prostitutes them at the brothel in order to have them whipped while he looks on, but this is not the same man of whom we have already spoken.

Whips with a cat-o'-nine-tails, from the nape of the neck to the calves of the legs; the girl is bound, he excoriates her entire back.

Whips breasts only; he insists that they be exceedingly large. And pays twice the sum when the woman is pregnant.

Rosette's cunt is delivered up to the society that evening; after Curval and the Duc have thoroughly fucked it, they and their colleagues thoroughly whip it. She is down on her hands and knees; Messieurs take care to drive the martinet's steel tips well up into her.

THE 31ST. 148.He whips the face only, using a bundle of dry switches; he must have charming faces. Desgranges will refer to him on the 7th of February.

Using switches, he impartially lashes the entire body, sparing nothing, face, cunt, and breasts included.

Gives two hundred blows of the bull's pizzle, these being distributed evenly up and down the backs of lads aged from sixteen to twenty.

He is in a room, four girls arouse and flog him; when at last he is all afire, he leaps upon a fifth girl, who is naked and awaiting him in the next room and, wielding a bull's pizzle, he assails whatever of her he can reach, maintaining the hail of blows until he discharges; but in order that his ejaculation arrive sooner and the patient suffer less, he is not sent into the second room until his discharge is imminent.

(Find out why there is one too many.)

Champville is applauded, the same honors are bestowed upon her that were given Duclos, and that evening both storytellers dine with Messieurs. Later, at the orgies, Adelaide, Aline, Augustine, and Zelmire are condemned to be whipped with switches all over the body save upon the breasts, but as the friends are to sport with them for another two months, they are treated circumspectly.

Part The Third

HE 150 CRIMINAL PASSIONS, OR THOSE BELONGING TO THE THIRD CLASS, COMPOSING THE THIRTY-ONE DAYS OF JANUARY PASSED IN HEARING THE NARRATIONS OF MADAME MARTAINE; INTERSPERSED AMONGST WHICH ARE THE SCANDALOUS DOINGS AT THE CHÂTEAU DURING THAT MONTH; ALL BEING SET DOWN IN THE FORM OF A JOURNAL.

(DRAFT. THE 1ST OF JANUARY. 1. He loves nothing but to have himself embuggered, and he is never able to find too thick a prick. But, says Martaine, she'll not lay much emphasis upon this passion which is too simple a taste and one wherewith her auditors are far too well acquainted.

He wishes to depucelate none but little girls between the ages of three and seven, in the bum. This is the man who had her pucelage in this manner: she was four years old, the ordeal caused her to fall ill, her mother implored this man to give aid, money. But his heart was of flint...

And this man is the same one of whom Duclos spoke on the 29th of November; the same again who appears in Champville's story of the 2nd of December. He has a prick of colossal proportions, he is enormously rich. He depucelates two little girls every day: one of them in the cunt, in the morning, as Champville related on the 2nd of December, the other in the bum, in the afternoon; and he has a quantity of other passions as well. Four women held Martaine when he embuggered her. His discharge lasts six minutes, and he bellows like a bull while it is in progress. His simple, straightforward, and adroit method of threading her needle, even though she was a young thing of four; describe all that.

Her mother sells the pucelage of Martaine's older brother to a man who sodomizes boys only, and who would have them exactly seven years old.

She is now thirteen, her brother fifteen; they go to the home of a man who constrains the brother to fuck his sister, and who alternately fucks now the boy's ass, now the girl's, while they are in each other's clutches.

Martaine proudly describes her ass; Messieurs request her to display it, she exhibits it from the platform.

The man she has just spoken of, she continues, is the same person who figured in Duclos' story of the 21st of November, the Comte, and who will appear in Desgranges' of the 24th of February.

He has himself fucked while embuggering the brother and sister; the same personage Desgranges will refer to on the 24th of February.

That same evening, the Duc depucelates the bum of Hébé, who is merely twelve. The operation succeeds only at the price of infinite trouble: she is held by the four duennas and administered by Duclos and Champville. And as there is to be a festival on the morrow, in order that things run smoothly then, Hébé's ass is also, on the evening of the 1st of January, surrendered to the society, and all four friends take full advantage of it. She is carried away unconscious; has been buggered seven times.

(Martaine must not say that she has a uterine deformity; that would be false.)

THE 2ND. 6. He has four girls fart in his mouth all the while he embuggers a fifth, then he changes girls. All rotate: all fart, all are embuggered; he does not discharge until he has finished with the fifth ass.

Amuses himself with three small boys: embuggers and has each of them shit, puts all three to each task, and frigs the boy who is inactive.

He fucks the sister in the mouth while having her brother shit into his mouth, then he reverses their roles, and during both exercises he is embuggered.

He embuggers none but girls of fifteen, but only after having, by way of preliminary, flogged them with all his strength.

For an hour he pinches and molests her buttocks and asshole, then embuggers her while she is flogged with exceeding violence.

The ninth week's festival is celebrated upon that day: Hercule weds Hébé and fucks her cuntwardly. Curval and the Duc take turns sodomizing first the husband, then the wife.

THE 3RD. 11. He embuggers only during mass, and discharges at the moment of the Elevation of the Host.

He embuggers only while kicking a crucifix about in the dust; the girl must treat it with like contempt.

The man who amused himself with Eugénie on Duclos' eleventh day has the girl shit, wipes the well-beshitted ass; he possesses an outsized prick, and embuggers, ploughing into the asshole behind a consecrated Host.

Embuggers a youth, has a second youth embugger him, both plough-ing, as above, behind a protective Host; upon the nape of the neck of the boy he is embuggering rests another Host, and a third youth shits there-upon. He discharges thus, without changing position, but while uttering fearful blasphemies.

He embuggers the priest while the latter is in the act of saying mass, and when the priest has performed the consecration, the fucker withdraws for a moment; profiting from this brief interval, the priest buries the Host in his ass, the fucker returns straightway to work and re-embuggers him, tamping in the wafer.

That evening, Curval, with a Host depucelates in the bum the young and charming Zélamir. And Antinoüs fucks the Président with another Host; while fucking, the Président's tongue pushes a third into Fanchon's asshole.

THE 4TH. 16. He likes to embugger none but very aged women while they are being lashed.

Embuggers only very aged men while being fucked.

Has a regular intrigue with his son.

Will embugger none but monsters, or blackamoors, or deformed persons.

In order to combine incest, adultery, sodomy and sacrilege, he embuggers his married daughter with a Host.

That evening the four friends avail themselves of Zélamir's ass.

THE 5TH. 21. He has two men alternately fuck and flagellate him while he embuggers a young boy and while an old man sheds a turd into his mouth. He eats the turd.

Two men take turns fucking him, one in the mouth, the other in the ass; this exercise must last no less than three hours by the clock. He swallows the fuck emanating from him who fucks him in the mouth.

He has himself fucked by ten men, whom he pays so much by the discharge; during a given day he withstands as many as twenty-four without himself discharging.

For the purposes of ass-fuckery, he prostitutes his wife, his daughter, and his sister, and watches the proceedings.

He employs eight men at a time: one in his mouth, one in his ass, one beneath his left testicle, one beneath his right; he frigs two others, each with one hand, he lodges a seventh between his thighs and the eighth frigs himself upon his face.

That evening, the Duc deflowers Michette's ass and causes her fright-ful pain.

THE 6TH. 26. He has an elderly man embuggered in his presence; several times over the prick is removed from that ancient asshole, it is placed in the mouth of the examiner, who sucks it, then sucks the old man's prick, sucks his asshole, and penetrates it while he who has been fucking the old man now embuggers the lecher, and is lashed by the lecher's governess. For the lecher is still a young man.

He vigorously constricts the neck of the fifteen-year-old girl he is embuggering -- choking her neck has the effect of tightening her anus; meanwhile, he is flogged with a bull's pizzle.

He has large spheres of quicksilver inserted into his bowels. These spheres rise up in his entrails, then descend, and during the excessive

titillation caused thereby, he sucks pricks, swallows fuck, has shit out of whores' asses, bolts turds. This ecstasy lasts a good two hours.

He would have himself embuggered by the father while he sodomizes that father's son and daughter.

Michette's ass is surrendered to the company that evening. Durcet selects Martaine for his bedroom companion, following the precedent established by the Duc, who has Duclos, and by Curval, who has Fanchon; Martaine has begun to exert upon Durcet much the same lubricious influence Duclos exerts upon Blangis.

THE 7TH. 30. He fucks a turkey whose head is gripped between the legs of a girl lying on her belly -- while in action he looks quite as if he were embuggering the girl. While he is at work he is being sodomized, and the moment he discharges, the girl cuts the turkey's throat.

He fucks a goat from behind while being flogged; the goat conceives and gives birth to a monster. Monster though it be, he embuggers it.

He embuggers bucks.

Wishes to see a woman discharge after having been frigged by a dog; and he shoots the dog dead while its head is between the woman's thighs. But he does not harm the woman.

Embuggers a swan after having popped a Host up into its ass; then strangles the bird upon discharging.

This same evening, the Bishop embuggers Cupidon for the first time.

THE 8TH. 35. He has himself placed in a specially prepared wicker-work structure provided with an opening at one end; against this opening he places his asshole after having anointed it with mare's fuck. The structure he is in represents a mare's body and is covered with horsehide. A genuine horse is fetched in, mounts the artificial mare, embuggers him and meanwhile he fucks a pretty white bitch he has with him in the basket.

He fucks a cow, it conceives and gives birth to a monster which, shortly thereafter, he fucks.

In a similar basket he places a woman who receives a bull's member in her cunt. He watches this entertaining spectacle.

He has a tamed serpent which he introduces into his anus; while being thus sodomized, he embuggers a cat in a basket. Firmly contained therein, the animal can do him no harm.

He fucks a she-ass while having himself embuggered by an ass. (For this delight an elaborate machine is indispensable. We will give a description of it elsewhere.)

That evening, Cupidon's ass is presented to the society.

THE 9TH. 40. He fucks the nostrils of a goat which meanwhile is licking his balls; and during this exercise, he is alternately flogged and has his asshole licked.

He embuggers a sheep while a dog is licking his asshole.

He embuggers a dog whose head is cut off while he discharges.

He obliges a whore to frig a donkey, he is fucked while observing this spectacle.

He fucks a monkey's asshole, the animal is enclosed in a basket; while being sodomized, the monkey is tormented in order that its anus will constrict about the libertine's member.

That evening, the tenth week's festival is celebrated by the marriage of Bum-Cleaver and Michette; the union is consummated, 'tis a dolorous experience for the bride.

THE 10TH. Martaine announces that she is going to move on to another passion, and that the whip, of central importance in Champville's contributions of December, will enjoy only a secondary one in hers.

The procuress is obliged to find him girls guilty of some felony or other; he arrives, frightens them, says that they are going certainly to be arrested but that he will take it upon himself to protect them provided they will submit to a violent fustigation, and, afraid as they are, they let themselves be whipped till they bleed.

Has a woman with beautiful hair brought to him, saying he simply wishes to examine her hair; but he cuts it off very traitorously and discharges upon seeing her melt into tears and bewail her misfortune, at which he laughs immoderately.

With all sorts of attendant ceremonies, she enters a dark room. She sees no one there, but overhears a conversation regarding her -- give details of this conversation -- which is of a nature to frighten her nearly to death. Finally, she receives a deluge of slaps and blows without knowing whence they come; she hears the cries accompanying a discharge, then is taken out of the room.

She enters a kind of subterranean sepulcher which is lit by nothing but a few oil lamps; they reveal all the horror of the place. After a moment, during which she is able to observe everything, all the lamps are extinguished, a horrible series of screams and the rattling of chains are heard, she collapses in a swoon; if she does not faint, the noises are multiplied until finally she does fall unconscious from terror. Once unconscious, a man swoops down upon her and embuggers her, then abandons her, and valets later come to her rescue; he must have very young and very inexperienced girls. Novices, if possible.

She enters a similar place, but provide a few details to distinguish it from the sepulcher above. She is stripped, thrust naked into a coffin, the coffin's lid is nailed down, and the rhythm of the hammer driving the nails finally excites the man's discharge.

That afternoon, Zelmire was taken down to the cellars we have previously mentioned, which had been prepared in the manner we have just described. The four friends are there, naked and equipped with weapons; Zelmire swoons, and while she is unconscious, Curval depucelates her bum. The Président has been seized by the very same sentiments of love (mixed with lubric rage) for this girl that the Duc has for Augustine.

THE 11TH. 50. The same Duc de Florville, of whom Duclos spoke on the 29th of November, and of whom Desgranges, in her fifth story, will speak on the 26th of February, wishes to have the corpse of a beautiful and recently murdered girl placed upon a bed covered with black satin; he fondles the body, explores its every nook and cranny, and embuggers it.

Another individual requires two corpses, those of a boy and of a girl, and he embuggers the youth's dead body while kissing the buttocks of the girl's and driving his tongue into its anus.

He receives the girl in a small room filled with most convincing wax representations of dead bodies, they are all pierced in various ways. He recommends that the girl make her choice, saying he intends to kill her in whatever way she prefers, inviting her to choose the corpse whose wounds please her most.

He binds her to an authentic corpse, knee to knee, mouth to mouth, and flogs her until the back of her body is covered with blood.

Zelmire's ass is made the evening's treat, but before being served up, she is subjected to a trial, and she is advised that she will be killed that night; she believes what she is told but, instead of dispatching her, Messieurs are content each to give her a hundred lashes after having generously embuggered her, and Curval takes her to bed with him. She is further embuggered all night.

THE 12TH. 54. The girl must be menstruating. She arrives at his home, a valet conducts her to a room in the cellar where the libertine stands awaiting her, but he is near a kind of reservoir of icy water, more than twelve feet across and eight deep; it is concealed in such a way the girl does not notice it. She approaches the man, he topples her into it, and discharges the instant he hears the splash; she is pulled back out at once, but as she is menstruating, severe disability is the very frequent result of her adventure.

He lowers her into a very deep well and shouts down after her that he is about to fill it with large stones; he flings in a few clods of earth to frighten her, and discharges into the well, his seed landing on the naked whore's head.

He has a pregnant woman brought to him and terrifies her with threats and words, flogs her, continuing his ill-treatment of her until she either has a miscarriage there and then, or will surely have one when she returns home. If she disgorges her fruit while under his roof, she receives double payment.

He locks her into a black dungeon, surrounded by cats, rats, and mice; he gives her to understand she has been put there for the rest of her life, and every day he goes to her door, frigs himself, and banters with her.

He inserts sheafs of straw in her ass, ignites them, and watches her buttocks sizzle as the straw burns short.

That evening, Curval announces he will take Zelmire to be his wife, and does indeed publicly marry her. The Bishop officiates at the wedding, the Président repudiates Julie who therewith falls into the greatest discredit, but her libertinage speaks strongly in her favor and the Bishop is disposed to protect her somewhat until the time shall arrive for him to declare himself entirely for her -- he will so declare himself later on.

More clearly than ever before, upon this particular evening his associates notice Durcet's teasing hatred for Adelaide; he torments her, vexes her, she wails and is melancholy. And her father, the Président, does not by any means give her his support.

THE 13TH. 59. He attaches a girl to a St. Andrew's cross suspended in the air, and whips her with all his might, flaying her entire back. After which, he unties her and casts her out through a window, but mattresses are there to lighten her fall, upon hearing which he discharges. Give further details of the scene in order to justify his reaction.

He has her swallow a drug which unhinges her imagination and causes her to see horrible things in the room. She fancies the room is being flooded, sees the water rise, climbs upon a chair, but still the water mounts, reaches her, and she is told that she has no alternative but to leap in and swim; she plunges, but falls upon the stone floor and injures herself badly. 'Tis at this point the libertine discharges; previously, he has taken much pleasure in kissing her ass.

He holds her suspended by a rope that runs up through a pulley affixed to the top of a tower; he stands at a window, she hangs directly outside and opposite him. He frigs himself and threatens to sever the rope as he discharges. While all this is afoot he is being flogged, and earlier he induces the whore to shit for him.

She is held by four slender cords, each attached to one of her limbs. She is held thus in a very cruel and painful position; a trap door is opened beneath her and a charcoal brazier, very hot, is discovered to her view: if the cords break, she falls thereupon. The roué meddles with the cords, strains them, cuts one while discharging. Sometimes he suspends the girl in the same attitude, places a weight upon her belly, then suddenly jerks all four cords, pulling her up, and in so doing rupturing her stomach and tearing her muscles. She remains where she is until he discharges.

He binds her to a low stool; suspended a foot above her head is a dagger whose point is filed needle sharp; the dagger hangs by a hair

-- if the hair snaps, the dagger drives into her skull. The libertine frigs himself while watching his victim's anxious contortions. An hour later, he frees her and bloodies her buttocks with light jabs of the same dagger which, he would like to have her remark, pricks very nicely; he discharges upon her blood-soaked ass.

That evening, the Bishop depucelates Colombe's bum, and after his discharge lashes her with a whip, for he cannot bear to have a girl cause him to discharge.

THE 14TH. 64. He embuggers a young novice who knows nothing of the ways of the world, and as he discharges, he fires two pistol shots very close to her ear. The powder singes her hair.

He makes her sit down in an armchair balanced on springs; her weight releases a number of springs connected to iron rings which bind her tightly to the chair. Certain levers and gears advance twenty daggers until their points graze her skin; the man frigs himself, the while explaining that the least movement of the chair will cause her to be stabbed. He sprays his fuck upon her, in so doing touching the chair very delicately with his foot.

A bascule carries her down into a small crypt hung in black and furnished with a prie-dieu, a coffin, and an assortment of death's heads. She sees six specters armed with clubs, swords, pistols, sabers, poignards, and lances, and each is about to pierce her in a different place. Overcome by fear, she sways, is about to fall; the man enters, catches her in his arms, and flogs her until he is weary, then discharges as he embuggers her. If she is unconscious at the time he enters, and this is frequently the case, his lash restores her to her senses.

She enters a room in a tower, in its center she sees a large charcoal brazier; upon a table, poison and a dirk; she is allowed to choose the manner whereby she is to perish. It generally happens that she selects poison. 'Tis a variety of opiate which plunges her into a profound drowsiness; while the spell lasts, the libertine embuggers her. He is the same personage Duclos cited on the 27th of November and of whom Desgranges will say more on the 6th of February.

The same gentleman who will figure in Desgranges' story of the 16th of February goes through the entire ceremony of preparing to decapitate the girl; just as the blow falls, a rope suddenly snatches the girl's body away, the axe-blade sinks three inches into the block. If the rope does not drag the girl away, she dies. He discharges while bringing down the axe. But prior to this, he has embuggered her as she lies with her neck upon the block.

Colombe's ass is plumbed by the society that evening, and Messieurs pretend to cut off her head. They are accomplished actors.

THE 15TH. 69. He slips a noose around the whore's throat and hangs her. Her feet rest upon a stool, a cord is tied to one leg of the stool, he sits in an armchair, watching and having the whore's daughter frig him. When he discharges, he pulls the cord, the whore hangs, he leaves, valets enter and cut the whore down. A leech lets some blood from one of her veins and she returns to life, but these attentions are given her without the libertine's knowledge. He goes off to bed with the whore's daughter and sodomizes her all night long, while doing so telling her he has hanged her mother. Have Martaine say that Desgranges will refer to him again.

He holds the girl by the ears and walks her around the room, discharging as he parades with her.

He pinches the girl's body, nipping her everywhere save upon the breast, till she turns black and blue.

He pinches her breasts, molests them, and kneads them until they are completely bruised.

He writes letters and words upon her breasts, working with a needle which has a poisoned tip; her breasts become infected, and she suffers excruciatingly.

Drives between one and two thousand pins into her breasts, and discharges when he has covered them.

More libertine with every passing day, Julie is discovered frigging herself with Champville. The Bishop affords her additional protection and thereafter admits her into his bedchamber, as the Duc has Duclos, Durcet Martaine, and Curval Fanchon. Julie confesses that at the time of her repudiation, having been condemned to sleep in the stables with the other animals, she appealed to Champville and was taken into her chamber; they have been bedding together ever since.

THE 16TH. 75. He buries large hatpins in the girl's flesh, dotting her entire body, her nipples included; he discharges after having driven home the last pin. Desgranges will return to the same enthusiast in her fourth story of the 27th of February.

He gives her a great deal to drink, then sews up her cunt and asshole; he leaves her thus sealed up till he remarks she is nigh to collapsing from the need to piss and shit, two activities which are impossible in the state she is in; or else he waits until the weight of the shit and the pressure of the piss finally breaks the stitches.

Four gentlemen enter the room and cuff the girl, strike and kick her until she falls. When she is down, all four mutually frig one another and discharge.

She is deprived of air, then given air, then 'tis taken away again. She is lodged within a pneumatic machine.

To celebrate the end of the eleventh week, the wedding of Colombe and Antinoüs takes place that day, and is consummated. The Duc, who has been indulging in some prodigious cunt-fuckery with Augustine, has been seized by a lubricious fury: he has had Duclos hold her, and has given her three hundred lashes distributed between the middle of her back and her calves, and, after that, has embuggered Duclos while kissing Augustine's flogged ass. Directly after having molested her, he does some foolish things, for his head is completely giddy: he has her sit beside him at table, will touch no food save what he has out of her mouth, dotes upon her, and does a thousand other things, all very illogical and very libertine. But he and his confreres are men of that strange turn of character.

THE 17TH. 79. He binds the girl belly down upon a dining table and eats a piping hot omelette served upon her buttocks. He uses an exceedingly sharp fork.

He immobilizes her head above a grill, lights a brisk fire, and roasts her until she loses consciousness, embuggering her steadily.

He gently toasts the skin of her breasts and buttocks, proceeding very gradually, and using sulphur-tipped matches.

He uses candles and extinguishes them again and again by snuffing them out in her cunt, her asshole, and upon her nipples.

With a match he sears her eyelids; this prevents her from sleeping soundly that night, for she cannot close her eyes.

That evening, the Duc depucelates Giton, who finds the experience discomfiting, for the Duc is enormous, fucks with great brutality, and Giton is, after all, only twelve.

THE 18TH. 84. Pointing a pistol at her heart, he obliges her to chew and swallow a live coal, and then he washes out her cunt with aqua fortis.

He has her dance the olivettes. Naked, she is to dance round four pillars; but the only path her naked feet can tread is studded with shards of broken glass and bits of sharp metal and pointed tacks and nails; by each pillar stands a man, a bundle of switches in his hand, and he lashes whichever side of her body she offers every time she passes by him. She is thus obliged to run a certain number of turns around, it all depending upon whether she is more or less attractive. The most beautiful are harried the most.

He strikes her violently in the face until the blows of his fist bring blood from her nose, and he continues yet a while longer, the blood notwithstanding; he discharges and mixes his fuck with the blood she has lost.

Employing very well-heated tongs, he pinches her flesh, and mainly her buttocks, her mons veneris and her breasts. Desgranges will have more to say about this personage.

Upon various parts of her naked, reclining body, especially the more sensitive areas, he places little mounds of gunpowder, then sets fire to them.

Giton's ass is made public property that evening, and after this ceremony, he is flogged by Curval, the Duc, and the Bishop, who have fucked him.

THE 19TH. 89. He inserts a cylinder of gunpowder in her cunt, removes the cylinder, leaves the powder there; he puts a match to the charge and ejaculates upon seeing the flames dart forth. Earlier, he has kissed her ass.

He soaks her everywhere from head to foot with brandy, brings a match near and entertains himself with the spectacle of this poor girl all covered with flames. Then he discharges. He repeats the same operation two or three times.

He gives her bowels a rinsing with boiling oil.

He introduces a red-hot iron into her anus, another into her cunt, after having thoroughly whipped the latter.

He likes to trample upon a pregnant woman until she aborts. Prior to this he whips her.

That same evening, Curval depucelates Sophie's bum, but this ordeal succeeds another: she has first been given one hundred lashes by each of the friends and is streaming blood. Directly Curval has discharged into her ass, he offers to pay the society five hundred louis for permission to take her down to the cellars that very evening and to be given a free hand with her. Curval's request is rejected, he re-embuggers her, and upon emerging from her ass after this second discharge, he gives her a kick which sends her sprawling upon a mattress fifteen feet away. He revenges himself upon Zelmire, whom he flogs till his arm aches.

THE 20TH. 94. He appears to be caressing the girl who is frigging him, she suspects nothing; but at the moment he discharges, he seizes her head and batters it against the wall. The blow is so strong and so unexpected that she usually falls unconscious.

They are four libertines assembled; they judge a girl, and, ultimately disagreeing upon what punishment to inflict, decide to sentence her individually. All in all, she receives one hundred strokes of the whip; each juror metes out twenty-five of them: the first flogs her from the back to the loins, the second from the loins to the calves, the third from the neck to the navel, breasts included, the fourth from the belly to the shins.

Using a pin, he pricks each of her eyes, each nipple, and her clitoris.

He drops molten sealing wax upon her buttocks, into her cunt, and upon her breasts.

He opens the veins in one arm and bleeds her until she faints.

Curval suggests they bleed Constance because of her pregnancy; and bled she is, until she collapses, 'tis Durcet who acts as her leech. That evening, Messieurs avail themselves of Sophie's ass, and the Duc proposes she be bled also, it could not possibly do her any harm, no, on the contrary, they might make a nice pudding of her blood for tomorrow's luncheon. His idea is acclaimed, Curval now plays the leech, Duclos frigs him while he operates, and he wishes to make the puncture at the same moment his fuck departs his balls; and he makes a generous puncture, but his blade finds the vein none the less. Despite it all, Sophie has pleased the Bishop, who adopts her for his wife, repudiating Aline, who falls into the greatest discredit.

THE 21ST. 99. He bleeds both of her arms and would have her remain standing while her blood flows; now and again he stops the bleeding and flogs her, then opens the wounds again, and this continues until she collapses. He only discharges when she faints. Earlier in the game he had her shit for him.

He bleeds her from all four of her limbs and from her jugular vein too, and frigs himself while watching the five fountains of blood.

He lightly scarifies her flesh, concentrating upon her buttocks, but neglecting her breasts.

He scarifies her vigorously, cutting deep, devoting particular attention to her breasts and especially to her nipples, and to the environs of her asshole when he turns his attentions to her behind. Next, he cauterizes the wounds with a red-hot iron.

He is bound hand and foot, as if he were a wild beast, and he is draped in a tiger's skin. When thus readied, he is excited, irritated, whipped, beaten, his ass is frigged; opposite him is a plump young girl, naked and tied by her feet to the floor, by her neck to the ceiling, in such wise she cannot stir. When the roué is all a-sweat, his captors free him, he leaps upon the girl, bites her everywhere and above all her clitoris and her nipples, which he generally manages to remove with his teeth. He roars and cries like a ferocious animal, and discharges while shrieking. The girl must shit, he eats her turd upon the floor.

That evening, the Bishop depucelates Narcisse; he is surrendered to the society the same evening, so that the festival of the 23rd will not be disturbed. Before embuggering him, the Duc has him shit into his mouth and render him, together with the turd, his predecessors' fuck. And then, after having sodomized the lad, Blangis scourges him.

THE 22ND. 104. He pulls out her teeth and scratches her gums with needles. Sometimes he heats the needles.

He breaks one of her fingers, several upon occasion.

Employing a heavy hammer, he flattens one of her feet.

He removes a hand, sawing through the wrist.

While discharging, he batters in her front teeth with a hammer. He is very fond of sucking her mouth before proceeding to the major phase of his operation.

The Duc depucelates Rosette in the rear that evening, and the same instant his prick sounds her ass, Curval extracts one of the little girl's teeth -- this in order that she may experience two terrible pains at the same time. So that the morrow's festival not be disturbed, her ass is made generally available that same evening. When Curval has discharged thereinto (and he is the last of the four to do so), he sends the child spinning with a blow of his fist.

THE 23RD. Because of the holiday, only four are related.

He amputates one foot.

He breaks one of her arms as he embuggers her.

Using a crowbar, he breaks a bone in her leg and embuggers her after doing so.

He ties her to a stepladder, her limbs being attached in a peculiar manner, a cord is tied to the ladder; he pulls the cord, the ladder falls. Sometimes she breaks one limb, sometimes another.

Upon that day Invictus was married to Rosette; their wedding celebrated the twelfth week's festival. That evening, Rosette is bled after she has been fucked, and Aline is likewise bled after Hercule has fucked her; both are bled in such a way their blood spurts upon our libertines' thighs and pricks. Messieurs frig themselves while looking on, and discharge when both have fainted.

THE 24TH. 113. He cuts off one of her ears. (See to it that you specify what these persons do by way of a prelude to their major stunt.)

He slits her lips and nostrils.

After having sucked and bitten it, he pierces her tongue with a hot iron.

He tears several nails from her fingers, and also from her toes.

He cuts off one of her fingers at the last joint.

And, upon close questioning, the storyteller having said that, provided the wound is dressed at once, such a mutilation has no undesirable aftereffects, Durcet straightway cuts the end off one of Adelaide's fingers, for his lewd jesting and teasing have been increasingly directed against her. His practical joke fetches a discharge from him, his flow of fuck is accompanied by unheard-of transports.

That same evening, Curval depucelates Augustine's ass, even though she is now the Duc's wife. Her anguish, her sufferings. Curval rages against her afterward; he conspires with the Duc to take her down to the cellars without further delay, and they tell Durcet that if they are granted permission to carry out the expedition, they in their turn will allow him to dispatch Adelaide at once, but the Bishop delivers an impassioned sermon to those truants, and obtains the promise that they will restrain themselves yet a little longer for the sake of their own pleasure. Curval and the Duc hence limit themselves to giving Augustine a ferocious whipping. Both lash her at once.

THE 25TH. 118. He distills fifteen or twenty drops of molten lead into her mouth and burns her gums with aqua fortis.

After having had her lick his beshitted ass with her tongue, he snips off the end of that same tongue, then, when once she is mutilated, he embuggers her.

He employs a machine involving a hollow steel bit which bores holes in the flesh and which, when removed, takes with it a round chunk of flesh which is as long as the drill has penetrated; the machine bores on automatically if not withdrawn.

He transforms a boy of ten or twelve into a eunuch.

With a pair of pliers isolating and raising each nipple, he cuts off the same with a pair of scissors.

That same evening, Augustine's ass is made generally available. While embuggering her, Curval had wished to kiss Constance's breast, and upon discharging, he made off with a nipple in his teeth, but as her wound was treated and bandaged at once, Messieurs assured one another that the accident would have no harmful effect upon the child in her womb. Curval says to his colleagues, in answer to their pleasantries upon his mounting rage against Constance, that he has no control over the fury she inspires in him.

When in his turn the Duc embuggers Augustine, his own powerful feelings for that beautiful girl are exhaled with incomparable violence: had the others not kept an eye upon him, he would have injured her, either while mauling her breasts or squeezing her neck with all his strength as he discharged. Once again he asks the society to put her in his power, but he is requested to wait for Desgranges' narrations. His brother entreats him to be patient and abstain until he himself sets an example by dispatching Aline; haste, the Bishop points out, makes waste; and why spoil the latter part of the holiday by upsetting a schedule admirably designed to guarantee them a daily fare of moderation, wherein only happiness lies? However, the Duc will not listen to reason, he cannot any longer hold himself in check, and so, since he absolutely must torture the lovely girl, he is allowed to inflict a light wound upon her arm. He executes it upon the fleshy part of her left forearm, sucks blood from the cut he has made, and discharges;

Augustine is so skillfully patched up that four days later no trace of the Duc's teeth marks is to be seen.

THE 26TH. 123. He breaks a bottle of thin glass against the face of the girl, who is bound and unable to protect herself; before doing so, he sucked her mouth with great vigor and sucked her tongue also.

He tears off both her legs, ties one of her hands behind her back, puts a little stick into her free hand, and invites her to defend herself. Then he attacks her, wielding his sword with great vigor and dexterity, wounds her here and there, and finally discharges upon her wounds.

He stretches her upon a St. Andrew's cross, goes through the ceremony of breaking her, strains but does not dislocate three of her limbs, but does definitely break the fourth, either an arm or a leg.

Pistol in hand, he has her stand facing to the right and lets fly with a charge which grazes her two breasts; he aims to shoot away one of her little nipples.

He has her crouch down twenty feet away and present her buttocks; he shoots a bullet up her ass.

That same evening, the Bishop depucelates Fanny's bum.

THE 27TH. 128. The same man of whom Desgranges will speak on the 24th of February flogs a pregnant woman upon the belly until she miscarries; she must lay the egg in his presence, and he lashes her till she does.

He very tidily castrates a young lad of sixteen or seventeen after having embuggered and whipped him.

He must have a maiden brought to him, he slices off her clitoris with a razor, then deflowers her with a cylinder of heated iron, driving the device home with hammer blows.

This personage performs an abortion when the woman's pregnancy has entered its eighth month. He forces her to drink a certain brew which brings the child out dead in a trice. Upon other occasions, this libertine by his art causes the child to be born from the mother's asshole. But the child emerges dead, and the woman's life is gravely imperiled.

He severs an arm.

That evening, Fanny's ass is made generally available, Durcet rescues her from a torture his colleagues had been preparing for her; he takes her to be his wife, has the Bishop perform the marriage, and repudiates Adelaide, who is submitted to the torture originally readied for Fanny. It is however a paltry business after all: the Duc embuggers her while Durcet breaks her finger.

THE 28TH. 133. He cuts off both hands at the wrist and cauterizes the wounds with a hot iron.

He removes the tongue, cutting it at the roots, and cauterizes it with a hot iron.

He amputates one leg, usually having someone else cut it off while he embuggers her.

He extracts all her teeth, replacing each one with a red-hot nail, which he secures in place with a hammer; he does this directly after having fucked the woman in the mouth.

He removes one eye.

Julie is roundly whipped by everyone that evening and all her fingers are pricked with a needle. This latter operation takes place while the Bishop, who is passing fond of her, embuggers her.

THE 29TH. 138. Allowing molten sealing wax to flow thereupon, he blinds and ultimately dissolves first one eye, then the other.

He neatly slices off one breast, then cauterizes the wound with a hot iron. Desgranges will here interject that 'tis this same man who made off with the nipple she is missing, and that she is positively certain he ate it after having cooked it upon a griddle.

He amputates both buttocks after having flogged and embuggered her. It is believed that he too eats the meat.

He shaves off both her ears.

Clips off all the extremities, to wit: ten fingers, ten toes, two nipples, one clitoris and the end of the tongue.

That evening, Aline, after a vigorous whipping given her by the four friends and an embuggery the Bishop performs for the last time, is condemned to have a finger on either hand and a toe on either foot cut off by each friend. Thus she loses a total of eight parts.

THE 30TH. 143. He carves away several chunks of flesh, selecting them from divers areas upon her body; he has them roasted and obliges her to eat them with him. Desgranges will mention the same man on the 8th and 17th of February.

He cuts off a young boy's four limbs, embuggers the trunk, feeds him well and allows him so to live; as the arms and legs were not severed too close to the body, the boy lives for quite a while. And the surgeon embuggers him steadily for approximately a year.

He chains one of the girl's hands and secures the chain to the wall; he leaves her thus, without food. Near her is a large knife, and just beyond her reach sits an excellent meal: if she wishes to eat, she has but to cut through her forearm; otherwise, she dies of starvation. Prior to this he has embuggered her. He observes her through a window.

He manacles both mother and daughter; in order that they both survive, one has got to get to the food placed not far away: survival, that is, means that one must sacrifice a hand. He amuses himself listening to them discuss their dilemma, and argue about who is to resolve it.

She recounts only four stories, for that evening the thirteenth week's festival is to take place. During it, the Duc, acting in the capacity of a woman, is married to Hercule, who is to be the husband; acting now as a man, the Duc takes Zéphyr to be his wife. The young bardash who, as the reader is aware, possesses the prettiest ass amongst the eight boys, is dressed as a girl, and so clad appears as beautiful as the goddess of love. The ceremony is consecrated by the Bishop and transpires within the sight of the entire household. The dear little Zéphyr surrenders his virginal bum to the Duc, who finds all his pleasure therein, but much trouble making a successful entry; Zéphyr is rather badly torn, and bleeds profusely. Hercule fucks the Duc throughout this operation.

THE 31ST. 147. He plucks out both her eyes and leaves her locked in a room, saying that she has before her what she needs to eat, that she has but to get up and search for it. But in order to reach the food she must cross a broad plate of iron, which, of course, she cannot see, and which is kept heated to a very high temperature. Situated at a window, he amuses himself watching how she manages: will she burn herself, or will she prefer to perish from hunger? She has been, previously, very soundly whipped.

He subjects her to the rope torture; this consists in having one's four limbs tied to ropes, then one is raised high in the air and suddenly dropped from a considerable height, then raised, then dropped; each fall dislocates and sometimes breaks the limbs, because one never quite falls to the ground, the ropes halting one just a short distance above it.

He inflicts upon her a quantity of deep wounds into which he pours boiling pitch and molten lead.

The moment after she gives birth to a child, he binds her hand and foot, and ties her child not far away from her. The infant wails, she is unable to get to it. And thus she must watch it expire. Then he steps up and lashes the mother, aiming his whip-strokes at her cunt and managing the thing so that the interior of her vagina is well tickled. He himself is usually the child's father.

He gives her copiously to drink, then sews up her cunt, her asshole and her mouth as well, and leaves her thus until the water bursts through its conduits, or until she dies.

(Determine why there is one too many; if one is to be deleted, suppress the last, for I believe I have already used it.)

That same evening, Messieurs avail themselves of Zéphyr's ass, and Adelaide is condemned to a rude fustigation, after which a hot iron is brought very close to the interior of her vagina, to her armpits, and she is slightly scorched beneath each nipple.

She endures it all like a heroine and frequently invokes God. This further arouses her persecutors.

Part The Fourth

HE 150 MURDEROUS PASSIONS, OR THOSE BELONGING TO THE FOURTH CLASS, COMPOSING THE TWENTY-EIGHT DAYS OF FEBRUARY SPENT IN HEARING THE NARRATIONS OF MADAME DESGRANGES; INTERSPERSED AMONGST WHICH ARE THE SCANDALOUS DOINGS AT THE CHÂTEAU DURING THAT MONTH; ALL BEING SET DOWN IN THE FORM OF A JOURNAL. (DRAFT)

Begin by giving a full description of the new situation which exists in February; there has been a radical change in the appearance of things. The four original wives have been repudiated, but the Bishop has extended his protection to Julie, whom he keeps near him as a kind of servant to wait upon him; Duclos has been allowed to share her quarters with Constance, whose fruit Messieurs are eager to keep from spoiling; Aline and Adelaide have been driven out of house and home and now sleep amongst animals intended for their Lordships' table. The sultanas Augustine, Zelmire, Fanny, and Sophie have replaced the wives and now fulfill all their functions, to wit: as wipers in the chapel, as waitresses at the meals, as couch companions, as Messieurs' bed companions at night. Apart from the fucker, who changes from day to day, Messieurs have:

The Duc: Augustine, Zéphyr, and Duclos in his bed, together with his fucker; he sleeps surrounded by the four of them, and Marie occupies a sofa in his bedchamber;

Curval: the Président likewise sleeps amidst Adonis, Zelmire, a fucker, and Fanchon; his room is otherwise empty;

Durcet sleeps amidst Hyacinthe, Fanny, a fucker, and Martaine (check the foregoing), and he has Louison lie upon a neighboring divan.

The Bishop sleeps amidst Céladon, Sophie, a fucker, and Julie; Thérèse sleeps upon the divan.

Which reveals that each of the little ménages, Zéphyr and Augustine, Adonis and Zelmire, Hyacinthe and Fanny, Céladon and Sophie, all of whom are married, belong, husband and wife, to a single master. Only four little girls remain in the girls' harem, and four in the boys'. Champville sleeps in the girls' quarters, Desgranges in the boys' quarters. Aline is in the stable, as we pointed out, and Constance is in Duclos' room, but alone there since Duclos spends every night in the Duc's bed.

Dinner is always served by the four sultanas (by, that is to say, the four new wives), and supper by the remaining four sultanas; a quatrain always serves coffee; but the quatrains formerly allocated to each niche in the auditorium are now reduced in number to one boy and one girl.

The reader will recall our mention of the pillars in the auditorium; at the beginning of each séance, Aline is attached to one of them, Adelaide to the other, their buttocks facing out toward the alcoves, and near each pillar is a little table covered with assorted punitive instruments; and so it is the two women are at all times ready to receive the lash. Constance has permission to sit with the storytellers. Each duenna keeps close to her couple, and Julie, completely unclothed, wanders from couch to couch, taking orders and executing them upon the spot. As always, one fucker per couch.

Such is the situation when Desgranges begins her narrations. The friends have also ruled, in a special decree, that, during this month, Aline, Adelaide, Augustine, and Zelmire shall be surrendered to Messieurs' brutal passions, and that Messieurs are at liberty, upon the described day, either to immolate them privately or to invite whichever of their friends they please to witness the sacrifice; and that with what regards Constance, she shall be employed for the celebration of the final week, a full explanation of which shall be given in due time and place. Should the Duc and Curval, who by this arrangement are to be made widowers, be disposed to take another wife to care for their needs until the end of the holiday, they shall be able to do so by making a selection from amongst the four remaining sultanas. But the pillars will remain ungarnished when the two women who garnish them now shall have been bidden a last farewell.

Desgranges starts, and after having reminded her auditors that henceforth the tales shall be those of an exclusively murderous character, she says that she will be careful, as their Lordships have enjoined her to be, to enter into the most minute details, and above all to indicate with what ordinary caprices these libertine assassins preface their more serious exercises; thus, their Lordships will be able to perceive and judge their relationships and associations, and to see how an example of simple libertinage, rectified and elaborated by an unmannerly and unprincipled individual, may lead straight to murder, and to what kind of murder. Then she begins.

THE 1ST OF FEBRUARY. 1. He used to enjoy amusing himself with a beggarwoman who had not had a bit to eat in three days, and his second passion is to leave a woman to die of hunger in a dungeon; he keeps a close watch upon her and frigs himself while examining her, but does not discharge until the day she perishes.

He maintains her in her prison cell, toying with her for a long season, gradually diminishing her daily portion of food; beforehand, he has her shit, and eats her turd upon a platter.

He formerly liked to suck the mouth and swallow its saliva; in recent days he has developed the passion of immuring a woman in a dungeon with food to last no more than a fortnight; on the thirtieth day, he enters her prison and frigs himself upon the corpse.

First, he would have her kiss, then he would slowly destroy her by preventing her from drinking although feeding her all she wanted to eat.

He would flog, then later kill the woman by depriving her of sleep.

That same evening, Michette, after having eaten a big supper, is hung head downward until she has vomited everything upon Curval, who stands frigging himself beneath her and eating the manna that descends from on high.

THE 2ND. 6. His first passion was to have her shit into his mouth, and he would eat it as it emerged; nowadays he feeds her a diet of worthless bread and cheap wine. A month on this fare and she starves to death.

He was once a great cunt-fucker; now he gives the woman a venereal distemper by injection, but of such virulence she croaks in very short order.

As a youth, he was fond of receiving vomit in his mouth, now, by means of a certain decoction, he gives her a deathly fever which results in her speedy demise.

He was once wont to gather shit from assholes, presently injects an enema containing toxic ingredients dissolved in boiling water or aqua fortis.

Once a famous fustigator, today he binds a woman to a pivot upon which she uninterruptedly revolves until dead.

That evening, an enema of boiling water is given to Rosette the moment after the Duc has finished embuggering her.

THE 3RD. 11. He used to like to slap the whore's face; as a mature man, he twists her head around until it faces backward. When so adjusted, one may simultaneously look at her face and at her buttocks.

Addicted to bestiality as a youngster, he now likes to have a girl depucelated by a stallion while he looks on. She ordinarily dies.

Once an ass-fucker, he now buries the girl up to her waist and maintains her thus till the lower half of her body rots.

Previously, he was wont to frig her clitoris, and he still does so, but more vigorously, employing one of his servants to keep at the work until the girl expires.

Gradually perfecting his passion over the years, a fustigator now flogs every part of a woman's body until she perishes.

That evening, the Duc would have Augustine, endowed with an unusually sensitive clitoris, frigged thereupon by Duclos and Champville, who relieve each other at the post and continue the task until the little lady falls unconscious.

THE 4TH. 16. His earlier passion was to squeeze the whore's neck, in later years he would tie the girl by the neck. Before her sits a sumptuous meal, but to reach it she must strangle; otherwise she dies of hunger.

The same man who slew Duclos' sister and whose taste is to subject the flesh to a prolonged mauling, abuses the breasts and buttocks with such furious violence that his treatment of the whore proves fatal to her.

The man Martaine mentioned on the 20th of January, he who formerly adored bleeding women, now kills them by dint of repeated bloodlettings.

He whose passion in times past was to make a naked woman run until she dropped from exhaustion, in this age of unbridled libertinage shuts her up in a steaming bathhouse where she dies of asphyxiation.

He whom Duclos cited earlier, the gentleman who liked to be wrapped in swaddling clothes and fed whoreshit in a spoon rather than pap, swathes a girl so tightly in baby's blankets that he kills her.

Shortly before the company moved into the auditorium that afternoon, Curval was found embuggering one of the scullery maids. He pays the fine; the girl is ordered to reappear at the evening's orgies, where the Duc and the Bishop embugger her in their turn, and she receives two hundred lashes from the hand of each of them. She's a strapping country girl, twenty-five, in satisfactory health, and has a fine ass.

THE 5TH. 21. His first passion is for bestiality, his second is to sew the girl into an untanned donkey's skin, her head protruding; he feeds and cares for her until the animal's skin shrinks and crushes her to death.

He of whom Martaine spoke on the 15th of January and who liked to hang a girl for his amusement, currently amuses himself by hanging her by her feet until the blood rushing to her head kills her.

Duclos' libertine of the 27th of November who liked to besot his whore, today inserts a funnel into her mouth and floods her with liquids till she dies therefrom.

Once he was wont to mistreat nipples, but has progressed since then and now buckles a sort of small iron pot over each breast and lowers her over a stove; the iron heats, and she is allowed to perish thus in frightful pain.

His whole delight used to consist in watching a woman swim, but he now casts her into a pond and fishes her out half-drowned, then hangs her by the feet to encourage the water to drain out of her. Once she has returned to her senses, into the pond she goes again, and so on and so forth, till she gives up the ghost.

Upon that day and at the same hour, another kitchen servant is found being embuggered, this time by the Duc; he pays the fine, the servant is summoned to the orgies, where everyone cavorts with her, Durcet making good use of her mouth, the others of her bum, and even of her cunt, for she is a virgin, and she is condemned to receive two hundred lashes from each of her employers. She is a girl of eighteen, tall and well made, her hair is auburn in color, and she owns a very fair ass.

That same evening, Curval utters the opinion that it is a matter of extreme urgency that Constance be bled again on account of her pregnancy; the Duc embuggers her, and Curval bleeds her while Augustine frigs his prick against Zelmire's buttocks and while someone else fucks Zelmire. Upon discharging, he executes the puncture; his aim is true.

THE 6TH. 26. As a young man he used to kick a woman in the ass, tumbling her into a brazier, whence she would emerge before suffering excessively. He has lately refined this stunt, now obliges a girl to stand upright between two blazing fires: one cooks her in front, the other behind; and there she remains until the fat on her body melts.

Desgranges announces that she is going to describe murders which, bringing on a prompt death, cause very little suffering.

In former times he would impede respiration by constricting the neck with his hands or by blocking the nose and mouth, but these days he deposits the whore between four mattresses and she suffocates.

He of whom Martaine said a few words and who used to allow his victim a choice from among three manners of dying (see the 14th of January) has of late begun to blow out the whore's brains, denying her any say in the matter; he embuggers, and upon discharging, pulls the trigger.

The man Champville referred to on the 22nd of December as the libertine who made the girl dance with the cat, presently flings the whore from the top of a tower. She lands on sharp gravel. He discharges upon hearing her land.

That gentleman who liked to throttle his partner while embuggering her, and whom Martaine described on the 6th of January, has advanced to the stage at which, as he embuggers her, he slips a black silk cord about her neck and strangles her while discharging; this delight, says Desgranges, is one of the most exquisite a libertine can procure himself.

Upon that day, Messieurs celebrate the festival of the fourteenth week, and, in the guise of a woman, Curval becomes Bum-Cleaver's wife, and, as a man, takes Adonis to be his helpmeet; 'tis not till then that child is depucelated, and the event occurs very publicly, while Bum-Cleaver is fucking the Président.

Messieurs besot themselves at supper. And they flog Zelmire and Augustine about the loins, the buttocks, the thighs, the belly, the cunt, and the groin, then Curval has Zelmire fucked by Adonis, his new wife, and embuggers both of them one after the other.

THE 7TH. 31. He once liked to fuck a drowsy woman; he does much better now: he kills her with a strong dose of opium and encunts her during her death-sleep.

The same roué she referred to very recently, and who subjects the whore to a series of duckings, has still another passion: tying a stone to her neck, he drowns the woman.

Whereas once he was content to slap her face, now he carries matters further: he pours molten lead into her ear while she is asleep.

He was fond of whipping her face; Champville spoke of him on the 30th of December (verify that); but now he dispatches the girl with a quick hammer blow upon the temple.

This libertine would previously allow a candle to burn out in a woman's anus; today, he attaches her to a lightning rod during a thunderstorm and awaits a fortuitous stroke.

A sometime fustigator. He has her bend over with her behind facing the muzzle of a small piece of artillery. The ball enters her ass.

That day 'tis the Bishop they discover with his prick lodged in the third kitchen servant's asshole. He pays the fine, the Duc and Curval embugger and cunt-fuck her, for she is also a virgin, then she is given a total of eight hundred stripes, two hundred by each friend. She is Swiss, nineteen, very fair of skin, very plump, and has a splendid ass.

The cooks complain and say that the service will not be able to continue any longer if Messieurs go on fussing about with the help, and the society agrees to a truce extending until March.

Rosette loses a finger that evening, and the wound is cauterized with fire. She is sandwiched between Curval and the Duc during the operation: one fucks her ass, the other her cunt. Adonis' ass is made generally available that same evening; and so it is that the Duc cunt-fucks one servant and Rosette at the orgies and ass-fucks the same servant, ass-fucks Rosette too, and Adonis. He is tired.

THE 8TH. 37. His whole delight once lay in beating a woman's entire body with a bull's pizzle; 'twas to him Martaine alluded as the man who strained all four of his victim's limbs on the rack and broke but one of them. He likes now thoroughly to break the woman on the wheel, but he chokes her to death when he has finished exercising her.

Martaine's gentleman who would feign a decapitation and have the woman snatched from beneath the blade at the last moment, now severs her head in all good faith. He discharges as the blow falls. He frigs himself.

Martaine's libertine of the 30th of January who was wont to perform an extensive scarification, now consigns his victims to perish in dungeons.

He used to be a whipper of pregnant women's bellies, has latterly perfected that by causing an enormous weight to fall on the pregnant woman's belly, thereby crushing her and her fruit at one stroke.

Formerly, he was known to be fond of the sight of a girl's bare neck, which he would squeeze and molest somewhat; that mild passion has been replaced by the insertion of a pin in a certain spot upon the woman's neck. The pin kills her at once.

At the beginning he would gently burn various parts of the body with a candle flame, more recently he has begun to hurl women into a glowing furnace where they are consumed instantly.

Durcet, his prick very stiff and who during the storytelling has ventured forth twice to flog Adelaide awaiting him at her pillar, proposes to lay her

lengthwise in the fire, and after she has had sufficient time to quake over an idea Messieurs would be nothing loath to put into execution, they burn her nipples for the sake of their convenience; Durcet, her husband, burns one, her father, Curval, burns the other. This exciting operation causes both to discharge.

THE 9TH. 43. In his young years a pin-pricker, he has got himself a more formidable weapon: discharges while thrice driving a dagger into the woman's heart.

He used to adore burning gunpowder in the cunt, but has since improved his passion: he attaches a slender but attractive girl to a large rocket, the fuse is ignited, the rocket ascends, then returns to earth with the girl still attached.

The same personage who put gunpowder in all the orifices of a woman's body, now wedges cartridges into them; they explode simultaneously, sending the members flying in every direction.

First passion: he enjoyed secreting an emetic in the girl's food, unbeknownst to her; his second passion: he mixes a certain powder with her snuff, or sprinkles it on some flowers, she inhales and straightway falls dead.

First passion: he would flog her breasts and neck; refinement thereof: he aims a blow of a crowbar at her throat, it fells her forever.

Duclos spoke of him on the 27th of November, Martaine on the 14th of January (verify the dates): the whore enters and shits before the rake, he scolds her; brandishing a whip, he pursues her, she thinks to take refuge in a loft. A door opens, she spies a little stairway, believes she will be safe, rushes up the steps, but one of them gives way and she plunges into a large vat of boiling water; she dies, scalded, drowned, asphyxiated. His tastes are previously to have the woman shit and to lash her while she is doing so.

Curval had solicited and obtained shit from Zelmire that morning; now, directly the aforementioned tale is concluded, the Duc demands further shit from her. She cannot produce any; she is promptly condemned to have her ass pricked with a golden needle until it is covered with blood; in that it is the Duc whose interests have suffered as a result of her refusal, he is the one who recovers damages.

Curval requests shit of Zéphyr; the latter replies, saying that the Duc had him shit that morning. This the Duc denies, Duclos is called to give evidence, she supports Blangis' contention even though it is false. Consequently, Curval has the right to punish Zéphyr, despite the fact he is the Duc's bardash, just as the Duc has punished Zelmire, who is Curval's wife. The Président flogs Zéphyr until the lad streams blood, then tweaks his nose six times; the tweaks fetch forth more blood, and that makes the Duc roar with laughter.

THE 10TH. Desgranges says that she is now going to discuss murders of imposture and duplicity in which the manner is of principal significance; that is to say, the murder itself is merely incidental. Wherewith, says she, poisonings will be presented first.

A man whose caprice consisted in bum-fuckery and in no other kind, now envenoms all his wives; he is presently on his twenty-second. Never does he fuck them save in the ass, nor have they ever been deflowered otherwise.

A bugger invites a number of friends to a banquet, and with each succeeding course a few of them are stricken with stomach cramps which prove fatal.

Duclos spoke of him on the 26th of November, Martaine on the 10th of January; he is a bugger, pretends that it is relief he is giving the poor, distributes food, but 'tis poisoned.

A treacherous bugger regularly employs a drug which, sprinkled on the ground, very wonderfully kills whosoever walks thereupon; he sprinkles it about rather frequently, and over wide areas.

A bugger, equally skilled in alchemy, uses another substance which causes death after inconceivable torture; the death throes last a good two weeks, and no doctor has ever been able to diagnose or treat the ailment. He takes the keenest pleasure in paying you a visit while you are in the toils.

A sodomizer of men and women makes use of yet another powder which deprives you of your senses and renders you as if dead. And such you are believed to be, you are buried, and full of despair, you die in your coffin, into which you have no sooner been placed than you regain consciousness. He endeavors to find the exact place you have been buried, to place an ear to the ground and listen for a few screams; if indeed he hears your cries, 'tis enough to make him swoon with pleasure. He thuswise slew part of his family.

While joking and making merry that evening, Messieurs give Julie a powder concealed in her food, which causes her frightful cramps; they advise her that she is poisoned, she believes it, she wails, is beside herself. While watching her convulsions, the Duc has Augustine frig him directly opposite Julie. Augustine has the great misfortune of allowing the prepuce to slip back over the Duc's glans, and that is something which displeases the Duc extremely: he was just about to discharge, the girl's carelessness prevents it. He declares he is going to cut off one of that buggress' fingers and, as good as his word, does so, slicing a digit from the hand that failed him, and while cutting, he has his daughter Julie, still persuaded she is poisoned, crawl up to him and complete his discharge. Julie is cured that same evening.

THE 11TH. 55. A consummate bugger would frequently dine at the home of friends or acquaintances and would never fail to poison the individual his host cherished most dearly amongst all living creatures. He employed a powder which finally slew after causing two days of atrocious agony.

An erstwhile breast-abuser has perfected his passion: he poisons infants being suckled by their nurses.

He once used to love to receive back into his mouth milk enemas he had injected into his partner's rectum; his later passion: he administers toxic injections which kill while causing horrible spasms and colics.

A crafty bugger of whom she will have occasion to say more on the 13th and the 26th, used to love to set fire to poorhouses, and would always see to it that a quantity of persons were consumed, above all children.

Another bugger liked to cause women to die in childbirth; he would come to pay his respects, bringing along a powder whose odor would cause spasms and convulsions ending in death.

The man to whom Duclos referred during her twenty-eighth evening enjoys watching a woman bear a child; he murders it immediately it emerges from the womb and within full view of the mother, and does so while feigning to caress it.

That evening, Adelaide is first dealt a hundred lashes by each friend, and then, when she is well bloodied, shit is demanded of her; she gave some that morning to Curval, who swears 'tis not so. Consequently, they burn her two breasts, the palm of each hand, spill drops of molten sealing wax upon her thighs and belly, fill her navel therewith, burn her pubic hair after having doused it with cognac. The Duc attempts to pick a quarrel with Zelmire, and the Président severs a finger from each of her hands.

Augustine is scourged about the cunt and asshole.

THE 12TH. Messieurs assemble in the morning and decide that the four governesses, who are no longer of much use to the society and whose functions the four storytellers shall henceforth be perfectly able to carry out, may just as well provide the society with a little amusement; Messieurs therefore decree that the elders shall be martyrized one after another, the first sacrifice being scheduled for the evening of that same day. The four storytellers are invited to replace the elders; they accept upon condition they shall suffer no ill-treatment. Messieurs promise to subject them to none.

The three friends, d'Aucourt, the abbot, and Desprès, of whom Duclos spoke on the 12th of November, are now living abroad and still enjoying each other's company, and this is one of their common passions: they require a woman whose pregnancy is in its eighth or begun its ninth month, they open her belly, snatch out the child, burn it before the mother's eyes, and in its place substitute a package containing sulphur and quicksilver, which they set afire, then stitch the belly up again, leaving the mother thus to perish in the midst of incredible agonies, while they look on and have themselves frigged by the girl they have with them. (Verify the girl's name.)

He was fond of depucelating, has gradually broadened his scope of activity: he has a great number of children by several women, then, when they reach the age of five or six, he depucelates them, boys and girls alike, and directly he has fucked them, throws them into a blazing oven. Or he sometimes throws them in at the same moment he discharges.

The man Duclos mentioned on the 27th of November, Martaine on the 15th of January, and she herself on the 5th of February, whose taste was to play at hanging, to see hanged, etc., this same fellow, I say, hides some of his personal effects in his domestics' wardrobes and declares he has been robbed. He strives to have his servants hanged, and if he succeeds goes to watch the spectacle; if not, he locks them in a room and strangles them to death. While operating, he discharges.

An inveterate shit-lover, he of whom Duclos spoke on the 14th of November, has a specially prepared commode at his home; he engages his intended victim to sit down upon it, and once the victim is seated, the seat buckles, gives way, and precipitates the sitter into a very deep ditch filled with shit, in which environment she is left to die.

A man to whom Martaine made reference and who would amuse himself watching a girl fall from a ladder, has perfected his passion thus (but find out which man):

He situates the girl upon a little trestle on the edge of a deep ditch filled with water; on the farther side of it is a wall which seems to be all the more inviting, what for the ladder leaning against it. But to reach the ladder she must cross the moat, and she becomes all the more will-

ing to spring into the water as the fire burning behind the trestle moves
gradually closer to her. If she hesitates too long, the fire will reach her,
consume her, and as she does not know how to swim, she will be drowned
if she plunges into the water. While she is considering what to do, the
fire approaches, and she finally elects to struggle with a different element
and endeavor to get to the wall. It frequently happens that she drowns;
if so, the game is over. But if by good fortune she reaches the other bank
and then the ladder, and starts to climb it, toward the top there is a rung
which breaks beneath her weight and she drops into a hole covered over
with a thin layer of earth, and the hole contains a bed of live coals upon
which she perishes. Hard by the scene, the libertine observes it with the
keenest interest, frigging himself industriously.

The same man Duclos spoke of on the 29th of November, the same
who bumwise depucelated Martaine when a little girl of five, and also
the same with whom Desgranges announces she will conclude her narrations (the hell episode), this individual, I say, embuggers the prettiest
girl of sixteen or eighteen the procuress can find for him. Sensing his
crisis about to arrive, he releases a spring, upon the bare and completely
unadorned neck of the girl descends a machine furnished with steel
teeth; the machine begins to move laterally and gradually saws through
the pinioned neck while the libertine occupies himself with completing
his discharge. Which always takes a very long time.

That very evening Messieurs discover the intrigue involving Augustine and one of the subaltern fuckers; he has not yet fucked her, but to
attain his ends has suggested that they both escape from the castle, and he
has outlined to her a very easy way to do so. Augustine confesses that she
was about to grant him what he sought from her in order to save herself
from a place where she believes her life to be in danger. 'Tis Fanchon
who discovers and reports everything. The traitorous quadrumvirate leap
upon the fucker without warning, bind him hand and foot, and take him
down to the cellars, where the Duc embuggers him with extreme vigor
and without pomade, while the Président saws through his neck and the
other two apply red-hot irons to all parts of his body.

This scene transpires directly after dinner is over and hence coffee
is omitted that day; the work completed, everyone repairs to the auditorium as usual, then to supper, and amongst themselves Messieurs debate
whether, in return for having disclosed the conspiracy, they ought not
accord Fanchon a reprieve, for their decision that morning was to maltreat
her the same evening. The Bishop declares himself against sparing her,
and says that it would be unworthy of them to yield to the sentiment of
gratitude, and that, for his part, he will always be seen to favor any decision
likely to afford the society one pleasure more, just as he will always vote
against any motion apt to deprive it of a pleasure. And so, after having
punished Augustine for lending herself to the subversive scheme, first by

obliging her to watch her lover's execution, then by embuggering her and making her believe her head would be cut off as well, next by actually pulling out two of her teeth, an operation performed by the Duc while Curval was embuggering that beautiful girl, finally by giving her a sound whipping, after all that, I say, Fanchon is led into the arena, made to shit, given a hundred lashes by each of the friends, and then the Duc deftly shaves off her left nipple. She raises a storm, criticizing their behavior toward her and describing it as unjust. "Were it just," says the Duc, wiping his razor, "it would surely fail to give us an erection." Whereupon they dress the old whore's wounds, eager to preserve her for further ordeals.

Their Lordships perceive that indeed there had been faint but definite rebellious stirrings amongst the subaltern fuckers; the prompt sacrifice of one of them has, however, thoroughly quelled their murmurs. Like Fanchon, the three other duennas are divested of all responsibility, removed from office, and replaced by the four storytellers and Julie. They tremble, do the old dames; but by what shifts are they to escape their fate?

THE 13TH. 67. A great connoisseur of the ass, he declares his love for a girl and, having arranged a boating party, lures her upon the water in a small boat, the which has been prepared for the outing, springs a leak, founders; the girl is drowned. He sometimes pursues his objective by different means: will, for example, lead a girl out upon a high balcony, have her lean upon the railing, which gives way; and once again the girl dies.

A man, while making his apprenticeship in life, was content first to whip and then to embugger; now, having reached a mature age, entices the girl to enter a specially prepared room; a trap door yields beneath her step, she falls into a cellar where the rake awaits her; he plunges a knife into her breasts, her cunt, and into her asshole as she lies stunned by her fall. Next, he casts her, dead or still alive, into another cellar, over which a stone drops into place; she tumbles upon a heap of other corpses, and she expires in a great fit if life has not already departed her sore-beset frame. And he is very careful to administer delicate stabs, for he would prefer that she live a little and finally perish in the cellar mentioned latterly. Prior to all this, he of course embuggers and flogs her and discharges; 'tis coolly and with utmost method he proceeds to her undoing.

A bugger has the girl mount astride an untamed, unbroken horse which unseats her, drags her along a rocky terrain, and finally pitches her over a precipice.

Martaine's hero of the 18th of January whose juvenile passion was to distribute little mounds of gunpowder upon the girl's body, has made significant progress. He lays the girl in a special bed; when properly tucked in, the bed gives way, dropping her into a large brazier of live coals, but she is able to scramble out of it; however, he is standing by and, as she repeats her attempts to escape the fire, he drives her back, wielding a pitchfork and with it aiming stout blows at her belly.

The gentleman she mentioned on the 11th, who likes to burn down poorhouses, endeavors to lure a beggar, whether a man or a woman, from out of one and into his own home, upon the pretense of bestowing charity; he embuggers his victim, then breaks his back and leaves him thus discomfited to die in a dungeon.

He who was wont to defenestrate a woman, hurling her upon a dung heap, the same man of whom Martaine spoke, by way of second passion executes the following one: he allows the girl to sleep in a room she is acquainted with and whose window she knows to be not far above the ground; she is given opium, when in a deep slumber she is conveyed to another chamber, identical with the first but having a window high above the ground which, on this side of the house, is strewn with sharp rocks. Next, the libertine enters where she lies sleeping, makes a dreadful noise, terrifies her; she is informed that she is about to die. Knowing the drop from the window to the ground to be short, she leaps through it, but falls thirty feet and lands upon the murderous rocks, killing herself. No one has so much as laid a finger upon her.

In the character of a woman, that great histrionic, the Bishop, marries Antinoüs, whose role is that of a husband, and also weds Céladon, whom he takes to be his wife, and 'tis that evening the child is embuggered for the first time.

This ceremony celebrates the festival of the fifteenth week; to complete the holiday, the prelate wishes to expose Aline to some severe vexations, for his libertine rage against her has been quietly but steadily mounting: she is hanged, then quickly cut down, but while seeing her however briefly aloft, everyone discharges. Durcet opens her veins, this treatment restores her to life; the next day she appears none the worse for wear, but suspension has added an inch to her height; she relates what she experienced during the ordeal.

The Bishop, for whom everything is an occasion of jollity and everyone the object of game that day, cuts one of old Louison's nipples clean off her breast; whereupon the other two duennas see very clearly what their fate is to be.

THE 14TH. 73. A man whose simple taste was to flog a girl, perfects it by every day removing morsels of flesh the size of a pea from the girl's body, but her wounds are not dressed, and thus she perishes over a low fire, as it were.

Desgranges announces that she will now deal with exceedingly painful murders wherein 'tis the extreme cruelty which comprises the main element; Messieurs more strongly than ever urge her to furnish abundant details.

He who was fond of letting blood daily relieves his victim of a half ounce of it, continuing till she is dead. Messieurs greet this example with hearty applause.

He who was wont to prick the ass with many pins every day administers a more or less superficial gash with a poignard. The blood is stanched,
but the wound is not treated, neither does it mend, and thus 'tis a slow
death she dies. A fustigator (75) quietly and slowly saws off all four limbs,
one after the other.

The Marquis de Mesanges, of whom Duclos spoke in connection with
the shoemaker Petignon's daughter, bought by the Marquis from Duclos,
and whose first passion was to undergo four hours of flogging without
discharging, for a second passion places a little girl in the hands of a giant
fellow who holds the child by the head over a large charcoal brazier which
burns her very slowly; the victims must be virgins.

His first passion: little by little to burn the breasts and buttocks with
the flame of a match; his second: over every part of the girl's body to plant
a forest of sulphur-coated slivers, which he lights one by one. He watches
her die in this way.

"Nor is there anymore painful way to die," observes the Duc, who
then confesses to having surrendered himself to this infamous pastime,
and to having discharged vigorously thanks to it. They say that the patient
lives six hours, sometimes eight.

Céladon's ass is made generally available that evening; the Duc and
Curval indulge themselves heavily. Constance's pregnancy is still on the
Président's mind; he suggests that she be bled, and bleeds her himself
while discharging in Céladon's ass, then he lops off one of Thérèse's nipples
while embuggering Zelmire, and the Duc sodomizes the duenna during
the amputation.

THE 15TH. 78. Once beguiled by the charms of a mouth to suck and
saliva to swallow, he is now of sterner stuff: every day he inserts a funnel
into the girl's mouth and pours a small dose of molten lead down her
throat; she gives up the ghost on the ninth day.

First a finger-twister, he currently breaks all her limbs, tears out her
tongue, gouges out her eyes, and leaves her thus to live, diminishing her
sustenance day by day.

A perpetrator of sacrilege, the second one Martaine mentioned on
the 3rd of January, he secures a beautiful youth to a tall cross, binding
him with cords and leaving him there as food for ravens.

An armpit-sniffer and -fucker, to whom Duclos alluded, binds a
woman hand and foot and hangs her by a rope looped under her arms;
he goes every day to prick some part of her body so that the blood will
attract flies; her death is by slow degrees.

A passionate admirer of asses rectifies his worship: he now seals a
girl in an underground cave where she has food to last three days; before
leaving her, he inflicts several wounds upon her body, thuswise to render
her death more painful. He wishes to have them virgins and spends a week
embracing their asses before organizing their destruction.

Formerly he loved to fuck very youthful mouths and asses; his later improvement consists in snatching out the heart of a living girl, widening the space that organ occupied, fucking the warm hole, replacing the heart in that pool of blood and fuck, sewing up the wound, and leaving the girl to her fate, without help of any kind. In which case the wait is not long.

Still wroth with the lovely Constance, Curval maintains that there is no reason under the sun why one cannot successfully bear a child even though one has a broken limb, and therefore they fracture that unlucky creature's arm the same evening. Durcet slices off one of Marie's nipples after she has been well warmed by the lash and made copiously to shit.

THE 16TH. 84. A fustigator refines his passion: he learns and then practices the art of gently removing flesh from bones; he then extracts the marrow, usually by sucking it out, and pours molten lead into the cavity.

At this point the Duc loudly exclaims that he'll not fuck another ass while he lives if that isn't the very ordeal he has had in mind for his beloved Augustine; that poor girl, whom Blangis has been embuggering for some time, utters cries and sheds a torrent of tears. And as thanks to her misbehavior she interferes with his discharge and frustrates it effectively, he withdraws, takes hold of his engine in one hand, and while with the other he gives her a dozen slaps which resound through that wing of the castle, he manages his discharge very satisfactorily by himself.

A bugger uses an ingenious machine to chop the girl into small pieces: this is a Chinese torture.

Weary of his early fondness for girls' pucelages, his latest passion is to impale a girl upon the point of a sharp pickaxe introduced into her cunt; there she sits, as if upon a horse, he ties a cannon ball to each of her legs, the pick works deeper, and she is left to her own devices and a slow death.

A fustigator flays the girl thrice over; he soaks her fourth layer of skin with a devouring escharotic which brings about death accompanied by hideous agonies.

His first passion was to sever a finger; his second is to pluck up some flesh with a pair of red-hot tongs, to cut off the flesh with a pair of scissors, then to burn the wound. He is quite apt to spend as long as four or five days whittling away a girl's body piecemeal, and she ordinarily dies while the cruel operation is still advancing.

Sophie and Céladon have been found amusing themselves together and are punished that evening; both are whipped over their entire bodies by the Bishop, whose chattels they are. Sophie loses two fingers to the shears, Céladon as many; but he recovers very quickly. The Bishop is no less eager to use them in his pleasures, however they be maimed.

Fanchon returns to the center of the stage. After having been beaten with a bull's pizzle, the soles of her feet are burned, each thigh, before and behind, is burned also, her forehead too, and each hand as well, and Messieurs extract all her remaining teeth. The Duc's prick is almost continually wedged into her ass throughout this lengthy operation.

Mention that it has been prescribed by law that a subject's buttocks shall be left intact until the day the said subject reaches the end of his career.

THE 17TH. 89. Martaine's gentleman of the 30th of January and the same one she herself described on the 5th of February, pares away a girl's breasts and buttocks, eats them, and upon her wounds puts plasters which so violently burn the flesh that they are her undoing. He also forces her to eat her own flesh, which he has had grilled.

A bugger cooks up a little girl in a double boiler.

A bugger: he has her roasted alive on a spit directly after embuggering her.

A man whose initial passion was to have little girls and boys embuggered in his presence by massive and ponderous pricks, impales the girl, a spear in her ass, and leaves her thus to die while he studies her contortions.

Another bugger: attaches a woman to a wheel, it is then set in motion and, without having done her any previous harm, he allows her to die a very pretty death.

That evening, the Bishop, his spirits in a great ferment, wishes to have Aline tormented, his rage against her has reached its fever pitch. She makes her appearance naked, he has her shit and embuggers her, then, without discharging, he withdraws in a towering fury from that enchanting ass and injects a rinse of boiling water into it, obliging her to squirt it out at once, while it is still boiling hot, upon Thérèse's face. After that, Messieurs hack off all the fingers and toes Aline has left, break both her arms and burn them with red-hot pokers. She is next flogged, beaten, and slapped, then the Bishop, still further aroused, cuts off one of her nipples, and discharges.

Wherewith they transfer their attentions to Thérèse, the interior of her vagina is seared, her nostrils, tongue, feet, and hands are all burned too; then she is given six hundred lashes with a bull's pizzle. Out come the rest of her teeth, fire is introduced into her throat. A witness to these harsh proceedings, Augustine falls to weeping; the

Duc lashes her belly and cunt until he has drawn a suitable amount of blood therefrom.

THE 18TH. 94. A flesh-sacrificer in his early days, his adult entertainment consists in quartering girls by bending four saplings, attaching an arm or leg to each, and releasing the trees, which spring back erect.

A fustigator suspends her from a machine which lowers a girl into and immediately lifts her out of a fire, then repeats the operation until there is very little left of the patient.

He once loved to extinguish candles by snuffing them out upon flesh; today, he envelopes her in sulphur and uses her for a torch, being careful to prevent the fumes for choking her.

A sodomist: rips the intestines from a young boy and a young girl, puts the boy's into the girl, inserts the girl's into the boy's body, stitches up the incisions, ties them back to back to a pillar which supports them both, and he watches them perish.

A man who was fond of inflicting light burns, improves his passion: he now roasts his victim upon a grill, turning him over and over again.

Michette is, that evening, exposed to the libertines' fury; all four begin by whipping her, then each tears out one of her teeth, they cut off four fingers (each friend amputates one), her thighs are burned in four places, two in front and two behind, the Duc manhandles one of her breasts until it is truly unrecognizable, sodomizing Giton in the meantime.

Louison is next on the bill of fare; she is made to shit, she is given eight hundred strokes with the bull's pizzle, she is divested of all her teeth, her tongue is burned, as is her asshole, her vagina, and her remaining nipple, and so are six places upon her thighs.

When everyone has retired to bed for the night, the Bishop goes in search of his brother, they wake Desgranges and Duclos, and the four of them take Aline down into the cellars; the Bishop embuggers her, the Duc embuggers her, they pronounce the death sentence, and by means of excessive torments which last until daybreak, they execute it. Upon returning, they exchange words of unqualified praise for these two storytellers and advise their colleagues to undertake no serious projects without their help.

THE 19TH. 99. He places the woman so that the base of her spine bears upon the sharpened head of a tall post, her four limbs are held in the air only by light cords; the effects of her suffering make the lecher laugh incontinently, the torture is frightful.

A man who used to enjoy cutting small steaks from the girl's rump has become absolutely a butcher: he has the girl sandwiched between two heavy planks, then slowly and carefully sawed in two.

An embuggerer of both sexes has brother and sister fetched in; he declares to the brother that he is about to die a horrible death, and shows the young man all the deployed tackle he proposes to use; however, the libertine continues, he will save the brother's life if he will fuck his sister and strangle her at once. The young man agrees, and while he fucks his sister, the libertine embuggers now one of them, now the other. Then the brother, fearing for his life, deprives her sister of hers, and the moment he completes that operation, both he and his dead sister tumble through a trap door into a capacious charcoal brazier, wherein the libertine watches them be consumed.

A bugger compels a father to fuck his daughter in his presence. Next, the father holds the daughter, the bugger sodomizes her; after which he informs the father that the girl absolutely has to perish, but that he has the alternatives of killing her himself by strangling her, which will cause her little suffering, or, in that other case, if her prefers not to kill his daughter, then he, the libertine, will do the work, but the father shall have to witness it all, and his child's agonies will be atrocious.

Rather than see her undergo frightful tortures, the father decides to kill his daughter with a noose of black silk, but while he is preparing to dispatch her, he is seized, bound, and before his eyes his child is flayed alive, then rolled upon burning iron nails, then cast into a brazier, and the father is strangled; this, says the libertine, is to teach him a lesson not to be so eager to choke the life out of his own children, for 'tis barbaric. Afterward, he is dumped into the same brazier wherein his daughter perished.

A great devotee of asses and of the lash brings together mother and daughter. He tells the girl that he is going to kill her mother if she, the girl, does not consent to the sacrifice of both her hands; the little one agrees, they are severed at the wrist. Whereupon these two creatures are separated; a rope suspended from the ceiling is slipped around the girl's neck, she stands upon a stool; another cord runs from the stool into the next room and the mother is requested to hold the end. She is then invited to tug on the cord: she pulls it without knowing what she is doing, she is led directly into the first room to contemplate her work, and during that moment of her keenest distress, she is smitten down by a saber blow aimed at her head from behind.

Jealous of the pleasure the two brothers had the night before, Durcet, that evening, is moved to suggest that they vex Adelaide, whose turn, he assures the society, is soon to come. And so Curval, her father, and Durcet, her husband, worry her thighs with white-hot thongs while the Duc's unlubricated member sounds her ass. The tip of her tongue is pierced, the ends of both her ears are shorn away, with the aid of instruments Messieurs dispossess her of four teeth, and then she is given a savage whipping. That same evening, the

Bishop bleeds Sophie while her dearly beloved friend, Adelaide, watches the blood issue from the child's veins; the fountains are kept turned on until Sophie loses consciousness; as he bleeds her, the Bishop embuggers her, remaining in her ass throughout the operation.

While Curval is sodomizing him, Narcisse loses a pair of fingers, then Marie is hailed into court, red-hot irons are thrust into her cunt and asshole, more irons are applied to six places upon her thighs, upon her clitoris, her tongue, upon her one remaining breast, and out come the remainder of her teeth.

THE 20TH. 104. Champville's of the 5th of December, the man who was wont to have the mother prostitute her son and hold him while he embuggered the lad, improves his taste by bringing the mother and son together. He tells the mother that he is about to kill her, but will spare her if she will murder her son. In case she refuses to do so, he slits the boy's throat before the woman's eyes. Or if she consents: then she is bound to her son's dead body and left quietly to meditate and finally to die.

A very incestuous personage assembles two sisters after having embuggered both of them; he binds them to a machine, each has a knife in her hand: the machine is set in motion, the girls are brought suddenly together and mutually kill each other.

Another devotee of incest requires a mother and her four children. They are locked into a room; he observes them through a small barred window. He gives them nothing to eat in order to study the effects of famine upon this woman, and to discover which of her children she will eat first.

Champville's of the 29th of December, who liked to flog pregnant women, calls for a mother and daughter, both of whom must be gravid: they are tied to a pair of steel plates one set above the other; the women face one another; the machine starts, the jaws of the vise close with great speed and power, the two women are ground to dust, together with their fruit.

A very buggerish gentleman entertains himself in the following manner: he assembles lover and mistress:

"There is in all the world but one person who stands in the way of your happiness," says he, taking the lover aside; "I am going to put that individual in your power."

And he leads him into an obscurely lit chamber containing a bed; upon it someone lies asleep. Greatly aroused, the young man takes dagger in hand and stabs his enemy. When he has had done, he is permitted to recognize his mistress' dead body: 'twas she he slew; he kills himself in despair, or if he does not, the libertine kills him with a shot from a rifle, fired at a distance, not daring to enter the room with the furious young man who still has a weapon in his hand. Previously, he fucked the youth and his beloved too, they singly yielded to him in the hope he would help them and bring them together, it is after having enjoyed them he rids the world of them.

In celebration of the sixteenth week, Durcet, as a woman, marries Invictus, who enacts a masculine role; and as a man he takes Hyacinthe to be his wife; the ceremonies are performed that evening and, by way of festivity, Durcet wishes to torment Fanny, his feminine wife. Consequently, her arms are burned, so are her thighs in six separate places, two teeth are extracted from her mouth, she is flogged; Hyacinthe, who loves her and who is her husband thanks to the voluptuous arrangements hitherto described. Hyacinthe, I say, is obliged to shit into Fanny's mouth, and she to eat the turd.

The Duc pulls out one of Augustine's teeth and immediately afterward fucks her in the mouth. Fanchon reappears, she is bled, and while blood flows from her arm, her arm is broken; next, they remove her toenails and sever the fingers from both her hands.

THE 21ST. She announces that the following examples are of buggers who wish to commit exclusively masculine murders.

He buries the muzzle of a shotgun in the boy's ass, the weapon is loaded with buckshot and he has just finished fucking the lad. He pulls the trigger; the gun and his prick discharge simultaneously.

He obliges the lad to watch his mistress being mutilated, and to eat her flesh, principally her buttocks, breasts, and heart. He has the option of eating these meats, or of dying of hunger. As soon as he has devoured them, if 'tis that he elects to do, the libertine inflicts several deep wounds upon him and leaves him thus to bleed to death; if he abstains from eating, he then starves to death.

He tears off the youth's testicles and, a short while later, serves them up to him in a ragout, then, in place of the stolen treasure, substitutes spheres of quicksilver and fills his voided scrotum with sulphur a-plenty, which cause such violent suffering that the patient succumbs. During his agony, the libertine embuggers him and increases the boy's trouble by burning him here, there and everywhere with sulphur-impregnated slivers, and by scratching, picking, and further burning these wounds.

He drives a long spike through the victim's asshole and thus nails him to a slender pole, and leaves him to sigh away his last hours, or days.

He embuggers, and whilst sodomizing, opens the cranium, removes the brain, and fills the cavity with molten lead.

Vigorously fustigated beforehand, Hyacinthe's ass is made generally available that evening. Narcisse is presented to the assembly: off come his balls with a snip of the scissors. Adelaide is summoned forth, a red-hot fire shovel is brushed over the rear of her thighs, they burn her clitoris, pierce her tongue, lash her breasts with cruel instruments, cut off the two little buttons on her breasts, break both her arms, carve away her remaining fingers, tear the hair from her cunt, tear a handful of hair from her head, pull out six of her teeth. Thus discomfited, she causes Messieurs to discharge every one save the Duc who, his livid prick straining upward, demands leave to exercise Thérèse all alone. Leave so to do is accorded him; using a pocketknife, he pries out all her nails and, as he proceeds, burns her fingers with a candle, then he fractures one of her arms, and still he does not discharge; very wroth, he leaps upon Augustine, encunts her and tears out one of her teeth as he spills his seed into her womb.

THE 22ND. 114. He breaks a young boy on the rack, then affixes him to a wheel upon which he is left to expire: upon the wheel he is turned in such a way as to expose his buttocks, and the scoundrel, his tormentor, has his table set beneath the wheel, and dines there every day until the patient is no more.

He flays a young boy, rubs his body with honey, and invites the flies to the feast.

He slices off his prick and breasts, nails one of his feet to a post, one of his hands to another post, and thus he is left to expire with however little dignity.

The same man who had made Duclos take supper with his dogs, owns a lion too, and, arming a boy with a light stick, introduces the youngster into the lion's cage. They boy's defense only further arouses the animal; the libertine watches the contest and discharges when the loser is completely devoured.

Clothed in a mare's skin, his asshole smeared with mare's fuck, a small boy is surrendered to an excited horse. The libertine observes their struggle and the boy's death.

Giton is subjected to tortures that evening: the Duc, Curval, Hercule, and Bum-Cleaver penetrate his ass ungreased. He is whipped very lustily, Messieurs extract four of his teeth, cut off four of his fingers (as always, each friend has a share in the despoiling of the victim), and Durcet crushes one of his balls between thumb and forefinger.

All four gentlemen soundly flog Augustine. Her glorious ass is soon washed in blood, the Duc embuggers her while Curval severs one of her fingers, then Curval marches into the breach while the Duc six times sears her thighs with a hot iron; Blangis snips away yet another finger the same instant his colleague discharges, and despite all this rough treatment, she spends the night, a stormy one, in the Duc's bed. Marie sustains a broken arm, her fingernails are drawn out, her fingers burned.

That same night, Durcet and Curval, seconded by Desgranges and Duclos, accompany Adelaide to the cellars. Curval gives her a farewell embuggering, then they cause her to die in the throes of terrible sufferings, which you will give in full detail.

THE 23RD. 119. He places a young boy in a machine which stretches him, dislocating his bones; he is meticulously and thoroughly broken, then removed from the machine, given a chance to recover his breath, exposed to the process again; and so it continues for several days, until the patient's death.

He has a pretty girl pollute and fatigue a young boy; he is drained very dry indeed, but still the girl toils over him, he is given no nourishment, and eventually dies in horrible convulsions.

In the space of a single day, he performs four operations upon the young man: a gallstone removal, a trepanning, the excision of a fistula in the eye, of one in the anus. He knows just enough about surgery to botch all four operations; then he abandons the patient, giving him no further help and watching him expire.

After having sheared off the boy's prick and balls, using a red-hot iron he hollows out a cunt in the place formerly occupied by his genitals; the iron makes the hole and cauterizes simultaneously: he fucks the patient's new orifice and strangles him with his hands upon discharging.

He massages him with a currycomb; when he has generally abraded his flesh in this fashion, he rubs him with alcohol, ignites it, resumes his combing, rubs again with alcohol, relights the torch, proceeding in this wise till death makes further care unnecessary.

That same evening, Narcisse's turn arrives to be vexed; fire is applied to his thighs and little prick, then Messieurs crush his two balls.

They turn again to Augustine upon the recommendation of the Duc, whose spiteful attitude toward her seems only to have worsened; they burn her thighs and armpits, a very hot bar of iron is rammed into her cunt. She faints, the Duc waxes all the more furious, he shears off one of her nipples, drinks her blood, breaks both her arms, and tears out her cunt hair, all her teeth, and cuts off every finger left on her hands, cauterizing the wounds with fire. And once again 'tis in his bed she sleeps, or rather lies, that night, for if one is to believe Duclos, he fucks her fore and aft the whole night long, repeatedly telling her that the day about to dawn will be her last.

Louison appears, they break one of her arms, burn her tongue, her clitoris, tear out all her nails, and burn the tips of her bleeding fingers. Curval sodomizes her in this state and, in his rage, twists and manhandles one of Zelmire's breasts while discharging. Not content with those abuses, he catches hold of her again and whips her until he cannot lift his arm.

THE 24TH. 124. The same man Martaine referred to on the 1st of January wishes to embugger the father while his two children observe, and as he discharges, he stabs one child to death with one hand, and with his other strangles the other.

His first passion was to flog the bellies of pregnant women; his second is to assemble six of them whose pregnancy has reached the end of the eighth month: he ties them back to back, their bellies prominently thrust forward: he splits open the belly of the first, perforates the belly of the second with dagger thrusts, gives a hundred kicks to the third's, a hundred blows of a club deflates the belly of the fourth, he burns the fifth's, applies a rasp to the sixth's, and then, using a truncheon upon her belly, he finishes off whichever amongst them has survived his treatment.

Curval interrupts the narrations with some furious scene or other, this passion having had a great effect upon his mind.

The seducer mentioned by Duclos assembles two women. Says he to the first: "Deny God and religion if you wish to live," but his valet has whispered to her, telling her to say nothing, for if she does, she shall surely be killed, but by keeping silent she shall have nothing to fear. Hence, she is mute; he blows out her brains, murmuring, "There's one for God." He calls the second; struck by the example of the first and remembering what she has been told before entering the room, that she has no choice but to renounce belief in God and religion if she is to save herself, she assents to all he proposes: he blows out her brains: "And there's another for the

Devil." The villain plays that little game every week.

He is a great bugger and he is fond of giving dances, but the ceiling in the salon is of a special order, it collapses as soon as the room is filled, and nearly everyone perishes. Were he to remain living in the same city for any length of time, he would be detected, but he moves frequently; he is eventually found out, but only after having given his fiftieth dance.

Martaine's of the 27th of January, whose taste is to promote abortions, establishes three pregnant women in three cruel postures, composing an artistic group. Thus situated, they give birth while he looks on, then he ties each infant to its mother's neck until the little creature either dies or is eaten, for the libertine keeps the women just where they are and gives them no food. The same personage has yet another passion: he has two women whelp in his presence, blindfolds them, and after having himself identified the infants by some mark, he puts them side by side and bids each woman go and recover each her own offspring; if the ladies are not mistaken, he permits their young to live, but if they are in error, he carves up the children with a saber.

Narcisse is presented at the evening orgies. While the Bishop sodomizes the little fellow, Durcet relieves him of his remaining digits and inserts a red-hot needle into his urethral canal. They bid Giton step forth, he is kicked about, 'tis a lively game of ball they play with him, three of the friends fracture one of his legs while the Duc embuggers him.

Zelmire's turn: they roast her clitoris, sear her tongue, bake her gums, extract four of her teeth, burn her thighs in six places before and behind, snip away her nipples, unfinger both her hands, and when she is thus prepared to afford pleasure, Curval embuggers her. But he does not discharge.

Up steps Fanchon. Their attentions cost her an eye.

Escorted by Desgranges and Duclos, the Duc and Curval make a journey to the cellars with Augustine in the course of that night; her ass has been preserved in excellent condition, 'tis now lashed to tatters, then the two brothers alternately embugger her, but guard their seed, and then the Duc gives her fifty-eight wounds in the buttocks, pours boiling oil into each gash. He drives a hot iron into her cunt, another into her ass, and fucks her wounded charms, his prick sheathed in a sealskin condom which worsens the already lamentable state of her privities. That accomplished, the flesh is peeled away from the bones of her arms and legs, which bones are sawed in several different places, then her nerves are laid bare in four adjacent places, the nerve ends are tied to a short stick which, like a tourniquet, is twisted, thus drawing forth the aforesaid nerves, which are very delicate parts of the human anatomy and, which, when mistreated, cause the patient to suffer much. Augustine's agonies are unheard-of.

She is given some respite and allowed to recruit her strength, then

Messieurs resume work, but this time, as the nerves are pulled into sight, they are scraped with the blade of a knife. The friends complete that operation and now move elsewhere; a hole is bored in her throat, her tongue is drawn back, down, and passed through it, 'tis a comical effect, they broil her remaining breast, then, clutching a scalpel, the Duc thrusts his hand into her cunt and cuts through the partition dividing the anus from the vagina; he throws aside the scalpel, reintroduces his hand, and rummaging about in her entrails, forces her to shit through her cunt, another amusing stunt; then, availing himself of the same entrance, he reaches up and tears open her stomach. Next, they concentrate upon her visage: cut away her ears, burn her nasal passages, blind her eyes with molten sealing wax, girdle her cranium, hang her by the hair, attach heavy stones to her feet, and allow her to drop: the top of the skull remains dangling.

She was still breathing when she fell, and the Duc encunted her in this sorry state; he discharged and came away only the more enraged. They split her belly, opened her, and applied fire to her entrails; scalpel in hand, the Président burrows in her chest and harasses her heart, puncturing it in several places. 'Twas only then her soul fled her body; at the age of fifteen years and eight months thus perished one of the most heavenly creatures ever formed by Nature's skillful hand. Etc. Her eulogy.

THE 25TH. That morning, the Duc takes Colombe to be his wife and hereafter she performs all a wife's functions.

A great connoisseur of the ass and a man mightily fond thereof, he embuggers the mistress while the lover looks on, then the lover while his mistress watches, then he nails the lover over the mistress' body and leaves them to expire, mouth to mouth.

Such will be the end of Céladon and Sophie, who are in love, and Messieurs interrupt the storyteller to oblige Céladon himself to spread a little hot sealing wax on his dear Sophie's thighs; while obeying the instructions, he collapses: while lying unconscious, he is embuggered by the Bishop.

He who was wont to amuse himself by throwing a girl into water and pulling her out, has as his second passion that of casting seven or eight whores into a pond and watching them thrash about, for they are poor swimmers. He tenders them an iron pike, but it is heated red hot; still they cling to it, but he thrusts them away, and that they the more certainly perish, he has amputated one limb from each of them before throwing them in.

His earlier caprice was to cause vomiting; his improvement thereof is, by using a secret means, to spread the plague throughout an entire provence: he has brought about the death of a truly incredible number of people. He also poisons wells and streams.

Fond of employing the whip, he has three pregnant women locked in an iron cage, and with them he imprisons their three children; a fire is lit beneath the cage, its occupants caper and dance more and more in earnest as the floor heats; the women take the children in their arms, and finally fall and die in this manner.

(That one belongs somewhere further above; move it to its proper place.)

'Twas he who pricked with an awl; more of a man today, he seals a pregnant woman in a chest whose interior is studded with sharp nails; he then has the chest rolled and dragged through the garden.

These tales of pregnant women being chastised have proven as woeful to Constance's ears as they have delighted Curval's; she sees only too well what the future holds in store for her. As her fatal hour is drawing nigh, Messieurs are of the opinion her vexations may be inaugurated: her thighs are burned in six places, molten wax is allowed to trickle upon her navel, and her breasts are teased with pins.

Giton appears, a burning needle is run through his little member, his little balls are stabbed, four of his teeth are extracted.

Then comes Zelmire, whose death is not far off; deep into her cunt runs a red-hot poker, six wounds are inflicted upon her breasts, a dozen upon her thighs, needles are driven into her navel, each friend bestows twenty strong blows upon her face. They forcibly remove four of her teeth, her eye is pricked, she is whipped, she is embuggered. While in the act of sodomizing her, Curval, her husband, gives her intelligence of her death, scheduled for the morrow; she declares she is not sorry to learn the tidings, for 'twill put a period to her sorrows.

Rosette steps forward; four teeth are jerked from her mouth, each of her shoulders is branded, her thighs and calves are gashed and hacked; she is then embuggered while several hands worry her breasts.

And now Thérèse advances; out comes an eye, a hundred blows of the bull's pizzle rain down upon her scrawny back.

THE 26TH. 134. A bugger takes his stand at the foot of a tower; the earth about him is studded with sharpened steel rods pointing upward; his associates pitch several children of both sexes from the top of the tower. He has previously embuggered them, and now enjoys seeing them impaled a second time. 'Tis, he considers, very thrilling to be splashed by their blood.

The same personage she cited on the 11th of February, whose tastes ran to instigating combustions, also delights in binding six pregnant women to bundles of inflammable materials; these he sets afire, and if his victims undertake to save themselves, he awaits them, pitchfork in hand, skewers them and hurls them back into the blaze. However, when half-roasted, the floor gives way and they spill into a large vat of boiling oil, wherein they finally perish.

He is the nobleman Duclos spoke of, who has no fondness for the poor and who bought Lucile, her mother, and her sister, and whom Desgranges has also cited (verify this); another of his passions is to assemble a family of beggars over a mine and to watch those luckless creatures blown to bits.

A notorious sodomist, in order to combine that crime with those of incest, murder, rape, sacrilege, and adultery, first inserts a Host in his ass, then has himself embuggered by his own son, rapes his married daughter, and kills his niece.

Greatly partisan to asses, he strangles a mother while embuggering her; when she is dead, he turns her over and cunt-fucks her corpse. While discharging, he kills her daughter with a knife, slashing her breasts, then he embuggers the girl even though she is dead; then apparently convinced there is still some life in his victims, and fancying they are jet capable of suffering, he hurls the cadavers into a fire and discharges as he watches them burn. Duclos spoke of this wealthy individual on the 29th of November: 'twas he who liked to see the girl lying on the pallet covered with black satin; he is also the same man who figured in Martaine's first tale of the 11th of January.

The evening's program begins with Narcisse. One of his hands is lopped off.

Giton loses a hand too.

The interior of Michette's cunt is burned, the same treatment is given Rosette's, and then both girls are burned upon the body and breasts.

But Curval, who has lost control of himself, violates the society's charter and cleaves an entire breast from Rosette's chest, all the while embuggering Michette.

Thérèse makes a further appearance; she receives two hundred blows of the bull's pizzle and loses her other eye.

Curval goes in search of the Duc that night when all is still and, accompanied by Desgranges and Duclos, those two champions take Zelmrire down to the cellars where the most refined tortures are put to use upon her: they are all much more painful, more severe than the others employed upon Augustine, and the two men are still hard at work by the time breakfast arrives the following morning. That enchanting girl dies at the age of fifteen years and two months. 'Twas she who could boast the most beautiful ass in the harem of little girls. And thus deprived of a wife, the Président weds Hébé the next day.

THE 27TH. The seventeeth and last week's festival is postponed until the morrow, in order that the holiday may coincide with the end of the narrations; Desgranges recounts the following passions:

A man Martaine described on the 12th of January, the one who set off fireworks in the woman's ass, has, for his second, this other passion: he ties two pregnant women together so that they form a ball and fires them from a large mortar.

He was a scratcher and scab picker; he now places two pregnant women in a room and obliges them to fight with knives (he observes them from a safe position); they are naked, he threatens them with a gun he keeps trained upon them, and promises to shoot them dead if they begin to dally and falter. If they kill each other, why, that is precisely what he wishes, if not, sword in hand, he rushes into the arena and, after killing one, he disembowels the other and burns her entrails with aqua fortis, or with pieces of red-hot metal.

A man who once liked to flog pregnant women's bellies has reformed: he presently binds a pregnant girl to a wheel and beneath it, fixed in a chair and unable to move, sits the girl's mother, her head flung back, her mouth open and ready to receive all the ordures and rubbish which flow out of the corpse, and the infant, too, if the girl gives birth to it.

Martaine's of the 16th of January, whose joy was to prick asses, attaches a girl to a machine studded with sharp iron points; he fucks her as she lies upon that bed, with every blow of his loins he drives her upon the nails, then he turns her over and fucks her asswise, that she may also be punctured on the other side. When he has finished that phase of the operation, he lays a second plank above her, and it is likewise provided with nails; the planks are brought together by means of bolts, thus dies the patient, crushed and stabbed in a multitude of places. The pressing is carried out gradually, she is given ample opportunity to savor her pain.

A fustigator stretches a pregnant woman out upon a table; he nails her thereto, first driving a fiery nail into each eye, one into her mouth, another into either breast, then he burns her clitoris and nipples with a taper, and slowly saws her knees halfway through, breaks her legs, and ends by hammering a red-hot spike, of enormous size, into her navel: it undoes both mother and child. He likes to have her ready to give birth.

Messieurs whip Julie and Duclos that evening, but from amusement, since they are both amongst the inhabitants of Silling who shall transfer their residence to Paris: nevertheless, Julie's thighs are burned in two places, and she is depilated.

Sentenced to die the next day but unaware of her impending fate, Constance appears; her nipples are scorched, molten wax is allowed to trickle down over her belly, she yields four teeth, Messieurs prick the white of her eyes with needles.

Narcisse, also due to be immolated on the 28th of February, enters upon the stage; he loses an eye and four teeth.

Giton, Michette, and Rosette, destined to accompany Constance to the grave, each surrenders an eye and four teeth, Rosette her two nipples to the knife and six chunks of flesh, some of them carved from her arms, some from her thighs; all her fingers are neatly severed, and hot irons are introduced into her cunt and bum. Both Curval and the Duc discharge twice.

Up steps Louison; she weathers a storm of one hundred blows of the bull's pizzle; Messieurs pluck out one of her eyes and, most cynically, bid her swallow it. Down it goes.

THE 28TH. 144. A bugger: has two girls brought to him, they are fast friends, he ties them mouth to mouth, and by their side sits an excellent meal; but they cannot get to it, and he watches them bite and eat each other when hunger begins to exert its influence upon them.

A man who as a boy was wont to flog pregnant women, now shuts six of this sort into a round cage formed by large iron hoops: they are all facing one another. Little by little, the hoops contract, little by little they are brought together, slowly they are flattened, gradually all six are crushed, their fruit crushed too. But prior to this he has cut a buttock and a breast from each and fashioned six collars therefrom; each woman wears one as you might a fur tippet.

Another pregnant-woman beater binds two of these objects each to the end of a long tilting pole; a clever machine, into which the other ends of the poles are inserted, bumps and bangs the women against each other. These repeated collisions are their mutual undoing, and he discharges. He makes every effort to procure himself a mother and daughter, or two sisters.

That Comte of whom Duclos spoke at length, and to whom Desgranges alluded once before on the 26th, he who purchased

Lucile, Lucile's mother, and Lucile's little sister, of whom Martaine also spoke in her fourth tale on the 1st of January, this Comte, I say, has another passion still: 'tis to suspend three women over three holes. The first woman hangs by her tongue, beneath her is a very deep well; the second hangs from her breasts, underneath her lies a charcoal brazier; the scalp of the third has been loosened, she hangs by her hair over a pit studded with pointed iron rods. When the weight of their bodies causes these women to fall free -- when the scalp is torn from the head of the third, when the breasts of the second tear loose from her torso, when the tongue of the first is torn from her mouth -- they only escape one difficulty in order to encounter a new one. Whenever possible, he suspends three pregnant women, or three women from the same family; such was his unkind use of Lucile, her sister, and her mother.

The last passion.

(But why the last? Where are the other two? They were all there in the original outline.)

Desgranges recounts the last passion:

The nobleman who indulges in this final passion we shall designate as the infernal caprice or, more simply, as the hell passion, has been cited four times: by Duclos in the last story she told on the 29th of November; by Champville, when referring to a personage who depucelates nine-year-olds only; by Martaine, as he who depucelates three-year-olds in the bum; by Desgranges who mentioned him in an early connection (establish that connection more precisely). He is a man of some forty years, enormous in stature and furnished with the member of a stallion: his prick is very near to nine inches in circumference and a foot in overall length; he is exceedingly wealthy, a very powerful lord, very harsh, very cruel, his heart is of stone. He has a house on the outskirts of Paris which he uses for no purposes other than the gratification of this passion.

The surroundings wherein he savors his delight is a spacious room, simply decked, but padded everywhere, the floor covered with mattresses; upon entering the room one sees a single long casement window, the room has no other opening save for the door; that window looks down upon an underground cellar, twenty feet below the salon where he busies himself, and looking out, one sees the mattresses which break the fall of the girls as he flings down into the cellar, a description whereof we shall give shortly. He requires fifteen girls for this party; their ages must be between fifteen and seventeen, neither more, nor less; he employs six procuresses in Paris, as well as twelve in the provinces, and they are to spare no efforts, no expense to find him everything of the most charming that may possibly be found of that age, and as it is collected, the material is sent to a country convent over which he has absolute control, and there, in that nursery, the girls ripen, and from it he selects the fifteen objects for his debauch, which is regularly executed every fortnight.

That evening before the ceremony begins, he personally examines the said material, the least defect in which warrants its rejection; he insists that his creatures be perfect models of beauty. Escorted by a procuress, they arrive at the house and are lodged in a room adjacent to the pleasure-salon. They are first exhibited to him in this adjoining chamber, all fifteen are naked. He touches, feels, fondles, experiments with them, he scrutinizes them, sucks their mouths, and one after the other has them all shit into his mouth. But he does not swallow.

This initial operation performed with dreadful seriousness, he brands each upon the shoulder, imprinting a number in her flesh; it is to indicate the order in which he will receive them. That done, he goes alone into the salon, where he remains for a brief space: no one knows what he does in this moment of solitude. Then he knocks. Girl Number 1 is cast into his lair. And she is properly cast into it: the procuress flings her toward him, he catches her in his arms, she is naked. He shuts the door, takes up switches and begins to flail her ass; after that he sodomizes her with his gigantic prick. Never does he need any help. He does not discharge. His prick retires, still rock-hard; he seizes the switches again and returns to lashing the girl's back, the front and back of her thighs, then he lays her down again and deflowers her cunt; next, he goes back to beating her, now upon the breasts, both of which he seizes and grinds and kneads with all his strength, and he is a strong man. And now he picks up an awl and six times stabs her body, driving his point once into each bruised breast.

After all that has been done, he opens the casement window, places the girl in the middle of the room, standing erect, at attention, facing the window; he stands behind her and, when all is ready, gives her a kick in the ass of such startling violence that she flies across the room, crashes against the windowsill, topples over it, and vanishes into the cellar. But before launching her, he slips a ribbon around her neck, thereby to signify which torture, according to his best belief, will be most suitable for that particular patient, which torture will prove most voluptuous to inflict upon her, and his acuity and judgment in these matters, his tact and discrimination are truly wonderful.

And thus the girls pass one by one through his hands, the identical ceremony awaits them all, and thus he makes away with thirty maidenheads in a given day, and performs those heroic feats unscathed: not a drop of fuck does he lose. The subterranean apartment into which the girl tumble is furnished with fifteen different assortments of frightful torture machines, and an executioner, wearing the mask and emblems of a demon, wearing also the colors of his specialty, presides over each apparatus. The ribbon placed about the girl's neck corresponds in color with the torture to which she has been condemned, and directly she falls into the pit, the appropriate executioner steps forward, having recognized his victim, and drags her to the machine of which he has charge, but the tortures do not begin until the fifteenth has entered the gallery and been claimed by her demon. As soon as the entire complement has descended, our man, by now in a furious state after having depucelated thirty orifices without discharging, I say, makes his entrance into the infernal repair; he is practically naked, his prick glued against his belly. Everything is ready, all the tortures are in motion, and they proceed simultaneously, amidst much noise.

The first torture engine is a wheel upon which the girl is strapped and which, rotating uninterruptedly, bears against an outer circle studded with razors which everywhere scratch and tear and slice the unfortunate victim, but as the blades do not bite deep, only superficially, she turns for at least two hours before dying.

The second: the girl lies two inches above a red-hot iron plate which slowly melts her.

Third: she is attached by the waist to a piece of burning iron, and all her limbs are twisted and frightfully dislocated.

Fourth: the four limbs attached each to a spring which slowly moves away, gradually stretching her arms and legs until they are detached and the trunk falls into a brazier.

Fifth: a red-hot cast-iron bell is place over her head, but the bonnet is several sizes too large, the iron does not touch her, but her brain slowly melts, her head is slowly grilled.

Sixth: she is chained inside an iron tub of boiling oil.

Seventh: she is held standing before a machine which, six times a minute, shoots a small dart into her body, and each time into a different place; the machine does not stop until she is entirely feathered.

Eighth: her feet anchored in a furnace, a mass of lead very gradually descends upon her head, thrusting her further into the oven.

Ninth: her executioner continually pricks her with a red-hot iron goad; she is bound before him, he thus meticulously works over every inch of her body.

Tenth: she is chained to a pillar underneath a large glass dome, twenty famished reptiles devour her alive.

Eleventh: a cannon ball attached to each foot, she is suspended by one hand, and if she falls, 'tis into a furnace.

Twelfth: a hook is driven through her mouth; thus she hangs, a deluge of burning pitch incessantly pouring over her body.

Thirteenth: the nerves are pulled from her flesh and tied to cords which draw them further, and meanwhile burning nails are driven into her body.

Fourteenth: alternately torn with tongs and whipped upon her cunt and ass with martinets whose steel tips are heated red hot, and from time to time scratched with burning iron rakes.

Fifteenth: she is poisoned by a drug which burns and rends her entrails, which hurls her into frightful convulsions, causes her to utter hideous screams, and insures her death; but it is slow, and she is the last to succumb. This is one of the most terrible of the ordeals.

The villain walks about the torture chamber as soon as he arrives there, spends fifteen minutes contemplating each operation while swearing like of the damned and overwhelming the patient with unmentionable invectives. When toward the end he can bear no more of it and his fuck, captive for so long, is ready to escape him, he falls into a comfortable armchair whence he can observe the entire spectacle, two of the demons approach him, display their asses and frig him, and he squirts his seed while pronouncing shouts so stentorian that they rise above and totally blot out the din his fifteen patients are producing. And now he gets to his feet and leaves the gallery, the coup de grâce is given the girls who are not yet dead, their bodies are buried, and there's an end to it until the next fortnight comes round.

Wherewith Desgranges terminates her contribution; she is congratulated, toasted, acclaimed, etc...

Upon the morning of that day there had been the most ominous preparations for the great holiday Messieurs were meditating. Curval, detesting Constance as he does, had been cunt-fucking her at a very early hour and while fucking her had imparted grave news to her. Coffee was served by the five victims, to wit: Constance, Narcisse, Giton, Michette, and Rosette. Horrid things were perpetrated in the salon; during the recitations the reader has just perused, the quatrains Messieurs had been able to arrange had been composed of naked children. And as soon as Desgranges had brought her narrations to a term, Fanny had been marched to the fore: her remaining fingers and toes had been hacked off, and Curval had embuggered her without pomade, so had the Duc, so had the four first-rank fuckers.

Sophie was led into the center of the stage; Céladon, her lover, had been obliged to burn the interior of her cunt, all her fingers had been severed, her four limbs bled, her right ear had been torn away, her left eye gouged out. Céladon had been constrained to lend his assistance in all these operations, and his least frown or lowest murmur was rewarded by a flogging with an iron-tipped martinet. Supper had come next, the meal had been voluptuous, Messieurs drank naught but sparkling champagne and liqueurs.

The torturing was arranged for the orgy hour; as the friends sat at dessert, word was brought to them that everything was in readiness, they descended and found the cellars agreeably festooned and very properly furnished. Constance lay upon a kind of mausoleum, the four children decorated its corners. As their asses were still in excellent condition, Messieurs were able to take considerable pleasure in molesting them; then at last the heavier work was begun: while embuggering Giton, Curval himself opened Constance's belly and tore out the fruit, already well-ripened and clearly of the masculine sex; then the society continued, inflicting tortures upon those five victims. Their sufferings were long, cruel, and various.

Upon THE 1ST DAY OF MARCH, remarking that the snows have not yet melted, Messieurs decide to dispatch the rest of the subjects one by one. Messieurs devise new arrangements whereby to keep their bed-chambers staffed, and agree to give a green ribbon to everyone whom they propose to take back with them to France; the green favor is bestowed, however, upon condition the recipient is willing to lend a hand with the destruction of the other victims. Nothing is said to the six women in the kitchen; Messieurs decide to do away with the three scullery maids, who are well worth toying over, but to spare the cooks, because of their considerable talents. And so a list is drawn up; 'tis found that, to date, the following creatures had already been sacrificed:

Wives: Aline, Adelaide, and Constance: 3

Sultanas: Augustine, Michette, Rosette, and Zelmire: 4 Bardashes: Giton and Narcisse: 2

Fuckers: one subaltern: 1 Total: 10

The new ménages are arranged:

The Duc takes unto himself, or under his protection: Hercule, Duclos, one cook: 4

Curval takes: Bum-Cleaver, Champville, one cook: 4 Durcet takes:

Invictus, Martaine, one cook: 4

And the Bishop: Antinoüs, Desgranges, Julie: 4 Total: 16

Messieurs decide that, upon a given signal, and with the aid of the four fuckers and the four storytellers, but not the cooks whom they do not wish to employ for these purposes, they will seize all the others, making use of the most treacherous possible means and when their victims least expect it; they will lay hands upon all the others, I say, save for the three scullions, who will not be seized until later on; it is further decided that the upstairs chambers will be converted into four prisons, that the three subaltern fuckers, manacled, will be lodged in the strongest of these prisons; Fanny, Colombe, Sophie, and Hébé in the second; Céladon, Zélamir, Cupidon, Zéphyr, Adonis, and Hyacinthe in the third; and the four elders in the fourth; that one subject will be dispatched every day; and that when the hour arrives to arrest the three scullions, they will be locked into whichever of the prison happens to be empty.

These agreements once reached, Messieurs appoint each storyteller the warden of one prison. And whenever they please, Messieurs will amuse themselves with these victims, either in their prison or in one of the larger rooms, or in their Lordships' bedchambers, depending upon Messieurs' individual preference. And so, as we have just indicated, one subject is dispatched daily, in the following order:

On the 1st of March: Fanchon. On the 2nd: Louison.

On the 3rd: Thérèse.

On the 4th: Marie. On the 5th: Fanny.

On the 6th and the 7th: Sophie and Céladon together, for they are lovers, and they perish nailed one to the other, as we have hitherto explained.

On the 8th: one subaltern fucker. On the 9th: Hébé.

On the 10th: another subaltern fucker. On the 11th: Colombe.

On the 12th: the last of the subaltern fuckers. On the 13th: Zélamir.

On the 14th: Cupidon. On the 15th: Zéphyr. On the 16th: Adonis. On the 17th: Hyacinthe.

On the morning of the 18th, Messieurs and their cohorts seize the three scullions, lock them in the prison formerly occupied by the elders, and dispatch one upon that day.

A second upon the 19th. And the last upon the 20th. Total: 20.

The following recapitulation lists the inhabitants of the Château of Silling during that memorable winter:

Masters: 4

Elders: 4

Kitchen staff: 6

Storytellers: 4

Fuckers: 8

Little boys: 8

Wives: 4
Little girls: 8
Total: 46
Whereof thirty were immolated and sixteen returned to Paris. FINAL ASSESSMENT
Massacred prior to the 1st of March, in the course of the orgies: 10 Massacred after the 1st of March: 20 Survived and came back: 16
Total: 46
With what regards the tortures and deaths of the last twenty subjects, and life such as it was in the household until the day of departure, you will give details at your leisure and where you see fit, you will say, first of all, that thirteen of the sixteen survivors (three of whom were cooks) took all their meals together; sprinkle in whatever tortures you like.

Notes

Under no circumstances deviate from this plan, everything has been worked out, the entirety several times re-examined with the greatest care and thoroughness.

Detail the departure. And throughout the whole, introduce a quantity of moral dissertation and diatribe, above all at the suppers.

When you produce the final version, keep a notebook; in it you will place the names of all the principal characters and the names of all those who play important roles, such as they who have several passions and who will appear several times in the romance, as, for example, the hell libertine; leave a wide margin beside their names and, as you recopy, fill it with everything you come across that has any bearing upon them; this note is very essential, it is the sole way to keep your work clear of obscurities and to avoid repetitions.

Edulcorate Part The First, it is much too strong; things develop too rapidly and too far in it, it cannot possibly be too soft, mild, feeble, subdued. Above all, never have the four friends do anything until it has first been recounted. You have not been sufficiently scrupulous in that connection.

In Part The First, say that the man who mouth-fucks the little girl prostituted by her father is the same man, of whom she has already spoken, who fucks with a dirty prick.

Do not forget to place somewhere in December the scene of the little girls serving supper, squirting liqueurs from their asses into Messieurs' glasses; you announced such a scene but failed to include it in the plan.

SUPPLEMENTARY TORTURES
-- By means of a hollow tube, a mouse is introduced into her cunt,

the tube is withdrawn, the cunt sewn up, and the animal, unable to get out, devours her entrails.

-- She is made to swallow a snake which in similar wise feeds upon her entrails.

ADDENDA

In general, describe Curval and the Duc as two hot-blooded and imperious scoundrels, 'tis thus you conceived them in the plan and in Part The First, and figure the Bishop as a cool, reasoning and tough-minded villain. As for Durcet, he must be mischievous, a teaser, false, traitorous, perfidious. In accordance with which, have them do everything that conforms with such characters.

Carefully recapitulate all the names and the qualities of all the personages your storytellers mention; this to avoid repetition.

Upon one page in your notebook of characters draw the plan of the chteau, room by room, and in the blank space next to this page, itemize all the things done in each room.

This entire great roll was begun the 22nd of October, 1785, and finished in thirty-seven days.

Place here the portrait of Durcet as it is in notebook 18, the one that's bound in pink, then, after having concluded this portrait with the words under (a) in the notebooks, continue with (b).

As Sade notes, the speed with which he wrote the final draft of The 120 Days, and because he was unable to reread and correct his manuscript, resulted in a number of minor discrepancies in dates, characters, and situations, which the careful reader will doubtless discover. None the less, given the large cast of characters, and the complexity of rules and procedures, his accuracy of detail is remarkable. -- Tr.

www.ingramcontent.com/pod-product-compliance
Lightning Source LLC
Chambersburg PA
CBHW070533260626
47161CB00002B/371